Dangerous Favor

Other works by Joyce DiPastena

Poitevin Hearts series

Loyalty's Web (Poitevin Hearts 1)
Illuminations of the Heart (Poitevin Hearts 2)
Loving Lucianna (Poitevin Hearts 3)

Additional Titles

Courting Cassandry
The Lady and the Minstrel
An Epiphany Gift for Robin: A short prequel scene to The Lady and the Minstrel (free on Amazon)
The Girl by the River: A short prequel scene to The Lady and the Minstrel (free on Amazon)
A Candlelight Courting
"Caroles on the Green," in *Timeless Romance Anthology: Winter Edition*

Non-fiction

Name Your Medieval Character: Medieval Christian Names (12th-13th Centuries)

A
POITEVIN
HEARTS
ROMANCE

Dangerous Favor

JOYCE DiPASTENA

Sable Tyger Books

Author's Note

It is a common misconception that the King Arthur legends are uniquely British and furthermore, owe their origins to Sir Thomas Malory's *Le Morte d'Arthur*. The truth is that Sir Thomas merely compiled and reinterpreted already existing tales that stretched back much earlier. Many of these legends flourished in the 12th Century among such medieval writers as Geoffrey of Monmouth (c. 1100 – c. 1155) and Wace (c. 1115 – c. 1183). But the 12 Century French poet, Chrétien de Troyes (flourished 1165–80), is recognized by historians as the first to have fashioned these tales into the courtly romances that we know today. Chrétien thrilled his medieval listeners with the daring deeds of Lancelot, Gawain, and Kay, Lancelot's love affair with Guinevere, and Percival's quest for the Holy Grail three hundred years before the publication of Malory's masterpiece. Chrétien also wrote poems about Arthurian heroes with whom we are less familiar today. One of these poems, *Erec and Enide*, you will soon discover is a particular favorite of my heroine's in *Dangerous Favor*.

Along with Chrétien's poetry, William Marshal also makes a few cameo appearances in my story. The younger son of a minor nobleman, William rose to great heights in his lifetime. He served three generations of Plantagenet kings, rising to become Regent of England after the death of King John. He was nearly unbeatable on the tournament field. This, together with his skill in battle combined with his high moral code, won him praise among his contemporaries as "the greatest knight who ever lived" (Stephen Langton, Archbishop of Canterbury, c 1150-1228). From 1170-1183, William served prominently in the household of Henry the Young King, (so called because he had been anointed co-ruler with his father, Henry II, at the age of fifteen). William's influence over his young master stirred deep jealousies among his rivals. The intrigues against William in *Dangerous Favor* are based on historical records, although for the purposes of this novel, I have given them my own spin.

Cast of Characters

Fictional characters (in alphabetical order)

Acelet de Cary (mentioned): cousin to Etienne and Triston de Brielle; introduced in *Illuminations of the Heart*

Alun d'Amville: formerly betrothed to Mathilde de Riavelle; a neighbor and contemporary of her father's

Aymor de Riavelle: father of Mathilde and Girard de Riavelle; holds his lands from Henry, the Young King

Beata: a lady-in-waiting to Queen Marguerite

Caterine de Guerre: Mathilde and Girard de Riavelle's deceased mother

Costane: Girard de Riavelle's squire

Etienne de Brielle: an impoverished younger son seeking to advance his career as a knight of Henry, the Young King's household; introduced in *Loyalty's Web*

Girard de Riavelle: son and heir of Lord Aymor de Riavelle, elder brother of Mathilde de Riavelle; a knight of Henry, the Young King's household

Heléne de Bury, Countess of Gunthar: Therri de Laurant's younger sister; wife of Hugh de Bury; introduced in *Loyalty's Web*

Hermaline: illegitimate daughter of Lord de Maloisel; step-daughter to Violette de Maloisel

Hugh de Bury, **Earl of Gunthar**: counselor to King Henry II; brother-in-law to Therri de Laurant; introduced in *Loyalty's Web*

Mathilde de Riavelle: daughter of the disgraced Lord Aymor de Riavelle; is determined to prove her father's innocence and restore his honor

Nevell de Chesnei: nephew of Sir Alun d'Amville

Siri de Brielle: wife of Triston de Brielle; introduced in *Illuminations of the Heart*

Therri de Laurant: son and heir to Lord Aumary de Laurant; brother-in-law to Hugh de Bury, Earl of Gunthar; best friend of Etienne de Brielle; introduced in *Loyalty's Web*

Triston de Brielle: Etienne de Brielle's older brother; heir to their father's lands; holds his lands from Richard, Duke of Aquitiane; appears in *Loyalty's Web* and *Illuminations of the Heart*

Violette de Maloisel: wealthy widow of Lord de Maloisel; mistress of Grantamur Castle; holds her lands from Henry, the Young King

Historical Characters

Adam of Churchdown: former vice-chancellor to Henry, the Young King

Adam d'Yquebeuf and **Thomas de Coulonces**: knights of Henry, the Young King's household; rivals of William Marshal

Chretién de Troyes: 12th Century poet; helped popularize the King Arthur legends in courtly romances

Eleanor of Aquitaine: first wife of Louis VII of France, divorced; married Henry II of England; mother of Henry, the Young King and Richard, Duke of Aquitaine

Henry II: king of England; father of Henry, the Young King and Richard, Duke of Aquitaine

Henry, the Young King: eldest son of King Henry II of England; crowned co-ruler with his father at the age of fifteen, but never granted any real power; holds his court in Normandy

Philip II of France: son of Louis VII's third wife; half-brother of Queen Marguerite, wife of Henry, the Young King

Queen Marguerite: wife of Henry, the Young King; daughter of King Louis VII of France's second wife; half-sister to King Louis' son and heir by his third wife, King Philip II

Richard, Duke of Aquitaine: younger brother of Henry, the Young King; rules over Poitou, the homeland of Etienne de Brielle and Therri de Laurant

The Plantagenets: the ruling house of England; sometimes called the Angevins from their original homeland of Anjou

William Marshal: a knight of Henry, the Young King's household, one of his inner circle; a master of the tournament field; praised by his contemporaries as "the greatest knight who ever lived."

One

Normandy ~ Autumn 1181

"Q uit gawking," Girard de Riavelle growled and dug a chiding elbow into his sister's ribs. "You're a lady, not some wide-eyed serf girl straight out of Father's fields. Attempt a little dignity, will you?"

Mathilde closed her mouth, which had popped open on entering the Great Hall of Grantamur Castle. It was like stepping into the world of King Arthur! She had never seen so many richly attired people in her life. Silken gowns and surcotes, lavishly embellished with embroidery and jewels, gleamed beneath the light of the torches. Tapestries with bright, glistening threads glittered in the torch light, their colors fresh and brilliant against the clean, whitewashed walls. Between them hung row after row of shields, some bearing emblems of birds or beasts, some painted with stripes or slashes that radiated out from gilded bosses.

"Those are the shields of the knights who will fight in the tournament tomorrow," her brother told her. "As soon as I've settled you somewhere, I'll hang mine alongside them."

Mathilde allowed Girard to maneuver her through the throng to stand beside one of the tapestries, then watched him disappear through the crowd. He had not been too happy when their father had insisted that he use some of his high and mighty connections in the Young King's court to find his eighteen-year-old sister a husband. Girard had grudgingly agreed to take Mathilde with him to Grantamur Castle where a great tournament of knights was soon to be held. But Mathilde knew that just *any* husband would not do. For her father's sake, she must marry a man of wealth and power. A man who could help to right her father's wrongs . . .

But there was nothing she could do about seeking a husband until Girard saw fit to introduce her to some gentlemen.

She sighed and turned to study the figures woven into the tapestry. The colors were much brighter than the soot-dulled ones that draped the walls in her father's smoky hall. The flowers and birds sprinkled amid the weaving reminded her of the enchanted garden the jongleur had sung of one night at her father's table. She closed her eyes and imagined again the jongleur's sweet voice, chanting the strains of a poet's lay of laughter, love and tears.

"I beg your pardon. Are you not Aymor de Riavelle's daughter?"

Mathilde started at the jovial male voice that intruded upon her dreams. The gentleman's jewels caught her eye first, diamonds flashing from a girdle about his waist, and chains with ruby and emerald studs slung across a broad, silk-clad chest. Her breath caught. *A man of wealth.*

She lifted her gaze to the speaker's face. Soft, round features smiled back at her. Thin ginger hair, topped by a jewel-banded cap, hung in limp tendrils to his shoulders. His ruddy cheeks bowed out a little with his smile. And his chest, she saw now, was not so much broad as plump.

She hoped he was married.

"Aye, aye," he continued in cheerful tones. "But of course you are. I saw you out riding near your father's fields not a fortnight ago."

She gazed doubtfully at the gentleman. "I do not think I know you, sir."

"Forgive me." He attempted a bow but his girth made him look more like a bobbing ball. "I should have introduced myself. I am your neighbor, Sir Nevell de Chesnei."

That startled her. "Neighbor?"

"From Martival."

"Sir Alun d'Amville's castle? I thought it had been abandoned."

Chesnei's jovial face sobered. "Aye, so it has stood these past three years, since my uncle's disappearance."

Her heart gave an unpleasant stumble. "Disappearance? My father said Lord d'Amville was killed by forest bandits." Pray heaven, it must be true! Far easier to challenge a dead man's lies than a living tongue of honeyed deceit.

"So the rumors say, but his body has never been found." Chesnei rubbed a pair of pink, fleshy hands together. "I believe he and your father were friends?"

"I-I was betrothed to Lord d'Amville."

Memories came rushing back of a large, handsome man her father's age, with reddish hair and gold-flecked hazel eyes. His soft, melodious voice had entranced her once. Before she heard that voice raised in threats against her father.

She had stood in the shadows, unseen by either man as they quarreled about her betrothal. Father wanted to annul it, but d'Amville had sworn that if he tried he would see her father's last manor stripped from him. He had the power to do it, d'Amville insisted, power to prove her father worse than merely a thief. This time, there would be no royal mercy for his crime. The bargain had been made, d'Amville reminded him, the documents signed, the betrothal words spoken. Her father could either choose to stand with Mathilde at her wedding, or learn of its details while he languished in a prison cell.

That had been three years ago. Her father said that d'Amville was dead, the threat to them both gone. But the stain of d'Amville's lies still lingered on her father's honor.

Her father and Girard seemed content to leave matters so. But Mathilde had made a silent vow to prove her father's innocence.

Chesnei's gaze—hazel and gold flecked, as she remembered d'Amville's—dropped from her face and traveled the length of her simple, unembellished silk gown. "Betrothed, eh? What a pity my uncle did not live to enjoy the fruits of a wedding."

She tried not to shrink from the warmth in his eyes. Might

d'Amville have confided his lies to his nephew? If Chesnei found her attractive, she might be able to persuade him to tell her how his uncle had incriminated her father in the theft. For she was convinced that was exactly what d'Amville had done.

But the idea of encouraging the gleam in Chesnei's eyes brought a sour lump to her throat.

"Is your father with you?" Chesnei asked abruptly. "Will he join the mêlée tomorrow?"

Mathilde swallowed hard. "Nay, I am here with my brother. Girard says that only knights between the ages of twenty-one and thirty-five are permitted to take part in the tournament." She wished Girard had not wandered away, wished her late mother's maid-servant, whom her father had sent as her chaperone, had not become ill and returned to her father's manor.

Chesnei flashed her a grin that puffed out his plump cheeks. "Then I qualify—just. Though I do not think my skill with the lance sufficient to give me much chance at the prize."

She followed his glance to Violette de Maloisel, standing at the center of a semi-circle of glittering maids-in-waiting on the hall's dais. A shimmering gold surcote of brocaded silk graced the lady's prettily curved figure. Sleek, mahogany hair swept up and away from her exquisite face, bound in the back with a golden net twinkling with diamonds and emeralds. Lady Violette had promised her hand in marriage to the winner of the morrow's tournament. The floor before the dais teemed with eager, hopeful men.

Mathilde sighed in wistful envy. Her own gown of simple blue silk clung becomingly, Father had said, to a figure he approvingly called "willowy". But another glance at Lady Violette's well-defined curves left her feeling as thin and unattractive as a dried-up reed. What man would look at her with Lady Violette in the hall?

"Tell me," Chesnei interrupted her thoughts, "how did you leave your father? Well, I hope?"

"Yes, sir, I thank you."

"I am glad to hear it. And your brother the same?"

"We are all well, I thank you, sir."

Nervous, she touched the embroidered ribbon that threaded her flaxen hair. Girard carried it as a favor from one of his lady-loves. It had been so pretty and so exotically scented, and Mathilde had had so little besides a simple jeweled necklet to liven her appearance, that she had pleaded with Girard to lend her the ribbon for the evening. At first he'd refused. But she had promised to weave it most carefully through her hair and to check it frequently to be sure it had not inadvertently fallen out, until at last he had reluctantly surrendered it to her.

Chesnei offered her a lopsided grin. "You must think me very bold, approaching you this way without a proper introduction. But I know no other ladies here and when I saw you, I recalled how we are neighbors and thought that perhaps you would—" He reached out and took her hand. "My lady, might you do me the honor of granting me a favor to wear in the tournament tomorrow?"

The feel of his soft, moist skin against hers sent through her a wave of panic. "I—" She tried to disengage her hand without appearing rude, but his plump fingers tightened around hers. "Wh-What about your wife?" she asked, praying she did not sound as desperate as she felt.

He laughed. "My dear, we are none of us married. That is the point of this tournament. Lady Violette means to choose herself a young husband to replace the old one she's recently buried. But only one of us can win that prize. The rest of us battle for honor and ransom—and for the smiles of the ladies whose favors we wear. I should consider myself much privileged if you would condescend to grant me yours."

"I—I shall have to ask my brother." The jongleur had sung of ladies bestowing tokens upon their chosen knights. But Custance, the maid-servant who had waited on Mathilde's mother when she and Lady Caterine had both lived in the royal court, had warned Mathilde about warm-eyed, smooth-tongued men eager to prey upon fortuneless innocents such as herself.

"Your brother will understand," Chesnei said. "He will no doubt wear some lady's favor himself. Surely you can spare some small token for me? Perhaps a tassel from your girdle or that ribbon in your hair . . ."

15

To her relief, he finally released her hand.

To her horror, the plump fingers swooped towards her face.

He could not have missed the way she flinched to avoid him, the way her hand flew up to guard her ribbon. "I shall ask my brother," she repeated breathlessly and slipped into the safety of the crowd before he could stop her.

Her panic ebbed as the milling company closed off her view of Chesnei. She looked at the dais, searching for her brother amongst the suitors gathered there. There was no sign of Girard. Violette de Maloisel still stood at the center of the dais, but she no longer smiled. She seemed to be exchanging sharp words with a tall, pale-haired gentleman who stood below her. The man's back was turned to Mathilde, but Lady Violette's brilliant dark eyes glared at him.

Mathilde's gaze drifted from the lady's fiery challenge to the exotic jeweled collar that graced her throat. Mathilde raised her fingers to touch her own necklet, a large sapphire framed in an ornamental setting of scrolling gold. She ran her fingers up the links of the chain and tentatively felt the clasp at the back of her neck. The clasp had been loose when she had checked it earlier today. Girard had promised to fix it for her, but it still did not feel right. The necklet had been the only piece of jewelry left to her by her mother. She would hate to have it break loose amid this crush of people.

She shifted into a little pocket of space in the crowd where she could look at her necklet without the risk of being jostled. Then she slid the chain around on her neck and tried to view the clasp. The chain was too short to see the small metal piece comfortably. She craned her neck back as far as she could and stretched out the chain to its utmost length, just past her chin.

"Fiend seize the wench, and all women like her! If she thinks, for her sake, that I am going to—"

"Therri, look out—"

Mathilde heard the two male voices, the first one growling almost in her ear, just before the speaker trod into her so hard that he sent her staggering across the floor.

Snap.

The clasp popped free in her fingers as the force of the collision threatened to hurl her into an ungainly sprawl. Her hands flew out to try to break her fall, but someone caught her and jerked her back.

"Devil take my clumsiness! Are you all right?"

Mathilde gasped, then flinched. A terrifying two-headed bird, with two equally fierce-looking beaks, soared out at her from tongues of wickedly leaping orange-red flames. She shivered and flapped out her hands in a protective movement as she backed hurriedly away.

"Lady? Forgive me, the fault was mine. I was not looking where I was going. Have I injured you?"

The voice drew Mathilde's gaze away from the horrible apparition.

And riveted it on the most heroically beautiful face she had ever beheld.

Above her towered a man with pale gold hair waving back from a strong, high forehead and clean-shaven cheeks bronzed warm by the sun. Features of impeccable perfection which might have been thought delicate in a woman, somehow imparted a manly confidence bordering on arrogance in this face. Eyes as clear and bright as her sapphire looked down on her from beneath fair, finely chiseled eyebrows. The brows quirked upwards slightly as she gazed silently back at him. Mathilde could not speak. Her breath had somehow become trapped in her throat in a snare of pleasurably painful delight.

"Lady?"

This time his voice fell on her ears like the mellifluous thrum of the jongleur's harp.

"I told you to look out. You've knocked the senses from her."

Her blissful trance shattered at this clipping remark, spoken from somewhere to the golden-haired gentleman's left. Mathilde dragged her gaze reluctantly away from the vision before her to stare at the new speaker. Two green eyes laughed down at her from a face tanned to a deep nut brown. A mass of wild black curls riotously framed features handsome in their regularity but falling short of the perfection of his companion. Across the breast of his forest green surcote was blazoned an emblem in gold cloth of a five-petaled rose with a crimson center shaped like a droplet of blood. She felt a warm wash of color sweep up into her cheeks and glanced furtively back at the Vision. The frightening two-headed bird was nothing more than a similar emblem rising out of a pattern of flames on his black silk surcote.

The Vision gazed down on her with concern at her continued silence. "Lady," he tried again, "did I hurt you when I stepped on you? You have my sorest regrets. I allowed irritation to distract me from where I was going."

He paused, the clarity of his blue eyes darkening as he cast a glance at the dais. Mathilde followed his gaze. Her spirits plunged. The tall, pale-haired gentleman with whom Lady Violette had been quarreling no longer stood at its foot, but their hostess's pouting glance across the floor at the Vision left no doubt in Mathilde's mind that the Vision and the quarrelsome gentleman were one and the same. A sigh of regret escaped the snare in her throat, more painful now than pleasurable. She allowed herself one more moment to imagine herself basking in the glow of those wonderful, sapphire-hued eyes . . .

Sapphire! She stiffened and raised a hand to her throat. The necklet was gone!

"My jewels," she whispered. "They must have fallen off when you bumped me."

She turned about, but saw no sign of the necklet. It must be buried somewhere in the rushes on the floor. Without thought for the dignity her brother had chided her to remember, she dropped to her knees and began searching frantically through the dried grasses and herbs. Her fingers crushed free a scent of wild mint, almost casting her back into the jongleur's world again. King Arthur's court had sprinkled their rushes with this same sweet-smelling plant . . .

The Vision's voice broke the spell before it could properly begin. "What the devil are you doing down there?"

He sounded as censorious as Girard.

"Don't be a thick wit," his companion said. "She's looking for something." He added as she resumed her search, "Maybe if you told me what you were looking *for*, I could be of more help."

18

She glanced up. The green-eyed gentleman with the errant black curls was on his knees, plunging hands as deeply tanned as his face repeatedly into the rushes.

"People are staring at us," the Vision muttered above them.

"Let 'em stare. A truly chivalrous knight cares more for a lady's distress than for his dignity." The green-eyed gentleman paused in his search to drive an elbow into the muscular calf of the Vision's silk-hosed leg.

"Ow! Oh, all right." The Vision knelt too.

By then, however, Mathilde had become aware of the decrease of humming around them and of all the shocked eyes turned their way. She felt the heat in her face as it stained with color.

"I-I'm sorry," she stammered. "But it was my mother's necklet. It is the only piece of jewelry she left me when she died. I dare not return home without it."

She searched more hurriedly, as eager to end this humiliating scene as she was to find the necklet. The Vision frowned, his perfectly molded mouth hinting of displeasure as he threaded his hands through the rushes with a half-hearted gesture. His companion scowled, whether at the Vision or at herself, Mathilde was not sure.

She felt herself on the verge of tears when the scowl vanished in a grin of triumph. Two wide, nut-brown hands swooped up, bearing in their palms her necklet lying in a bed of grasses and mint.

"Is this it?"

"Oh, yes!" She snatched the necklet out of his hands, picked the strands of dried grass out of the chain . . . "Oh, but you've broken the clasp!"

The green eyes widened. "I—? I merely picked it up for you."

"I mean—" Mathilde blushed again. "I mean it must have broken when you bumped into me."

"*I* didn't—"

The Vision cut him off. "I'm the one who bumped into you. If I've broken it, I'll take it and see it mended."

Mathilde hesitated. Before she could answer, he drove a hand under her elbow and raised her firmly back to her feet. He cast a sharp glance at the crowd. Those who had been staring turned away, but not without a few titters and smirks.

"I apologize again for walking into you," the Vision said. "I'm sorry I broke your necklet. But I promise I'll see it repaired and returned to you safely."

Mathilde observed that even his frown could not mar the beauty of his face. If she refused his offer, she might never speak to him again. But if he repaired the necklet, then he would have to return it. Surely by then she would have thought of something lively and witty to say, rather than embarrassing him or standing before him like a besmitten stock?

She held out the necklet. "Thank you. It is very kind of you, my lord."

He snatched it out of her palm, sketched her a polite bow, then turned on his heel and strode towards the exit of the hall.

Mathilde gazed after him, holding her breath until he disappeared through the exit. She pressed her hand to her fluttering heart, her palm still tingling from the brief touch of his fingers.

She whispered on a long, almost dizzying sigh, "He is as beautiful as I imagined Prince Erec to be."

"Therri? You think he's beautiful, eh? Well, most women do."

She spun about at the laughing voice. The green-eyed gentleman still stood beside her, watching her with his dark head tilted at a quizzing, considering angle.

"Who's Prince Erec?" he asked.

To Mathilde's exasperation, she felt her face turn rosy again. Had she done anything but blush since these two men had blundered into her? "He was the son of King Lac, and a knight of King Arthur's Round Table. No knight was more handsome or valiant than he, and only Sir Gawain was stronger. The great poet of Champagne, Chrétien de Troyes, wrote a poem about him and his love for the beautiful Enide."

"You have met Chrétien de Troyes?"

His gaze dropped from her face to sweep her gown, reminding her briefly of Chesnei's perusal. But there was nothing lewd in this glance. She guessed he merely sought to assess her status from the simple, unembellished silk. The beads on her girdle were painted wood, her shoes plain white linen. Only the fine silk of her gown and her sapphire necklet suggested that she merited even a lowly place amidst this glittering company. Certainly it made her seeming claim to have sat in the court of Champagne nothing less than ludicrous.

Embarrassment lent a defensive crispness to her voice. "Of course I've not met him. But my father is a great lover of poetry and music, and though he has not much otherwise to give them, any jongleur seeking a warm hearth and a meal is welcome in our hall. One of them repaid my father's generosity by telling us the tale of Erec and Enide, as he claimed to have heard it from the lips of Chrétien himself."

"My master, the Young King, loves poetry as well. He sought to engage Chrétien in his court after the Count of Champagne's death last year. But Chrétien elected to accept the patronage of the Count of Flanders, instead."

That caught her interest. "You are a knight of the Young King's court?"

Even the Vision could not have sketched her a more flawlessly courteous bow. "Etienne de Brielle, at your service, my lady. Might you do me the honor of entrusting me with your name as well?"

"I am Mathilde de Riavelle. My brother, Girard, also serves the Young King. Do you know him, sir?"

The laughter in his eyes shaded with an expression Mathilde could not interpret.

"Girard de Riavelle? Aye, I know him. He never mentioned he had a sister." He must have seen the dismayed way Mathilde's face fell, for he hastened to add, "But we are not *close* friends. Perhaps he hoped to guard you from any dishonorable intentions amongst his cronies. Most of us in the Young King's court are younger sons with little hope of advancement beyond the strength of our swords or a well-dowered wife."

"My father is a poor man. I shall have little dowry when I wed." That was, she knew, more likely the reason Girard had never mentioned her.

But the gentleman insisted, "Nay, then your brother must have held his silence to guard your pretty face. A woman with beauty but no dowry bears a different kind of risk than an equally beautiful woman who bears a fat purse."

Mathilde studied him through narrowed eyes. Why would this man flatter her? Only her father ever called her pretty, and even he had never called her beautiful. There stirred in her mind her mother's maid's warning about smooth-tongued men.

"Is that why you have come to Grantamur Castle? To wed Lady Violette's fat purse?" The pert words slipped out before she could stop them. His soot-colored brows twitched down slightly, the good humor fading from his face, but to her relief, he tossed his glance of displeasure not at her, but at their hostess.

The pout had vanished from Lady Violette's lovely face, replaced with a fresh glow of pleasure as she bent down and allowed some gentleman below the dais to kiss her hand. Mathilde noticed that two of her ladies-in-waiting seemed to be staring in Mathilde's direction. Had her bumbling search for her necklet been observed as far away as the dais?

"I'm as dependent on the Young King's generosity as the rest of his court," the gentleman said after a frowning moment, "and if his father, King Henry, tightens his purse-strings again, it'll send a number of us crawling home to our fathers. Or in my case, my brother. I'd sooner wed Violette the Termagant than choke down my pride to do that."

Mathilde gasped. "Does Lady Violette know you call her that?"

His humor returned with a rueful grin. "I hope not. She'd probably rip the tongue out of the man she caught doing so. You won't betray me, my lady?"

She saw the twinkle in his eyes. He was laughing at her! She drew herself up proudly. "I am not a tattler, sir. And I wish you luck with your prize."

She took a step away from him, but he touched her sleeve.

"Wait, I pray you. I was wondering . . . my lady, have you already bestowed your favor on some knight for tomorrow's tourney?"

She turned, startled. Again, that too-ready color seeped into her face. She drew her arm pointedly away from his hand.

"No one has requested a favor of me yet," she lied, unwilling to admit to Chesnei's offer, "but I have not been long in the hall. I expect as soon as my brother introduces me to a few of his friends, I will—"

"Might I beg the boon of you first?"

She stole a glance at the dais, where Lady Violette was casting coy smiles at a large, bluff-featured man with light brown hair.

"What about the Fair Violette?" Thus had Mathilde heard Lady Violette called by her brother. "Since you hope to marry her, I should think it would be *her* favor you wish to wear."

His lips parted, preparing, she suspected, to issue a stream of false flattery to win her acquiescence. But she had no intention of serving as a pawn in his game to make another woman jealous. She ground her slippered heel into the rushes, releasing a minty burst of aroma as she prepared to spin away from him.

But in the instant before she moved, he uttered abruptly, "The Fair Vi won't have me. She won't have any of us. She went back on her word to give Therri her favor and claims she scorns us all except Sir William. She'd like us all to play hangdog for her, but I'll not give her the satisfaction. Let Therri skulk off and sulk if he likes, but I mean to show her she's not the only wench in Normandy."

His frankness took Mathilde aback. She had not expected him to admit to his purpose. "But if you wish to make her jealous, why choose me? There are many prettier ladies in the hall than I."

He studied her for another weighing moment. "You remind me of someone. Besides, I like the way your eyes sparkle when you're angry and go all dreamy when you're thinking of that jongleur's poetry."

The smile he flashed along with these words held an unanticipated charm. Mathilde's heart gave a disturbing thump and she observed very suddenly that his eyes were quite as vibrantly green as the Vision's had been blue.

No, she did not wish to be used as a pawn—

—but on the other hand, it seemed a shame to allow pride to prevent her from having *some* champion in the field tomorrow. Girard's continued absence from her side bespoke, she feared, little interest in finding a champion for her. At least this gentleman, irritating though his game with Violette was, looked lithe enough to win a joust or two in her honor.

Lithe, broad-shouldered, nearly as tall as the Vision . . .

Her hand fluttered to her bare neck, then fell away again. Disappointment twitched through her in a bewilderingly strong pang. "I'm afraid I don't have anything to give you."

His gaze drifted again down the length of her blue silk gown, more slowly and lingeringly this time. She backed away a little, dismayed by the rush of warmth that tingled over her flesh. When his eyes lifted again to her face, the green seemed subtly darker.

"What about this?" He reached out a hand to touch the embroidered silk ribbon.

"Oh, I could not. It is not mi—"

The rest caught in her throat. His hand hovered near her face, distracting her with its wide brown palm and the odd heat that seemed to radiate from it. Before she could regain her voice to stop him, his fingers clasped the ribbon. Slowly, like a seductive whisper against her scalp, he threaded it out of her hair.

"I shall wear it on my sleeve tomorrow," he murmured, "and do battle in your honor."

"But—" Her scalp tingled, but her voice returned once his hand retreated from her face. "But you said you were fighting for Lady Violette."

The corners of his mouth twitched up and a gleam of— mischief?—glimmered briefly in his eyes. "Perhaps. But the glory of my victories shall belong to you."

He bowed to her, his mouth curving up the rest of the way into another of his wickedly engaging smiles. Then he bade her good-even, and strode off the way the Vision had gone.

The disconcerting trance broke as soon as he vanished into the crowd. Again disappointment wove through her, more bitter than before. What use was the glory of his victories, when he, like all the other men still thronging the dais, had eyes only for Lady Violette?

Or had she misinterpreted his motive entirely? She frowned, remembering her reaction when he had taken her ribbon. Why had she not shrank from him as she had from Chesnei? What sort of trick had this gentleman used to freeze her voice and make her body flush the way he had? He had professed his intention of pursuing Lady Violette's wealth. But he had also spoken of dowerless women at risk from dishonorable men.

Perhaps he knew of such men because he was one of them! Aye, he was undoubtedly the very sort of seducer her mother's maid-servant had warned her of. What further evidence did she need than her own perplexing reaction to his nearness? It must be a small trick for a seducer to tantalize a woman, as he had tantalized her, with the mere proximity of his hand.

No doubt he thought her poverty and her unremarkable face would make her an easy target for his dishonest advances. She had been warned of men who lured unsuspecting women to ruin with soft-spoken flattery. But her mother's maid had not had the foresight to caution Mathilde against men with delicious black curls and laughing green eyes and smiles that sent every thought from her head except the firm conviction that she had never seen anything quite as beguiling as the flash of this man's grin.

Mathilde found herself drawing a dismayingly shaky breath. She must keep her distance from him, this green-eyed seducer. If his advances became too overwhelming, she would seek protection from the Vision. She closed her eyes and drew comfort in the memory of their meeting. Unlike his seducer friend, honor lay in every line of the Vision's countenance and frame. A man of such valiant visage would warn his friend off, would no doubt even do battle to defend a lady's honor. Aye, the contrast of the pleasant tingling the Vision had left in her palm to the provocative heat his friend had imparted without even a touch, told the tale of their conflicting characters more loudly than any words could have done.

The corners of her frown tilted upwards as her mind filled with the thrilling image of the Vision riding to her rescue, thundering to save her from a wicked abduction at the hands of his base, lascivious former-friend.

"Mathilde?"

She opened her eyes, her pleasant dream shimmering away at her brother's voice.

"I'm through here," he said. He held up a strip of blue cloth. "I drew the south end of the field for tomorrow. I'll find you a seat in one of the stands near there where you can watch. Now we had better retire. I'll need a clear head and a good night's sleep if I'm going to have a chance tomorrow of—"

He broke off, his gaze suddenly riveted on her hair. The flesh above his beard went pasty white. "Where's the ribbon?"

She raised a hand to her hair. What had she been thinking? "Girard, I—"

"Where is it?"

She cast a glance about the hall in a search for the green-eyed gentleman before she remembered he had left. "He asked me for a favor for the tournament tomorrow. He took it from me before I could stop him."

"'He' who?"

"I-I can't remember his name. He had black curls and green eyes and—"

"I don't care what color his eyes are, curse you!" He seized her by the shoulders so hard that his fingers pinched painfully into her flesh. "I should have known better than to trust it to you. How could you be such a fool? I need that ribbon back. *Think.* What was the fellow's name?"

She racked her brains for the answer. She remembered he had introduced himself with a flourishing bow worthy of a master seducer. But she could not for the life of her remember the name he had told her, and the only name she could think of for his companion was the Vision.

"*Curse* you!" Girard shook her. "We're not leaving this hall until we find him. Your memory for faces had better be keener than your memory for names."

He started to drag her into the crowd.

"There is no use looking for him here," she said. "He has left the hall."

He swung around on her, and she saw fury mingled with panic in his eyes. "Left? Great heavens, Mathilde, have you any idea what you've done?" His voice came in a strangled wail.

"Girard, it was only a ribbon."

"Only a ribbon? *Only a ribbon?*" For a moment, he looked so enraged she thought he might strike her. His free hand formed a fist, but he cast a sharp glance at the surrounding crowd and only growled, "We'll settle this back at the tent."

He jerked her towards the exit, all dignity abandoned as his angry strides forced her to alternately run and stumble through the crowd in an attempt to keep up with him.

E tienne de Brielle hunched down on his cot and drew his cloak closer as the early autumn wind outside rustled the flaps of the tent and sent a cold draft swirling on the air. This tournament of Lady Violette de Maloisel's would likely be the last of the season. Outside he could hear the jovial laughter and camaraderie of knights gathered around makeshift fires scattered amongst the tents set up on the field below Grantamur Castle. Etienne had sent the squires out to warm themselves at one of those fires, since the brazier had been pushed into a far corner inside the tent to clear a path for Therri's pacings.

Nothing but friendship could have kept Etienne sitting in this dismal cold, rather than joining the squires. The candle beside the cot sputtered and nearly went out. He grimaced and pushed the candle across the table until its flame sprang up again, albeit dangerously near the cloth of the tent.

"For heaven's sake, Therri, can't you at least slow down?" he said. "Every time you stride past the table, you create a wind that threatens to cast us into darkness. And I, for one, am not ready to sleep."

"I can see that," his companion snapped. Therri de Laurant cast a dour glance at Etienne as he swept past the cot again. "Do you plan to sit there sniffing that all night?"

Etienne raised the white, gilt-embroidered ribbon to his nose and breathed deeply of its lingering scent. "Ahhhh. A bit musky."

Somehow he had expected a breezier fragrance to cling from her hair. Still, this scent was pretty, although . . . "I can't quite place it. "

Therri spun on his heel at the far side of the tent and strode back, snatching the ribbon out of Etienne's hand as he paced towards the entrance. He sniffed at the ribbon without breaking his long-legged stride. "Angelica," he stated, turned again, and tossed it back at his friend.

Etienne caught the strip. He rubbed a thumb absently along the tiny stitches on the back and watched Therri's restless movements from beneath his lashes. He murmured, "I should have known you'd be an expert at recognizing ladies' perfumes."

"It has nothing to do with ladies. You'd know the scent too, if you had any sisters."

"I'd know the scent if I had a beautiful face that set the ladies swooning."

Therri paused long enough to glower at his friend. Not for the first time, Etienne marveled that such perfectly cast features could impart so fierce an expression. Few men would pursue a quarrel with Therri when he scowled like that.

"Devil take my face," Therri muttered. "And fiend seize those silly, sighing women! Violette must know that they mean nothing to me!" He lunged back into his pacing.

Finally, his friend was ready to talk. Etienne had sat in the murky cold a long while, watching Therri's restless strides, waiting for him to speak.

Violette de Maloisel. His friend clearly had eyes for no one else. But Therri's reputation with women had preceded him to Grantamur Castle. They had swarmed around him in the Young King's palace in Rouen and Therri had not been immune to their flattery. He had teased and flirted so outrageously with them all, that it had not taken long for rumors to spread that he might have indulged in more than a few stolen kisses with some of them. Etienne knew better, but Therri had found it amusing to maintain a smug silence on the matter when the other knights of the court had tried to draw the truth from him. But the game had taken a perverse twist when Violette had paid a visit to Rouen. Therri had fallen headlong in love. He and the lovely widow had enjoyed a few blissful weeks together, laughing over games of chess, dancing together night after night, and lingering in long, private conversations in the palace gardens, until whispers of Therri's "reputation" had at last drifted to Violette's ears. Still, Etienne suspected she might have been willing to leave the past in the past had Therri not committed a disasterous "present" mistake right under her nose. She had departed from Rouen in a tiny whirlwind of indignation and promptly announced this tournament to choose her future husband. Therri had stormed after her, but any hopes he had had of soothing her ruffled feathers remained frustrated by the gaggle of ladies who trailed him about even here in Violette's court, hoping to become his next "conquest".

"If anyone should stand rebuked, it is she," Therri lashed out. "I have never seen such a shameless flirt in my life as Violette de Maloisel. Did you see her tonight, laughing with those men, fluttering her lashes at them, enticing them so coyly with her honeyed words and captivating smiles . . . ?" He trailed off and even in the dim light of the tent, Etienne caught the darkling look directed at himself. "But of course you saw. She fluttered her lashes hardest of all at you."

Etienne refused to rise to that bait. Only a love-sick, jealousy-blinded fool could have missed the sly glances the Fair Violette sent Therri's way while she laughed and flattered his friend. Etienne had not been able to resist the temptation of teasing Therri by flattering Violette in return. But after a twenty-four year friendship that had begun almost from the hour of their births, Therri should have known better than to suspect Etienne of intending to disrupt what was clearly, to Therri, a serious affair of the heart.

Therri stopped suddenly and whirled towards the cot. "Where *did* you get that ribbon, anyway?"

"Oh, go stick your head in a bucket," Etienne said. "Preferably one filled with cold water. De Riavelle's sister gave it to me."

"De Riavelle? *Girard* de Riavelle? He has a sister?"

"Aye, that pretty, awkward lass you bumped into tonight. The one whose necklet you broke."

"Oh . . . aye." The vague way Therri said it convinced Etienne that his friend bore no memory whatsoever of the poor girl's face.

"You do mean to mend it, don't you?" Etienne said.

"What?"

"Her necklet. You said you would mend it and return it to her."

"Oh. Aye," Therri said again. "After the tournament, I'll find a goldsmith to attend to it. I can't believe you accepted a favor from her. De Riavelle's sister! *De Riavelle.*"

Etienne shrugged. "I know. But I felt sorry for her. I'll wager this is her first time away from her parents' doting arms. She reminded me a bit of Heléne—except for the doting parents."

"My sister?" Therri ignored the dig at his sire and dame. "The girl was nothing like Heléne."

"How do you know? You don't even remember her face."

"Exactly. If she'd looked like Heléne, I'd remember."

"I didn't say she *looked* like Heléne—except that she's as slender as your sister, and her hair is flaxen. Her eyes are darker, though, something like the color of violets. But the sad way she looked when I said her brother never spoke of her, and the suspicious way her eyes narrowed when I called her 'pretty' . . . Heléne had that same awkward uncertainty about her looks before she married Gunthar."

"The only thing *I* remember is the embarrassing way the wench had us both crawling about the floor. If you don't want your brother storming Rouen again demanding your return home, I'd sever that connection at once."

Etienne's good humor dissolved in the brief space it took to divide two heartbeats. "Who I choose to bestow my attentions on is none of my brother's business."

"Bestowing them on de Riavelle's sister is not going to convince Triston that your judgment has improved since Rousillon tricked you into trying to murder my brother-in-law."

The reminder of Etienne's youthful error stung. "Gunthar wasn't your brother-in-law when I attacked him," he muttered. "And I'd never have done it if Rousillon hadn't told me that Gunthar had come to imprison Father." Such imprisonment would have been a death-sentence for Etienne's frail, crippled sire. Etienne could still taste the bittersweet tang of panicked disappointment mingled with heart-pounding relief at his failure, the two emotions barely submerged beneath the pain of the Earl of Gunthar snapping his wrist as Gunthar had wrestled Etienne's dagger away.

Etienne frowned and rubbed his wrist. Though once more hale and strong, it ached a little in the cold. He had made a mistake with Gunthar, and he owned it. But his brother's patronizing presumption that Etienne had been foolishly manipulated yet again when he had chosen to declare his allegiance to King Henry II's eldest son and titular co-ruler, Henry the Young King, stung Etienne's pride past bearing.

That pride had prompted him to angrily reject the offer his brother had extended six months past, to make Etienne his seneschal. When Etienne had challenged him, his brother admitted that the offer was designed to fetch Etienne away from the Young King's court. Worse, he knew that beneath his brother's openly admitted political goal had lain a silent conviction that Etienne, their late father's younger, pampered son, was not capable of carving himself an independent and successful place in the world.

Etienne had sworn to prove his brother wrong.

A lifetime of friendship, and a brief, tragic marriage between Therri's older sister and Etienne's brother, had left Therri too well acquainted with the tensions in Etienne's family. No doubt, Etienne told himself, his friend only meant to be helpful by persisting.

"Still, you'd better take care. Your brother inherited quite a windfall when he remarried, and if de Riavelle sees you flirting with his sister, he's likely to push for a connection that he thinks might land a steady stream of gold into his congenitally-empty purse. You'd be better off marrying Hermaline."

Etienne barely repressed a shudder at the mention of Violette's saucy step-daughter. "I'd sooner throw myself off a cliff."

Therri gave a sympathetic crack of laughter, but insisted, "At least she'd bring you some gold and the lordship of a castle. Admittedly her birth is unfortunate. De Maloisel's by-blow. But he left her a generous dowry and no other stain on her name, and —"

"And you think she's the best I can aspire to."

"I did not say that. But I think you can aspire to higher than de Riavelle's penniless sister. It's not just that she's poor. There are whispers about her father, although I've not listened to the gossip myself. But I know her brother is a shirking weasel. A connection like that is sure to bring Triston's wrath crashing down about your head."

"Blazes!" Etienne swore. "I haven't asked the girl to marry me. I only offered to wear her favor."

"Aye, and for the life of me, I can't fathom why!"

"Because she looked like she didn't have a friend in that hall, apart from her wretched brother. And then you blundered into her and—"

"And what?"

And set her poor head spinning at your arrogantly beautiful face. Etienne bit off the words before they could cut his friend anew.

"And what?" Therri repeated.

Etienne shook his head. The ribbon flapped in the air as he waved the answer away. He was relieved when Therri resumed his pacing. His friend's exquisitely chiseled features had, he knew, caused Therri as much grief as pleasure in life. If women swarmed to him, men were wont to taunt him—until they met him lance to lance in the field. No wonder he had learned to look so fierce! A keen battle-eye and hard-honed reflexes sufficed to reassure Therri's mockers of his masculinity. But he was not above exploiting his physical charm when he wished to make a lady blush.

Mathilde de Riavelle, alas, had not even pricked his conceit sufficiently to win herself so much as one of his absent-mindedly sensuous smiles. It hadn't mattered. Etienne had seen the glow in her wide, violet eyes. One brief, awkward encounter, and she'd thought herself head-over-ears in love with his friend.

Etienne was not sure what had prompted him to linger behind Therri's departure from the hall to flirt with her. Perhaps he'd hoped to smooth over Therri's curt manners. She had looked so young in that pretty but unpretentious blue gown. He remembered the pink blush of embarrassment on her high-boned cheeks when he'd surveyed her beaded girdle and little, prosaic linen shoes, the nervous way her hand had fluttered to her neck when he'd asked for a favor . . . There had been something touchingly vulnerable about that gesture. A poignant fragility to her slender fingers, a curious, childlike innocence in the tilt of her head . . .

Therri interrupted his musings with sudden savagery. "I'll wager Violette gave her favor to Marshal after I left the hall. Do you suppose she means to abide by that absurd vow she made to wed tomorrow's champion, whoever he may be?"

Etienne reluctantly shook away his thoughts of Mathilde. "You did not think the vow so absurd before William Marshal entered his name for the tourney."

"I could have won. Fiend seize it, Etienne, I could have won against *anyone* but him! What do I do now?"

Etienne heard the ill-smothered despair in Therri's voice. Young though he was, Therri's reputation on the tournament field was formidable. But in nearly fourteen years, William Marshal had never been defeated in the mêlée.

Etienne watched his friend's pacings another moment. The last thing Therri needed was to be encouraged to wallow in self-pity. Better to try to tease him out of it.

Etienne exhaled an exaggerated sigh and flung himself dramatically down on his cot. "Go to bed and let me get some sleep."

Even with his eyes closed, he could feel Therri's glare. "I thought you weren't tired."

"I changed my mind. I'd rather dream of de Riavelle's sister than listen to you make a fool of yourself over the Fair Violette." She of the shrewish tongue, Etienne added to himself. The way she had snapped at Therri tonight when he had pressed her for her favor had been appalling. But he cracked open one eye and said, for Therri's sake, "If she loves you, she won't marry Marshal, no matter how grandly he wins the day. And if she does marry him—well, then, you're well rid of a shameless flirt for a wife."

Therri grunted. Etienne turned his back to him and told him to blow out the candle. His friend growled something but snuffed the flame. Etienne reached down to jerk up the blanket at the end of the cot and nearly dropped the ribbon. His hand clenched around the embroidered strip, then he loosened a forefinger to hook the blanket and pulled it up around him. Once shrouded in the extra warmth, he looped the ribbon around his palm for safety, and tucked them both under the bolster beneath his head. A whiff of angelica eased upward to his nostrils. With that musky perfume weaving through his senses, he was not surprised to find the pretty, piquant face of the ribbon's owner dancing against his closed lids.

"Curious," he murmured.

"What is?" He heard the resumption of Therri's pacings in the dark.

"You'd think Violette would be the one with violet eyes." He laughed. But he drew out his beribboned hand and laid it alongside his head on the bolster before he fell asleep.

Mathilde squinted against the bright autumn sun and raised a hand to shade her eyes. They had been searching for well-nigh three quarters of an hour. The wedge-shaped pennons posted above the tents that dotted the field below Grantamur Castle had appeared as little more than black rippling cloth in the night, their colorful devices hidden in the shadows or distorted by the leaping flames of camp fires. Now, in the early morning light she could clearly make out the various emblems on the fluttering banners.

"Well?" Girard demanded. "Do you see it?"

Mathilde tilted her head to study her brother. She suspected that he had not slept a wink all night. Smudges like dark puddles rimmed his bloodshot eyes. His mouth trembled briefly within his beard, then tensed into a line as he waited for her answer. He must, she thought, be very deeply in love indeed with the woman who had given him the ribbon. Why else would he have been so upset at its loss?

She turned her attention back to the banners. "I don't think so. I remember that it was some kind of bird, but none of these seem to be right."

Mathilde had endured her brother's roaring anger until late into the night. He had called her witless and feather-brained and cursed himself for a fool for agreeing to bring her to Grantamur Castle. None of his railings had, however, prompted her to remember the name of either the Vision who had taken her necklet or his green-eyed friend who had seduced the ribbon from her hair. Only after Girard had thrown himself onto his cot in apparent exhaustion and despair had she curled up on her own cot and drifted off to sleep. But she had been beset with the most frightful dreams. Screeching birds and flapping wings and angry tongues of bright orange flame . . .

She must have cried out in her sleep for Girard had shaken her awake, ordering his squire to light a lantern. As the light helped dispel the last shreds of the oppressive nightmares, their source gradually became clear in her mind. The emblem she had seen woven into the Vision's tunic, the two-headed bird rising from the flames . . .

Girard gave a shout when she mumbled out the memory. At first light, he exclaimed, they would seek out the tent that flew the banner she described. Surely her Vision, whoever he was, would be able to point them in the direction of his friend who had taken the ribbon?

"What about that one, my lady?" Girard's squire pointed at a round-eyed owl poised over a nest of three vipers.

His flat voice made Mathilde's skin twitch. Costane was at least ten years her brother's senior, with colorless hair, colorless flesh, colorless eyes—eyes that frightened Mathilde in the flatness of their gaze.

She shivered at Costane's unblinking regard and drew a little closer to Girard. Her brother might be impatient and rough, but he had also always been fiercely protective of her when she was growing up. She shook her head to the squire's question.

"That one, then?" Costane shifted his finger to another banner.

"That is a falcon," she said. "I told you it was some bird I had never seen before. And it had two heads."

"Sir Adam Bearce employs the double-headed eagle in his standard," Costane said to Girard. "I believe his tent lies in that direction." He pointed to the north end of the field.

Girard gave a curt nod and fell into step beside the squire.

Mathilde called out after them, "But I don't think it was an eagle, Girard. I would have recognized an eagle."

"You're too dizzy-headed to recall what your last meal was," Girard retorted. "Now come along."

"But I am sure it was not an eagle!"

She turned and swept stubbornly in the opposite direction from where Costane had pointed.

Outside the tents, chain mail rattled and steel blades rasped as squires assisted their knights to arm for the upcoming tourney. Armor gleamed white in the morning sun. Mathilde slowed her pace to admire the scene. Just as in the jongleur's poem of the brave Erec, these knights wore surcotes bearing every imaginable heraldic device and hefted great round or kite-shaped shields painted in bright colors like their lances. Several of the knights turned to stare as Mathilde strolled past. She returned their gazes with a dreamy sigh and a smile.

Girard caught up with her and broke the spell with a fierce grasp on her arm. "Where do you think you're going?"

"I'm looking for the Vision's banner," she replied. "Costane is wrong. It was not an eagle."

"Well, don't go traipsing about the field without Costane or me beside you. At least half these fellows staring at you are members of the Young King's court. I know them, and how quick they are to misinterpret a pretty, unattended woman."

She stopped, a faint blush of pleasure warming her cheeks. "Do you think I am pretty, Girard? You've never said so before."

"Aye," he muttered, "a pretty goose with feathers for brains."

A half-smile tugged at his troubled mouth. It held a hint of fondness that she recalled he had sometimes betrayed for her when she had been small and he had rumpled her hair to comfort her after rebuking her for some annoyance she had caused him that had brought her to tears.

Before she could reply, someone called out her name.

"Lady Mathilde!"

She turned, then silently berated herself for doing so. Nevell de

Chesnei, as yet unarmed and wearing a tunic that looked too tight across the central part of his girth, raised a hand to salute her. She fought an urge to shrink. She supposed she must acknowledge him, for politeness' sake . . .

Girard caught her hand before she could return Chesnei's salute, tucked it into the crook of his arm and bowed coldly in Chesnei's direction. Chesnei returned the bow with a jovial grin.

"Did you not wish me to speak with him, Girard?" Mathilde asked as her brother pulled her away.

"Nay," he said curtly.

She waited for more but he offered no explanation. "He is d'Amville's nephew," she ventured into his grim-faced silence. "Perhaps he knows something that can help us to clear Father's name."

"There is nothing to clear," Girard said. "Let it alone, Mathilde. Father's honor is as dead as D'Amville. Nothing that Chesnei might know is going to change Father's disgrace."

Mathilde tugged on Girard's arm, forcing him to stop beside her. "Father did not steal from the crown!"

"You know nothing about it, you weren't even born. D'Amville had proof of Father's guilt."

"Father told me he did not take that ring from the Royal Wardrobe!"

"And the candlesticks and the jeweled plates? Did he deny taking those, too?"

She hesitated, remembering the way her father had clamped his lips together when she had asked him about those items. Items which, unlike the king's ring, had never been recovered.

"But I am sure there is something more to the story," she insisted, "something that Father is not telling us. I heard him and d'Amville arguing shortly before d'Amville died. D'Amville said my marriage to him would set 'the seal' upon his revenge on Father."

"Revenge for what?" Girard demanded.

"He did not say. Father must have injured him in some way. But does it not suggest that d'Amville might have planted that ring on Father out of spite?"

"How would he have done so? Father worked in King Henry's Wardrobe, not d'Amville. D'Amville had no access to any of those items."

"But—"

"Give it up, Mathilde. I admit that d'Amville was cruel and twisted, and I thank the stars he did not live to marry you. But 'twas Father, not d'Amville, who thirsted for revenge. D'Amville destroyed Father's future by exposing his crime to King Henry, then enticed Father into that drunken game of dice that lost us our inheritance. Aye, it was Father, not d'Amville, who wanted revenge." He broke off, then repeated sharply, "Let it alone, Mathilde."

"But Father was innocent, I am sure of it," she insisted. "And if you will not help me to prove it, then I will find a man who will."

Girard's patience snapped. "Fine. Shall I take you back to Chesnei? Perhaps he will marry you in d'Amville's place. You can try wheedling 'the truth' out of him while he pants for you on your wedding night."

Mathilde's face flamed. She pulled her hand out of Girard's arm and marched deeper into the field of tents, appalled not at his sarcastic suggestion, but at her own cowardice for having rejected that very same idea in Grantamur's hall last night. Chesnei had repulsed her. But if she truly loved her father, surely no sacrifice would be too great to make for him?

"Tillot, wait. I—"

She knew from Girard's use of her pet name that he was about to apologize, but before he could do so Costane appeared in their path. She had not realized the squire had left them until he spoke to her brother.

"I have been to Sir Adam's tent, sir," he said in his dull voice. "He knows nothing about my lady's ribbon."

Girard swore softly. "A two-headed bird. I thought sure it must be Sir Adam's eagle."

"I told you it was not," Mathilde said.

Still ruffled at her brother and unnerved by the thought of Chesnei, she made a random turn and strode briskly past a half-dozen tents. Girard followed, cursing her softly.

"Costane, you search the tents that way. I'll keep an eye on Mathilde."

Mathilde swept on, wishing Girard would go away with his squire. Thoroughly irritated with her brother, she veered to the right, swept through a fresh cluster of tents, then stopped suddenly and pointed at a banner flapping in the autumn breeze.

"Girard, there it is!"

She gazed up at a fancifully feathered bird with two great hooked beaks, its body rising with sweeping, outstretched wings from an angry pattern of orange-red flames. Even in the cool clarity of the morning sun, the creature still looked frightening.

But it was not fear that dissolved her annoyance with Girard and set her heart to fluttering. In the space before the tent sat a half-dozen mounted men in rich mantles, the same number of richly garbed women, and two elegant but empty-saddled palfreys. The Vision must be a man of great importance that such a grand company had come to pay homage to him!

Girard groaned from beside her. "Nay, not the double-headed phoenix. Not Laurant. Tillot, are you sure you're not mistaken?"

"Nay," she breathed, "'tis the Vision's tent."

In mere moments, she would stand in his presence again. She was certain she would have no need of Chesnei if she could only win such a knight as the Vision to her cause. But how should she ever catch the eye of a man so beautiful, valiant and important as he?

She raised her hands to try to smooth her hair. Did she look as frightfully tousled as she felt? At least her blue silk gown had been hung all night so that it had not become rumpled. But her shabby mantle and dull linen shoes . . . Well, there was no help for it. She had nothing better to wear of the other clothes she had brought from home. She must impress the Vision with her spirit instead. He admired Lady Violette. Perhaps he liked his women proud and haughty. She lifted her chin and threw back her shoulders. This time she would *not* behave like a stuttering fool. She would dazzle him with her smile and her clever, amusing tongue.

Reassuring herself that something clever and amusing would

pop into her mouth once she stood in his presence, she took three quick, determined steps towards the tent.

Just then, the horse of one of the mounted ladies whinnied and sidled a bit, creating a brief opening in the semi-circle of waiting attendants. Through the space she saw a lady attended by a maid, conversing with a knight near the tent's entrance. The Vision! How tall he looked, how broad-shouldered and strong, how . . .

Her breath caught away in a wrench. 'Twas *not* the Vision. This knight's breeze-stirred curls were the color of soot.

'Twas the green-eyed Seducer. Over his silver-hued hauberk, he wore an emerald green tunic blazoned with a five-petaled gilded rose. An impossibly huge ruby flashed from the emblem's center. In his hand he held her white silk ribbon.

But what was he doing at the Vision's tent? She glanced back up at the Vision's banner, then let her gaze sweep a little beyond. Flanking the other side of the tent flapped a second banner, this one bearing a slightly more sober rendition of the same emblem that graced the Seducer's surcote.

"Lady Mathilde!"

Mathilde started. He had seen her! And she noted with a dismaying thump in her breast that his wickedly disarming smile had lost none its beguiling power over night.

Etienne grinned with relief at the sight of her. He glimpsed Mathilde just as Hermaline laughed her coy laugh and started to extend to him a gauzy apple green veil sprinkled with silver stars. Hermaline had been on the verge of thrusting it upon him half a dozen times last night. Fortunately, Violette had been flirting so extravagantly with him in a bid to make Therri jealous, that Etienne had been able to pretend he was too preoccupied to understand her step-daughter's broadly inviting hints.

This morning, he could claim no such distraction. Hermaline had brought with her a dozen attendants, no doubt hoping to impress upon him what an auspicious marriage partner she would make. Etienne knew the attendants had been borrowed from Violette, for Hermaline had no such great standing of her own. De Maloisel had bequeathed his illegitimate daughter some gold, but not enough to win a husband from among the higher nobility. But the single modest castle he had left her, along with its adjoining village and fields, might be enough to lure an improvident younger son—like Etienne.

He admitted he had toyed with the idea when he had first met her, when she had come to Rouen with Violette to buy the Young King's permission for Violette to remarry. One castle and a village might not seem much, but other men had built great and ambitious estates from equally small beginnings.

But one dance with Hermaline at the Young King's court had convinced Etienne that behind her pretty, pouting face with it's summer blue eyes and her tumble of burnished gold curls, hid a managing, ill-tempered cat. But a clever cat. Once she had that apple green veil wrapped around his arm as a favor, he feared she would use it to spread such sly rumors that he would find himself bound to her before he knew it.

He executed his most courteous bow to Hermaline now and said, before she could offer the veil to him, "Pray excuse me, my lady, I must speak to Lady Mathilde. She most kindly bestowed her favor on me last night and has come to tie it around my sleeve for luck."

He did not give Hermaline a chance to protest, but strode purposefully towards Mathilde and her brother. Knowing Hermaline's gaze to be riveted on them, Etienne greeted Mathilde with a resounding "My lady!", boldly took her hand and set upon it a kiss.

He only vaguely registered her gasp. Her fingers looked so slender and fragile in his that he was smitten with a sudden fear lest they break in his firm grasp. He eased his hold on them but found himself reluctant to release them.

Girard's censorious voice broke across Etienne's bemusement. "I beg your pardon, de Brielle. Just what do you think you're doing?"

Mathilde's face went scarlet. She snatched her hand out of Etienne's and stepped back so hastily that she nearly tripped over the hem of her gown. He moved to steady her, but found Girard in his path.

"Forgive my presumption, de Riavelle," Etienne said. "Your sister and I met in Grantamur's hall last night. She granted me her favor for the tournament today, and I was hoping that she might—"

"The ribbon!" Girard exclaimed. "*You* are the one she gave it to?"

Etienne glanced at the slip of embroidered white silk in his hand, but before he could answer, a voice thundered from behind him.

"De Riavelle?"

Girard's head snapped up and Etienne saw him pale. Etienne glanced back at the tent. Therri had appeared in the entrance.

His friend jabbed a finger in the air in Girard's direction. "I want a word with you, de Riavelle."

Girard made a helpless, sputtering sound.

"Girard, what is it?" Mathilde asked anxiously.

"Nothing," he said in a strangled voice. "I—de Brielle, that ribbon. I need it back now!"

Etienne held up the strand. "This? Why?"

"There's been a mistake. I need it back. Why is none of your affair."

Etienne glanced over his shoulder at Hermaline. She watched him as keenly as a blue-eyed falcon, her star-spangled veil fluttering in the breeze. His grasp tightened on the ribbon as he turned back to Girard. "Your lady sister has honored me with her token. I'll not surrender it until I've achieved a victory or two for her on the field.

"The devil you won't—" Girard broke off as Etienne's brows plunged down.

Etienne saw him cast a nervous glance at where Therri stood glaring at him outside the tent. He seized Etienne's arm and pulled him away from Mathilde.

Girard made an obvious attempt to moderate his words. "The thing is, de Brielle, the ribbon was not my sister's to give. 'Tis *my* lady's token, granted to me before we left Rouen. I promised her I'd wear it in her honor this day."

43

Etienne's frown deepened. "The last wench I saw you with at Rouen was that strumpet Parnelle. Don't tell me you've taken to wearing harlots' favors when you joust?"

Girard's face went red but before he could answer, Therri's voice boomed out again. "I'm waiting, de Riavelle. Shall we settle this in private or before all my lady's attendants?" He gestured at Hermaline and her court.

Etienne said, "He's in a foul enough temper over Lady Violette's teasing. I wouldn't provoke him further than you already have."

Girard groaned. He moved with open reluctance towards Therri, only pausing to growl at Mathilde, "Get back the ribbon."

Etienne returned to Mathilde's side. At first he thought it was worry for her brother that fixed her gaze towards the tent. He opened his mouth to reassure her that it was merely a disagreement over gambling debts. Then he saw the soft glow in her eyes — the same glow he had seen last night in Grantamur's hall — and heard her dreamy sigh.

"How well that proud scowl suits his valiant face," she breathed before he could speak. "No man would dare threaten my father if we had the Vision to defend us."

Etienne glanced from her to Therri but only said, "Does someone threaten your father, my lady?"

His voice seemed to startle her. Her violet gaze drifted to his. Again she stepped back from him. He watched the mistiness in her eyes disperse, replaced with a puzzling wariness.

"No — that is —" A faint blush washed her translucent cheeks in pink. "My family's business is not your concern, sir. My brother and I have only come for the ribbon."

"You granted it to me as your favor for the tournament today."

"But I had no right to do so. It belongs to my brother. I mean," she said when Etienne raised his brows, "it belongs to one of his ladies."

"*One* of his ladies?"

She looked defensive at his surprise. "My brother is a handsome man. I have heard him boast to my father's squire that he has many conquests in the Young King's court."

Etienne had to bite his lip to keep from snorting. The only women he had seen fawning over Girard de Riavelle these past three years were the painted harlots Girard picked up in the streets of Rouen. Etienne knew Girard would not have dared to bring one of his strumpets with him to Grantamur Castle—certainly not when he was sharing a tent with his sister.

Etienne felt sickened at the thought of Girard giving Mathilde a harlot's ribbon to wear. Yet when he looked at the silken strip, he remembered only how prettily entangled he had found it in her trailing, flaxen hair and how its musky fragrance had kept her piquant face hovering in his dreams all night.

He glanced again at Hermaline, who stood watching him with her hands planted on her pretty, plump hips. By contrast, Mathilde was a slender willow-maid. He returned his gaze to her, taking in the blue silk gown that in the morning light set off sylphlike curves hidden from his vision in the shadows of the evening's torchlight.

"I pray you, sir."

Her breathless voice brought his gaze back to her face. The color in her cheeks had deepened and with a small, jerking movement, she drew her threadbare mantle closer around her.

"My brother insists that you give back the ribbon."

Etienne told himself that he would be wise to do just that. Her blushes set too many disconcerting emotions churning in his breast. She was a lady, he reminded himself. An impoverished lady, but a lady nonetheless. 'Twas foolish to encourage an attraction that he knew he could not afford to pursue in an honorable way.

Yet if he surrendered the ribbon to Mathilde while Hermaline was watching, there would be no evading that spangled veil and Hermaline's insinuating whispers. He clutched the ribbon as though it were a shield in his hand.

"You have told me of your brother's demands," he said, "but what of you, my lady? Have you no desire for a champion in the field today?" He saw her glance at Therri. He should have felt relieved to know that he had not raised expectations in her mind with his flirting last night in the hall. But instead, he experienced an unfamiliar stir of resentment. He was not generally one to boast of his accomplishments, but he heard himself adding, "I would not shame you. I have won accolades from the Young King himself for my skill in the mêlée."

On his left hand shone a clear red jacinth stone in a silver ring, a gift from his master, the Young King, in praise of his performance in a tourney five months ago.

Mathilde's gaze returned to him as Therri and Girard vanished inside the tent. Etienne straightened his shoulders a bit as she appeared to study his height and muscular build. He thought she took a quickened breath before that strange wariness stole back into her eyes.

"I-I should like to have a champion," she owned. "And I do not think you would shame me. But Girard will not let you keep my ribbon."

"Unfortunately for your brother," he said, "'twas not *his* person I found it on. I won it from you fairly, my lady—and I mean to wear it in your honor this day."

"But Girard says he *must* have it back. I do not think he slept at all last night because of it. He was so angry when he saw it missing from my hair. I think he must be *painfully* in love with some lady at court. What will she think if she sees you wearing the favor she gave to Girard?"

"She will not see it. She did not come with him to Grantamur."

"You know her, then? Is she very beautiful? She must be for Girard to be so stricken at losing her favor."

Her violet eyes turned misty again. Etienne imagined she longed for some man to be thus stricken over her. No doubt it was of Therri she dreamed. What had she called him? The Vision? Etienne's mouth quirked up in rare envy of his friend.

She sighed and forced her gaze—reluctantly, he thought—to refocus on his face.

"Pray, sir, it is most unchivalrous of you to tease me this way. If you are a true knight, you will honor my request and give me back the ribbon."

Etienne hesitated. He wanted to wear her favor, but he realized it was equally important to him that she should think well of him. If he continued to refuse her request, she would think him a churlish brute.

Before he could decide how to answer, Hermaline swept through her half-circle of mounted attendants, apparently tired of waiting for her would-be champion to return. She bore down upon Etienne and Mathilde with sparkling eyes, her star-spangled veil fluttering in her hand like a banner of war. If he were to surrender Mathilde's ribbon, he told himself, then he must at least arm himself with some other shield in its place.

"If I give it back to you," he said quickly to Mathilde, "what will you give me in exchange?"

"In exchange?"

"You agreed last night to grant me your favor for the tournament today. If you insist that I behave as a 'true knight' and return the ribbon you gave me, then I demand you keep your word as a 'lady' and grant me some other favor in its stead."

"But I told you last night that I have nothing else to give you."

Hermaline was nearly upon them.

"Then," he murmured to Mathilde, "I hope you will forgive me, for I am about to behave most unchivalrously."

Three

"Come, Maude, do not tease me so cruelly. Either tie your favor about my sleeve or pay the forfeit you promised me."

Mathilde wrinkled her nose as the previously soft-voiced Seducer boomed out this command. Her father and brother sometimes called her 'Tillot', but no one had ever called her 'Maude'. Whatever game this gentleman was playing at now, his choice of diminutive did nothing to endear him to her. And why did he have to state it so loudly? That lady sweeping towards them in the elegant, fur-trimmed cloak must have heard his use of the wretched sobriquet.

"I did not promise you any 'forfeit'," Mathilde said. "I'm not even sure I promised you the ribbon. Now that I think back, you did not wait for me to acquiesce last night before you pulled it out of my hair."

He laughed—a disconcertingly engaging sound that caused an odd skip in her breast, even though the laugh seemed tinged with nervousness.

"Your memory has always been charmingly capricious, my dear." He turned to greet the blue-eyed lady with the bright, burnished curls as she joined them. "Lady Hermaline, pray judge this matter between us. Six weeks ago, Lady Mathilde lost to me a game of hoodman blind. Our fellow players decreed her penalty should be a kiss. To spare her embarrassment before the laughing company, I agreed to forgo that sweet pleasure so long as she consented that I should wear her favor in the next tournament I fought in. Now here she is, obstinately demanding her favor back. Have I not the right, then, to insist that she surrender the kiss in its place?"

Mathilde gasped. What insane fancy had possessed him now, that he should recite so arrantly false a tale to this lady?

"I never—" Mathilde began heatedly, but something in his devilishly mischievous smile snatched her breath away again.

Lady Hermaline's blue eyes narrowed at Mathilde and her small, rosebud mouth pinched in disapproval. "I fear, Sir Etienne, that my step-mamma says such familiarities are improper between gentlemen and ladies of slight acquaintance."

Etienne—had that been his name?—laughed again, a little more harshly, Mathilde thought.

He said, "Lady Violette, as I recall, enjoyed the game as much as anyone on her visit to Rouen, until Lord Therri mistook Lady Barbary for her. Besides," he added as Lady Hermaline appeared about to speak another protest, "Lady Mathilde and I are more than 'slight acquaintances'. Aren't we, Maude?"

If his smile had made it difficult for her to breathe, Mathilde's lungs threatened to collapse in shock when he slid one mailed arm around her waist. His height and the strength of his embrace suddenly became intimately more real than her earlier appraisal by mere sight had prepared her for.

She thought the breath he drew sounded somewhat ragged, but he said to Lady Hermaline, "Maude and I have been friends—oh, for years! Grew up together, in fact. There can be no harm in the exchange of one quick kiss. You shall stand as witness that I do not take advantage of her."

"I am not going to kiss you!" Mathilde hissed. She squirmed, trying to free herself from his hold, but he only clamped his arm more firmly around her.

"Lady Maude appears most uncomfortable with your game, sir," Lady Hermaline said. "I judge 'twould be gentlemanly of you to release her from the penalty of both kiss and favor. If you desire a token for the tournament" —she held out a gauzy apple green veil with silver stars— "then I would be most happy to give you my—"

"Nay," Etienne said quickly, "Maude is only being contrary because I teased her last night in the hall. But I appeal to you, Lady Hermaline, ought not a lady to keep her word? If you stood in her shoes, would you deny me the prize you had promised me?"

Lady Hermaline's gaze slid with an ill-concealed longing to Etienne's lips. *She wants him. And he . . . ?*

Mathilde stopped squirming and took closer stock of the blue-eyed lady. Hermaline was not as small as Lady Violette, but was slightly shorter than Mathilde and, Mathilde guessed, a year or two younger. Beneath Hermaline's fur-trimmed mantle, a kirtle of green silk with an embroidered neckline molded itself like a form-fitting glove across her voluptuous bosom. The skirt fell in draping folds over attractively plump hips. Bright, burnished-gold curls clustered in a shimmering frame about her pretty, round face and tumbled in disarray down her back. Hermaline appeared all softness and light.

But there was nothing soft in the disdainful glance she raked Mathilde with. In that instant Mathilde realized that she had seen her before. Hermaline had been one of the two ladies-in-waiting on Lady Violette's dais who had witnessed her fumbling search for the necklet and her subsequent exchange with Etienne in Grantamur's hall.

A sudden suspicion flashed through Mathilde's mind. At first blush, she had interpreted Etienne's request for her favor last night as an attempt to make Lady Violette jealous. But what had been his response when Mathilde had challenged him with Lady Violette's name? An enigmatic, "Perhaps."

Perhaps . . . it had been the watching Hermaline whose jealousy he had hoped to stir, and not Lady Violette's at all!

With one haughty glance, Hermaline communicated to Mathilde not only that she, too, remembered the scene in the hall, but that she judged Mathilde's slight figure insipid at best and the wearing of her blue silk gown two days in a row little more than gauche.

Hermaline nudged her mantle behind her shoulders, displaying her buxom figure for Etienne's view. Her moist, red lips curved up in a smile of supreme self-confidence as she cast a dismissive look at Mathilde before returning her gaze to Etienne.

"I suppose," Hermaline said, "there can be no harm in one quick kiss. Mind you keep it brotherly. Then Lady Maude may take her favor back and perhaps you will condescend to look kindly on mine in its place." She coyly fluttered her veil, then gave a girlish giggle and batted her lashes against her cheeks. "And perhaps when we gather this eve in my step-mamma's hall to celebrate the tournament's end, you and your friends will teach hoodman blind to a few of us who had not the good fortune to learn the game when we accompanied my step-mamma to Rouen."

Aye, Mathilde thought, *so that you might have an excuse to kiss him yourself.* She checked herself. What did she care if this provoking man showered a veritable thunderstorm of passion on so haughty and ill-mannered a cat as Hermaline?

Mathilde did not care, not one bit. Then why didn't he just go off with Hermaline somewhere and do so? Hermaline appeared eager enough. Why continue to tease her with Mathilde?

Mathilde could think of only one reason. Custance, her mother's maid-servant, had warned Mathilde about such games. "Court games," Custance had called them, witnessed for herself in the days when she had waited on Mathilde's mother at the court of the Young King's father. Custance claimed to have seen certain knights who were little more than base seducers, deriving perverse pleasure from fanning a woman's passion by flirting with some poor innocent who, in fact, meant nothing to him.

The way Etienne was fanning Hermaline's eagerness by flirting with Mathilde now.

The arm around her waist tightened, causing Mathilde to glance up into Etienne's face. She expected to find him grinning with smug satisfaction at Hermaline's bold request.

Instead, his green gaze slid to Mathilde's and sent her wits into an unexpected tumble.

Did he spend dawn to dusk of every day in the sun, to make his cheeks so brown, she wondered? Had he been blessed by nature, or did he cheat, as she had heard some women did, and employ hot

51

irons to create those wondrously wayward black curls? Had gems ever sparkled more deeply than the gleam in his grass-green eyes? And if she let his firm, strong mouth touch hers, would it send fiery chills clear down to her toes the way it had when he had kissed the back of her hand?

"Well, Maude, which is it to be?" he demanded. "The kiss or your favor?"

His voice sounded husky now and the green of his eyes seemed to darken. She tried to speak but her throat felt paralyzed. Her hand crept up until it lay against the huge ruby on his breast, but whether she meant to encourage him or push him away, her tumbling thoughts would not tell her. His low sigh vibrated through her body. Then inch by tantalizing inch, she saw his mouth lowering towards hers.

She told herself that it was for Girard's sake she closed her eyes and curled her toes inside her slippers, bracing herself for a rush of mind-whirling sensations. One kiss and she would have the ribbon back. One kiss. What could be the harm?

"If you are going to force me to accept that wretched veil," he whispered, so close that she felt his breath on her lips, "then I warn you, my lady, I mean to console myself with much more than a 'brotherly kiss' from you."

Her lashes flew up in time to catch the gleam of vexation mingled with warm desire in his eyes before his mouth swooped the final inch towards the target of her lips.

An instant. But in that breath's space, Mathilde comprehended the shameful truth in her heart. Her imminent surrender had nothing to do with Girard. She coveted Etienne's kiss as intensely as Hermaline did.

Horrified, she twisted her head aside so that his mouth merely grazed her cheek. The fiery shock of that brief contact mingled so keenly with her mortification that it brought tears to her eyes.

"Let me go!" She shoved against his chest, but he held her fast.

"'Tis done!" Hermaline cried. "You've had your kiss. Now you must surrender the ribbon. And you shall take my —"

"Nay," Etienne said sharply, "the penalty declared was a kiss on the lips. Come, Maude, we must try again."

"No." The word strangled out of her throat. She had *wanted* him to kiss her, had wanted to immerse herself in a thrill his earlier caress of her hand had only hinted he had the capacity to impart. She must escape his seductive power while she still had a shred of modesty left to save.

"Maude—" He spoke the name through his teeth and put up a hand to her chin.

But she jerked away. "Nay! I will give you the ribbon!" Better to endure Girard's fury than risk her virtue to this man's devilish sway.

"'Tis not fair," Hermaline protested. "You said simply 'a kiss.'"

"On the lips," Etienne repeated stubbornly. Then, more softly, again, "On the lips."

Mathilde ducked her head, hoping to regain her composure by avoiding his ensnaring gaze. But he breached her defenses by brushing his thumb across her mouth, sending quivering shivers dancing through her body.

Slowly, his arm relaxed about her waist so that she was able to draw away. Then he held out his hand with the ribbon draped across his palm.

Taking care not to glance into his face again, she grabbed the ribbon and started to loop it around his right sleeve.

"Favors must be tied to the left," he said. "Our right arms will bear the color of the team we fight on today."

Mathilde shifted the ribbon quickly to his left sleeve. Her fingers shook so badly that she could scarcely make the knot.

"If your brother rebukes you," he said, his voice low to escape Hermaline's ears, "assure him that I will return the ribbon to him at the tournament's end."

Mathilde nodded and blinked the sting of tears away from her eyes. His intention to be rid of her favor immediately after the tournament confirmed that her token had meant nothing to him but a means to tease Hermaline. He had used Mathilde very neatly indeed. Hermaline was glaring blue icicles at her. It was just as Custance had said. He was nothing but a vain seducer, who had satisfied his conceit by manipulating Mathilde to respond to his charms while concurrently driving the woman he truly wanted wild with jealousy. Mathilde had no doubt that he desired Hermaline. What man would *not* desire so much voluptuous beauty?

She finished tying off the ribbon and fled before he could try again to stay her. To her relief, Girard came striding red-faced out of the tent. Etienne would not dare to pursue his dishonorable game with her in her brother's presence. She ran to meet Girard as he swept between Lady Hermaline's attendants. The Vision stood in the tent's entrance, one hand holding open the flap.

"I mean it, de Riavelle!" he shouted after Girard. "Either settle your debts with me and the others, or I swear we'll see you drummed out of Rouen. And if you don't want to add your armor and horse to what you already owe me, you had better stay out of my way on the field today!"

Girard swore a blasphemy under his breath. He grabbed Mathilde's arm and swept her so quickly past Etienne and Hermaline that she thankfully did not have a chance to spare either of them a glance.

"Why didn't you tell me you had given your necklet to Laurant?" Girard demanded.

"I-I didn't think of it," Mathilde said. No, she would not steal a peek over her shoulder at the wretched couple. "He broke it in the hall last night and promised to fix it for me."

Girard gave a harsh laugh. "Well, you needn't hope to see it again any time soon. Laurant refuses to return it until my debts to him are paid."

In spite of her determination not to look behind her, an irresistible curiosity had her head turning when her brother's words swept her gaze back to his face. "But Girard, that was Mother's necklet! Father will be furious if he learns you have used it for your gambling debts."

The sapphire had been one of two stones possessing unusual beauty and value. The second had studded the pommel of her father's favorite dagger. Twin stones, representing twin souls, her father had murmured when he gave Mathilde the necklet. Mathilde had never known her mother. But the tender memory she'd seen in her father's eyes had brought tears into her own. Her deepest, most heartfelt dream of all was to find a man who might love her someday as much as her father had loved her mother.

But three years past, he had lost his dagger with the sapphire stone. If he learned that she had now lost the necklet as well . . .

"Girard, did you not remind him that the necklet was mine?" A man as noble and honest as the Vision would surely return it to Mathilde at once, undoubtedly with a very pretty request that she pardon him for trying to use it to punish her brother.

"Nay, I told him I'd lent it to you," Girard said. "I hoped it might satisfy his demands on me, but no! Laurant insists that I redeem it in coin. Devil take him! 'Tis not as if he has not fountains of gold at his command that he must harass me for a few francs lost to him over a game or two of dice. The fellow thinks he can lord it over the rest of us because of his high and mighty title. He needs to be knocked down a peg or two. If I were only expert enough with the lance, I'd deal him a sound drubbing on the field today."

Mathilde had always thought her brother well and strongly built, but beside her memory of the Vision, or even Etienne, he looked stocky, his muscles more burly than sleek. She tugged on his arm, trying to slow his strides. "Girard—"

Girard strode on, still furious. "Chastise me, will he? Dressed me down like I was an errant squire! Well, we shall see—"

"Girard, stop! You have got to go back and explain to the Vision about the necklet."

"Not now, Mathilde. I scarcely have time to change for the tournament. Mayhap there is a way to take Laurant unawares on the field, before his guard is up—"

"But Girard—"

He stopped and whirled on her, irritation loosing an impatient curse on her head. Then he stiffened. His gaze raked her empty hands. The angry color drained slowly out of his face.

"Mathilde—where—is—the ribbon?"

The ribbon. In her upset over her brother's lies to the Vision about the necklet, she had forgotten about the ribbon!

He followed her glance to Etienne. The white strand fluttered against the polished mail of his sleeve, clearly discernible as he lifted

Hermaline onto her palfrey.

She took a deep breath. "Girard, I can explain . . ."

Etienne stepped back from Hermaline's mount and executed one of the flourishing bows he'd mastered while serving in the Young King's court. "Till this evening, my lady."

He smothered a sigh at the flush of triumph in Hermaline's cheeks. She had refused to leave until she had won a promise from Etienne that he would teach her and the other ladies of her step-mother's court the game of hoodman blind following the evening's banquet to celebrate the tournament's victor. Etienne had only agreed out of desperation to be rid of her. He would just have to make sure that during the game, when it was Hermaline's turn to have her eyes veiled, some matter of urgent business should call him quickly, and silently, out of the circle.

He deliberately avoided Therri's eyes as Hermaline and her attendants rode away. He knew Therri had been inside their tent earlier, listening with fiendish humor to Etienne's harried attempts to preempt Hermaline's offer of her favor. Etienne had twice heard a snort of laughter from within the tent. No doubt curiosity at the sudden silence when he had gone to greet Mathilde had prompted Therri to peek out of the tent's entrance in time to see Girard's arrival with his sister.

Etienne heard a sharp intake of breath behind him and snapped, "Stow it, Therri. At least I'm not wearing her favor."

There was a choking sound, but apparently Therri lost the battle to spare Etienne's feelings, for a sound of wheezing laughter followed. Etienne whirled to find his friend doubled over.

"Nay, Etienne," Therri gasped. "I-I admire you, truly I do. I thought sure Hermaline would make short shrift of Lady Mathilde's ribbon. I commend your cunning in using it to fend off Hermaline's token."

"Then what's so funny?"

"The sly anticipation on her face when you promised to teach her hoodman blind—and the look of consternation on yours. She's got you dancing like a panicked puppet. Every time you think you've snipped a string, she yanks two more and pulls you back into line. What protection will Lady Mathilde's ribbon be to you tonight? Do you think Hermaline won't cheat to catch you in the circle?"

"I am not Hermaline's puppet, and you may be sure we will not be playing for kisses, the way we sometimes do to tease the ladies at Rouen."

"If Violette tells her about those stakes, Hermaline will insist." Some of the humor left Therri's face.

Etienne knew Therri was remembering his own disastrous misguess in the game when, when his turn had come to wear the hood, he had mistook Lady Barbary's kiss for Violette's. For Etienne's part, he knew it would not matter what Violette told Hermaline. Hermaline already knew about the forfeited kisses from Etienne's maneuvering to keep Mathilde's ribbon.

He glanced to where Mathilde stood conversing with her brother. They were too far away for Etienne to hear their words, but Girard's hands waved in a gesture of agitation. Mathilde's hands fluttered in nervous accompaniment to her response. No doubt Girard was rebuking her for not retrieving his harlot's ribbon. Disgust at Girard's morals vied with guilt in Etienne's breast. He had played a reprehensible trick on her with his wildly fabricated story to Hermaline. Mathilde must have thought him an absolute lout.

He would have to find some way to make things right with her. Some way to prove to her that he was *not* —

Girard's hand drew back, then flashed across Mathilde's face in a slap.

Etienne felt the blow reverberate through his own bones. *"The dog!"*

He took a furious step towards Girard, his fingers clenching into fists.

Therri's hand clamped on his arm. "Etienne—"

"Let me go, Therri."

"Nay, listen." A trumpet blast sounded in the air. "'Tis the warning call for the tournament. De Riavelle needs chastising, aye, for that slap to his sister and for other things. But there's not time now. Save it for the tournament field."

Etienne struggled to free himself another moment, then stopped. Therri was right, this was neither the time nor the place to start a row with Girard. But guilt at the "harmless game" Etienne had played with Mathilde over her ribbon nearly choked him.

"'Tis my fault," he whispered. *His* fault that Mathilde now stood with that frightened look on her face, rubbing her reddening cheek. Had he not been so insistent on keeping the ribbon—

Therri's hand moved to Etienne's shoulder. "She'll be safe enough for now. De Riavelle has not even changed into his armor yet. He hasn't time to pursue a quarrel with his sister. You can crack a lance over his head in the mêlée—if I don't do it first."

The mêlée. Aye, there Etienne would use his lance to deal Girard more than a dash of his own medicine. When Etienne was through with him, he would think twice before raising a hand to his sister again.

Girard grabbed Mathilde's arm and dragged her stumbling away. It took every ounce of control that Etienne possessed—and Therri's tightened grip on his shoulder—to prevent him from striding after them. He watched them until they vanished amid the tents. Then he turned to Therri.

"Send your squire after them," he said abruptly. "Have him tell Mathilde that Violette has invited her to watch the tournament from her castle walls."

"What? Why?"

"Because I don't trust de Riavelle not to squeeze in another slap to his sister while he's strapping on his armor."

"Why don't you send your own squire after them?"

Etienne's mouth twisted bitterly. "Mathilde doesn't trust me. I pulled a rather boorish trick on her to keep her favor. She's not about to trust herself with any squire of mine, now."

"What makes you think she would trust herself with a squire of mine?"

"Because she's smitten with you. Thinks you're the embodiment of one of those knights-errant in Chrétien de Troyes' poems. I expect she envisions you a champion of the helpless and a protector of defenseless womanhood."

Therri's jaw dropped. Though Mathilde's infatuation irked Etienne, he could not resist a grin at the dismay on his friend's face.

"If you think," Therri said, "that I'm going to do anything to encourage her to view me in such a ridiculous light as that—!"

He broke off suddenly, then uttered a soft curse, his gaze narrowing at some point over Etienne's shoulder. Etienne turned to see what had commanded his friend's scowling attention.

William Marshal rode past their tent astride a stamping bay destrier, trailed by no less than a half-dozen squires and twice as many grooms. Marshal wore a divided surcote of green and yellow, with a red lion rampant blazoned across his breast. The same heraldic device danced on the parti-colored banner that fluttered on a pole held at the fore of the group by one of the young, straight-backed squires.

"Look at the arrogant way he struts," Therri muttered. "*I* might have brought six squires with me as well, but I did not wish to appear such a braggart."

"At least he wears no lady's token upon his armor," Etienne said.

Therri's scowl lightened only slightly. Unlike Therri, who stood heir to a barony, Marshal was of but middling birth. But he was a man of both ambition and talent. His prowess on the tournament field had won him the Young King's friendship and esteem, along with a place of honor and trust in the Young King's household. But though he had accumulated considerable wealth of his own and wielded an enviable degree of power over his young master, two bolts in his quiver of honors yet eluded him. Land and a title. And Lady Violette de Maloisel had vowed to bestow both upon the victor of this day through the boon of her hand in marriage.

"She will find some way to declare you the winner," Etienne said, reading the dour direction of his friend's thoughts. "Or else she will alter the intention of her vow. She does not want to marry Marshal. If she did, she would have granted him her favor last night after she refused to give it to you."

59

"Marshal has never been unhorsed." Therri's voice sounded strained. "And Violette has given her word—"

"Violette is a woman and women are allowed to change their minds." Etienne grabbed Therri's arm and pulled him toward their tent, forcing his attention away from Marshal's procession. "If you do not wish to lose by default, you had better finish arming yourself. But not," he added, "until you have sent your squire to escort Mathilde up to Grantamur Castle."

Four

T was a fool's choice, Etienne," Therri chided. "You should have left your surcote the way it was. Think of the target you will make on the field!"

Etienne glanced down at his outward garment. He had had this surcote cut from fresh cloth only a sennight ago, abandoning the traditional dreary dark green of his house in favor of a brighter, emerald hue. The five petals of the emblem across his breast had been overlaid with a soft, gold foil that glistened in the sunlight. And where a piece of red cloth cut in the shape of a droplet of blood had formerly been sewn to the flower's center, the surcote now sported a huge and sparkling glass stud that, from a distance, resembled a ruby.

Aye, he would make a fine target indeed.

He and Therri sat astride their destriers in the roped off refuge at the north end of the tournament field, where they awaited the herald's shout and the blast of trumpets that would set the mêlée into motion.

"You look like a peacock," Therri muttered as Etienne raised a hand to return the salute of a knightly acquaintance just entering the refuge.

Etienne laughed. "All the better to lure some fat-pursed rivals on the field."

And to catch the eye of an admiring lady or two.

Thus had been his hopes before encountering Hermaline. A well-dowered wife still seemed the quickest and surest way to establish his independence in the world. But the odds that Hermaline would permit him to pursue any other possible partners while at Grantamur now appeared little less than nil.

Etienne touched his sleeve, readjusting the white, gilt-edged ribbon that fluttered there. He glanced at Therri, saw that something had drawn his friend's attention away, and raised his arm to breathe the ribbon's scent. A soft, sultry whiff of angelica still lingered on the strand. Though Etienne's head warned him the perfume probably belonged to Girard's harlot, it's musky scent brought memories of Mathilde with a warm thump to his breast.

Nay, he must not dwell thus upon her. She had nothing to bring him, and he had even less to give her. He must content himself with knowing that he had arranged her protection this day from her brother's anger. He would do his best to deal that brother a sound rebuke on the field today and after that, he must force himself to forget that he had ever met Mathilde de Riavelle.

"A pity we're fighting with blunted weapons," Therri uttered with a savagery that startled Etienne. "I should like to see that swaggerer's blood flow."

Etienne looked about to see who had provoked this violent response. Not surprisingly, he found the narrowed direction of Therri's eyes fixed on William Marshal.

"Then send your squire to stir up his followers to shout 'God for the Marshal' as they have at the last half-dozen tourneys," Etienne said. "The cry has infuriated the Young King and laid Marshal open to Adam d'Yquebeuf's charges of *lèse majesté*."

He spoke teasingly, knowing Therri would never sink to such depths of desperation as to throw in his lot with a plotter like d'Yquebeuf to accuse the honest Marshal of treason. D'Yquebeuf burned with jealousy of Marshal's influence over the Young King. Etienne had heard the hatred in d'Yquebeuf's voice that evening he had inadvertently stumbled upon d'Yquebeuf and his cohort, Thomas de Coulonces, in a shadowed corridor in Rouen. The two knights hoped that Marshal's arrogance on the tournament field would goad the Young King into lending an ear to their more sinister whispers against him. Etienne had listened in the shadows long enough to know that they were planning something . . . some way to trap Marshal.

He frowned and shifted uneasily in his saddle. His attempt at warning Marshal had been waved away by that self-confident knight. Etienne had tried.

But had he tried hard enough?

"Rouen was rife with rumors when we left," Therri murmured, still glaring after Marshal. "They say the Young King is planning an invasion of Poitou and that Marshal is arguing against it."

"I've heard the rumors, too," Etienne said. He had not told Therri about the exchange in the corridor.

"Do you think it's true? You've known the Young King longer than I."

"I was only a squire when the Young King joined Duke Richard in the assault on the Castle Chateauneuf five years ago," Etienne said, "and was hardly in his confidence, then or now. But there were whispers even then that while he was in Poitou, he entered into a covert alliance with some of our barons to return someday and depose Duke Richard from his tyrant's throne."

"Is that why when the Young King withdrew from the assault, you went with him? I always knew it must have had something to do with your dislike of Duke Richard."

They had never before discussed Etienne's motives for leaving his homeland. Therri had been in England serving as squire to his brother-in-law, the Earl of Gunthar, in the days of Chateauneuf and had lingered there after his knighting two years later. Tensions between Etienne's family and the earl had discouraged correspondence between Etienne and Therri during that time. Etienne had been completely surprised when Therri had suddenly joined him in the Young King's court a year past, out of curiosity, Therri said, to learn for himself what manner of man Etienne had chosen to serve in Duke Richard's place.

Etienne gripped his lips hard together. When one was a landless younger son, one made one's way in the world as best one could. He had entered the Young King's service with the loftiest of hopes and the most noble of ambitions. He had thought he could advance a career independent of his brother while at the same time throwing his support to a faction that would free his native county of its tyrannical ruler. It had all seemed so simple and clear . . .

Until, little by little, the Young King had begun to expose his true character. Etienne had not forgotten the last outburst at court. The Young King had become so enraged at some message delivered to him from his father, King Henry II of England, that he had seized the courier by the hair and dragged him up and down the hall, roaring obscenities at the absent King Henry.

He caught Therri studying him, and knew what he was thinking.

"I did *not* make a mistake when I chose to throw my allegiance to the Young King over his wretched brother," Etienne said. "Duke Richard is a scourge on Poitou. He has razed our castles and trampled our rights. I should think you would care more about the land of our birth than to accept his tyranny with equanimity."

"They are both a little mad," Therri said of King Henry II's two eldest sons. "All the Plantagenets are. Nay, I am not condoning Duke Richard's abuses. But I spent time in his father's court when I served Gunthar, and I tell you King Henry will never allow one of his sons to depose the other. The Young King may forgive you for your father's sins, Etienne, but Duke Richard never will. Come down on the wrong side in this question, and while the Young King may suffer no more than a sharp rebuke from his doting father, that father as wrathful king may grant Duke Richard *your* head."

"What do you want me to do? Go crawling back to my brother?"

"There are worse things than swallowing your pride. Triston would welcome you home, and you know it. Why don't you reconsider his offer?"

"Because he made it out of pity. He thinks I cannot support myself without his aid. And he is afraid that my allegiance to the Young King reflects badly on the depths of his own loyalty to Duke Richard. Nay, I'll enter no service that owes fealty to such a devil, not even my brother's."

A trumpet blared from the castle walls, followed by shouts of,

"Peace! Peace! Our lady of Grantamur Castle would address those who come to fight in her honor this day!"

Etienne wrenched his angry gaze away from Therri's and looked up the castle's crennelated curtain wall. The ladies of Violette de Maloisel's court flitted above them in brightly colored gowns, like flowers in a garden being tumbled about by the wind. Before he could stop himself, his gaze swept among them in search of a flaxen-haired, violet-eyed damsel. Therri's squire had assured them that he had escorted Lady Mathilde to the castle gates, together with the written request Etienne had coaxed Therri to write requesting that Violette allow Mathilde to watch the mêlée from the walls with her court.

But Etienne saw no sign of Mathilde. Had Violette rejected Therri's request? Or had Girard sent one of his servants to demand her return?

It took several minutes for the marshals of the field to impose enough order on the assembling knights so that Violette could be heard. Violette appeared on the curtain wall, standing proudly in the gap between two square-toothed merlons. A gauzy, blue-green veil lifted away from her face with the breeze, revealing her mahogany hair plaited in elaborate braids on either side of her head. The sleeve of her gown fluttered as she raised an elegant hand in a gesture to command attention.

"Fair knights," she called, "battle well this day, but adhere strictly to my rules."

She nodded at her herald, who had ridden into position at the center of the tournament field. He proceeded in a thunderous voice to recite the rules of battle laid down for the day.

"Sir Knights, attend! By Lady de Maloisel's order, only blunted weapons are permitted in this competition, and that of swords and lances only. Use of darts, crossbows, maces, battle axes or any other weapon will be grounds for disqualification. Once a knight is unseated, it shall be considered a defeat. He must pledge a ransom to his victor, though for the course of the tourney he may retain his horse and rejoin the competition against other challengers, if he wishes. Points will be garnered by the number of challengers each knight unhorses. The combat will end at sundown when you hear three blasts from the trumpets. Any who are unwilling to be bound by these rules should now withdraw from the field of combatants."

No knight stirred from either refuge, north or south, whence the volley of the opposing teams would begin.

"Fair knights," Violette called again, "my judges will be watching you closely." She gestured at the half-dozen men dressed in yellow and black livery, positioned at strategic points along the wall where they might track the action of the mêlée. "Upon the three knights who fight most valiantly in the field this day, my ladies will bestow rich prizes. And to he who fights with such grace and skill as to surpass all others . . ."

She left the promise unfinished, her unspoken words hovering tantalizingly in the air. What need had she to complete the phrase? All knew she offered herself as the greatest prize of all.

Etienne saw the plunging of Therri's brows as William Marshal boldly, and with great gallantry, touched his fingers to his lips and raised them in a salute to Violette.

"To our Queen of Love and Beauty!" he cried.

The other knights quickly copied Marshal's gesture, adding shouts of praise and devotion to the exotic lady who laughed in open delight above them.

"Nay, good knights," her voice floated above their cries. "This day's champion alone shall have the privilege of choosing our queen."

Her gaze might have flitted in Therri's direction on the words, but she was too far away for Etienne to be sure. Therri turned sharply away. Etienne allowed his gaze to linger on the wall a moment too long and caught an earnest wave in his direction from Lady Hermaline, poised in the embrasure next to Violette. Reluctantly, he lifted his hand in acknowledgment.

"Gentlemen," the herald shouted, "arm yourselves for battle!"

Etienne turned away from the wall in relief. He pulled his mail coif up over his hair and signaled to his squire. Unlike Therri, whose father had sent him a well-trained squire on the eve of his knighting, Etienne had had to settle for an obscure knight's son even poorer than himself. He had offered to instruct the youth in knightly skills, share a portion of any spoils he won at tourneying, and keep him fed, and Walter had accepted with eager gratitude. The youth ran forward now with the final trappings of Etienne's armor. Moment's later, with his helmet donned, his shield strapped securely to his left arm, and his lance couched tightly under his right, Etienne braced himself in the saddle and waited for the herald's raised hand to fall.

"Sir Knights, in God's name and for Lady de Maloisel's honor — do your battle!"

Mathilde stretched onto her toes, straining to see over the head of Lady Cassandry. After exchanging whispers with Lady Hermaline, the red-head had rudely inserted herself between Mathilde and the gap between the merlons through which Mathilde had been viewing the tournament. Mathilde bit her lip in annoyance. She had only just caught sight of the Vision's colors again when Cassandry had shouldered her away from the wall. Mathilde had found and lost the Vision's form a dozen times as the sun slid across the sky. Each time she had done so, Hermaline and Cassandry distracted her with a drift of loudly whispered words mocking Mathilde's mantle, her gown, the painted beads on her girdle, her plain linen shoes.

But Mathilde dared not complain. That she should be viewing this grand tournament spectacle from Lady Violette's curtain wall was a stroke of good fortune which still held her in awe.

At least, she had been viewing it before Cassandry's impudent maneuver.

"Cassandry." Lady Violette's voice sounded crisply from behind them. "You have seen many a tournament. Step aside and let Lady Mathilde resume her place on the wall."

Cassandry's pert face fell, but she moved away to rejoin Hermaline at a neighboring embrasure. Mathilde sent her hostess a grateful smile. She did not think there could be a kinder person on earth than Violette de Maloisel.

Except, of course, for the Vision. Like a true hero of romance, he had appeared in her hour of need to save her from her brother's wrath. Or to be more accurate, he had sent his squire. Girard had been roaring curses at her for failing to retrieve the ribbon from Etienne, when the squire had interrupted him. The squire's announcement that Mathilde had been invited to view the tournament from Lady Violette's castle had taken them both aback. But Mathilde, fearful of receiving a second slap from her brother, had taken advantage of Girard's surprise to dart out on the squire's arm before Girard could stop her.

What perceptive impulse had prompted the Vision to come to her aid, she could not guess. She thought she had made too clumsy an impression upon him for him to recall her to mind with such a generous act. Her heart soared to realize how blissfully wrong she had been. He *must* remember her with fondness, to have sought for her such a wonderful boon as a privileged place in Lady Violette's circle.

Mathilde had been admitted to the castle and led onto the curtain wall just in time to hear Lady Violette's trill of laughter at some scene that took place on the field below her, followed by a man's roar and an explosion of shouted war cries. At the servant's announcement of Mathilde's arrival, Violette turned, causing Mathilde to catch her breath. Violette's flawless beauty cast even Hermaline's loveliness in the shade.

With elegant brows raised, Violette accepted a folded sheet of parchment handed to her by the servant. She read its contents through without a word, then lifted her brilliant dark eyes to study Mathilde. A moment passed, so silent and long that Mathilde began to pluck nervously at the folds of her well-worn mantle. Then Violette's exquisite lips had curved up in a courteous smile and she bade Mathilde join her ladies along the wall.

Mathilde drew a breath of pure joy and leaned forward now, straining to recapture some sight of the Vision. Violette slipped into the embrasure alongside her, studied the field of battling, armored knights below them, then pointed an elegant finger.

"There. I believe that is who you were watching before Cassandry moved to block your view."

Mathilde blushed as Violette's gesture guided her once more to the Vision's colors but she fixed her gaze firmly on his figure so as not to lose sight of him again. 'Twas no easy task to follow his movements in the chaos of the mêlée. In his silver armor, he looked very much like all the other knights thrashing about. From this distance she could scarcely keep track of his surcote amidst all the blues and reds and yellows worn by his opponents.

They all blurred together—except for that knight in the bright emerald green surcote. The vibrant hue of Etienne's cloth made him stand out like some exotically feathered cock in a farmyard. Despite her most valiant efforts to ignore him, the sunlight flashed off the arrogantly huge ruby on his breast, repeatedly drawing her gaze as irresistibly as it attracted one challenger after another to his lance.

But she refused to acknowledge a thrill when the force of that lance sent those challengers flying from their saddles. She did not care how many knights he tumbled to the earth in her honor. He had used her shamefully in his provoking game with Hermaline. Etienne might wear Mathilde's favor on his strong, cocky arm, but 'twas the Vision who had come to her rescue with Girard. The Vision alone fought as her true champion this day, and no matter the temptation, she would not let her gaze stray from him again for so much as a heartbeat.

"Have you known Lord Therri a long while, my lady?" Violette asked. She added when Mathilde hesitated, "Forgive my curiosity. I only wonder because I do not recall meeting you when I visited the Young King's court at Rouen a few months ago. Perhaps you know Lord Therri from Poitou?"

Before Mathilde could answer, Hermaline's voice floated from the neighboring embrasure. "She grew up with Sir Etienne, and as 'tis said his and Lord Therri's lands march together, she was no doubt boon companions with the both of them."

Her words almost startled Mathilde into glancing away from the field. She caught herself in time, and kept her gaze fixed on the Vision. How was she to respond? If she contradicted Hermaline, Etienne would be exposed as a liar and *she* would be judged, at best, a shameless flirt for accepting kisses from a man she scarcely knew. At worst—

"Yes," she said in a nervous whisper. "I-I know Lord Therri from Poitou."

She hoped her cheeks did not look as hot as they felt. *Oh!* What way was this to repay the Vision's generosity, with falsehoods to their hostess?

To her relief, Violette did not pursue the question further. After a few moments, Mathilde's guilt and embarrassment faded, supplanted with a fresh ripple of excitement at the scene below her. The Vision whirled his horse and aimed his lance at some knight wearing a blue and gold quartered surcote. She held her breath as they charged each other three times. The fourth time the Vision's lance slipped beneath his opponent's shield and knocked the other knight from the saddle.

"Ah," Violette murmured. "There goes Beaujeu. That makes Lord Therri's score four to William Marshal's five."

Mathilde did not know which knight on the field might be William Marshal, but she thought she heard a note of regret in Violette's voice. A disturbing thought suddenly occurred to Mathilde. If the Vision won the tournament by capturing the greatest number of knights, then he would also win Violette's hand in marriage. Did he fight for gold, like Etienne? Or did he fight for love?

Nay, he wore no woman's favor. That clearly meant that his heart remained unclaimed. And Girard had said the Vision already had "fountains of gold" at his fingertips. Then surely he fought only for honor and glory, as did the heroes in the jongleur's ballads. Mathilde had as much right to try to win his affections as any other woman in this court.

But what if the Vision won the tournament and Violette's hand? Mathilde should never then have an opportunity to prove to him that, though her face be plain, she had faith and loyalty and love enough to challenge the most dazzling beauties.

Time. Mathilde only needed time. She closed her eyes and whispered a silent prayer that the mysterious Marshal's prowess would, just this once, surpass the Vision's.

When she opened her eyes again, the Vision had blended once

more into the chaos of the mêlée. After several minutes of fruitless searching, her gaze reluctantly slid to the only other knight she recognized on the field. She located him by the flash of his ruby, just as he sent another challenger tumbling to the ground.

Sweat trickled into Etienne's eyes, stinging and momentarily blurring his vision. With a few rapid blinks, he squeezed the moisture away. His ears rang with the surrounding cacophony of men's war cries. Steel clashed against steel, wood splintered from shattered lances and rended shields. In the midst of this confusion, he caught the reins of the destrier whose rider he had just laid in the dust.

He leveled his lance at the fallen knight's breast. "Do you yield, sir?" he shouted. The knight nodded. "Then ransom, equivalent to the value of your mail and this destrier, will be paid to Etienne de Brielle. You may find him when the tourney is over on the field of tents beneath the twin banners of the gilded rose and the double-headed phoenix."

The knight nodded again, accepting Etienne's terms. Etienne relinquished the man's destrier, then turned and maneuvered his way through the tumult of the mêlée in search of a fresh opponent.

As Therri had predicted, Etienne's boldly colored surcote and the huge faux-ruby flashing from his breast had attracted challengers like bees to an insolently brilliant summer rose. He had unhorsed three knights already and stalemated two so that they had finally gone off looking for easier prey. There were hours yet to go before a vanishing sun would call a halt to this game. If his luck and skill held, he might collect ransoms enough to enable him to take a respite from the Young King's court without being forced to throw himself on either his brother's or Hermaline's mercy.

"You there!"

The shout might have been directed at anyone in the bedlam around him. Etienne continued his forward advance through the chaos, then drew up abruptly when three knights with unmarked surcotes suddenly appeared in his path.

"Violette, remember you promised that I should bestow the prizes on the runners-up today."

"I have not forgotten, Hermaline," Violette said.

Hermaline turned to Cassandry and said in a voice that carried clearly to Mathilde's ears, "Sir Etienne bids fair to come in third at the very least. I have in mind such a favor to award him as to make him forget that drab little ribbon he wears now about his sleeve."

"I heard he requested it of some obscure girl who came up with her brother to view the tournament," Cassandry said in like tones.

Hermaline nodded her burnished head. "I saw her. Insipid as milk. I believe Sir Etienne pitied her distress at being slighted by all the other knights. Sir Etienne is such a kind-hearted gentleman."

Mathilde's face burned, but she kept her gaze fixed stoically on the field below. If Hermaline mocked her one more time, she thought she might push her tormentor off the wall. As for Sir Etienne—whether he'd taken her favor for pity or in some calculating game of flirtation with Hermaline, she utterly scorned him. She hoped fervently that those three knights now blocking his path would deal him the drubbing he deserved.

Etienne raised his weapon and braced himself in the stirrups.

"We've no wish to break lances with you, de Brielle," one of the knights shouted.

Which one of the three actually spoke Etienne could not tell, for helmets concealed their faces. They wore black surcotes, but lacked any insignia by which he might have identified his challengers. Their right arms remained bare of either blue or red scarves to signify the team they fought for. Yet challengers they clearly were, whether they professed themselves to be or not.

"Then that is your misfortune," Etienne returned. "I had my eye on unhorsing that fellow with the falcon crest over there, but your delay has delivered him into Marshal's hands. The only way to appease my disappointment is to replace his loss with ransoms from the three of you."

"We're united against you, de Brielle," a different voice growled from the trio before him. "Three to one. Lady Violette neglected to set any rule against such odds. There are easier pickings for you than us on the field. Give us what we want and we will leave you to pluck them without further interference."

Etienne lowered his lance until it rested across his saddlebow. "What is it you want, then, if not a joust?"

"That ribbon you wear on your arm. A meaningless bit of cloth. Hand it to my friend here, and we will be out of your way."

The knight on the left held out a mailed hand.

Mathilde's ribbon? Etienne stared at them through the slits of his helmet. "De Riavelle, is that you?"

The three men answered him with stony silence. But it must be Girard. The man had earlier been wearing a grey and blue surcote, but Etienne supposed he might have slipped back to one of the refuges and exchanged it for black. But why would he? If he were so determined to win back his sister's token, why not meet Etienne in open and fair competition on the field?

Etienne's mouth curved up in derisive anger. Because the man was a coward. Etienne had fought with him in mêlées before and knew him no more than adequate with a lance. He must fear himself outmatched by Etienne's skill, so he'd brought these cohorts with him to guarantee success. But to take things to such extremes over a woman's token? Surely 'twas no common harlot Girard jousted for.

But it did not matter to Etienne if the ribbon belonged to Queen Marguerite herself. No urgency to retrieve it could justify Girard slapping Mathilde.

He glanced up at Grantamur's curtain wall. Her face had appeared at one of the embrasures just as he had met his first challenger this day. He had won three victories for her, and disgraced her with two stalemates. He saw her now still watching him. He was not about to humiliate her by tamely handing over her token to any man without a struggle. And Girard would not leave this field without receiving the harsh rebuke of Etienne's lance for that brutish slap of his sister.

"You're pathetic, de Riavelle," Etienne shouted. "If you want her ribbon, you will have to take it."

The three knights drew together and conferred for a moment. Then they turned back toward Etienne and leveled the points of their lances.

"So be it," Etienne snapped. He brought up his lance and charged.

O h, my!" Violette exclaimed. "What colors did you say your brother is wearing?"

"Blue and grey," Mathilde said. "Why?"

"If I am not mistaken, Lord Therri has just intercepted Sir Girard on the field."

Mathilde dragged her gaze away from Etienne just as he spurred his destrier towards his trio of challengers. Even following the helpful direction of Violette's pointing finger, it took her a moment to locate the knights her hostess referred to.

"Oh!" Mathilde echoed Violette's dismay. She gripped the edge of the embrasure and leaned anxiously forward. She was certain that blue and grey surcote did indeed belong to her brother.

Girard tried to weave his mount around the Vision, but the Vision galloped forward to cut him off. Girard made an angry gesture with his lance. Mathilde thought he pointed it towards Etienne's battle, but she could not be sure that was Girard's intent. Her brother again tried to circumvent his would-be challenger. The Vision blocked him as before.

"I don't think Girard wants to fight him." Mathilde remembered what Etienne had said about her brother's gambling debts. "I fear he cannot afford to pay a ransom if he is unhorsed, and Father has no money to pay it for him. And I am sure he has not the skill to defeat the Vision."

Violette raised her elegant brows.

Mathilde blushed. "I mean, Lord Therri. Oh, I do wish Lord Therri would let him pass!"

"Lord Therri appears to have no such intention," Violette murmured. "He seems determined to force a joust on your brother."

"Is there no way to stop them?"

"La, my dear, it is just a game. Your brother will find his ransom somewhere. Is he not a member of the Young King's court?"

"But what if he is injured by Lord Therri's lance?"

"By my own order, all weapons today have been blunted. Your brother may be bruised, but no blood will be shed, I can promise you."

Etienne registered the gleaming point of the lance's sharpened blade one instant before it glanced off his shield. His own well-aimed blow struck truer, square in the center of his opponent's shield, hurling the knight on the right out of his stirrups and into the dirt.

There was no time to question the appearance of a malignant weapon in the midst of a battlefield of dulled swords and blunted lances. The razor-sharp point of a second lance flashed towards him from the left. He twisted in his saddle and flung up his shield. The blade struck a little off-center. His opponent's shaft broke, sending a shower of splinters over Etienne's head.

Etienne swayed at the impact of the blow, but he kept his seat and recovered before his newly unarmed opponent did. He whipped out his left hand, banging the shield on his arm into his rival's chest as he caught hold of the broken shaft the man still held. Etienne jerked on the shaft. The man pitched forward. Etienne released the shaft and brought his shield down full-force into the back of the knight's helmet. The knight rolled out of the saddle and hit the earth with a thud.

"We've no wish to harm you, de Brielle. The ribbon is all we want."

Etienne whirled at the growling voice and found the glistening point of a third lance aimed at the base of his throat.

He knew the mail ventail that guarded that part of his body from slashing blows in the heat of battle would not protect him from a thrust flung quick and hard at so near a proximity as this. He guessed de Riavelle to be the knight who spoke, the man who had formerly been at the center of the trio. Etienne's gaze flicked to the ragged tear in his shield's leather covering where his prior opponent's lance blade had struck before the shaft shattered.

Fury hardened his voice. "Does your sister know what a coward you are, de Riavelle? Exchanging sharpened weapons for blunted ones to gain an unfair advantage over your rivals?"

A pair of gold-flecked eyes weighed him through the slits of the knight's unmarked helmet. "We merely wish to demonstrate the sincerity of our request." The knight's voice rasped as though spoken through a throat filled with gravel. "Is some wench's trivial favor worth spilling your blood over?"

"You tell me? You are the one so driven with misguided lust that you would risk what shreds of reputation you have left with this foul attack on me."

"Drop your lance and surrender the ribbon."

Etienne's hand tightened on his shaft, but defiance was futile with that lance-blade at his throat. Reluctantly he let his own lance fall into the dust.

"And your sword."

Etienne hesitated, then drew his sword and tossed it down after his lance.

"I don't need them to thrash you, de Riavelle," he said. "That I will gladly do with my bare hands. If you intend to turn a sportly match into a game of blood, then do it now. Otherwise I guarantee you will have to crawl back to your tent where I will hear you beg your sister's forgiveness on your knees."

The lance-blade did not flinch. The first knight Etienne had unhorsed retrieved his destrier. He remounted and ranged himself alongside de Riavelle. Etienne hoped his second opponent was still trying to gather his wits. Surely de Riavelle would not dare to follow through with the threat his poised lance-blade implied, not before so many potential witnesses on the field?

The blade nudged up beneath Etienne's chin. The gold flecks in de Riavelle's hazel eyes glittered eerily. Saints! The man *was* serious! To turn a friendly competition lethal over a woman's favor—! Either the ribbon on Etienne's arm held greater significance than de Riavelle had thus far admitted, or the man must be slightly unhinged.

"*Now*, de Brielle."

Again Etienne hesitated. De Riavelle's companion drew his sword and Etienne saw the sun's bright rays bounce off its well-honed edge. He looked one last time into de Riavelle's menacingly glistering eyes. Then slowly, he reached around to untie the ribbon.

Mathilde winced as the Vision's lance lifted Girard into the air and deposited him several feet behind his destrier. What would be Girard's temper when he returned to their tent this evening, bruised, worsted in battle, and in debt to the Vision for his ransom? Involuntarily, she raised a hand and rubbed her cheek. He had never struck her before, but then she had never seen him so angry as he had been earlier today. She glanced to where she had last seen Etienne, that dishonorable knight whose roguish game over her ribbon had won her a slap from her brother. She hoped his three challengers had humbled him. He deserved to be trounced for the way he had used her.

Hermaline's voice sounded in an annoying whine. "Violette, it is not fair! Your rules expressly state that once a knight is unhorsed, his ransom must be forfeit. He cannot reenter the battle against the same challenger, as that knight with the sword is doing with Sir Etienne!"

Etienne's position had shifted, but a flash of light so bright that it dazzled Mathilde bounced off the facets of the huge ruby on his breast, helping her to relocate him. She must have missed some important maneuvering while she watched Girard and the Vision, for one of Etienne's opponents was down. But two more still confronted him, one with a lance held at his throat, the other with a sword. Etienne sat empty-handed upon his destrier. Those weapons lying beside his mount's hooves must belong to him. What did it mean if a knight were unarmed by his challengers, but still retained his seat in the saddle?

"Is it over?" Mathilde asked Violette. "Must Sir Etienne yield? Or has he already done so?"

An unaccountable twinge of disappointment twitched through her. Of course, she had wanted to see him vanquished to punish him for his impudent amusement at her expense. But it was still *her* favor that fluttered from his arm. A knight's discomfiture must also reflect on the lady who had granted him her token. And what could be more awkwardly embarrassing than to have one's champion disarmed so easily that the struggle hadn't even tumbled him onto the ground?

Hermaline protested again. "Violette, I saw Sir Etienne unhorse that knight with the sword. You must award Sir Etienne two more points at least, for that knight and his fellow, the one whose lance broke."

"The judges will sort it all out," Violette promised. "But while Sir Etienne retains his seat, he should be allowed a fresh lance and another pass at his challengers. Where is his squire? Why has the boy not brought him a fresh weapon?"

"Look," Mathilde said. "What is Sir Etienne doing?"

She watched with dismay as Etienne untied her ribbon from his arm. The knight with the sword extended a hand, but Etienne's helmet shook in a gesture of negation. Some words appeared to pass between the three men.

"Violette, they are cheating!" Hermaline cried. "You banned crossbows from the tourney!"

Mathilde's head whipped around. With horror, she watched a knight break from the surging chaos a short distance from Etienne and level a crossbow's arrow at his back. The knight wore a black surcote and unmarked helmet like Etienne's other challengers, masking his identity.

Except that Mathilde's mind reeled with shocked recognition.

She grasped Violette's arm, her fingers spasming into Violette's sleeve so hard that it made her hostess gasp. "My lady, you must do something to stop this!"

The crossbowman could be no one else. Unless there were some other knight in the mêlée requiring a surcote and mail of such exaggerated girth . . . *it was Chesnei.*

Etienne pulled loose the ribbon. "Nay." He shook his head as the man with the sword held out his hand. "You are the one who orchestrated this absurd confrontation, de Riavelle. I'll surrender the token to you and none other."

"You are in no position to make demands, de Brielle."

"What, are you too cowardly to lower your lance to take it?"

"No man calls me a coward!"

The gold flecks fairly sizzled in their hazel beds. The lance's point made a small, stabbing movement that thrust the links of Etienne's iron-linked ventail so hard against his windpipe that it choked him. Had it not been for the mail, he knew his flesh would have been pierced clean through.

Apparently satisfied with the warning jab, de Riavelle withdrew the lance and shifted his destrier near enough to reach out his hand for the ribbon. If they believed the lance's jab had injured Etienne's throat . . . Etienne drew a rasping breath and burst into a coughing fit. He flopped the ribbon towards de Riavelle's hand, taking care to miss his mark, hoping they would lay his inaccuracy to his convulsive coughs. A second time he slapped and missed. The coughs threatened to double him over. The third time he flapped out the ribbon, he grazed de Riavelle's gauntlet, but whipped the strip of cloth away before de Riavelle's fingers could close on it.

Somewhere in the distance, a trumpet blared.

"Curse you, de Brielle! Just—" De Riavelle made a grab for the ribbon.

This time Etienne met his hand, locked and pulled.

Again the trumpet sounded.

The swordsman flashed his blade at Etienne, but Etienne jerked de Riavelle between them. Etienne's yank succeeded in pitching de Riavelle half-way out of his saddle. His companion's sword crashed down between de Riavelle's shoulder-blades, flinging him the rest of the way into the dirt.

Etienne caught and pulled free de Riavelle's lance as he fell, then swung it about towards the startled swordsman.

One moment he had the lance's sharpened point poised at the swordsman's breast.

The next, his shoulder exploded in a crackle of white-hot pain.

Some impelling force hurled him across his destrier's neck. The clamor of contending knights around them erupted to a deafening roar, then faded away to a mere buzz. He felt the reins slipping from his grasp, his body pitching through insubstantial air, and then a bone-jolting thud.

The impact of hitting the ground briefly restored his senses. But everything looked hazy. He must have gotten some dust in his helmet. He struggled to sit up and pressed a hand to a shoulder gone fiery and numb all at once. Someone pulled his hand away, sought to pry apart his fingers . . .

Mathilde's ribbon. It remained tangled in his hand. Someone—de Riavelle?—struggled to rip it away. If only he could see clearly! The haze before his eyes was turning to a reddish mist. His muscles felt like water. Still, he hung doggedly on to the ribbon. He could not see the face of his attacker, but Mathilde's reproachful violet gaze focused vividly against the shade of his lids as they threatened to sink shut.

He had wanted to shower victories upon her. Instead, he had failed her, shamed her. Like a callow squire, he had allowed a moment of distraction to lay himself vulnerable to some opponent's rearward blow. And now, to compound a humiliating defeat, he was about to lose her favor to a man who claimed it as a harlot's trinket.

The thought enraged him. Fresh strength flowed briefly through his limbs. His fingers flexed with convulsive vigor to resist de

Riavelle's efforts to wrest the ribbon away. Dimly he heard hooves clamoring around them. Men shouted and swore. And off in the distance the trumpets blasted and blasted and blasted . . .

"Curse you, de Brielle," de Riavelle growled. Then, as though tossed at someone else, "Nay, can't you see I am trying to help him? I—"

"Get back!" a familiar voice snapped. A tussling sound, then the voice spoke again. "Etienne?"

Therri?

"No, de Riavelle," he heard Therri say sharply. "Don't—"

The sound of snapping wood coincided with a fresh sear of agony through Etienne's shoulder, so wrenching that this time he cried out. Mathilde's violet gaze exploded into a flash of white light, then plunged into blackness.

Had Mathilde not been clinging to the rim of the embrasure, her knees would have given way. She had wanted Etienne humbled, she had not wanted him dead!

At a frantic wave of Violette's hand, her trumpeters blasted out the signal that called a premature end to the tourney. But the alarm had not come in time to stop the bowman from loosing his arrow. Mathilde saw Etienne hit the ground, the bolt from the crossbow planted in his back. Immediately, Etienne's black-surcoted challengers converged around his prone body, all except the stout bowman who disappeared like a fat puff of smoke into the surrounding tumult of the mêlée.

The repetitive blare of the trumpets gradually reined the tumult in. The Vision must have seen his friend fall, for he thundered through the confusion of knights to Etienne's side. To Mathilde's surprise, Girard rode close at his heels.

"Violette," Hermaline said, "we must send someone to help him."

Violette turned to the thickset servant who had announced

Mathilde. "Hugon, take a cart to the field and bring Sir Etienne back to the castle. We will attend to him here."

The man bowed and started towards the tower stairs.

Mathilde turned to Violette, her face cold. "You think he still lives, my lady?"

Violette's smooth forehead creased. She patted one of Mathilde's hands, still clutching the embrasure's stones. "We must all pray that he does, my dear. Hermaline, where are you going?"

"With Hugon. I am going to ride with him to the field."

"Sir Etienne does not need you there. Stay here and help me prepare a chamber for him."

Hermaline crossed her arms over her generous bosom, her full lower lip thrust out in a stubborn pout. "I am going."

Violette shrugged.

Mathilde touched her sleeve. "My lady, you must let me go too."

She must tell the Vision what she suspected, that Chesnei was the man with the crossbow. The Vision might be able to intercept him before he escaped from the tournament field. But she had not seen Chesnei's face. She might be wrong. She did not wish to slander his name before Violette and her ladies, lest he should after all prove to be innocent of the deed. But the Vision would know how to learn the truth. He would be clever and resourceful, just like the heroes of the jongleur's ballads.

"I do not want *her* along!" Hermaline said.

Violette frowned. "Hermaline."

But Mathilde ignored her rudeness. "Please, my lady." What excuse could she give to join Hermaline? "Sir Etienne—he was my champion."

Her voice wavered and threatened to break. She saw Etienne in her mind's eye, lying in a pool of blood. However he had used her, he had not deserved that. She dashed away a genuine tear.

"Sir Etienne was wearing your favor?" Violette said.

Mathilde nodded.

"But I thought—" Violette's dark eyes narrowed at Mathilde. She murmured, "What game is this he plays?"

83

"Game, my lady?" Mathilde said.

Violette weighed her for a moment with an enigmatic gaze. Then she gently disengaged Mathilde's hand from her sleeve. "Go, my dear."

Mathilde whispered her thanks and hurried after Hermaline.

By the time the cart reached the field, the trumpets had ceased blaring and the last knightly scuffle had drawn to a standstill. Blocked by the crowd that surrounded Etienne, Hugon drew up the cart and sprang down. At Hermaline's insistence, he lifted her, then Mathilde, to the ground, then shouted for a path to be made through the wall of knights. Drawn by curiosity to Etienne's plight, the knights were slow to heed the command. Mathilde danced impatiently on her toes. Time was slipping away. Chesnei—or whoever the bowman had been—would be gone before anything could be done to stop him.

Hermaline grabbed Hugon's arm and berated him for being so slow to make the knights move. Mathilde's own fear flushed hotly through her body. Not only was Chesnei slipping away, but so might be Etienne's life!

She ran to a knight at the edge of the crowd and tugged on the skirt of his surcote. He had removed his helmet and turned with a startled look.

"Please, sir, can you help us to—?" She broke off as the knight's gaze slid over her tangled, windblown hair and the threadbare mantle that covered her gown. A leering grin twisted up the side of his mouth.

She dropped his surcote and backed away.

Hugon must have seen. He pulled away from Hermaline's grasp and joined Mathilde, placing himself firmly between Mathilde and the grinning knight. Mathilde glimpsed the knight's crestfallen face at Hugon's blocking move, but Hugon distracted him with a stream of rapid orders. The knight nodded and nudged a nearby companion. Soon they were adding their shouts to Hugon's, causing the crowd at last to begin to break apart.

Hermaline ran forward and shouldered Mathilde out of the way so that she might be first to follow Hugon as he began maneuvering into the group of milling knights. She paused and whispered something to the knight who had leered at Mathilde, then turned and swept after Hugon.

With an effort, Mathilde swallowed her resentment of Hermaline's rudeness, tossed her head and took a step towards the crowd.

"Ho, there." The knight who had leered at her grabbed her boldly by the arm. "You are to await your mistress over there by the cart."

Mathilde stared at him. "My mistress?"

"Lady Hermaline. She said she had no need of her servant to help her attend Sir Etienne. You are to return to the cart and await her orders."

"S-servant?" Mathilde gasped. "I am *not* – "

"She told me you might prove saucy about it. Must I escort you myself?"

He looked altogether too eager to do so. Mathilde shook her head and backed away from him. He shrugged and turned back to the crowd, closing off her entry to the path he had helped to clear.

Now what was she to do? How should she ever get the Vision's attention in time to –

Her thoughts broke off as she saw four knights push their way free from the far side of the crowd. Three of them wore helmets and black surcotes. The third wore a surcote of blue and grey, his helmet tucked under his arm. Short dark hair, a dark, fringing beard . . . *Girard.*

Two of the knights with black surcotes seemed to be dragging him. Mathilde saw her brother's heels dig into the dirt as though to resist, before he was jerked forward so hard his feet briefly left the ground. He dropped his helmet and it rolled to a stop a few feet away.

Chesnei, or whoever Etienne's attacker had been, had worn a black surcote, just like these men. Together they had attacked and wounded—perhaps killed!—Etienne. Now what did they want with her brother?

She waited until she thought they had moved far enough away not to notice her, then ran and picked up Girard's helmet. She hugged it to her chest and moved cautiously after the knights. Hermaline would not let her help Etienne, but she must find some way to help her brother. And if she crept near enough, she might hear the knights speak the name of the bowman who had so arrantly planted his arrow in Etienne's back.

The men pulled Girard, still stumbling and resisting, over to a bay destrier some distance from the crowd. Mathilde followed, her heart pounding.

The destrier sidled nervously as the two men who held Girard pushed him roughly against the horse's side. She recognized her brother's mount from the white stocking on its foreleg. She crept closer as the third man, the largest of the three, waved the other two away. He stepped forward and slowly twisted a mailed hand into the front of her brother's surcote.

"You thought yourself very clever, did you not?" she heard him growl at Girard. "But your game to hide the ribbon has failed. Did you think I would not recognize it tied around de Brielle's arm?"

Girard stammered, "I—I don't kn-know what you—"

The knight's free hand swiped across his face. Mathilde winced and raised a hand to her own cheek, almost dropping the helmet. Her brother's bare palm had been painful enough. One clad in mail would be brutal. She saw a trickle of blood ooze from the corner of her brother's mouth and drip into his beard.

"Don't try my patience, de Riavelle," the knight warned. "We know you are the courier. Retrieve the ribbon for us, and I'll let you live to report your failure to your lady. Continue this foolish play of ignorance and I'll kill you here and now."

Alarmed by this threat, Mathilde shot a look around the field. There must be someone who had seen her brother's plight and would come to his aid?

But most of the knights remained gathered around Etienne. The few milling in the refuges were there because of wounds incurred in mêlée. Even had they not been too injured to help, they, like the spectators watching from the stands, were too far away to intervene between Girard and his captors.

She glanced back at her brother, just as he sent a panicked look over the knight's shoulder, as though similarly hopeful of some rescue. He gave an audible gasp when his eyes locked with Mathilde's.

"Don't think to cry out," the knight warned him, misinterpreting Girard's sharp intake of breath. "You'll be dead before the crowd can even turn this way."

"Sir," one of his companions suggested, "perhaps we should discuss our strategy to regain the ribbon somewhere else? Somewhere there are not so many potential witnesses to our persuasion of Sir Girard."

The first knight, the apparent leader, gave a curt nod. "Fetch the horses," he snapped.

The man so ordered turned to obey. And saw Mathilde.

"Sir — we have an audience."

The leader turned, one hand still clenched on her brother's surcote.

Mathilde stood frozen in the space of silence that followed. She saw the shift of the leader's eyes through the slits in his helmet as he surveyed her.

"Lady Mathilde. A lady now, indeed." The leader's rough voice rumbled across the air. "You've not changed, child. You still have your mother's eyes." His gruff voice hardened. "And, I fear, your mother's heart."

This man knew her? His gold-flecked gaze . . . Nay, his gravel tones betrayed the impossibility of the thought that flashed through her mind.

He glanced away from her, back to Girard. "Your sister has solved your dilemma for you, de Riavelle. De Brielle believes it is her token he defended. His fierce determination to hold on to the ribbon, even with that crossbolt in his shoulder, betrayed his passion for its owner. I suspect he will agree to an exchange quickly enough. The ribbon for Lady Mathilde's safe return to him."

"But sir, what if de Brielle is dead?" one of his companions asked.

Mathilde's flesh prickled as though a whisper of frost had brushed her skin at the words.

"Then we will bargain with Laurant," the leader said. "He will not turn his back on his late friend's paramour. Take her."

His two companions stepped towards Mathilde.

"No!" Girard shouted. "Mathilde, run!"

She hesitated. "Girard—"

"You can't help me! Run for the crowd!"

She flung her brother's helmet at the pair of advancing knights. It caught one of them on his own iron helm, staggering him with an awful clang.

Then she turned and ran for the safety of the crowd.

The helmet did not slow her pursuers for long. She heard their pounding feet at her heels. They were faster than she, their strides longer and more powerful. She drew breath into her burning lungs and screamed, "Lord Therri! Hugo—"

A curse thundered behind her. Two mailed arms clamped around her waist, cutting off her cry. The force of her pursuer's lunge hurled them both onto the ground. Mathilde fell face down, her mouth filling with dirt. For a terrifying moment, she feared the weight of the knight atop her back would crush her.

Then somewhere above them echoed a *whirrr*, a *thump*, and a *thud*.

"Get up," a voice rapped out. "Step away from her."

The weight lifted from her back. Mathilde sat up, shaking. Tears streamed from her eyes, stinging from both dirt and terror. She coughed and spat out the dirt from her mouth.

"Lady Mathilde, are you injured?"

She coughed and spat again, then tried to focus on the horseman who seemed to have appeared from out of nowhere. His image danced blurrily, but she recognized the weapon in his hands. *A crossbow. Had Chesnei returned to kill her and Girard?*

She rubbed the heels of her shaking palms into her eyes, trying desperately to clear her vision.

"Lady Mathilde?"

The voice prodded her more urgently. Slowly, she lowered her hands—and gasped in relief. She recognized the colorless tendrils of hair, the bland, blank eyes— "C-Costane?"

Nay, the eyes were not blank now, but fixed with a grim determination. Her brother's squire held his crossbow trained on the knight who had tumbled her to the ground. The other knight lay crumpled nearby, one hand clasped around an arrow's shaft protruding from his chest. From the way his helmeted head lolled to one side, Mathilde knew that he was dead.

Visions of Etienne flashed through her mind. She glanced at the crowd behind her, her eyes blurring with fresh tears, then gasped again and scrambled to her knees.

The crowd had parted anew, but the three men emerging from it kept the milling knights distracted from her and the squire. Mathilde's heart lurched so hard she thought it might burst out of her ribs. Hugon and the Vision supported a white-faced but apparently conscious Etienne as he stumbled towards the cart. A broken arrow shaft still jutted from his left shoulder. Hermaline hovered beside him, saying something. Mathilde saw the vehement shake of Etienne's head.

He was alive. *He was alive.* And in his hand still fluttered her gilt-edged ribbon.

"My lady, can you stand?"

Mathilde stumbled numbly to her feet at Costane's query, her gaze still riveted on Etienne.

"Give me your hand."

She took a step towards the cart. "I must go to him—"

"Lady Mathilde." She found herself blocked by Costane's horse. "Give me your hand and mount behind me."

His crossbow still trained on her former pursuer, he reached down his free hand and waited for her to obey.

She strained to see around the horse. Etienne now leaned against the cart, still shaking his head at Hermaline. His face looked pasty and drawn. "But Sir Etienne—"

"Your brother needs my help, my lady. Delay may cost him his life."

Mathilde tore her gaze away from Etienne. Her brother had somehow freed himself from his captor's hold. He and the black-surcoted leader had drawn their swords and were engaged in a heated battle.

"Your brother fights with blunted steel, my lady. His challenger has a well-honed blade. If I do not ride to his aid soon—"

Etienne had the Vision and Hermaline to care for him, she reminded herself. Her duty was to Girard.

She put her hand in Costane's. He pulled her up onto the back of his horse, then turned in the saddle and released the spring of his crossbow. The arrow whistled cleanly into her former pursuer's breast. Mathilde stared in horror as the knight reeled and fell.

"He might have followed us," Costane said, his voice as chill as his deed. "Hold tight to me, my lady."

Mathilde wound her arms around the squire's waist as he spurred his horse into a gallop across the field. They covered the ground quickly to Girard and his opponent. Costane drew up, reloaded the crossbow, and called out, "Master, step away."

Girard disengaged his sword from his attacker's and sprang to his destrier's side.

"Hold!" Costane snapped at the black-surcoted knight.

The knight froze, then turned slowly to face Costane. Girard shoved his foot into his destrier's stirrup and threw himself into the saddle as Costane leveled his arrow at the knight's breast.

Mathilde shuddered and squeezed shut her eyes.

"Wait, de Riavelle," the knight rasped. "Are you not man enough to look me in the face before your squire kills me?"

"Your face will make no difference to your fate," Girard snapped.

The knight snorted. "And de Brielle called *me* coward."

Mathilde re-opened her eyes at Etienne's name. She saw Girard stiffen.

"As you wish," he said. "Drop your sword, then you may remove your helmet. It shall spare you a few seconds only."

The sword fell with a soft *thump* into the dirt. Slowly, the knight lifted the unmarked helmet from his head, then pushed back his mail coif. He ran a hand over the back of his neck, loosing long waves of sweat-dampened grey hair to tumble over his shoulders. Again, uneasy memory prickled over Mathilde's skin. His nose hooked like a falcon's beak. Flecks of disturbing gold nested in the hazel beds of his eyes. Deep, shadowed creases split his leathern cheeks as his heavy lips twitched, twisting up into such a baleful grimace that Mathilde shrank against Costane's back.

"Your death-wish has been granted," Costane snapped at the knight. "Now —"

"No!" The strangled word croaked from Girard. He pushed his destrier alongside Costane's horse and tore the crossbow out of his squire's hands. He stared ashen-faced at the knight.

"You are wise not to kill me," the knight growled. "My men know you and the message you bear. They would avenge me and you would die—a most unpleasant death. Now perhaps we can serve one another. I can make it worth your while to help me obtain the ribbon —" he paused and his gold-flecked gaze slid to Mathilde " —and surrender what was promised me."

She clung closer to Costane, but could not tear her gaze away from the knight's face. She knew him, yet she did not. He was like a grotesque caricature of the sleek, honey-voiced man she recalled.

Mathilde sent a confused glance at her brother and saw his pale face flush.

"If you come one step near my sister, I will send you back to hell where you belong!"

With his threat still quivering in the air, Girard whipped up Costane's crossbow and released the spring. The arrow sailed into the knight's right thigh, piercing his mail chausses. The knight fell with a howl of pain.

"Come," Girard croaked at Costane, and set spurs to his destrier to gallop away from the field.

Costane thundered after him until they reached the field of tents. Girard dismounted, then turned and dragged Mathilde off Costane's horse.

She swayed in her brother's hold. "Girard, who was that man? He looked like—b-but he could not be! His voice, his face—all were different—and yet —"

Girard released her so quickly that she stumbled back against Costane's horse.

Costane nudged her away with his foot, then swung himself out of the saddle. "Master, you should not have let that cur live."

"You heard him!" Girard roared. "If I had killed him, his cohorts would have tracked me down and—" He shuddered. "You do not know him, what he is capable of, even in death. Nay, I daresay he is so evil he *cannot* die. My father tried and here he is, returned to haunt us."

These words about their father took Mathilde aback, but before she could protest them, Costane said, "Master, I do not know who that knight was or why you fear him, but we must get back the ribbon from de Brielle."

Girard groaned. "I tried. I broke the shaft in his shoulder, hoping it would send him into a faint so I could slip free the ribbon from his hand. Laurant thrust me out of the way before I could do so." He began to pace back and forth in front of their tent, his pale cheeks hollow with agitation. "How did that devil know to find me here? How did he know I had the ribbon? Someone has betrayed us, Costane. Ah, Saints! He will want more than that curst token, now. He will want my blood for that bolt I sent into his leg. And Mathilde—" He stopped and stared white-faced at her. "He wants Mathilde!"

"Send her back to your father," Costane said, "and let us be about our business."

"Nay, that is what he will expect me to do, now that he knows I have recognized him. He will set men to watch the road to seize her along the way. We have got to hide her. Somehow, somewhere we have got to—"

"Master." Costane betrayed his own agitation by grabbing Girard by the arm. "What we must do is retrieve the ribbon. You have sworn on your honor to see it safely delivered!"

"But Mathil—"

"Curse your ninnyhammered sister! She is not impor—" Costane's colorless eyes flicked to Mathilde and suddenly locked. Slowly his gaze shifted to survey her from the top of her head to her linen-slippered toes. Its eerie blankness repulsed her even more than the leering knight's much hotter perusal had done. Costane's gaze traveled slowly back up to her face. He took an abrupt step forward and stopped just in front of her. Mathilde tried to back away, but found Costane's horse behind her. Costane touched the palm of his hand to the top of his head, then moved it forward until it brushed the top of Mathilde's flaxen hair.

They were nearly the same height.

"Nay, master," he said. "You wish to protect your sister. I want to see you keep your oath. Perhaps there is a way to do both."

Six

*S*aints! *He must be dead. Else what was this angel's face doing above him?*

Etienne squeezed his eyes shut. Nay, his shoulder throbbed too fiercely for him to be dead. And that angel had looked altogether too familiar to be a celestial spirit. Perhaps he was hallucinating? Aye, that must be it. He was feverish, delirious.

But he did not feel hot and damp. Cautiously, he cracked open one eye. Definitely a hallucination. He had dreamed himself drowning in waves of flaxen hair. His head had whirled with the musky fragrance of angelica, his skin luxuriating in a bath of silken tresses. But the lingering pleasure of those sensations fled as he squinted up at the cropped off ends of the angel's pale yellow mane. The hair just brushed against the angel's shoulders—shoulders clad not in some white, celestial robe, but in a squire's sober brown tunic. The garment bloused over a belt to conceal the sylphlike figure he recalled from Lady Violette's hall. But he noted with pleasure that the hem fell just below the knees of legs tantalizingly encased in a pair of clinging buff-colored hose.

He tried to blink away the absurd vision, but it stubbornly continued to hover above him. Wide violet eyes gazed down on him with flattering anxiety. A pair of petal-pink lips trembled softly. His heart gave a thump. If an angel, then surely those lips would taste of heaven?

He closed his eyes again and shook his head against the bolster. Nay, he *must* be dreaming. But when he looked again, the angel was still there, still ridiculously clad in some squire's clothes, the previously flowing hair cropped bluntly to the shoulders, but the face unmistakably that of . . .

"Mathilde?" His voice came out in a croak. He tried to swallow the lump of wool that seemed lodged in his throat, then queried hoarsely, "What the devil are you doing h—*mmph!*"

Her hands slammed down over his mouth, catching his nose in the slap. He lay stunned by her move, until he realized that she had cut off his air. He tried to pull away her fingers, flinching at a sharp twinge in his shoulder, but her hands only pressed down harder.

"*Shhh!*" she hissed. "You must not betray me to the Vision!"

He tugged again, desperation lending strength to muscles grown sluggish and weak. He did not want to hurt her, but she had caught him on an exhale and his lungs threatened to burst in a frantic demand for air. The harder he pried, the more determinedly she thrust her palms against his mouth and nose. At last, chivalry deserted him and he clawed her hands free with the gentleness of a bear swiping its dinner out of the stream.

"By all the saints—!" he gasped, wheezing in a chestful of air. "Are you trying to smother m—"

"Etienne? Mathieu, I told you to call me the minute he woke up."

Mathilde shrank away at the rebuking male voice. Therri's tall frame surged in front of her, eclipsing her from Etienne's view. His friend's gaze held the same anxious expression that had greeted him when he had first opened his eyes upon Mathilde.

"How do you feel?" Therri asked.

Etienne tried again to clear the wool from his mouth. "Confused," he muttered. He stretched his neck, trying to see the slight figure cowering behind his friend.

"Well, that's not surprising," Therri said. "You've lain abed two days with a fever. Thank the Saints it broke last night. Your shoulder seems to be healing cleanly now, thanks to Lady Hermaline's salves."

"Hmph." The sound snorted softly from behind Therri.

Therri didn't spare it a glance, but Etienne stretched his neck still further. "Therri, what is she doing here?"

"Hermaline?"

"Nay, Mathi—"

Mathilde's face flashed out from behind his friend with that same look of panic it had held just before her hands had smacked down over his mouth. Her violet eyes looked stricken, but being too far away to muffle him again, she was reduced to waving her hands frantically in the air. Etienne paused, took in again her shortened locks and the odd tunic she wore, then leaned back against the bolster and rubbed his eyes with his fingers.

"Are you sure I don't still have a fever?" he asked Therri.

"Nay," Therri said. "You'll be back on your feet in no time, and Hermaline will have no more excuse to haunt our tent."

Etienne dropped his hand and stared at the stretch of canvas over his head. He remembered the scuffle with de Riavelle and his cronies, some blow to his shoulder, falling from his horse and fainting, then regaining his senses to find Therri and Hermaline bent over him. Hermaline had wanted him carried to Grantamur Castle, but even through the distracting pain in his shoulder, something in Etienne had shrank from delivering himself so totally to Hermaline's power. Fortunately, Therri had seconded his insistence that he be allowed to recover in his own tent.

"Did you say Hermaline is here now?" Etienne asked.

"Outside." Therri jerked his head towards the tent door. "Warming you some gruel over the fire."

Etienne groaned. "I'd rather have some wine to wash this wool out of my mouth."

Therri glanced behind him. "Mathieu, there's a flask and a cup over there by my cot."

Mathilde sent one last pleading look at Etienne, then moved away as ordered.

Etienne watched her, baffled both by her presence and by his friend's seeming ignorance as to who—and what—she was. He waited until she returned with the cup.

"Can you sit up?" Therri asked.

"Perhaps if—Mathieu?—helped me."

Therri took the cup and nodded at Mathilde. She hesitated and Etienne saw the way she blushed. She glanced nervously from Therri back to Etienne, then drew a deep breath and reached towards his shoulders.

She stopped just short of touching him. "I-I don't want to hurt you."

"'Tis my left shoulder that seems to be injured," he said. "If you will just slide your hands under my right shoulder and help me to lift . . ."

Her blush deepened. He followed the direction of her glance, then touched his bare chest to see what might be amiss. He felt nothing but a linen strip holding in place the bandage around his left shoulder.

"Here, I'll help you," Therri said impatiently when Mathilde continued to hesitate.

He held out the cup to her, but she said quickly, "Nay, I will do it," and bent over to plunge her hands under Etienne's shoulder.

For an instant, her face hovered mere inches from his. A lock of her hair swung forward to brush his cheek, a mere tickle of silk, but the sensation threatened to stifle his lungs anew.

"I-I cannot lift you by myself."

He had a disconcerting urge to kiss the lips that whispered this complaint. As if sensing the danger, she drew back a little. With an effort, he reined in his bemused wits and used his right elbow to lever himself up as she heaved at his weight.

The movement wrenched his left shoulder. He gasped and nearly fell back, but she caught him around the waist and pulled until he managed to roll onto his right side and prop himself up with his elbow.

"There, I said I would hurt you!" Her voice brimmed with self-reproach.

He bit his lip against the pain, but moved his right hand to trap her fingers as they slid to his left arm and sought to balance him.

"Nay," he gritted. It must be the pain that made it so difficult to breathe. It could not be the disturbing warmth of her fingers against his skin, the sweet scent wafting from her . . .

Curious. His dreams had wreathed him in musky angelica, the fragrance that had clung to her ribbon. But now, despite the autumn wind whistling outside, with Mathilde's piquant face once again mere inches from his he smelled only sunshine and fresh spring breezes.

He shook himself out of her spell and slowly released her fingers. She jerked them away as if he had held them against a firebrand and fled to the other side of the tent.

Therri thrust the cup into Etienne's hand. "Drink that," he said. "It will brace you for Hermaline's return."

Grateful for the distraction, Etienne tilted some wine into his mouth. His tongue and throat felt parched, and he gulped greedily at the liquid.

But Therri pulled the cup away before Etienne could finish draining it. "That's enough, until you've had something to eat. We don't want to unsettle your wits anew. Mathieu, call Lady Hermaline —"

"Wait," Etienne said, his gaze fixed on Mathilde's stiffening back. He asked Therri, "Can you and I talk a moment — alone?"

Mathilde whirled around, her hands clasped at her breast, the pleading panic back in her eyes.

"With pleasure," Therri said. "I'm in no hurry to endure another of Hermaline's lectures on the bumbling way I've cared for you. Mathieu —"

Mathilde dropped her hands when Therri turned around to address her, her hasty attempt to look suddenly blank so comical that Etienne had to bite his lip to keep from laughing.

"Tell Sir Etienne's squire to ride to Grantamur Castle and inform Lady Violette of his recovery. And see if you can keep Lady Hermaline occupied for a few minutes. Don't let her into this tent until I call you. Do you understand?"

"I— Y-Yes. Yes, of course, my lord," Mathilde answered breathlessly. She lingered just long enough to grab up a hat with a high, pointed crown from the stool in the corner of the tent, slap the hat onto her head, and roll the brim down over her eyes, before hurrying out of the tent.

Therri shook his head and pulled up the stool to sit next to Etienne's cot. "First time he's gone with just one telling. Usually I have to repeat myself at least twice before he obeys. I tell you, Etienne, that's the queerest boy I've ever seen. Always heaving these dramatic sighs and when I ask him what is wrong, he just says 'Nothing, my lord,' then smiles and gazes at me with the oddest glow in his eyes. I swear, it's enough to make a man wonder if he's simpleminded—or worse."

Worse indeed, Etienne thought. *She's in love with you, you idiot—and you can't even see her for the woman that she is!*

But Etienne had to admit that with the loosely bloused tunic and with her hair cropped off, Mathilde might pass for a young squire to someone who had no reason to think her otherwise. Had her face not been so prevalent in his delirious dreams, he might have doubted his own eyes upon awakening, as well. Therri had only seen her once before, and had been so distracted with Violette upon that occasion, that Etienne supposed he could forgive his friend for being taken in by Mathilde's ridiculous disguise—at least temporarily. Two days, Therri had said, since Etienne's injury. She could not, then, have been masquerading longer than that.

Dreamy sighs and glowing eyes—all directed at Therri. Aye, she still fancied herself in love with his friend. Etienne felt an odd hollowness spread inside him. It must be the residual effects of the fever and the blood he had lost. Therri was right, he needed something more nourishing than wine in his stomach.

But first he needed to know what Mathilde was doing in their tent.

"Mathieu. Where did he come from?" he asked Therri.

Therri looked disgusted. "He's de Riavelle's brother, palmed off on me as 'surety' that de Riavelle will return to pay the ransom he owes me from the tourney. The dodger hadn't even the backbone to meet me face to face to plead for my 'indulgence'. Not that I would have granted it. And he probably knew it, so I suppose from his vantage point it was safer to send that poor whelp in his stead to say he hadn't the money. Apparently he'd rather throw his brother on my mercy than to part with his armor and horse."

Etienne's own memories of de Riavelle were less than charitable. "I think the man is a little crazed. He and two of his cronies attacked me with sharpened weapons. I had nearly bested the three of them, when—what *did* happen to me back there on the field?"

"Someone shot you with a crossbolt. I just happened to glance round in time to see you fall. If anyone saw the archer, he's not come forward with a name. But what do you mean de Riavelle attacked you? When?"

"Just before the crossbolt hit me."

Therri shook his head. "Couldn't have. I had just finished knocking him out of the saddle myself. He remounted and rode with me to see how badly you were hurt. In fact, he's the one who broke the arrow shaft while it was still in your shoulder and sent you into that faint."

"Then who—?" Etienne frowned. "I assumed it was de Riavelle when he demanded I give him Mathilde's ribbon. If it wasn't he— who else would care so much about a lady's trinket to attack me in that way?"

"You say they had sharpened weapons?"

"Aye. One of their lance-heads left a rip in my shield the length of my forearm."

"Over his sister's ribbon? Nay, that is too out-of-bounds even for de Riavelle. It must have been someone with a personal grudge against you."

Etienne strained to recall the details of the skirmish, but his head was starting to swim from the wine. "Nay, they only wanted the ribbon. I remember—"

"Etienne—do you recall any of your dreams while you were feverish?"

"What do my dreams have to do with—"

"You kept muttering about the ribbon de Riavelle's sister gave you, and once or twice I heard you mumble the girl's name. Mathilde. I'd lay odds, by the way, that Mathieu is her twin, though he hasn't said. But with names like those—'Mathieu' and 'Mathilde'—both flaxen haired, and you said the girl had violet eyes, too . . . But the point is, you must have been dreaming about her. If you didn't know your attacker, perhaps you dreamed him with de Riavelle's face."

"And fixed on Mathilde's ribbon as the reason for the attack?" Etienne pulled the bolster alongside him, shifting his weight to lean into it. The movement made his shoulder ache, but it was better than lying directly on his wound. The small effort left him exhausted. Blazes! He felt as weak as a kitten! He said stubbornly to Therri, "Nay, that part I *do* remember. The man I thought was de Riavelle had his lance-point at my throat, demanding the ribbon for my life."

He saw the skepticism in Therri's face, but Therri only said, "You look like death warmed over. We'll sort your memories out later. Go back to sleep. I'll bar Hermaline from the tent until you wake up."

Etienne sighed. He leaned his head against the bolster and almost immediately felt his eyes drifting shut.

"Where's the ribbon now?" he murmured. He remembered it had still been in his hand before he had fainted again in the cart.

"In my saddle bag, along with that curst necklet I broke. Why?"

"I spilled my blood for it. I want to know for myself that it's safe."

"The way you cling to that bit of cloth, you'd think the two of you were betrothed. I've never seen a man as smitten as you."

Etienne shifted his cheek against the bolster. "I'm not smitten. I can't afford to be. She's poor as a churchmouse and I cannot support a wife who comes without a dowry."

"Unless you swallowed your pride and—"

"Don't say it," Etienne warned sharply. "I'm not crawling back home to my brother."

He imagined he could see Therri's shrug, even with his eyes closed. Therri said, "Have done and marry Hermaline, then. She's eager enough to take you, poor as you are."

Aye, Etienne thought, *to take and twist and spin me into her notion of an ideal husband.* She would never let the man she married forget to whom he owed the good fortune her small dowry had brought him. He frowned as Hermaline's pouty face glimmered against his closed lids. The wine pulled powerfully at him. A few more moments and he would slide into sleep. He did not want Hermaline to be waiting for him in his dreams.

"The ribbon," he murmured.

"What about it?" Therri said.

"Let me have it."

There was a moment of silence during which Etienne imagined Therri was debating whether or not to humor him. Finally he heard the stool scrape and Therri's footsteps crunching across the dirt floor of the tent.

"Here."

Etienne tried to force open his eyes as Therri put the ribbon into his hand, but the wine held them firmly shut. The scent wreathed him at once. Angelica. A cheat. But the fragrance succeeded in chasing Hermaline's image away. He rubbed his thumb against the silk. Some of the tiny stitches at the back had come loose. It must have happened during the struggle on the field. He hoped he had not ruined it beyond repair.

"Perhaps she will be able to mend it," he murmured. "I suppose I shall have to give it back to her—Lady Mathilde—even though de Riavelle intends to snatch it away from her and return it to his harlot." The thought made Etienne's blood sizzle, even through the wine. Perhaps he should wait to return it until his strength returned, until he could at least teach de Riavelle a sharp lesson in manners toward his sister.

Therri's voice broke across the pleasant image of Etienne's sword whacking Girard de Riavelle to his knees.

"I should have told you this sooner, Etienne. Lady Mathilde has vanished along with her brother. He's no doubt whisked her off home to help plead the ransom he owes me from his father."

"Mmm . . ." Etienne resettled his cheek more comfortably against the bolster. "Gone, eh? Then I suppose I will have to entrust the ribbon to Mathieu to hold it for his sister." He laughed softly at his own joke, knowing Therri would not understand it, then gave up his struggle against the wine. In spite of the ribbon's exotic fragrance, this time when he slept, he dreamed of spring breezes and sunshine.

Mathilde watched him while he slept. Outside the tent she could hear Hermaline's shrill voice, upbraiding the Vision for not having called her when Etienne awoke. The Vision had sent Mathilde to sit with Etienne while he endured Hermaline's wrath. To Mathilde's relief, the Vision still seemed to think her a boy. That meant Etienne had not betrayed her.

Yet. She must retrieve the ribbon before he changed his mind. It was what Girard had sent her to do.

Girard had explained that he dared not attempt to retrieve the ribbon himself. The grey-haired knight and his men would be watching him. Girard hoped to lead them away from Grantamur Castle, then circle back and meet Mathilde in the woods in a sennight.

Her brother had hustled Mathilde into Costane's clothes so quickly that she had not had a chance to ask the questions hovering on her tongue. Why had the grey-haired knight looked so eerily familiar, and yet so strange? Why did he want the ribbon so badly that he had threatened to kill Girard on the open tournament field? Why were Girard and Costane so urgent to have the ribbon back that they were forcing her into a squire's tunic and sending her to risk her reputation by spending a sennight with two unmarried knights?

She picked up one end of the ribbon that trailed from Etienne's sleeping hand. What mystery did this embroidered strand hold?

When she saw her brother again, she would demand some answers. But first, she must slide the ribbon away from Etienne.

He had draped his arm across the bolster against which he leaned in his slumber. She did not think the position looked very comfortable but he seemed to be sleeping soundly.

At her first gentle pull his fingers flexed around the ribbon. She stopped, waited till his hand relaxed, then tried again. Again his fingers tightened on the embroidered strand.

Drat him! How could he be so sensitive in his sleep?

She sighed and sat down on the stool beside the cot. She must wait until he slept more deeply. At least that frightening flush no longer stained his cheeks. His skin looked cool and dry, but the wanness beneath his tan disturbed her.

For the first time in two days he lay quiet, his breathing steady. Lashes, thick and black, spread like tiny fans against the clay-like pallor of his cheeks. His sooty hair tumbled across his brow in curls more unruly than ever after his feverish tossings. Their waywardness intrigued her, for his curls looked altogether too soft to be so rebellious. She leaned forward and slid a tentative finger into one tightly coiled ringlet near his ear. It wrapped itself about her touch like some sleek serpent, smooth and sensuous. Its silky texture seduced her. She fondled a second curl and then a third until nearly the whole of her hand had slid into his tangled mane.

She scarcely realized what she was doing until her fingers hit a snag amid the tangles. He murmured and moved his head on the bolster to escape her inadvertent pull. Appalled at her own boldness, her hand instantly recoiled, but her fleeing fingers became caught in a silken knot.

This time Etienne grunted and jerked his head, resulting in a yank on the knot that brought his lashes fluttering up on sleep-hazed eyes.

"Ow! What the—?"

His hand with the ribbon flew up towards the source of the pain and captured Mathilde's retreating fingers.

He blinked several times, trying to focus on her face. She knew he was about to blurt out her name again. What if the Vision and Hermaline should step inside the tent just as he did so? After Etienne's wicked game to enflame Hermaline's jealousy, Hermaline would be all too ready to think the worst. After all, what sort of woman decked herself out in squire's clothes and hid herself in a man's tent? If Hermaline spread word of this, Mathilde's reputation would be ruined. And the Vision—! She could not bear to have the Vision recognize her like this!

She slid to her knees beside the cot. "Hush. *Please.* You must call me Mathieu."

He stared at her, his green eyes foggy and perplexed. "Mathieu?"

She could smell a lingering trace of wine on his breath. After two days of fever and fasting, the intoxicant must have left his head in a spin. He looked thoroughly muddled.

"I cannot explain it just now," she said, "and I think you need to go back to sleep anyway. But *please* try to remember when you wake up again to call me Mathieu."

"Mmm . . ." His lids drooped. He brought her hand with his to lay against the bolster and laced their fingers together, her ribbon caught between them. The clear red stone of his jacinth ring gleamed beside the embroidered strand. "But you *will* explain when I wake up."

"I-I'm not sure I can." She tried to ignore the soft quiver that wove through her at his touch. How white her fingers looked trapped between his tanned own! But his skin was cool against hers. Then why, when he had held her hand against his bare arm earlier, had she felt as though she'd been scorched?

"I think you had better," he murmured, "if you expect me to keep your secret from Therri."

He was not so muddled after all. He watched her through eyes narrowed now to mere slits. She tried to pull her hand free but he tightened his hold. *Seducer,* she thought. 'Twas the only explanation for these inexplicable sensations.

"Lord Therri will think it very odd if he comes in and sees you holding my hand," she warned. "He thinks I'm a boy."

"Does he?"

"Yes. And if you are a truly chivalrous knight, you will not betray me to him."

"You cannot play both boy and damsel in distress, my dear." His eyes closed but he held onto her hand. "And I've already shown you how unchivalrous I can be. All I want is your promise that when I wake up, you will tell me why you're strutting around my tent disguised as your own male twin. Else I shall indeed inform Therri that his new 'squire' is—"

"Very well," she said quickly. She thought she heard footsteps. He left her no choice. "I promise. Now let go of my hand."

He slid his fingers slowly free of hers. She did not realize how pleasant the strength of his touch had been until it was gone. Her hand felt curiously empty once it rested alone on the bolster.

"Can you help me get this back under my head?" His voice slurred a little with the request, the wine renumbing his tongue.

She drew a bracing breath and stood up. She had to help him lift his head before she shifted the bolster beneath it and before she could resist the temptation, she found herself caressing his silky curls anew. From his deepened breathing she knew he was asleep even before she laid his head back down on the bolster. She stepped away from the cot with a frown. What sort of man was he that he had skill to entice her even in his sleep?

"I tell you, I heard voices. He is awake again."

A flutter of the tent flap followed these words. Mathilde turned in time to catch a glimpse of Hermaline's pretty, petulant face before the flap fell closed on it again.

"Nay," the Vision's voice sounded, "Mathieu would have called us if he had reawakened."

"How many times have I heard you curse that boy for not remembering your commands? I am sure I heard voices. If I find Sir Etienne awake, I trust you will reward your new squire's disobedience with the good, stiff rod he deserves."

Mathilde drew an indignant breath, but when the flap fluttered again, she recollected her danger. She did not trust Hermaline to be as carelessly forgetful of her face as the Vision had proven. She snatched up her hat with the high, pointed crown and pulled it hurriedly onto her head, rolling the brim down to shade her eyes.

Not a moment too soon. The tent flap snapped open and Hermaline marched in.

"See? I told you—" Hermaline broke off and stared at Etienne slumbering on the cot. Her face fell, then reddened with anger as she turned on Mathilde. "He *was* awake. I heard him! You wretched whelp, you let him fall back to sleep again."

"Not so loud," Therri said. "You'll wake him. If you truly cared about him, you would know that he needs to sleep."

Hermaline tossed her head and crossed her arms over her chest.

Mathilde moved protectively closer to Etienne. Hermaline might be possessive of him in health, but Mathilde could not forget her cold indifference to the details of his care while he had burned two days with fever. Mathilde gave the other girl grudging credit for bringing the salve that had stemmed the inflammation in Etienne's wound. But Hermaline had made it clear from the first that she thought the salve's actual application and the wound's subsequent tending a task better fulfilled by a servant. Mathilde, only just arrived in the tent in her squire's disguise, remembered the way the Vision had cursed, snatched the jar out of Hermaline's hand, and cleaned and treated his friend's wound himself.

"Well," Hermaline said now, "'tis my face he will see the next time he awakes and not your whey-faced squire's. Move away from the cot, boy, and let me sit down on that stool."

"Fine," Therri said. "You can change his bandage the next time he wakes up, too. Mathieu, come."

Hermaline cried, "*I* am not going to—" She checked herself, then said simply, "I should not be strong enough to lift him. See that your squire lingers near enough to come at my call."

Therri shrugged and turned to lift the tent flap, letting in a haze of sunlight that illuminated his tall, broad-shouldered fame. Embraced by the soft, golden glow, he looked to Mathilde more like a heroic Vision than ever.

"Mathieu?"

Usually he attempted to keep his distance from Mathilde, assigning her to sit with Etienne whenever some errand called him away from the tent, then setting her to some task outside while he resumed the watch-care over his friend. Now he was inviting her to leave the tent in his company. For two days Mathilde had yearned to linger in his presence. Yet now, with her wish about to be fulfilled, she found herself edging backwards towards the cot.

"I— Perhaps I should stay to help Lady Hermaline."

"I don't need you *now*," Hermaline snapped. "Take him away, my lord."

"You heard my lady," he said. "She doesn't need either of us. Let's go, Mathieu."

Mathilde glanced at Etienne's sleeping form. Seducer he might be, but just now he was also wounded and vulnerable. Hermaline swept across the tent, her skirts swishing like the wings of a gerfalcon swooping down on its prey. How could Mathilde abandon Etienne to this . . .

"Go," Hermaline hissed at Mathilde, "or I shall take a rod to your back myself."

. . . *harpy.* Did Etienne know what manner of woman he had given his heart to?

"No one rebukes my squires except me," Therri snapped at Hermaline. "And if you wake Etienne up before he's ready I'll see you barred from this tent for good." He turned his frown on Mathilde. "Mathieu, I'm not going to tell you to come again."

Mathilde did not dare to defy his stern gaze. She moved reluctantly away from the cot, but she had not quite reached Therri's side when Hermaline gave an enraged squeal.

"What is this?"

Mathilde turned as Hermaline bent over the cot and came up with a strip of white, gilt-embroidered silk. The ribbon! Mathilde had been so bewitched by Etienne's enigmatic charms that she had left it tangled in his hand.

She saw Etienne's hand move against the cot as though in protest at its lost prize. He muttered something and shifted his head on the bolster, then settled back into sleep.

"*Be quiet,*" Therri said, obviously struggling to keep his voice low against his exasperation. "You almost woke him. What's the problem now?"

Hermaline shook the ribbon in the air. "This is the problem. It belongs to that insipid little hussy." She flung it angrily onto the dirt floor, then lifted her skirts above her ankle and ground her heel into the cloth.

Mathilde started forward in horror, but Therri brushed past her and whipped the ribbon to safety himself.

"Spiteful cat," he muttered.

"Call me what you like," Hermaline said, "if I see that again I will burn it."

Therri looked furious enough to shake Hermaline. He strode across the tent and stuffed the ribbon into his saddlebag, then jerked open the tent flap. "Mathieu."

Mathilde scurried out at his fierce glare.

"Don't—wake—him," Therri warned in a voice Mathilde thought even Hermaline would not dare to defy, then strode out on Mathilde's heels.

Seven

Mathilde smothered a sneeze in the crook of her sleeve. Hermaline's gruel reeked of so much pepper that it burned her throat and made her eyes stream. The liquid bubbled and gurgled in its iron pot. Hermaline had made the Vision build the fire so high, that despite the brisk autumn breeze, the heat beaded Mathilde's face with perspiration.

The Vision had ordered Mathilde to tend the broth while Hermaline sat with Etienne. Mathilde gave the gruel another swish with the wooden spoon. It had boiled so long now that it had grown quite thick. She hoped that it might boil dry. Forcing Etienne to swallow this spicy concoction would be sure to send him into such paroxysms of sneezing and choking that he would be certain to wrench his shoulder again.

She stirred the brew twice more, then sneezed again so hard that her hat flew off her head. She wiped her tearing eyes with her sleeve and turned away from the peppery fumes. The Vision sat on a stool near the tent, buffing his sword with a piece of soft cloth. She never grew weary of gazing at him! She had been terrified at first that he would recognize her instantly through her squire's disguise, but he had accepted her as Girard's "brother" without a blink. Of course, he had been distracted by other concerns when she had arrived at his tent.

Her lip quivered at the memory of the scene that had greeted

110

her. Blood-stained cloths and water, and Etienne sprawled face down on a cot while the Vision, his heroic face pale and taut, worked determinedly to staunch the flow of blood from his friend's wound. After roundly cursing Girard, the Vision had told "Mathieu" to make himself useful by tearing some linen for bandages. By the time Hermaline had come with her healing salves and the Vision had finished anointing and binding up his friend's shoulder, he had already accepted Mathilde as a boy.

The situation brought Mathilde both joy and frustration. Joy that she should be able to admire the Vision's beauty at her leisure and witness the truth of his valiant character reflected in his diligent care of his friend. Yet frustration that while she was forced to maintain this masquerade, she could do nothing to encourage the promising attention he had shown her in obtaining for her, however briefly, a privileged place in Violette de Maloisel's circle.

He had only asked "Mathieu" once about the whereabouts of his "sister". When she had stammered out that Girard had taken her home, the Vision had simply nodded and sent her off to fetch some fresh water for bathing Etienne's feverish face. But surely that steadfast frown upon the Vision's fair brow hinted of regret for opportunities lost?

"My lord." Her voice came out in a whisper, as it did every time she addressed him. Even after two days in his tent, his proud comeliness still awed her. She cleared her throat and repeated more loudly, "My lord."

The Vision looked up from his sword. "What is it, Mathieu?"

"I— Lady Hermaline's gruel. I do not think Sir Etienne should eat it."

"He's got to eat something when he wakes up. What the devil is wrong with the gruel?"

"Come and see."

He looked as if he meant to protest, then set his sword down and strode over to the pot. A soft glow enveloped her as he stopped beside her. *So different from the fiery tingles that Etienne stirred.* She shook the thought away. 'Twas the difference between a knight of honor and a beguiling knave.

"Well?" he demanded curtly.

She sighed and motioned toward the pot. "Smell it."

He hesitated, then leaned down and breathed in a lungful of steam.

A gasping sound raked out of his chest, followed by a rapid volley of sneezes. The Vision reeled away from the pot, the sneezes giving way to some very unheroic gagging sounds as he staggered back over to the stool.

"F-For the l-love of— Is she tr-trying to poison him?"

In spite of herself, Mathilde giggled. The Vision did not hear her, for he was sneezing again.

"G-Get—*choo!*—r-rid of it—*choo!*"

Mathilde willingly plucked the pot from the fire, holding it by its wooden handle as far away from herself as she could to escape the fumes. But she said, "What shall we feed Sir Etienne instead?"

A cool, feminine voice floated the answer on the air behind her. "If you will fetch some fresh water, I have brought some meal and a bit of beef bone. We will boil something a little less pungent than I fear my step-daughter's taste runs."

Mathilde turned in surprise and saw Violette de Maloisel wrapped in a fur-trimmed cloak, sitting astride a prancing grey palfrey. Etienne's squire and a maid carrying a basket covered with white linen accompanied her.

"Pungent," the Vision gasped, wiping his streaming eyes. "You mean something less lethal. Fiend seize it, Vi, what were you about, to let Hermaline loose on us like this?"

For a moment, with his face red from sneezing and his cheeks wet with pepper-induced tears, he almost wobbled off Mathilde's pedestal of perfection to the ranks of the merely mortal. To her relief the sneezes stopped, together with the unheroic choking sounds, and his color slowly returned to normal in the course of Violette's reply.

"When Hermaline sets her mind to something, it is useless to try to gainsay her," Violette said. "I knew she could do no harm so long as Sir Etienne remained in his faint. But she has never stepped foot in Grantamur's kitchen before this morning and I feared she would make a muddle of the gruel. As soon as his squire brought word that Sir Etienne had regained his senses, I gave orders to gather some healthful food and a bottle of wine." Violette paused. "Am I to remain sitting in this saddle all morning or are you going to ask your squire to assist me to dismount?"

Mathilde started at Violette's words. Though Violette was a diminutive woman and Mathilde stood slightly taller than the average, she did not think she was strong enough to lift Violette off her horse.

To her relief, the Vision strode over to the palfrey and held up his hands. "Allow me."

Violette seemed to hesitate, then set her hands to the Vision's broad shoulders and allowed him to lift her down.

She shook herself free immediately of the Vision's grasp on her waist, but Mathilde thought her voice sounded somewhat breathless.

"Thank you, my lord. Now if you will send your squire down to the river to fetch us some fresh—" She broke off and stared at Mathilde. "This is not your squire."

Mathilde hurriedly ducked her head, hoping the move would be taken as a gesture of respect for a lady and a superior. Why had she not redonned her hat? If Violette recognized her—

"The curst boy seems to have run off," the Vision said of his squire. "Disappeared just after the tournament. This is—" He paused.

Mathilde, on Girard's orders, had begged the Vision not to tell anyone that she was Girard's "brother". 'Twas to protect her from the grey-haired knight, Girard had told her. He might have men looking for her, as well as for Girard.

"I picked up this whelp in his place," the Vision finished vaguely, none too gracefully but nonetheless protecting her identity. "Mathieu, you may bow to Lady Violette."

Mathilde hesitated. Bow? She found curtsying awkward enough. But surely bows were simple. One simply bent forward at the waist.

She remembered Etienne's flourishing bows and attempted to imitate one now. But in her nervous haste to perform the gesture she bent forward too far too fast, and with the added weight of the iron pot still in her hands, she nearly lost her balance.

The Vision's hand shot out and pulled her back before she could pitch into Violette.

A snickering sound froze the embarrassed apology on Mathilde's lips.

Hermaline, apparently bored with waiting for Etienne to wake up, stood in the tent's entrance, laughing at Mathilde's clumsiness. "Wherever did you find such a bumbling boy, my lord?"

The Vision had looked angry at Mathilde's bungled bow, but he abruptly turned his displeasure on Hermaline.

"You might well ask," he said. "The boy is so bumbling that he has burned your gruel. Fortunately, your step-mamma has brought you the means to make more. Mathieu, give the pot to Lady Hermaline so that she may take it down to the river and wash it."

"Wash it?" Hermaline's small hands fluttered in horror. "You cannot think that I— That is servant's work. Send your squire to do it."

Mathilde said quickly, "I should be sure to bungle the cleaning of it, my lady, as I did my bow and the cooking."

"But I—I am *not* going to— Violette!"

Hermaline's dismay brought Mathilde a quirk of ill-smothered satisfaction.

But Violette sought to soothe the growing storm on her step-daughter's face. "Do not look so appalled, my dear. My maid will go down to the river with you and do the washing. Yes, yes, she will carry the pot, but you must carry the basket. She will help you to prepare some fresh gruel with the ingredients I've brought."

"But why must I go with her? Your maid can prepare the ingredients while I sit with Etienne."

"I thought you wished Etienne to know what an excellent cook you are? You would not wish to be dishonest with him, claiming the gruel was cooked by your hands when in fact it was made by others?"

Mathilde suspected that Hermaline was more than willing to lie about the gruel, but the Vision looked in no humor to guard her secret. Hermaline must have recognized the challenging lift of the Vision's brows.

"Oh, very well," Hermaline said, her lower lip thrust out in a pout. She snapped her fingers and Violette's maid, assisted by Etienne's squire, dismounted from her horse.

The maid paused while Violette removed something from the basket. Then the maid hurried forward to hand the basket to Hermaline and take the pot from Mathilde.

Hermaline moved out of the tent's entrance, then abruptly whirled when she came abreast of Mathilde. Her fingers flashed out to lock on Mathilde's arm in so painful a pinch that it made Mathilde yelp.

"That is for burning my gruel," Hermaline said. "And this" — the second pinch was even crueler than the first— "is for your impertinence. If Sir Etienne awakes again, you are to call me at once. At once! Do you understand?"

Hermaline's pretty, petulant face blurred through the tears of pain in Mathilde's eyes. She pried her arm loose of Hermaline's grasp and rubbed the stinging flesh through her sleeve. "Aye, my lady," she ground out, lowering her gaze to the ground to hide the glare she longed to direct at Hermaline.

"So help me, Vi," the Vision said as Hermaline swept away with the maid, "if she lays another hand on my squire—"

"You forget yourself, my lord," Violette cut him off in tones of frigid dignity. "I do not recall giving you leave to address me in this familiar way."

Her reply distracted the Vision from his complaints of her step-daughter, kindling a fire in his sapphire-hued eyes. "Oh, do you not? Then your memory is marvelously arbitrary, for *I* recall one night in the gardens of Rouen when you—"

This time, Violette's interruption bit like a whip. "I trust you are not about to sully my good name before these youths with your scurrilous remembrances?"

"Scurrilous—?" The Vision broke off with a glance at Mathilde and Etienne's squire. "Walter, go down to the river and guard Lady Hermaline and Lady Violette's maid. And you, Mathieu, go back inside the tent and sit with Etienne."

Mathilde realized that she had been holding her breath, torn between curiosity and dread of hearing the rest of the Vision's statement about the gardens at Rouen. 'Twas none of her business what he and Violette might have done there, she told herself fiercely, and turned towards the tent.

"Mathieu—" 'twas Violette who spoke, her voice softening " — wait a moment."

Mathilde turned.

Violette held out the linen-wrapped bundle she had removed from the basket. "Some fresh bread and soft, sweet cheese. In case Sir Etienne should awake before the gruel is ready and find himself hungry."

Her dark eyes, which but a moment ago had sparkled with such haughty spirit at the Vision, now warmed with compassion.

Mathilde darted a glance from Violette to the Vision, then forced her lips into a smile and accepted the bundle. "Thank you, my lady."

"I apologize for Hermaline's manners," Violette said, touching Mathilde's arm gently where Hermaline had pinched her. "Be assured I will rebuke her for—" She broke off, her eyes widening as they gazed into Mathilde's.

Mathilde ducked her head quickly, thanked Violette again, and hurried into the tent.

Had Violette recognized her? She stood inside the entrance, straining to hear whether Violette might express a suspicion to the Vision. Again Mathilde cursed herself for not retrieving her hat. And Hermaline! Hermaline had seen her without it, too!

She heard a soft murmur from Violette, then the Vision's louder, impatient reply.

"Nay. If there is any resemblance, it is because— Your pardon, Vi—*Lady Violette*—but I have given my word not to speak of it."

Another murmur.

Then the Vision: "Don't be ridiculous. If you must know—but you must not spread it about, for I promised him I'd keep it quiet— he's her brother. Twins I think. Etienne seems thick as thieves with the girl. Wore her favor in the tournament. You can ask him, if you doubt me, when he wakes up."

She heard a stirring sound behind her, then a sleepy voice slurred, "What is it I am supposed to know?"

Mathilde turned toward the cot. Etienne eyes were open, but they still looked hazy.

"'Tis nothing," she said. "Go back to sleep."

He lifted his head and appeared to gaze around the tent. "Is she gone?" he murmured.

"Is who gone?"

"Hermaline."

"Lady Violette sent her down to the river. But I am supposed to call her when you awake. Do you wish me to—?" She reached out a hand to pull back the tent flap.

"No!"

His vehemence startled her. Perhaps he was angry because Hermaline had not remained at his side until he awoke. Did he think the woman he loved was neglecting him in his hour of need? Mathilde had no fondness for Hermaline—her arm still throbbed from her cruel pinches—but Etienne had a right to know that she had been attending him as faithfully as Mathilde supposed Hermaline's selfish nature would permit her to attend to any man.

"Lady Hermaline has been sitting by your side for hours, waiting for you to wake up," Mathilde told him.

"I know." He spoke with an odd twist to his mouth. "I squinted my eyes open twice and glimpsed her on the stool."

So he *had* seen Hermaline. Why had he not spoken to her then? Perhaps he had been too tired. But that did not explain why he did not wish Mathilde to call her now.

She said, with more generosity than she knew Hermaline deserved, "She cooked you some gruel, too, but left me to tend it and I'm afraid I let it burn."

There was no need to tell him what a dreadful cook Hermaline was. No doubt the girl's efforts had been sincerely meant. It occurred to Mathilde, however, that Etienne might interpret her remark as evidence of her own lack of skill in the kitchen.

She added hastily, "I am not in the habit of burning something as simple as gruel. Since my father was forced to let our cook go, I have been responsible for all our meals. Father teases me that if he had known he had such a talented cook for a daughter, he would have turned Gilles off years earlier."

"You cook?" A flicker of surprise animated his drowsy gaze. With an effort, he drew his right elbow under him to prop himself up. "Nay, your fragile fingers never wielded a flesh-hook or turned the weight of a boar on a spit."

"Father drafted a scullery boy from the fields to help me lift the heavier pots and to dress game as large as boars. And my fingers are not fragile!"

"They are so slight I wonder their delicate bones have not shattered 'ere now. Such ethereal extremities were intended only for the gentle drawing of an embroidery needle or the sweet plucking of a harp's strings."

"I play the flute, not the harp. And I will prove to you that my fingers are quite strong!"

She crossed the tent, set the bundle of bread and cheese on the stool next to the cot, then grabbed Etienne's hand and squeezed.

"Mercy, my lady!" he cried.

But his green eyes twinkled as they had that first night she had met him in Grantamur's hall. Her squeeze had as much effect on his strong, broad palm as she imagined it would have had on a stone. She flushed with embarrassment at her boast—and with confusion at the disturbing tremor she felt as his long brown fingers wrapped themselves about her own.

"Let me go," she whispered.

"Afraid Therri will see me holding his squire's hand?" he said, echoing her earlier warning. "I suppose that would give him a jolt."

He laughed softly, an utterly disarming sound that caused a catch in her breath.

"I'm not holding them tightly, you know," he said after a moment of flustered silence on her part.

"What?"

"Your fingers. I don't want to break them. I am only holding them lightly—see?" He lifted her hand, bouncing it slightly as though weighing it in his.

He was right. He cradled her fingers as gently as a mother might cradle her cherished babe. 'Twas not by force of strength that he held her trapped, though quiet power emanated from his touch. If her fingers continued to nestle in his, 'twas because *she* willed them to.

Somewhere in some far corner of her mind the word *seducer* whispered. But 'twas more than his mysterious charm that held her now. She did not know why she thought suddenly of the grey-haired knight and his menacing gaze. But with her hand in Etienne's, the threat of that memory seemed to ebb, replaced with a warm promise of safety.

Safety? With a man who disordered her wits and stirred in her such inexplicable longings? A man who used her in perverse games of flirtation to fan another woman's passion, whose lack of chivalry had brought upon her a slap from her brother? Nay, she had reason rather to fear this man, to loathe and detest him . . .

Etienne sighed and released her hand. "Now what have I done?"

"D-Done?" she stammered.

"You've gone all wary of me again. I would remind you that *you* were the one who grabbed *my* hand, so don't go accusing me of being unchivalrous."

Mathilde flushed. "I-I wasn't going to— I am not—"

"What's in there?"

He broke through her guilty denials with a gesture at the stool. Relieved at the distraction, she snatched up the linen-wrapped bundle.

"Some bread and cheese. Lady Violette sent it. She thought you might become hungry before Lady Hermaline's gruel is ready."

He wrinkled his nose. "Gruel, bread and cheese . . . These aren't meals to satisfy a man who's not eaten for two days."

"As ill as you've been, I doubt you could consume much else."

"I could consume a chicken. Several chickens. Tell me, sweet Maude, how you cook a chicken for your father."

She sat down on the stool, holding the bundle to her breast as if it might somehow prove a shield against his too-potent charms. Only

119

a skilled seducer could take such a plain name as "Maude" and make it sound like a caress.

"He says he likes it simply gilded," she said. "Brushed with egg yolks while it bastes and seasoned with salt. And with saffron when we can get it."

"You do not sound so sure that is his favorite dish."

"It is simple to prepare and does not stretch our meager resources. That is why he says he likes it, even though I remember how very much he praised the chicken I once stuffed with lentils, cherries and cheese. But the cherries were expensive and difficult to obtain. We should not have had them but for Sir Alun d'Amville's generosity."

A chill whispered over her flesh as she spoke the name aloud.

"D'Amville? Alun d'Amville?" He repeated the name as though it were familiar to him.

"Did you know him?" Her heart gave a little leap. Might Etienne know something of the man that could help to prove her father's innocence?

But after a frowning moment, he shook his head. "Nay, I can't recall where I have heard the name before."

She sighed with disappointment. "Perhaps you heard Girard speak it. I was betrothed to Sir Alun before his death."

Etienne looked as if he were trying to remember, then shook his head again. "Sir Alun bought you cherries, though?"

"Aye, sweet, plump, dark crimson cherries."

It should have been a happy memory. She had thought d'Amville so kind when he had presented the fruit to her in a silver bowl. He had called her "poppet" in his smooth, honeyed voice, the way he had from childhood, though she had just passed her fifteenth year. She had not thought any maid more fortunate than she, to be betrothed to a man so generous.

How he had deceived her!

"What happened?" Etienne reached out his left hand, wincing a little as the movement stretched his wounded shoulder, but he persevered until his fingers brushed lightly across her brow. "Your face should never wear such a cloud as this. Is it because you mourn d'Amville still?"

120

She tried not to shiver in traitorous pleasure at Etienne's touch. "Nay, I do not mourn him at all," she said stoutly.

"Then why such a frown?" His hand fell away on a grunt of pain he could not quite muffle.

"You have hurt yourself!"

"Nay," he said through gritted teeth. The planes of his pale face were drawn tight, but he insisted, "I'm fine. Tell me about d'Amville. Perhaps it will help me to recall where I have heard the name."

Hope stirred afresh in her. "Sir Alun was a handsome man," she said, "even though his nose hooked proudly, like an eagle's. And he was very large of frame. Almost as tall as the Vision." She blushed. "I mean Lord Therri."

Etienne's mouth twitched a little at her slip over his friend's name, but whether 'twas in amusement or annoyance, she could not quite tell.

"What coloring was he?" he asked.

"Ruddy complexion." She remembered dark, leathern cheeks cracked in a grimacing smile. "Reddish hair." Long, grey, sweat-soaked locks falling over shoulders clad in a black surcote. "Hazel eyes that were flecked with gold." That had not changed. Again the chill. Was it possible—? "And the most beautiful voice I ever heard." She exhaled a sigh of relief. Nay, the harsh, gravely voice that had threatened her brother had been the voice of a stranger.

"How old was he?"

"Near my father's age. That would have made him somewhere near fifty when last I saw him."

"Fifty? You were betrothed to a man old enough to be your father?"

"'Tis not so uncommon," she said, defensive at his surprise. "And I did not mind until he—" She broke off. To confess d'Amville's threats against her father would be to confess the crime of which her father still stood accused. If Etienne did not already know of her father's disgrace—and he had given no indication that he did—she saw no reason to reveal it to him.

"Until he what?" Etienne demanded.

His green eyes gleamed so brightly that she wondered if his fever had returned. She started to lean forward, extending her hand to feel his brow for warmth.

"Until he what, Mathilde?"

She jumped, the sharpness of his demand causing her to jerk back her hand.

He must have seen her alarm, for although his voice throbbed a little, his next question came more softly. "Did he try to take advantage of your betrothal bonds?"

"Take advantage?"

"Some men see no difference between a promise of future marriage and the marriage itself. Did he touch you — use you — as if you were already his wife?"

Anger. 'Twas anger she saw in his eyes. She was not sure she fully understood his question or why he looked so fierce, but she shook her head. "He wooed me as gently as Yvain wooed the lovely lady of Landuc."

The anger slid away from his face and his breath sounded like one of relief, but he said, "I thought his name was Prince Erec."

She felt her cheeks color again. "That was a different ballad."

"Hmmm." The gleam in his eye bespoke amusement rather than anger now.

Embarrassed, she said, "I have no chicken for you, but if you are hungry, Lady Violette said the bread is fresh and the cheese sweet and soft."

"Do you have any more wine to wash it down?"

"Lady Violette said she brought some, but it must still be in the basket she gave to Lady Hermaline."

"Pity. Vi keeps superb wines in her cellar, if what she served in her hall the other night was any sample."

"Lady Hermaline insisted I was to call her when you awoke. I will run down to the river and fetch her . . ."

"Nay!" He reached out his left hand as if to stay her, then winced again when the movement jarred his wound.

"You must keep your shoulder still if it is to heal," she chided. "Perhaps I should make you a sling?"

"Aye," he said, his voice tight against the pain. "But help me to sit up first."

"You are too weak to sit up. You have already exhausted yourself by pulling yourself up to lean that way on your arm."

"An arm that is rapidly turning numb. How am I going to eat if my right arm is deadened by my weight and my left arm is in a sling?"

He had a point.

"Very well." She stood up, placed the bundle onto the stool, then drew a deep, bracing breath. She was *not* going to quiver or flutter when she touched him again.

"You look as if you expect me to eat *you*," he murmured.

Nor would she allow him to provoke any more blushes. "Just give me your right hand."

"But what if you break?"

"I am not going to break. I was strong enough to nearly smother you this morning. Or so you accused me when you ripped my hands away from your mouth. You did not seem worried about breaking me then."

He cocked a considering eyebrow at her. "Very well, I suppose you are stronger than you look. But I think I will need my right hand as a lever against the cot. Grab my shoulder—my *right* shoulder—and heave on the count of three."

Mathilde had too many turbulent memories of the emotions she had suffered the last time she had touched his bare shoulder.

"Don't you think you would be warmer wearing a smock?" she asked.

"I would be glad to don a smock, if it pleases you," he said. "But I can't do it from this position."

No, he could not. She had no choice.

"One." Etienne raised both brows at her on the word.

She grabbed his shoulder, determined not to admire the rippling muscles beneath her hands.

"Two."

Determined not to surrender to the temptation to caress his young, smooth skin, tanned so deeply that it made her fingers look like tendrils of foaming cream.

"Three!"

Determined that her knees should not go weak as she heaved at his weight, that she should not drop down on the cot beside him as he swung into a sitting position, nor melt against him when his right arm slid suddenly about her waist—nor moan with bewildered pleasure when his mouth caught hers on a mingled gasp of pain and desire.

Eight

Of all the erratic sensations he had thus far stirred in her, none of them prepared her for the scorching conflagration that exploded through her at his kiss. Time and thought ceased. There was only his mouth on hers and this terrifying, wonderful blaze that licked at her innermost soul. Like a moth compelled towards an irresistible flame, she hurled herself mindlessly into the white-hot incandescence.

An instant of rapture. An eternity of bliss.

A rumble. A groan. Then a blast of cold as his mouth wrenched away from hers.

"Saints, Maude, you kiss like an angel of vengeance."

Dimly, she realized that her arms were wound tightly around his neck. She stared into eyes so darkened they resembled the green forest floor at dusk. In their depths gleamed laughter, and another emotion . . . tenderness? She had not time to identify it before his coal-black lashes swept down against his tanned cheeks and his mouth settled warmly once more over hers.

The fire coiled through her slowly this time. Beginning in the pit of her stomach, it writhed upwards towards her pounding heart and downward to her ecstatically curling toes. One of his arms still bound her waist. She felt his other hand sliding up the back of her neck, sending her mind into fresh whirls so that his wincing movement only vaguely registered with the breath he caught against her lips. She moved her hands to his face and determinedly recaptured his kiss.

"Mmm . . . til . . . thilde." The vibration of his murmurs tickled her lips. He gave a gentle tug on the ends of her cropped off hair and pulled his mouth a breath's space away. "If you think your Vision would be startled to see me holding his squire's hand, how do you imagine he would react to this?"

He laughed softly, then kissed her again. Soundly. Thoroughly.

But this time through the bursting pleasure, one corner of her mind recoiled instead of whirled. These incinerating kisses were not the kisses of a hero. She had dreamed of a hero's caresses. Golden. Glowing. Falling on her lips like soft showers of silken rose petals. She had dreamed them once with d'Amville. She had dreamed them with the Vision.

But from this day on, she knew she would dream only of the exquisite reality of Etienne's terrifyingly intoxicating kisses.

No wonder Hermaline coveted him so! How many other women had he seduced with his devastating lips? Her vivid imagination envisioned dozens, perhaps hundreds of beautiful ladies—blonde and buxom like Hermaline, dark and elegant like Violette, fiery of hair and spirit like Cassandry—glorying in their surrender to his insatiable desires.

Insatiable. Only that could explain his determined assault upon Mathilde, who surely had none of the charms of his other conquests? Her mother's maid had been right about such men. Beautiful or plain, Etienne must have every woman he met at his feet. *Seducer. Villain. Knave.*

And in one more heartbeat she would no longer care. Her arms already were creeping back around his neck, her mouth zealously returning his caress.

A sob welled up into her throat. She must not—*would* not—let him add her to his string of used and cast-off lovers.

Only by focusing her mind on that imminent humiliation was she able to force her arms free of embracing him. She tried to pull her mouth away, but after returning his kisses with such eager abandon, she could not blame him for catching the back of her head and pulling her close again. *He must think her little better than a strumpet.* The shame of that thought, coupled with the mortifying yearnings he continued to rouse in her, sent her into a panic. She pushed against his chest, and when he continued to hold her locked against him, balled her hands into fists and struck at his shoulders.

His mouth wrenched free of hers on a gasp. She sprang to her feet as he flinched away with a groan of pain. He clamped his right hand to his injured shoulder, his face gone white.

"Oh!" Guilt flooded through her. How could she have been so thoughtless of his wound? She dropped back onto the cot and covered his gripping fingers with her own. "I am so *sorry!*"

She could see his white knuckles and his teeth biting into his lower lip, but before he could answer, the tent flap snapped back.

"Etienne?" The Vision surged into the tent. "I heard him cry out. What's wrong?"

Without releasing his lip, Etienne ground out, "Nothing."

It sounded more like *nuffing* to Mathilde. She slid off the cot towards the stool and would have sat on the bundle of cheese and bread had Violette, who had followed the Vision, not swept forward to save the food.

Etienne muttered something too muffled to be understood, then withdrew his teeth from his lip and said more clearly, "I'm fine. Mathil—Mathieu was just helping me to sit up and I accidentally wrenched my shoulder."

Quailing before the Vision's accusing gaze, Mathilde stammered, "H-He—I-I—W-We did not think he should eat lying down."

"Very wise," Violette said, her calm voice checking whatever angry response the Vision might have intended to make.

Mathilde realized Violette was staring at her, and hurriedly rose from the stool. "Would you like to sit, my lady?"

Violette's gaze narrowed. Mathilde ducked her head and respectfully backed away. From beneath her lashes, she saw Violette watch her retreat. Violette turned slightly and caught the Vision's eye. For the briefest second their gazes held.

Then Violette whirled towards the cot. She bent over Etienne and with one elegant hand, swept his tumbled locks back from his brow. "Poor dear. Our poor wounded, valiant champion," she purred in tones of sweet, musical sympathy.

Where Mathilde had caressed those silken curls in secret wonder, Violette now fondled them boldly before her and the Vision's gaze. Envy so strong she could taste it welled up in Mathilde as she saw Violette's fingers threading their way through Etienne's sensuous halo of whorls, ringlets and loops.

"How bravely you fought against overwhelming odds." Violette's hand left the coiling mass and traced lightly down the planes of his face. "Had it not been for that cowardly archer, you might have been champion of the day."

"His defeat of those three dastards put him one point ahead of Marshal," Therri said drily. "Had he fallen at your self-imposed deadline of sundown, instead of at midday, your choice of bridegroom would have been made."

Etienne, who's white-knuckled grip on his shoulder had relaxed a bit during Violette's ministrations, glanced up at the mahogany-haired beauty for the first time. "Is that true? Did I really have more points than Marshal?"

Mathilde chided herself for the bitter pang that wove through her at the startled pleasure on Etienne's face. Why should she be surprised? Had he not admitted to her in Grantamur Hall that he coveted Lady Violette for his wife? He desired her gold, even while he lusted for her step-daughter's charms. Did Lady Violette realize how base a scoundrel she caressed?

Apparently not, for Violette gave an eloquent sigh. "Indeed, it is true . . . and such a pity that the tournament ended in that unfortunate and premature way. You would indeed have proved a worthy bride-groom. But alas, that dishonorable attack on you cast a suspicious shadow over the whole affair. Other knights are already crying 'foul' and accusing their victors of employing dishonest means to defeat them. I have pledged my word to devise some new competition for choosing my husband . . . but not, of course, until you are well enough to take your place once more among the contenders."

"'Tis like to be months before his shoulder is healed sufficiently to let him balance a lance again," the Vision protested.

Violette sent him a scathing glance. "Are feats of arms the only games you know? I suppose that explains your lamentable lack of skill at hoodman blind." Her lovely cheeks flushed. "Or is it because you have kissed so many girls that you can no longer tell one from the other?"

"Dash it, Vi!" the Vision exploded. "Barbary had drenched herself in rose-water, the same scent you always wear. If you'd choose a more distinctive fragrance, I'd not have made the mistake."

The sparks in Violette's eyes flashed so hot, Mathilde wondered they did not set the Vision afire. As fiercely as Violette glared at the Vision, she turned and offered an dazzling smile to Etienne.

"Are you hungry?" She sat down in the spot where Mathilde had enjoyed Etienne's embrace and unwrapped the bundle in her lap. "Here." She broke off a piece of bread and popped it into Etienne's mouth before he could protest. "There, now, you must be famished. Perhaps Sir Therri will go down to the river and fetch the wine I left with Hermaline."

"The devil I will," the Vision muttered. "He can finish this." He grabbed up the flask and cup he had earlier made Mathilde serve Etienne from, emptied the last of the wine and thrust the cup between Etienne and Violette.

"Allow me." Violette took the cup. "He must not strain himself."

She pressed the cup to Etienne's lips. Etienne appeared to hesitate. His gaze slid briefly to the Vision. Then his lips quirked and he tilted back his head to allow Violette to pour the wine into his mouth. Some of the wine spilled and trickled down his chin.

"Oh, dear!" Violette giggled with a coyness worthy of Hermaline. "Mathieu, will you fetch me a cloth?"

Mathilde turned away from the scene in disgust. Had she needed further proof that Etienne was exactly what she believed him—a shameless seducer—she had her final evidence. Even the coolly self-possessed Violette turned into a simpering fool in his presence.

She found a linen strip in the pile she had torn for Etienne's bandages and handed it to Violette.

"Thank you," Violette said. She dabbed at Etienne's chin, a commonplace motion that she somehow managed to draw out into a long, sensuous gesture.

Mathilde heard the Vision swear under his breath. His friend's blatant charms must repel his noble nature as well. Mathilde inched closer to the Vision, hoping to reassure herself with the familiar glow she always experienced when she stood beside him. The glow of true love, rather than the allure of base profligacy.

She paused, waiting for the reassuring aura to surround her. A moment pulsed by. She must not be close enough to him. She took another step. Nothing. Another step . . .

Nay, she had never had such difficulty capturing at least a tiny thrill. Another step . . .

The Vision's head swiveled as she brushed up against his sleeve. "Mathieu, what are you doing?"

She retreated hastily from his reproving glance. Horror wove through her. In less than a half-dozen kisses, Etienne had despoiled her pure and chaste attraction to the Vision, replacing it with unholy longings for his own fiery embrace.

"I-I must fetch Lady Hermaline," she stammered. "I mean, have I your leave to fetch her? She told me to call her the very instant Sir Etienne awoke."

"No!" Etienne said. "Therri, don—"

Violette popped a piece of cheese into his mouth. "Yes," she said, "go fetch her, Mathieu. Why don't you go with him, my lord?"

"And leave you two alone?" the Vision said.

Etienne made a protesting gurgle, but when his lips parted Violette added a chunk of bread to join the cheese. "There is nothing improper about a lady caring for the injured," she said sweetly. "Even if Sir Etienne wished to press dishonorable advances on me, he is too weak to do so." She sighed, then murmured just loud enough for the word to fall not quite under her breath, "Alas."

The Vision glared at the back of her head for a moment, then snapped, "Fine!" and turned on his heel. "Come, Mathieu."

Mathilde hurried to keep up with his long-legged strides as he lunged out of the tent. A burst of crisp, autumn air greeted their escape. If only the chill of the breeze could quell the heated memories still churning inside her. *Somehow* she must banish them! She longed for the courage to slip her hand into the Vision's. If only she could touch him, surely she would re-experience the sweet tingles she had felt when his fingers had brushed her palm in Violette's hall? Curse Girard for trapping her in this wretched squire's disguise! While Etienne laughed at her secret and sought to seduce her, the Vision remained blindly ignorant of her danger at his friend's hands. A danger so real, so powerful, that for a few incomprehensible moments it had succeeded in supplanting the Vision's nobler influence over her heart.

An influence she was certain would reassert itself any moment, now that she had left Etienne's wicked temptations behind in the tent.

"Nay, Vi, that's enough!" Etienne caught Violette's wrist as she sought to stuff another chunk of cheese into his mouth. She had already put to the lie his boast that he was hungry enough to eat several chickens. Two days of fever and fasting had left him famished but had also shrunken his capacity to consume more than the few admittedly rather large mouthfuls of bread and cheese she had pressed upon him. She had fed him more grimly than tenderly since Therri and Mathilde had left them alone in the tent.

"You had better take one more bite," Violette said. "It may be some time before Hermaline's gruel is ready again."

Etienne clamped his mouth firmly shut and shook his head.

Violette sighed. "Another sip of wine, then?"

The bread and cheese had left his mouth dry. He nodded, then smiled when she raised the cup to his lips.

"There's no need to continue the charade, Vi. I can hold the cup myself."

She blushed but surrendered the cup. "Perhaps you should lie back down," she said when he had finished drinking. "You look exhausted." She took the cup and set it on the ground beside the cot.

He owned that he felt tired. His shoulder still throbbed from Mathilde's blow, although he knew she had not meant to hurt him. What had turned her in a heartbeat from a woman returning his kisses with breathtaking fervor to an inexplicably erupting fury, he could not fathom.

Or perhaps, he thought with a ripple of reflective shame, he could fathom it too well. He had known the instant his mouth touched hers that she had never been kissed before. He had felt her surprise, her confusion, followed by her delighted wonder as her lips had warmed, then ignited against his in an ingenuous response to his passion.

A passion that must have frightened her in an moment of rationality. Although poor, she had clearly been gently bred. And no gently bred young lady should be sitting alone in a tent with a gentleman, indulging in ardent kisses.

With a gentleman? Nay, no gentleman would have teased such kisses from a lady to begin with!

He groaned and dropped his head into his hand.

"Is something wrong?" Violette sounded anxious.

Wrong? Aye, everything was wrong! He should never have kissed Mathilde. Now every fiber in his body ached to do it again . . . and again . . . and again . . . He would never have her out of his mind after this. Never have her out of his heart.

His head snapped up. *His heart?*

"Etienne?"

"Is there any more wine?" he croaked. He suddenly had a desperate urge to drink himself back into oblivion. Perhaps when he woke up, he would find this had all been a nightmare. For thus, he feared, his life would become if he began to obsess over a woman whom circumstances forbade him from ever possessing.

"You drank it all, I'm afraid," Violette said. "But Hermaline should return soon with more. Are you in pain? Perhaps your wound has broken open. Let me look at your bandage."

"Nay, 'tis not my wound." Its throbbing paled beside the searing discomfort in his breast.

She moved behind him to study his injured shoulder, then said in relief, "There's no blood that I can see. Those salves I sent should keep any inflammation at bay. But you must keep your arm still until your shoulder has a chance to mend."

"Mathieu—" he barely caught himself from saying *Mathilde* "—was going to make me a sling."

"A very sensible idea."

She moved to the pile of linen strips that lay neatly folded near Therri's saddlebag and began searching among them for one of sufficient length to fashion a sling. Etienne thought he saw her pause and stiffen, but before he could question what was wrong, something she had said clicked in his head.

"Vi, *you* sent the salves for my shoulder? Not Hermaline?"

Violette glanced up, guilt easing the odd tightness in her face. "Oh, my, I wasn't supposed to tell you that. Hermaline does not know much of healing. Yes, I made the salves and agreed that she might take credit for them."

"Why?" Irritation at Violette's collusion almost dulled some of the pain in his chest. He must nourish this resentment. Perhaps it would bring him some ease from this merciless yearning . . .

"Well, she is my step-daughter. My husband made me swear I would not cast her off after he died." A dark shadow of memory flittered across her face. "He feared that I would, in revenge for all the harlots he flaunted before me. But Hermaline's mother died before I married him, and I do not believe in punishing children for their parents' crimes. She was the only child he ever fathered, which I suppose is why he doted on her so. But she is too much like him, I fear. Willful, selfish, easily angered—" Her hand fluttered briefly to her cheek, but promptly fell away again. "She needs some strong, level-headed man to moderate her nature."

Etienne fairly shrank at her unmistakable implication. "Me?"

The smile she turned on him would have sent Therri into transports of bliss. "You are the sweetest-tempered man I know. If you cannot charm her into behaving herself, then I know of no man that can."

"Blazes, Vi, I don't want to charm Hermaline!"

"She is very pretty," she said coaxingly. "And my husband left her a manor and castle as dowry. I know that you are in some need — "

"Who told you I was in need?" She hesitated, but Etienne guessed the answer. "Therri?"

She crossed the tent to sit down once more on the cot and draped the linen strip about his neck. "Before we quarreled at Rouen. He told me that your brother had offered to make you seneschal of his estates, but that you refused him. Nay, I understand perfectly. It is laudable for a man to make his own way in the world, to not wish to depend on others for his maintenance. Hermaline would bring you the land, but once married, it would be yours to rule as you please."

Etienne swallowed with difficulty his swelling vexation at Therri's loose tongue. His friend had had no right to go babbling of Etienne's embarrassments to anyone, not even Violette.

She lifted his arm gently to fit it in the sling, then when he failed to answer, added, "Hermaline cannot manage the manor herself, still less defend the keep her father left her. You would be doing her — and me — a service to govern both in her name."

Etienne met her dark eyes and saw the hopeful plea that hovered there. Such an offer would have been the answer to his prayers, had it been attached to anyone but Hermaline. It was only his determination to avoid binding himself to that comely shrew that prompted him to answer, "Forgive me, Vi, but I cannot."

Violette shifted on the cot so that he gazed at her profile. "Because your affections are otherwise engaged?"

"No," he said shortly. Mathilde had nothing to do with his decision. But in the awkward silence that followed this denial, the throbbing in his breast threatened to betray him. It pounded so loudly in his ears that he was certain any moment Violette would turn and call him 'liar'. Dismayed, he said hastily to distract them both, "What about you and Therri, Vi?"

Violette stiffened.

But he continued, "You must know Therri's head-over-ears in love with you? He would be your slave, if you'd only let him. And he would cut off his own hand before he would ever raise it to you in anger." He had guessed the meaning of that brief touch of her cheek. "Why don't you just marry him?"

134

She sat silent for a moment, then murmured, "There are betrayals that cut more deeply than a blow from a fist."

"Therri would not betray you."

"No? He has loved so many women that they are all become alike to him."

Lady Barbary again. Poor Therri. Women swarmed to him because of his beautiful face, and it had pleased his vanity to let men think him rake enough to take advantage of the blatant lures they threw his way. In fact, Etienne knew that Therri had avoided succumbing to their blandishments. Oh, he liked to corner them in the gardens and kiss them. He had been a great tease before Violette had soured his temper. But Etienne suspected he had never kissed Lady Barbary before, and had had no desire to once he'd met Violette. Which no doubt accounted for Lady Barbary's subterfuge in dousing herself with the rose-watered scent Violette was known for wearing.

Etienne cleared his throat. Therri would not thank him for this. His friend was perversely proud of his amorous reputation. But if it would help to win him the woman he loved —

"Vi, about Therri and those women . . . There has been some exaggeration . . ."

"I trust," Violette broke in coldly, "you are not going to try to deceive me with lies about his virtuous rectitude? I have heard the rumors. I have seen the way women fawn at his feet. I was willing to turn my head to his past, but I will not be insulted — be *shamed* again in present and future by my own husband!"

"Therri would never shame you. He's as loyal a man as you'll ever find! Blazes, I should know. He's been my best friend for over twenty years."

"And as his best friend, you would no doubt go to any lengths to help him achieve his ends."

"I wouldn't lie for him."

"No?" Her lovely lips tightened. Abruptly, she rose from the cot and swept across to Therri's saddle bag.

Etienne saw what looked like a narrow fabric strip trailing from the bag. Violette seized the visible end and pulled until the whole length sprang free, then spun with it back towards the cot.

"Tell me truthfully, Etienne. Does this belong to you or him?"

Mathilde's ribbon! Surely Violette did not think—"It's mine. That is, Lady Mathilde de Riavelle gave it to me as her favor for the tournament."

"Then what is it doing in Lord Therri's saddle bag?"

"I don't know. It was in my hand when I fell asleep." Violette clearly did not believe him. "Blazes, Vi, you know Therri rode into the mêlée without wearing any woman's favor."

"Because he knew that to do so would expose his passionate declarations of devotion to me as lies! How many other tokens from his many lovers does he have stashed away in there?"

"Why don't you comb through his bag and see? Little good it will do you. There aren't any tokens from any lovers. That one is mine, I tell you. And—" he held out his right hand "—I would like it back, if you please."

"Not until I have the truth."

"I have told you the truth."

"Nay, you have told me a pack of lies to protect him. He gave you this ribbon and told you to wear it for him in the tourney."

"Why on earth would he do a thing like that?"

"Because it belongs to his lover and he did not want me to know it. It pleases his twisted humor to taunt me with his mistress right under my nose while thinking me ignorant of the insult."

"Vi, Therri would never—"

"First he mocks me with this ribbon on the field," she said stubbornly.

"*I* was wearing the ribbon."

"Because he wished its origin concealed from me, yet still wanted to honor his mistress. De Maloisel did exactly the same at our wedding tournament. He dared not shame me openly before my father, so he gave his mistress's favor to one of his knights and told him to wear it in his behalf in the mêlée. He thought it so funny, he continued to mock me with the trick throughout our marriage, even after I discovered the truth. And now Therri—Lord Therri—thinks it equally amusing to persuade me to invite his mistress into my own castle to watch the tournament with me from my walls."

"Invite his mistress into your—?" He broke off. Great heavens! He realized with a flash of horror where this was going. "Vi—"

Violette's eyes were bright, but not with anger alone. A tear splashed down her flawless cheek. She swiped it impatiently away. "I wish I could at least hate her. But he chose a pretty, guileless child to mock me with. She was so artless, she could scarce tear her gaze away from his form as he fought in the mêlée, even though she tried to assure me that *you* were her champion. But the adoration in her eyes betrayed her. And does he really think me so indescribably stupid as to believe that I would not recognize her, though her hair is cropped and she wears a squire's tunic?"

Etienne regretted ever opening his eyes upon this day. 'Twas not enough that Mathilde had entirely destroyed his own peace of mind, now she threatened to destroy Therri's, as well. And the worst of it was, he could not even defend her presence in their tent because he had not the least understanding of what she was doing there.

Desperate to protect both Therri's innocence and Mathilde's reputation—for he shuddered at the thought of what would follow if it became known that she had been sharing an unchaperoned tent with two knights—he threw back his head and laughed. Pray heaven it did not sound as strained to Violette as it did to himself!

"Violette, you think that Mathieu—? Ha ha ha! Oh, but Therri will think this is rich when he hears!" He laughed louder and wiped his cheeks as though to dry tears of amusement.

"If you think," Violette said, "that these hollow chortles are going to convince me—"

"Nay, Violette, but 'tis you who will be made to look foolish if you insist on clinging to such an absurd suspicion. I'll grant you, the similarities are striking. But their likeness is easily enough explained by—" he racked his brains for some explanation that might satisfy her and recalled Therri's own conclusion "—by the fact that Mathilde and Mathieu are twins."

"Hmmph," she snorted. "So Therri tried to persuade me. But I studied the girl carefully while she watched the mêlée. I tell you, 'tis the same face."

"*Twins*, Vi," he repeated. "Of course they have the same face. Except that there's just a shade more blue in the violet of Mathilde's eyes than in her brother's, and the line of Mathieu's jaw is not quite so soft. Mathieu stands an inch or two taller than Mathilde, as well. If you saw them side by side, you'd realize how ridiculous your suspicion is."

She folded her arms across her chest. "I would be delighted to have you show them to me side by side."

"Well—I'm afraid I can't arrange for that just now. Sir Girard has taken Mathilde off with him—somewhere." Ah, saints! How could he have uttered such an obviously vague remark as that? He tried to remember what Therri had told him about "Mathieu's" appearance in their tent. "Sir Girard owes Therri a ransom from the mêlée. He did not wish to part with his armor and horse, so he sent Mathieu to stand as surety for him while he attempts to raise the sum. I think . . . I was a bit groggy when I woke up from my fever and heard Therri explain it all, but I think—ah, yes, I am certain that Therri said Sir Girard had gone home to borrow the ransom from his father."

"And took his sister with him?"

"Aye. At least, I'm fairly sure that's what he said. But I was—"

"—a bit groggy. That has only been since this morning, Etienne."

"Therri said I lost a lot of blood," Etienne muttered faintly. "My head is still in a spin." That was beginning to be true enough. He had sat up a long while now, longer, no doubt, than he should have. He lowered himself carefully onto his right arm.

"But not in such a spin that you could possibly confuse Mathilde with Mathieu?" Violette said.

He tried to look shocked. "Heavens, no. No one that knew them well could ever confuse them."

"And you know them both well? Is de Riavelle not a Norman family? Yet Hermaline tells me that you and Mathilde grew up together."

And Violette knew that Etienne's family came from Poitou. "They—had an aunt who was Poitevin. Their mother's sister, I think.

138

Or maybe it was their father's? No I think it was— Of course it was their mother's. Their father's line is Norman. Blazes, children are not as lineage-mad as adults. I don't remember the family connections for sure. And Mathieu and Mathilde only visited Poitou occasionally during the summers."

He dropped his head onto the bolster and closed his eyes with what he hoped was a look of fatigue. In truth, he did not realize how spent he felt until he lay full-length on the cot again.

Several minutes of silence pulsed by. A sudden, numbing weariness almost lulled Etienne back to sleep in its interval. But he fought the temptation until he heard Violette speak again.

"You almost persuade me to believe you."

He dragged his eyes open to gaze at her as she continued.

"Your story is remarkably consistent with Therri's. At least about Sir Girard. Odd that he never mentioned knowing the twins in Poitou, though. I thought your lands and Therri's marched alongside each other?"

"They do. Of course Therri knew the twins, too. I don't know why he didn't mention it."

"Then it was merely for 'friendship's' sake that he wished Mathilde to view the tournament from my walls?"

"Aye." He had better warn Therri about this new-found "friendship" between him and the de Riavelle "twins". Therri was not going to be happy about anything aligning his name, even in pretense, to Girard de Riavelle. How long would they be able to pull off this charade without Violette learning the truth? What would Therri do when *he* learned the truth?

Violette's figure danced unsteadily before Etienne's eyes. He would worry about it all when he woke up again. But before he surrendered to the weariness that dogged him . . .

He stretched out his right hand. "Violette, the ribbon."

She glanced at the strip. He thought she considered it frowningly, but her expression was as hazy as her figure. After a moment, she started to place it in his hand. But when his fingers tried to close around it, they clasped Violette's small fist instead.

"Etienne—" she bent down until her face was so close that he could see her dark eyes clearly " — please do not lie to me in this. Did Mathilde give this ribbon to you or to Therri?"

"I told you, she gave it to me."

"She asked *you* to be her champion? I implore you to be truthful."

He stretched his mind back to that night. The memory that met him brought an empty echo to his chest. "I asked her for a favor. I drew the ribbon from her hair. She did not stop me, but — " Even had his mind not been too foggy to concoct any further deceptions, he could not have resisted the compelling plea in Violette's gaze. "She did not offer it frankly to me, either."

"She wanted Therri to have her ribbon, didn't she?"

Etienne did not answer. It was the one truth he could not hide from her — or from himself.

Violette laid the ribbon in his hand.

He closed his eyes. "If you don't mind, Vi, I'd like to sleep."

"Of course. Hermaline will be disappointed, but I will keep her quiet until you have rested. But you will speak to her when you wake up again, won't you?"

He did not think he could face Hermaline just yet, but he knew he could not avoid her forever. "Tomorrow," he said. "I will see her tomorrow."

When Violette was gone, he opened his eyes and gazed at Mathilde's ribbon. Mathilde. He had been right. Her lips had tasted of heaven. Yet slowly but surely, she was leading him into purgatory.

Why had he kissed her? His mind had screamed a warning the instant before he'd found her mouth. *Kiss her and your peace is gone. Kiss her and you're lost.*

Lost. Aye, without her, now, he would be. But he could not have her. Not the way he wanted her. She was no low born maiden with whom to enjoy a transitory affair of passion. She was a lady. An indigent lady. A lady around whose family name unsavory whispers gathered. But a lady, nonetheless. Some men might have let the former facts blind them to the latter. To many of his comrades in the Young King's court, poor, discredited and defenseless meant a woman was fair prey for seduction—or worse. Had she fallen into other hands than his and Therri's—

He shuddered. But his blood boiled through veins of limbs grown too leaden to even move. He must regain his strength. He must protect her. He must find a way to make her—to make her—

His.

He closed his eyes and fought off the impossible thought. He had nothing to offer her except the strength of his arm and the intelligence of his mind. Traits a woman in Hermaline's position, with a manor and castle that needed governing, might find valuable. But to a woman as poor as himself—to Mathilde—his talents could be little more than dross.

Although he had attached himself to the Young King's court, the truth was that he, like all those knights who were not members of their master's personal household, sustained himself with the ransoms he earned from tourney to tourney. A precarious way to live, both financially and physically. Not all sponsors were as scrupulous as Violette in forbidding the use of sharpened weapons.

Nay, such an uncertain life would be little more than misery for a wife.

For a wife . . . In spite of his seemingly dour future, he smiled. That word had never been more to him than a cold but necessary option to spending his life as either a court parasite, a tournament follower or a mercenary. But now, if he pictured the woman just so— slender as a willow-maiden, with trailing waves of flaxen hair, a piquant face with petal-pink lips fashioned just for his kisses and ingenuous violet eyes that gazed with adoration at him rather than at Therri—aye, the word "wife" no longer seemed cold or necessary, but something—someone—to be warmly and vibrantly desired.

He felt his thoughts drifting away. To sleep. To dream. But first, he used his last shred of wakefulness and strength to wrap the ribbon several times around his palm, then push his fist under the bolster. Whoever had removed the ribbon before would have to fight him to do it again. He would guard it fiercely this time, even in his sleep.

Nine

She looked more like an angel than ever. A sleepy, blinking, adorably tousled angel.

Etienne watched as Mathilde brushed a strand of hair away from her eyes, then rolled onto her back and stared a moment at the tent's ceiling. She yawned, then sat up on the pallet where she had slept alongside Therri's cot. Her arms stretched over her head, lengthening her body. She had removed her squire's tunic, but the large, loose smock she wore veiled her woman's charms. She ran both hands through her cropped, tangled hair, then jerked down her smock as though to smooth it. For the barest instant, he thought he caught a glimpse of a few soft curves. But as soon as she released the smock, it bloused back to a formless covering. He smothered a sigh of regret.

She drew her legs up beneath the blanket. She leaned her elbows on her knees and propped her chin in her hands. A slant of early morning sunlight crept around the edge of the tent flap and touched a soft glow to her pale hair. An angel. With lips like heaven. Lips he had savored again and again in his dreams of the night.

As if unconsciously echoing his thoughts, her fingers slid round to touch her mouth. His dreams dissipated in a rush of pounding memory. Her soft mouth pressed to his . . .

This time, 'twas a groan he smothered. Inadequately. She turned her head and saw him watching her. She blushed. So deeply that he almost let himself believe she was thinking of the kisses they had shared, as well.

'Twould have been a mistake. She had no thoughts for any man but Therri. He hurled himself from his side onto his back, welcoming the burst of pain as his bandaged shoulder thumped against the cot.

Welcoming, but not insensible to it. Another groan broke from him, this one loud enough to rouse both his squire and Therri.

Walter, his squire, scrambled up from his pallet beside Etienne's cot. "Sir, are you all right?"

"Etienne —?" Therri rolled free of his blankets onto to his feet.

"I'm fine," Etienne growled and waved Therri back to his cot. "Just devilishly tired of lying on my side. Tired of lying down at all. I want to get up today."

Therri rubbed the sleep from his eyes. "Do you think that's wise?"

"Blazes, I don't care if it's wise. I want to get up. I'm *going* to get up. On my feet. And out of this stifling tent."

Stifling. Cool air nipped around the edges of the heat radiating from the brazier. Nay, 'twas not the tent that stifled Etienne. 'Twas desire. And frustration. And a yearning so strong he could taste it's bittersweet tang in his mouth. Sweet like her kisses. Bitter like the acrid, inflexible truth. She did not want him. And even if she had, his pathetically straitened circumstances forbade him ever seeking or accepting her love.

Dreams were dreams. But now it was morning. And reality stared cold and hard into his soul.

Mathilde fumbled on her tunic while Etienne snapped at the Vision. She slid from the tent, her boots in one hand, her belt in the other, and her hat under her arm. She had risen before the men every morn, dressed, and awaited the Vision's commands outside. The Vision had never rebuked her for her absence at his awakening, nor objected to turning to Etienne's squire to help him dress.

Only this morning she had not been the first to wake. Etienne had been watching her. He had seen her touch her lips. Had he known she was reliving his kiss?

Her cheeks warmed anew. She sat down on the stool beside the tent's entrance and began to tug on her boots. Just as she had feared, Etienne had ruined her dreams. She had lingered with the Vision down at the river bank after he had sent Hermaline and her companions back to the tent. While the Vision had sat on a broken log and stared broodingly across the waters, Mathilde had sat on the bank and stared at his face. Devoured his face. Sought desperately to brand his beautiful, noble features into her memory so that he alone would be waiting for her when she fell asleep.

But the Vision's golden beauty had not met her in her dreams. She rubbed the heels of her palms against her eyes, trying to banish the dark, teasing face that had greeted her instead. Twice she had woken gasping, Etienne's embrace had felt so real. And his kisses. And his caresses . . .

She stood and jerked her belt around her waist. She paced a few steps away from the tent. She ought to go look for the signs Girard had promised would point her in the direction of their rendezvous. The banner of the charging boar. The triangular shaped stone at the base of a half-grown beech tree that stood at the edge of Grantamur Forest. The identifying mark he had promised Costane would carve into the base of the tree.

But she dared not wander too far afield, lest the Vision should wish her to attend to some chore.

From inside the tent, she could hear voices raised, Etienne and the Vision, apparently arguing.

"Fine," Etienne snapped. "I'll dress myself. And you, Walter, can take yourself off back to Rouen. I've no use for a disobedient squire."

The squire's voice sounded alarmed. "But, sir, I was only following Lord Therri's orders."

"You seem to have forgotten which of us is your master. You can think the matter over in the Young King's court until I return."

"But—"

"I said, go!"

The squire came charging out of the tent, his face as red as a radish. Mathilde's curious regard seemed to deepen his humiliation, for he pointedly dodged her gaze while he saddled his horse.

"Have you lost your last wits, Etienne?" the Vision exclaimed. "Dismissing Walter because I ordered him not to hand you your tunic? You must have lost more blood than I thought, to be so addleheaded. *Now* who is going to attend us? You've left us both at the mercy of that woolgathering whelp, Mathieu!"

Mathilde flushed. Etienne's response was drown out by the thunder of Walter's horse as the squire mounted and rode away.

There was a pause.

Then a grunt.

"Serves you right," the Vision said. "Your shoulder's going to hurt a good deal worse if you insist on moving your arm about that way. Where's your sling? Fiend seize your stubbornness. Here, at least sit down again and let me change your bandage before you pull on your tunic."

The voices lowered to a level that she could no longer hear. A brisk wind tossed her hair back from her face, cooling cheeks still heated from the Vision's insult. The twin banners flanking the tent flapped overhead. The sound drew her gaze to their emblems, the Vision's frightful two-headed phoenix and Etienne's gilded rose.

She focused on Etienne's emblem. Muted gold petals and a dull crimson center, against the background of forest green. But she remembered the livelier rendition Etienne had worn in the tournament, his surcote of emerald green with shimmering gold foil forming the five petals of his rose and the huge, flashing ruby at the flower's center.

Her brother had confirmed that the Vision was wealthy. But surely Etienne too must have considerable means, else how could he afford such a jewel?

She wrinkled her brow, puzzled. Etienne had told her at their first meeting that he was dependent upon the Young King's generosity. Was it possible his words had been a ploy, a calculated stratagem to conceal the truth? In the jongleurs' ballads, young men of wealth and rank sometimes traveled *incognito* to prove that their courage and valor stemmed from a chivalrous heart rather than merely a stroke of good fortune or birth.

Absently, she set her hat on her head and pulled it down to shade her eyes. Etienne had not behaved very chivalrously to her. He had refused to return her ribbon. He had told shocking lies to Hermaline about some mythical game of hoodman blind. And he had lured wicked kisses from her.

But he had also fought bravely in the tournament. And successfully, until the dastardly archer's arrow had struck him down. And he had appeared to know *something* of d'Amville.

What if . . . She caught her breath at the unspeakable thought that flashed through her mind. What if she had been wrong all along? She had come to Grantamur Castle hoping to find a husband of wealth and power who could help her prove her father's innocence. She had thought she had found such a man in Lord Therri. But if Etienne were actually the heir to some great nobleman, if he had known d'Amville—perhaps it was *Etienne* whom the fates had sent her to Grantamur Castle to find!

She shivered. She told herself she did so out of revulsion at the very prospect. But when she heard the rustle of the tent flap and turned to see Etienne standing in the entry, 'twas not revulsion that caused her heart to skip. She had forgotten how tall he was, how broad his shoulders, how wickedly handsome his face. A forest green tunic enhanced his dark coloring. His soot-colored locks tumbled romantically over his forehead, while his slinged arm stood a stark reminder of his bold prowess on the battle-field.

Seducer, she reminded herself. And yet . . . it might prove highly satisfying to be the woman who reformed the rake.

He took two steps outside the tent and grabbed her by the arm. "We need to talk."

He did not wait for her to reply, but pulled her along beside him as he strode rather unsteadily away from the tent. Even through her sleeve, his touch set tiny wildfires licking through her veins. But he looked more grim than pleased to be drawing her off alone. Perhaps he only frowned so because his shoulder pained him.

"Etienne, where are you going?" Therri called

"Down to the river. Mathieu's going to attend me."

"Wait. Let me speak to him first. Mathieu, come here."

Etienne stopped and let Mathilde slip from his grasp. Therri stood in the tent's entrance, glowing in all his golden beauty. Because he felt impatient with Mathieu-the-squire, she told herself, that did not mean that he did not still nurse fond memories of Lady Mathilde. Would it wound his heart too sorely to learn that fate had destined her for another man? She walked slowly back towards the tent, fearful that he would forbid her to accompany Etienne.

But Therri only handed her a basket—the same basket that Violette had brought yesterday.

"Don't go too far," he warned her. "And see that he eats something out of this. Lady Hermaline will be coming to see him soon, so don't be gone too long. If there's a problem—" He glanced at Etienne, then ran his gaze over Mathilde's slender frame. "If you need help with him, if he feels weak and is too heavy for you to support him, come and call me."

"Yes, my lord."

Therri waved her away and she hurried back to Etienne's side.

"Do you wish to lean on me?" she asked as Etienne took another wavering step.

He glanced down at her. His mouth quirked. "Are you asking if I'd enjoy having your arms around me? Saints, if you had any notion how charmingly you blush . . ." He broke off, sighed, then took her arm and pulled it around his waist. "Don't worry," he said when she stiffened, "I'm not taking you away to ravish you. I don't imagine I'd have the stamina. I only want to talk."

He draped his hale arm over her shoulder. A carefully negligent gesture that threatened to turn the wildfires in her veins into a flaming deluge.

For several steps she could not even breathe. But slowly, by infinitesimal degrees, the fire ebbed. By the time she and Etienne reached the river bank, the last flames had not quite died—she doubted they could ever be entirely extinguished when he was near her—but other emotions had begun to mingle with the heat. An odd reassurance at the strength of his body. A curious contentment in the shelter of his arm.

He released her and lowered himself slowly onto the bank, leaning his back against the log where Therri had sat yesterday.

"We should not have walked so far," she said, viewing his pallor with concern. "You have exhausted yourself."

"Nay," he said a bit breathlessly. "I'm fine. I just need to rest a moment."

She hesitated, then seated herself on the ground a few feet away from him. They sat for several minutes in silence, until his breathing steadied. He stared across the river. Broodingly, the way Therri had. At length, his frown eased a little and he sighed.

"I wish I had a pole," he murmured. "I always used to think more clearly when fishing." He glanced at her. "Do you fish, Maude?"

She shook her head, surprised. "My father would never permit such a thing. Just because we are poor does not mean he did not raise me as a lady."

Etienne grinned. A frank, boyish smile that made her heart skip anew. "I taught Therri's sister to fish. It enraged their mother, but we did not care. Saints, but Heléne was a sport! She could pull the fish in like a wizard, but she hated to take them off the line. Said they were too slimy."

He flashed his grin at Mathilde. She forced herself to smile back, but she heard the affection in his voice when he spoke of Therri's sister. Another love? How many had there been?

"I suppose you think fish are slimy, too?" he said.

"I have prepared too many fish for dinner to give a second thought to how they feel."

Something warm and tender lurked in his eyes as he watched her. "And how do you prepare a meal of fish?"

Nay, she must be imagining that gentle gleam. "My father likes salmon cold and poached, or in an onion broth."

"Your father. But how do *you* like your salmon, Maude?"

She tilted her head and thought. No one had ever asked her the question before. "I like it in a pie with figs and dates and raisins. But my favorite is salmon roasted in ginger sauce."

He raised his brows. "Ginger? That is a rare and expensive spice."

She sighed. "I know. That's why I could only make it when I was betrothed to Sir Alun d'Amville."

"He bought you ginger like he bought you cherries? You must have meant a great deal to him."

She thought she had, once. Before she had heard her name on his honeyed lips, coupled with vengeful threats against her father.

She started as Etienne leaned forward and brushed the back of his hand against her cheek.

"I would bring you cherries every day if you were mine."

He sounded softly earnest, but this time she took care not to look into his eyes. Surely their gleam would reveal his words no more than another game to entice her?

She whispered through a suddenly constricted throat, "Cherries only grow in the warmth of summer."

"Then I would fill the long winter months with barrels of ginger. And cinnamon. Do you like cinnamon, Maude?"

She nodded. *Barrels* of such expensive spices? He must truly be some great man's heir. She peeped at him from beneath the brim of her hat. Just in time to see his mouth sober and his hand retreat from her face to clamp itself on his knee.

"I have not the means to keep those promises, of course," he said, "and I never shall. But I *can* pledge to you my courage and the strength of my arm. At least, my good *right* arm." His mouth grimaced. "My left arm too, when it heals. But one arm or two, if there is someone who threatens you, you may rest assured that so far as it lies in my power, I will keep you safe."

This surprising declaration overshadowed his attempt to conceal his slip about his wealth.

"What makes you think someone threatens me?" she asked.

"I have been racking my brains trying to imagine some other reason for this." His hand unlocked his knee and pulled gently on a shoulder-length strand of her hair. "You promised to tell me the truth when I awoke. I want to hear it now." When she hesitated, he swept the hat off her head and lifted her chin in his hand. "Now, Mathilde."

149

His eyes gazed with unwonted sternness into hers. She could not resist his demand. But how much could she tell him? Not about the ribbon. Girard had ordered her not to speak of it to Etienne or Therri. When she had questioned why, Girard had muttered something about not knowing whether he could trust them.

What other explanation could she give Etienne? She pulled away from his grasp on her chin and hid her reluctance to answer in a search of the basket's contents. "Lord Therri said you were to eat something from here."

"Mathilde." His tone of voice warned her that he would not be distracted from his purpose.

She found a tansy cake and held it out to him before admitting, "'Tis as you suspected. Girard dressed me this way and sent me to your tent to protect me." Girard had not forbidden her to speak of the grey-haired knight.

Etienne seemed to debate whether to pursue her answer first or accept the proffered food, but hunger won out. He took the cake, bit off a piece, chewed and swallowed, before asking, "To protect you from what? Or from whom?"

"I-I do not know his name." Or did she? Again two faces struggled to merge, one middle-aged and roughly handsome, the other coarsened in lines of cruelty, the features similar yet subtly different. "I do not know why he wished to harm Girard, or why Girard thinks he would try to harm me. But Girard assured me the danger to us both was real."

"Why did he not take you home to your father?"

"Girard said that the knight would attempt to seize me along the way."

"A knight? If you do not know his name, then describe him." He broke off another piece of cake.

"He was tall and strongly built," she said. "He wore his grey hair long, to his shoulders. His face looked as though it had been baked in the sun, tanned even darker than yours and his skin looked coarse, like leather. There was a hook to his nose which made it look something like a beak, and—" she hesitated, uncertainty flickering again across her mind "—his eyes were hazel, flecked with specks of gold."

"Hmmm." He finished off the tansy cake while he considered her words. Then he said, "The hooked nose and gold-flecked eyes sound something like the way you described d'Amville."

"It was not d'Amville!"

Etienne raised his brows.

She struggled to speak more calmly. "D'Amville is dead."

His face creased with a puzzled frown. "So you told me before. But—" He shook his head slowly, as though something were troubling him. "What else do you have in that basket?"

She searched the contents. "Two stuffed beef rolls, a pork tart and a chicken pasty. And a bottle of wine."

"Give me the chicken pasty and pour me some wine. Only you might want to water it first. I'd like to keep my wits about me today." He tossed her one of his heart-thumping smiles before adding, "The river seems to run clear here. Dip the cup in it before you pour the wine."

Mathilde obeyed and handed him the cup.

"Find yourself something in that basket to eat," he said. "There's room to sit beside me here, if you'd like to lean against the log."

She hesitated. She should not . . .

But *why* should she not? Yesterday she had wanted to escape his dangerous influence on her. But today . . .

Everything looked different today. Yesterday she had thought him an impoverished seducer of defenseless women. Now she knew that he was not impoverished at all. And while he was undoubtedly still a seducer, she hoped he was not an unredeemable one.

She chose a beef roll from the basket and settled herself on the ground beside him. The heat of his nearness swept round her again, no longer disconcerting but strangely comforting. She inched a little closer, glad that he was some great baron's heir, certain that he would agree to use his wealth to help her father. If only she could win him. She *must* win him. She suddenly wanted very much to bask in this wonderful warmth forever.

His gaze remained fixed thoughtfully at some point across the river. Mathilde watched his profile and indulged herself, while she nibbled on her roll, with a dozen different stratagems to win his heart. 'Twould be no easy task, with such beautiful rivals as Hermaline and Violette. But at the end of the jongleur's ballad, it had not been beauty alone that had made Prince Erec realize the jewel he had found in Enide. It had been Enide's loyalty and courage and selfless devotion to Erec, her husband and lover.

Mathilde wanted nothing more than to give all her loyalty and courage and devotion to some man who might one day view *her* as the jewel of his life. D'Amville had betrayed her. Lord Therri had curiously ceased to cause the slightest flutter in her pulse. But Etienne—surely one day he would thank her for saving him from a life of reckless waywardness? Surely, on that day, she would shine in his eyes more brightly than his own magnificent ruby?

"Maude," he said abruptly, "who told you that d'Amville was dead?"

It took a moment for her to rearrange her thoughts to comprehend his question. "My father. He said he had been attacked and killed by forest bandits and that I need not worry about him any more."

Etienne shot her a sharp glance. "Not worry? I thought you *wanted* to marry him."

She shook her head, then checked herself. "I did once," she admitted. "But that was before—"

She broke off. If Etienne were going to help her, then he had to know the truth. But could she trust him? Girard had not been sure, hence her enforced silence about the ribbon.

She drew her legs up under her and stared earnestly into his eyes. "If I tell you, will you swear not to repeat what I say to anyone? Not even to Lord Therri?

He cocked a brow at her and she realized this was the first time she had not nearly called his friend "the Vision".

Her cheeks warmed, but she insisted, "It is *very* important. It would mean renewed shame and embarrassment for my father. He does not deserve that. I am determined to prove that he *never* deserved it. Only—only I need someone to help me, and I do not know if I can trust you."

His sooty brows plunged into a frown. "I would never betray you, Mathilde."

She sensed that her doubt had hurt him. For some unaccountable reason, that troubled her so deeply that she nearly blurted out her father's story without any further attempt to extract a promise of silence from him. But what if she told him the truth and he shrank from her? The daughter of a thief! What if he would not believe her protestations of her father's innocence? And worse, what if he revived the story of her father's past? Girard would be shunned in the Young King's court, her father would be humiliated afresh . . .

"I want to believe you," she said, praying he would read the earnest plea in her eyes "but I have to be sure."

He held her gaze a long moment, so long that she wondered if time had somehow ceased to pulse by. She heard the slow, shivery exhale of his hard held breath.

"I'll tell you what," he said at last. "If it will ease your mind, I'll exchange secret for secret with you." His mouth twisted wryly. "Nay, 'tis no secret, really, but scandal enough that I would find it most unpleasant to have it stirred up again. Thus far, the Young King has turned his head to my past. But if enough of my companions decided to shun me, I doubt the Young King would continue to countenance me in his court. If I betray your trust, you have only to drop a few reminders of my notorious youth in the proper ears and I will undoubtedly find myself banished from all knightly society."

Banished? She had thought perhaps he was about to reveal his true identity to her, but— Banished? She had not expected that.

"What did you do?" she whispered.

He gave a caustic laugh, but sipped some more wine and swallowed his last bite of pasty while he appeared to consider his next words.

He dusted his fingers on his knee, then gave a small shrug. "I know no other way to put this. My father, sweet Maude, was a traitor."

His green gaze slid to hers somewhat warily. Her eyes widened, but she bit off a gasp and waited for an explanation.

"He had sworn allegiance to King Henry II of England for our lands in Poitou," Etienne continued. "But he broke his fealty and joined a scheme conceived by the King of France to pit Duke Richard of Aquitaine in war against his father, King Henry, for authority over my native county of Poitou. While father and son were locked in battle, it was the hope of the King of France to swoop into Normandy and reclaim it from the English throne.

"I was nineteen at the time. I did not know the exact nature of the plot or the extent of my father's involvement in it. But I knew he was angry with King Henry and that he hated and feared the English earl the King had sent to confirm the loyalty of the barons in Poitou. A man named Rousillon, a man I thought my father trusted, told me that the earl knew of my father's treason and that he had come to imprison my father. My father had been crippled in a former battle and his health was frail. I knew that imprisonment would kill him. Rousillon told me that the only way to save my father's life was to kill the earl first, so he could not betray my father's guilt."

From the subtle trembling of his voice, Mathilde knew that he had loved his father deeply. She tried to picture Etienne just older than she, torn between desperation to protect his sire and horror at the thought of murdering a man to do so.

"What did you do?" she breathed.

He drank again, a longer draught this time, then set the cup down and slowly wiped his mouth with his sleeve. "I could not let my father go to prison," he said at last. "So I took a dagger and tried to assassinate the Earl of Gunthar."

He followed these words with a sharp glance at her face. To see her reaction?

But she had caught his qualifying word. "Tried?"

He gave a harsh laugh. "Aye. If I had succeeded, it would have precipitated the war the French king wanted. That was Rousillon's hope. But my aim was bad and Therri's sister warned the earl with a scream. He turned, we struggled . . . he broke my wrist wrestling the dagger away. He threw *me* into prison, where he should have left me to rot."

She shivered. The thought of Etienne locked in some cold, dank cell riddled with vermin . . .

Without thinking, she touched his wrist, then slid her hand into his.

He looked down at her, his eyes narrowing. "You are not repulsed by my crime?"

She shook her head. "You did not kill anyone."

"I tried."

"You said your aim was bad. Perhaps because you did not really want to kill him. Perhaps because you hoped he would see and stop you in the end." He looked startled. Had he not thought of it before? "You're not a murderer, Etienne. How can you believe that of yourself?"

He closed his eyes and she saw the skin tighten along his cheekbones. She sensed his struggle to accept her faith in him.

"I pray you are right, Maude," he whispered. He shook his hand free and put his arm around her. When she made no protest, he pulled her against his hale shoulder.

For comfort, she told herself as she slid her arms around his waist. She only meant to comfort him with her embrace.

"How did you get out of the prison?" she asked.

"The plot fell apart. Rousillon murdered my father and the earl captured Rousillon before he could succeed in finding another way to instigate the war. Therri's sister, Heléne, told the earl how Rousillon had manipulated me with his lies. She pled mercy for me from the earl. He was in love with her and wanted to please her, so he won me a pardon from King Henry."

"I am sorry about your father," she murmured. She sensed his still smoldering grief at his father's death.

His hand rubbed absently at her shoulder. "When you deal with the devil, you pay the price."

The strokes sent quivers of pleasure through her. So she had been wrong. He was not some great baron's heir pretending to be poor to prove his valor independent from his birth. His father was dead.

That meant that Etienne must now be baron himself!

His arm around her tightened, stilling the excited jump of her body. But her mind raced. 'Twas the stain of his past he hoped to erase by his game of pretense. If he could prove himself incontestably honorable as "Sir Etienne the Impoverished", then surely men would pardon the youthful mistakes of "Lord Etienne the Traitor's Son".

A wealthy baron. 'Twas even better for her and her father. Etienne would not now have to obtain his sire's leave to use his money and influence to help them establish her father's innocence. And surely he would *want* to help them now? His own tragic past would make him but the more sympathetic to the sad plight of her father.

But her father's innocence would not be easy to prove. As Girard had said, d'Amville had had evidence of their father's guilt and had given that evidence to King Henry. Mathilde was certain the evidence had been fabricated, but it might cost a great deal of money and would undoubtedly take an even greater degree of effort to prove it. 'Twould be too much to expect Etienne to volunteer so much to her cause without offering him something in return.

And the only thing Mathilde had to give him was herself.

She shifted, then pulled away and knelt on the ground in front of him so that she could watch the reaction on his face.

"Etienne, you must tell me the truth. Are you in love with Lady Hermaline? Or with Lady Violette?" She added in a breathless rush, "Because if you are—I mean, if you are *truly* in love with one of them, then I will not try to win you away from her. But if you are only flirting with them for amusement, then— I know I am not beautiful, but I know you do not find me repulsive because you have teased me and kissed me and tried to seduce me, and I cannot imagine you would have bothered if you had thought me repellent—"

Etienne's gasp cut her off. "Tried to seduce you? I never—I wouldn't— Great heavens, Maude, what are you talking about?"

"Wearing my ribbon in the tournament, and telling those lies to Lady Hermaline so that you would have an excuse to kiss me, then *actually* kissing me in your tent yesterday. You kiss very skillfully, you know. You had my head quite in a whirl and if you had not inadvertently reminded me that I was supposed to be in love with Lord Therri, there is no telling what I might have let you do." A rush of fire surged into her cheeks. "Of course I realize now how silly I have been about Lord Therri. He has never made me feel anything like this."

She pressed a hand to her breast. Her heart seemed to tumble as fast as her words.

"I was terribly tempted by your kisses. I am tempted now . . ." She swayed towards him, then drew herself back quickly. "I—I will give you anything you want, if you will help my father. Only—only I would rather not be your mistress, if I can be your wife. I would be a very *good* wife. I can cook and sew. And I can play the flute. You said you liked the flute, did you not? And I am very thrifty. I would not ask a denier more of you than it takes to help my father. And—and if you grew tired of me and wanted a beautiful woman for a mistress, I vow I will never complain or upbraid you."

Her lip quivered at the thought of him with other lovers, but she caught her lip firmly between her teeth. For her father's sake, she would bear the pain somehow.

Etienne looked stunned as she finally fell silent. She turned her head away. What must he think of her after such a plea? Oh, what did it matter? If only he would help her father.

"Mathilde." His voice throbbed. "Saints, Maude, if you had any idea how I—How much I want to—But I can't. I can't marry you. Blazes, I can't even love you!"

She pressed her hands to her mouth. Her heart stopped tumbling and shattered.

For several minutes, her throat ached so badly that she could not choke out a response. She should have expected this, she told herself. How could she ever have thought Etienne would want her for his wife? Hermaline or Violette could bring him both beauty and the land and gold of a dowry. Even an already wealthy man would not scorn such gifts as those. What use to him were loyalty and courage and devotion, when Mathilde had not a denier to her name?

But he wanted her. She knew he wanted her. The kisses in his tent had been clear evidence of that.

Etienne muttered a curse under his breath. "Mathilde, what I meant to say is—"

"No." The word came muffled from behind her fingers. "Please. 'Twas my mistake." She gulped at the burning lump in her throat, then swallowed twice more before she lowered her hands. "I understand. I'm afraid, in my heart—I have always understood." Her voice broke and she lowered her head, hoping he would not see the tear trickling from the corner of her eye. "You do not want me to redeem you. You want me—for your mistress."

M y miss—" Etienne choked. He scrambled to his feet so fast, he knocked over the cup of wine. "Get up," he snapped.

He saw Mathilde shrink, a flicker of dismay in her eyes. Did he look as furious as he felt?

"Get up!"

When she still hesitated, he grabbed her arm and jerked her to her feet.

She gave a little cry. He knew his fingers were digging into her flesh through her sleeve. He tried to ease his grip, but he was so angry he was shaking.

"I-I thought—" she stammered. "The way you teased and kissed me—I th-thought you—"

"Blazes! You have made it clear what you thought."

Disgust struggled in his breast with anger. He had brought this on himself. He had taken disgraceful liberties with her in front of Hermaline over that blasted ribbon and then, the moment he had her alone in his tent, he had smothered her with kisses. What did he expect her to think?

Nay, his anger was not for her. 'Twas for himself.

"Oh, please," she pleaded. "I need your help, but I don't have anything else to give you in return. And I thought you wanted me."

"Wanted you—?" Saints, he ached for her! But to take her as his mistress would be an empty cheat for all he craved from her. The life he yearned for *with* her. He wanted her kisses, her passion, aye. But he also wanted her *his*, to cherish, to protect, to possess and adore to his dying breath. Not in the shadows. Not skulking to her arms in secret shame.

He wanted her *his* before all the world. He wanted her with honor.

He released her arm and paced down to the edge of the river. Her breathless plea to marry her had taken him aback. He had thought her smitten with Therri. But the look in her eyes when she had pressed her hand to her heart and said "Lord Therri never made me feel anything like this . . ." 'Twas the look he had dreamed of in his days of fever, the look he had dreamed this night just past. Not love—not yet. But a kind of awe and longing that might one day be nourished into something more.

That "something more" had already rooted itself firmly in Etienne's breast. He had told her that he could not love her, but the moment the cruel words had left his mouth, he had recognized them for the lie that they were. He did love her. But he could not afford to marry her. And if he could not have her in honor, he would not spoil her for the man who would one day be fortunate enough to have her for his wife.

"Etienne?" Her voice trembled behind him.

He stared at the water foaming past in cheerful rapids. A mockery of the pulsing misery in his breast.

"Your sacrifice isn't necessary, Mathilde," he said over his shoulder. "I don't want you for my mistress."

The words came out with a cruel edge he did not intend. But he made no effort to soften them. If he could not be her hero, at least he would squash her belief that he wanted to seduce her.

A moment of silence followed. When she spoke again, it sounded as though she had drawn closer.

"Then—then why did you kiss me?"

He spread his hand in frustration. What could he say? "I—I was tempted. I admit, you tempted me. You are not repulsive, Maude." He spoke this last sharply, remembering suddenly the words she had used in her plea—repulsive, repellent. Saints! Did she truly not realize how lovely she was?

He turned and saw her standing behind him, her eyes lowered, her lip caught between her teeth. That *was* what she feared. That he had rejected her—twice—because she was not attractive.

He took her chin in his hand. "You tempted me," he repeated firmly, "with your dreamy eyes and your angel's face and an ethereal figure that puts to shame every so-called beauty I have ever known. You are a prize worthy of a better man than I."

Her lids remained lowered, refusing to meet his gaze, but her mouth quivered. His fingers tightened on her chin. Then he released her and stepped back. It was either that or kiss her. And if he kissed her once, he knew he would kiss her again and again. He might never be able to stop.

A tremulous smile flitted across her lips. "You are kind, sir. I did not realize how kind until this moment." She brushed a hand against her cheek. A deft, furtive movement, but not deft enough to hide the tear she wiped away. "I am glad—that you are not the seducer I thought you. I suppose you do not covet Lady Violette's gold, either?"

How many sins had she been laying at his feet? "Therri is in love with Vi. I've teased him a little, I'll admit, by allowing her to flirt with me, but she's as mad for him as he is for her, if she would only admit it."

A flicker of dismay passed over Mathilde's face. Caused by his revelation to her about Therri and Violette?

She nodded slowly, her eyes still closed. "I see. Then Lady Violette was teasing Lord Therri with you, the way you teased Lady Hermaline with me? It is Hermaline you love, isn't it?"

Hermaline? He opened his mouth to protest, but before he could speak, Mathilde turned sharply and walked back over to the log. He followed her, determined to disabuse her mind of its latest suspicion. But at the last minute, he bit off the words. From the droop of her shoulders, he knew she did not believe his avowal of her charms. He would sooner have her think he had rejected her out of loyalty to another woman than because he had found her too plain for his passions.

"We have agreed to keep it quiet for the moment," he said. He carefully avoided specifying exactly what "it" referred to,

But Mathilde wanted clarity. "You mean your betrothal?"

He hesitated. *It would go no further*, he told himself. He would speak the word, swear Mathilde to silence, and Hermaline would never know. "Aye, our — betrothal. The Young King is her guardian since her father's death, you see, and I have not yet received his permission to wed her." In fact, by filling the Young King's perennially empty coffers with her late husband's gold, Violette had won their royal guardian's permission to choose husbands for both herself and Hermaline without his interference.

"I see," Mathilde said again. Etienne saw the way she twisted her hands together. "Then I was right. That day you teased me into letting you keep my ribbon, 'twas only a game, as I thought."

He felt another twinge of shame at the memory. He wished he had never seen that curst strip of cloth in her hair! His conscience would not now be in shreds, and his future would not look so empty.

He touched a hand to the breast of his tunic. Inside he had tucked the ribbon. Here, close to his heart. He had been angry that morning to find the white silk dusty and stained, the threads fraying along the back. Therri had told him of Hermaline's mistreatment of the trifle. It galled him now to maintain his lie. He spoke it because he had left himself no choice. But his words came out with a harshened edge.

"Aye, 'twas only a game. We had quarreled, you see — "

"And you wanted to make her jealous." He heard the mournful crack in her voice.

"Aye," he repeated more strongly. "And do you imagine the game could have worked if you had not been lovely enough to stir her jealousy?"

That startled her into looking at him. "L-Lovely? Not just a little pretty?"

He brushed the tips of his fingers across her cheek. Thank heavens one arm was bound in a sling, else he might have swept her against his chest.

His voice went husky. "I was tempted, Maude. Sorely tempted by your charms."

Her gaze searched his face and apparently found reassurance there of his sincerity. She broke into a smile—an angel's smile—and whispered, "As I was tempted by your kisses."

Her cheek fit perfectly in the cup of his hand. He tilted up her face. Caution be hanged!

He lowered his mouth to hers. Their lips mingled together for only a moment. He dared not linger longer. She still smelled of sunshine, still tasted like some heady confection of honey and wine . . .

He heard her shivery breath as he drew away. Could she hear the answering throb of his heart?

"There," he whispered. He ran his thumb across her parted lips. "That must hold us both for a lifetime."

He could not resist tangling his fingers with hers. He drew her down beside him on the log, determinedly pushing away the memory of her arms around his waist. How something that had felt so gloriously right could be so abysmally wrong—

He steadied himself with a bracing breath. "You did not need to try to barter yourself, Maude. Whoever threatens you or your father, whatever you require my help with, you had only to ask."

"But—" She stared down at their entwined hands. "But it may be very difficult—and expensive. I do not have any money or land or even a title—though I know you would have no need of these things if I did. And if you do not want *me* — "

He shook his hand free and laid a finger to her lips. "'Tis not a matter of wanting. I simply cannot accept your sacrifice. Sweethear—" He bit the word off. "Maude, it is not needful to offer me anything. Just tell me what you're afraid of. Who was this grey-haired man with the hooked nose and the gold-flecked eyes " —*where had he seen gold-flecked eyes?* — "your brother sent you to my tent to protect you from? Come, I shared my secret with you. It is your turn to trust me now."

He frowned as she glanced away. The memory nagged him. Eyes. Hazel eyes. With glittering gold flecks. Staring into his. Mocking . . . *Mad . . .*

The tournament field!

"Mathilde—" The sound of crackling twigs made him break off.

Footsteps, heavy and lumbering, approached. A moment later, a rotund man, puffing with exertion, burst upon their privacy.

"Sir Etienne? Sir Etienne de Brielle?"

Etienne rose. "Aye."

He heard a soft gasp from Mathilde. He glanced at her and saw her shift along the log behind him as though to block herself from the newcomer's view. When he turned back to the man, he thought for a moment he understood why. Hazel eyes with flecks of gold gazed back at him. Etienne's muscles tensed and his free hand formed itself into a fist. He longed for nothing more than to land it in the face of the man who had led the craven attack on him in the mêlée. The man who threatened Mathilde.

But a moment later, his fist relaxed. Nay, his attacker had been large of build but not fat. And Mathilde said the man she feared had grey hair. This man's hair was ginger, falling in limp tendrils over his plump cheeks. Yet still, he seemed familiar.

The man broke into a broad grin. "Lord Therri told me I might find you here. I am Sir Nevell de Chesnei."

Etienne bowed coldly. Whoever this man was, Mathilde did not want to be seen by him. 'Twas reason enough for Etienne to view him with suspicion.

Chesnei bobbed a bow in return and continued with the jovial smile still pinned to his lips. "I am a friend of Sir Girard de Riavelle. You know him, sir?"

"Aye," Etienne said. "We serve together in the Young King's court. I do not believe you are one of our number, though?" Then where had he seen this man before, if not at Rouen?

"Nay, nay, I am Sir Girard's neighbor. I dined with him and his father a few days ago at his father's manor. When Girard heard I was headed for Grantamur Castle, he asked me if I would speak to you for him."

Etienne raised his brows. "Speak to me? About—"

"His sister, the Lady Mathilde."

Etienne held Chesnei's gaze with his own and casually strolled away from the log in a quarter-arc that turned Chesnei's back to Mathilde.

"Is that name supposed to mean something to me?" Etienne asked.

Chesnei chuckled. "Young men. So coy about their conquests. As, of course, is fitting when one deals with a lady. But Girard confided to me her indiscretion. She awarded you her ribbon for the tournament, did she not?"

"And if she did?"

"The little minx was supposed to have given it to me."

Etienne shot a glance over Chesnei's shoulder and saw Mathilde's mouth pop open with surprise. *One lie*, he thought as he returned his regard to Chesnei.

"'Tis a lady's prerogative," Etienne said, "to choose her own champion."

"Oh, true, true," Chesnei replied, clapping his hands together in a cheerful gesture. "But it had been agreed beforehand that her favor should go to me. I am her betrothed, after all."

"Betrothed?" Another glance at Mathilde. She shook her head vehemently and accompanied it with a shudder. *Two lies.* He hoped. "'Twas a small solecism, if she chose to tease you a little, sir, by granting her favor to me."

"Oh, indeed. I was willing to overlook the matter completely. 'Twas her first tournament, and I realize . . . well . . ." Chesnei slapped good-naturedly at his belly. "You have something of the advantage of me, sir. Young, tall, lean, handsome. I own I am none of these things. But I will be a good husband to her, as her father knows, and my fortune makes it possible for me to excuse her lack of dowry."

Etienne noted a ring on every one of Chesnei's plump fingers, including both his thumbs. Diamonds, emeralds, sapphires, rubies— real rubies. Etienne knew the difference between true jewels and glass. The same combinations of stones sprinkled liberally among the tangle of chains that draped Chesnei's stout chest.

Etienne had sold what little jewelry his father had left him to purchase his armor for knighthood. The silver chain the Young King had given him for Easter last, Etienne had given to the seamstress who had obtained the emerald-hued cloth, gold foil and glass rubyesque stud for the surcote he had worn for Violette's tournament. He glanced at his last remaining prize, the starkly simple jacinth ring that graced his left hand. Its modest silver setting bore no elaborate swirls in the white metal, as did Chesnei's settings of gold.

Though Etienne wished sufficient means to be independent, he had never coveted wealth before. But now, envy so strong he could taste it flooded his mouth. He suspected the rings and chains were but a sampling of Chesnei's fortune. Had Etienne owned but half as much, he would have had Mathilde before a priest this very night.

Chesnei was still talking in that good-natured drone. "But she is quite a charming girl and I'm afraid I have vanity enough yet to wish to impress her. So I listed my name in the tournament. Vanity goeth before a fall, eh, sir? I was unhorsed by my very first challenger." He shook his head ruefully. "I see you met with a similar misfortune?"

He gestured at Etienne's sling. Etienne replied with a curt nod. Lacking encouragement in that vein, Chesnei returned to his own recent history.

"I immediately retired to Martival Castle to fetch my ransom, and found Sir Girard in the neighborhood attempting to raise the same from his father. Lord Aymor was furious with his son. The family is in serious straits, you know, have been ever since the night Lord Aymor got drunk and gambled away his last two castles to my late uncle. All Lord Aymor has left now is the fortified manor house that lies across the river from Martival. His fields scarcely produce enough to support Lord Aymor and his daughter. That he should be able to scrape together enough to pay off Girard's ransom is doubtful." Chesnei paused, then said, as though struck by a thought, "Perhaps I will settle the debt for him. If I can't impress my betrothed with my fighting prowess, perhaps I can do so with my generosity, instead."

He beamed at Etienne, as though expecting confirmation of his brilliance.

Etienne smiled stiffly back at him. "I am sure Sir Girard would be grateful."

"But not his sister? Oh, come, sir, I think perhaps you envy me.

She is a charming minx, after all. Those azure eyes of hers and cherry lips . . . Aye, I shall demand a kiss from those lips as reward for helping her brother."

Etienne's hand curled itself into a fist again. Only Chesnei's patently flawed description of Mathilde stayed him from an urge to strangle the man. Her eyes were violet, her lips more pink than cherry. Perhaps Chesnei had never met Mathilde at all?

"Her appreciation of your generosity might be doubled if you added a trinket for her raven hair," Etienne suggested.

Chesnei's belly jiggled as he chortled. "You jest with me, sir. The Lady Mathilde has hair the color of straw."

So he had glimpsed her, at least. Etienne continued to smile. "A jest, sir, as you say." He glanced at the sun. It was approaching noon. "Forgive me, Sir Nevell, but I do not understand exactly what it is you wish from me."

"Have I not said? The Lady Mathilde is in some disgrace with her father over the matter of her ribbon. Sir Girard suggested that if I were to fetch it back from you, their father might more quickly forgive her lapse in judgment."

Etienne studied the rotund man. Chesnei's hazel eyes gazed cheerfully back. He seemed harmless. And sincere. Was it possible his words were true? The thought of Mathilde clasped in Chesnei's pudgy arms flooded Etienne with revulsion.

"I can see your reluctance," Chesnei said when Etienne did not immediately reply, "but she shall be my wife, and the truth is, I prefer not to have another man walking about with her token. 'Tis the way rumors are started, and I would spare her the embarrassment of unfounded gossip. I explained this to her yesterday. She did not understand, of course, but—"

"You explained it to her when?" Etienne interrupted.

"Yesterday morning, when I took my leave of her. She was most unhappy about my demanding her favor back, but if I am to forgo a dowry, I shall at least demand a wife whose reputation cannot be sullied by malicious tongues."

Yesterday morning. *Three lies.*

"Mathieu," Etienne said abruptly, "fetch your hat."

Mathilde hesitated, then obediently slid off the log. She found her hat in the grass and rolled down the brim over her eyes. Etienne picked up the basket and thrust it into her hands.

"Forgive me, Sir Nevell," he said, "but I cannot help you. I no longer have Lady Mathilde's ribbon."

"No longer— Nay, I believe you jest again. Come, sir, I admit I have kept a token to remind me of a former love or two as well. But this is different. 'Tis not I alone who demand the ribbon back. 'Tis her father. He is most strict in his views—"

"I cannot help you," Etienne repeated. "I'm afraid I lost the ribbon in the mêlée. It got torn off my sleeve in the struggle that left me with this injured shoulder. It is probably in a thousand shreds by now somewhere out on that field, trampled by scores of destriers' hooves."

Chesnei's jovial grin faltered for the first time. "I-I cannot believe it, sir."

"'Tis true, I fear. Pray reassure Lord Aymor that I could not boast of his daughter's token even if I wished to. Not that I would ever succumb to behavior so dishonorable."

"N-No, of course not," Chesnei stammered through the remains of a smile that looked numb.

But ..." Etienne drew closer to Chesnei and lowered his voice conspiratorially. "Pray don't tell the Lady Mathilde. I should hate to have her remember me as the blundering knight who lost her favor. If she is like other women, 'twill please her to have cause to think you carry a bit of jealousy in your breast over the favor she gave to another man." He laughed and raised his voice again. "I trust you're listening, Mathieu. Jealousy can add a welcome bit of spice between a man and woman. Remember that when you're older."

Mathilde nodded her head. Her hat shaded her eyes, but he could see by her whitened knuckles on the basket how nervous she was. Chesnei threw an annoyed glance at the "squire", but gave no sign that he suspected her of being anything other than the youth she appeared.

"Will you walk with us back to the tents?" Etienne offered.

Chesnei's eyes, no longer quite so cheerful, measured him for a moment. Then he nodded and fell into step alongside Etienne. Mathilde kept pace several feet behind them. Far enough away that Etienne judged she could not overhear his next words.

"You may have done me a favor by coming here today, Sir Nevell."

"A favor?"

"Aye. I had no notion the Lady Mathilde was so poor. I confess, I had entertained a few thoughts of pursuing her. A pity, but I am something in need of a rich wife, you see. Clearly, the Lady Mathilde would have been a mistake. Not," Etienne added quickly, "that I would ever have so much as glanced her way had I known she was already betrothed."

Chesnei nodded again. His plump face had begun to look almost glum.

Etienne continued in tones of mild interest, "Her father gambled away her inheritance, you say?"

"To my uncle," Chesnei repeated in a mumble.

"High stakes," Etienne remarked when Chesnei failed to offer more. "You said he lost two castles?"

"Actually, 'twas five in all. Lady Mathilde's grandfather was a wealthy and powerful member of King Henry's court when Henry was still just Duke of Normandy." Chesnei graced Etienne with a dismal perusal. "I suppose you are too young to remember her father's disgrace."

"I am Poitevin," Etienne said.

"Ah. So you are new to our Norman scandals. Well, sir, let me enlighten you. Perhaps it will quicken the mending of your wounded heart over losing to me the Lady Mathilde." Chesnei's heavy lips twitched with a sullen humor Etienne found jarring after his earlier display of joviality.

Etienne casually slowed his pace to give Chesnei time to tell his story before they reached the tents.

"Lord Aymor was the second son of Lord Guiscard de Riavelle," Chesnei began. "According to my late uncle, Aymor's father desired him to enter the Church, but Aymor resolutely refused. He wished to serve in Duke Henry's court, so Lord Aymor eventually obtained for him a position on Duke Henry's Wardrobe staff. Six months into Aymor's service, however, certain items were found missing from the Wardrobe. Some jeweled plates, a number of silver candlesticks, and a ring that Duke Henry had inherited from his grandfather and namesake, King Henry I of England.

"A few weeks later, the ring appeared as the stake in a game of dice between my uncle and another drunken young man in Rouen. When my uncle recovered the next morning from the night's carousals, he recognized the prize he'd won as the ring missing from the Wardrobe. Compelled by his oath of knighthood, he carried the ring to Duke Henry and revealed that the man who had lost the ring to him was Aymor de Riavelle."

Etienne barely caught himself from spinning his head round to stare at Mathilde. Had she drawn close enough to hear these charges? Or did she already know them? Was this the "shame and embarrassment" she had hesitated to revive by confiding in him?

"What happened to Aymor when Duke Henry found out?" he asked Chesnei.

"My uncle told me that Aymor denied everything. Insisted he had never stolen so much as a pinch of spice from the Wardrobe. But when questioned about the game of dice, he admitted he'd been so drunk he could not recall the stakes of the game or who had won or lost. My uncle, however, had the proof in his hand. Lord Guiscard pled mercy for his son with tears and swore he would restore treble the value of the items that Aymor had stolen. The plate and candlesticks were never found. It was assumed that Aymor had already sold them—or gambled them away to less scrupulous companions than my uncle."

A footstep crunched softly behind them. This time Etienne glanced over his shoulder and briefly caught Mathilde's eyes, flashing at him from beneath the brim of her hat. Aye, she had heard. But surely she would realize that he would be the last man to judge her for her father's crimes?

"After several days of rage," Chesnei continued, "Duke Henry finally allowed himself to be appeased. For Lord Guiscard's sake, to whom Duke Henry owed many debts for loyal service, he agreed to pardon Aymor, on condition that Aymor never show his face at any of his courts again."

"How, then, did Lord Aymor eventually end up inheriting his father's title?" Etienne asked. He had as well draw out the rest of the story. He had bared his past to Mathilde. It was time she learned to trust him in return.

"Lord Guiscard banished Aymor and the wife he had recently married to one of his manors. A few months later, Aymor's brother fell ill, so ill that it quickly became obvious that Aymor would soon take his place as his father's heir. Anticipation of his future wealth made Aymor reckless. He had never forgiven my uncle for betraying him to Duke Henry. So one night when he was too drunk to think of the risks, he challenged my uncle to another game of dice. The most important castle in his father's barony against my uncle's single keep, a small but formidable fortress that lay across the river from Aymor's manor.

"The loss would have impoverished my uncle. He refused until Aymor, flushed in his cups, called him a coward. No man called my uncle a coward, not after his own father beat him senseless for freezing in battle when he and his sire helped Duke Henry defend his Norman title from King Louis of France over thirty years ago. My uncle never panicked in a fight again. And he never let any man slur his courage. Three rolls of the dice. The luck was with my uncle. He insisted that Aymor sign a document acknowledging that on the day Aymor's father died, the named castle would come into my uncle's possession."

Etienne gave a low whistle. "I imagine Lord Guiscard was none too pleased with his son."

"He did not know," Chesnei replied. "Aymor panicked when he sobered up enough to realize what he had done. He concealed the loss from his father and pleaded with my uncle to grant him a chance to win the castle back. My uncle's friends convinced him 'twas only fair that Aymor be given a chance to redeem himself. So they set another game. Aymor pledged his father's second best castle as stake for retrieving the first. And lost again. And so with the third—and the fourth—and finally the fifth. This did not all happen in a night, you understand. But in time, over the years, Aymor thus forfeited his once vast inheritance. My uncle agreed to keep the losses secret until Aymor's father died. But on that day, he presented the documents Aymor had signed to Duke Henry, who had since won the throne of England. And the now *King* Henry, already mistrusting Aymor for his former dishonesty and theft, allowed him to inherit his father's title, but confirmed the castles in my uncle's hands."

They were in sight of the field of tents. Etienne stopped and turned to Chesnei. From the corner of his eye, he could see Mathilde hovering near them. "Forgive my boldness, Sir Nevell, but it seems a bit odd to me that Lord Aymor would agree to betroth his daughter to the nephew of the man who had made him a pauper."

"Ah." Chesnei rubbed his hands together. His lips twitched upwards in a failed attempt to regain his joviality. The best he could manage, it seemed, was a rather wry grimace. "Actually, the betrothal came to me by default. Lady Mathilde is a charming minx, but—" He leaned a little closer to Etienne and lowered his voice. "Truth be told, she is a bit—how shall I say this?—ahh, spindly for my taste. I prefer my women rather more voluptuous. Like that beauty over there."

He winked, and bobbed his head towards the lady with burnished gold curls who stood conversing with Therri in front of their tent. This time Chesnei's mouth curved into a full-fledged grin, tinged with a shade of a leer.

Etienne resisted the impulse to grin himself. "Lady Hermaline? Aye, she is pleasingly buxom, is she not? Would you like me to introduce you to her?"

Chesnei's eyes lit up. "You know her?"

"We're acquainted. I would be glad to— Ah, wait a moment. She has no doubt come to retrieve the goblet she lent me. Mathieu, you remembered to put it back in the basket, didn't you?" Mathilde looked blank, but Etienne knew they had left it on the ground beside the log. "I don't know where the boy's wits are sometimes," he said to Chesnei, feigning tones of disgust. "The goblet was an expensive piece belonging to Lady Hermaline's father. She would never forgive me if I were to lose it. Come, Mathieu, we'd better go back and fetch it. I would be much obliged, Sir Nevell, if you would distract Lady Hermaline until I return."

Chesnei rubbed his hands together as though anticipating plunging into a succulent morsel of venison. "I should be happy to assist you, sir. Do you think Lord Therri will make the introduction for you?"

"I am sure he will. Give us only a moment to slip out of sight again." Etienne took a step away, then paused and turned back to Chesnei. He hoped the man would remain too absorbed in his lust to think anything suspicious of Etienne's next question. "Sir Nevell, one more thing. You say you came into your betrothal to the Lady Mathilde by default. What exactly did you mean?"

"She was betrothed to my uncle while she was still a child."

"Betrothed to your uncle?" The hair on the back of Etienne's neck suddenly prickled.

Chesnei looked impatient, as though anxious to join the duo outside the tent. "He was not completely without a conscience. So that the de Riavelle lands would not become entirely alienated to the blood that had so long ruled them, he offered to marry Aymor's daughter. But he died before the marriage could take place. The de Riavelle lands now belong to me. It seemed only proper that I should honor the oaths my uncle left unfulfilled, including his oath of betrothal."

"And your uncle's name, sir?" Etienne needed to hear it confirmed.

"My uncle was Sir Alun d'Amville."

Eleven

My uncle is Sir Alun d'Amville.

M The verb had changed, but Etienne had heard those words before. Spoken in that same jovial voice. Chesnei's voice. In a darkened corridor in Rouen.

His foot caught the goblet and sent it flying as he paced past the log. Mathilde's legs scrambled up out of reach of his strides. She balanced herself parallel on the log and wrapped her arms around her knees, hugging them to her chest.

"It isn't true," she said.

"What isn't true?"

"I'm not betrothed to Sir Nevell de Chesnei. I never met him before Girard brought me to Grantamur Castle."

Etienne was only half-listening. His mind raced, trying to remember—

"Etienne."

"What?"

"There—there is something I think I should tell you, though. About Sir Nevell . . ."

"I would rather you told me the truth about d'Amville."

"The truth?"

"The knight who threatened you and your brother was Sir Alun d'Amville, wasn't it?"

She swung her legs over the side of the log, her violet eyes stormy

174

beneath the brim of her hat. "No! D'Amville is dead."

He stopped and turned towards her. "He's not dead, Mathilde. Either your father lied to you or—"

She shot to her feet. "My father is not a liar! And he is not a thief! And he doesn't drink any more or gamble or—"

Etienne laid his free hand on her shoulder and pushed her back down on the log. "Quiet. I don't care a fig for what your father did in the past." He crouched in the grass in front of her and gazed into her stormy eyes. Devil take his bothersome sling! He pulled it off and let it fall into the grass, then wound her hands in his. "We do not have much time," he said. "I expect Hermaline to come looking for us any moment. Listen to me, Mathilde. D'Amville is alive. I remember now where I have heard his name before, and why Chesnei looks so familiar. I saw Chesnei in Rouen at the Young King's court the day my brother asked me to become his seneschal."

"Your brother?"

He heard the startled dismay in her voice, but his gaze had already drifted away from her face, as his mind raced back to the memory of . . .

Shadows. Someone had doused the torch that usually lit this corridor of the palace. Etienne brushed one hand along the wall to steady himself in the dark. He had just finished telling his brother to take his offer and go to blazes, then rewarded himself for his stance of independence by downing several tankards of wine. He was not drunk. Nay, had there only been sufficient light he was certain he could walk a line as straight as an arrow. In the dark he owned he was slightly unsteady. But his wits were not wine-addled. Even hushed, he recognized the voices issuing from the dimness up ahead.

"Do you know whom she has chosen?"

Sir Adam d'Yquebeuf. One of the Young King's *mesnie privée*, his inner retinue of most trusted knights. Etienne stopped. What was d'Yquebeuf doing lurking in a darkened corridor?

"Nay," a second voice spoke. "But she has promised to choose a messenger soon." The answer to d'Yquebeuf's question came in the imperturbable tones of his boon companion of recent days, Thomas de Coulonces.

"That letter must not reach its destination," d'Yquebeuf warned.

"I agree," de Coulonces replied. "But does it not occur to you, Adam, that we might be thinking too small?"

A pause. Etienne felt a swirl of cool air graze his cheeks in the dark. They must be near an exit of the palace. He remembered one lay this way and had bent his steps to find it, hoping a turn in the evening mists would dissipate the effects of his slight inebriation. But why had they left the door ajar?

"Too small?" d'Yquebeuf repeated.

"When the Young King seizes the ducal throne of Aquitaine and Poitou, why should you not be the one to stand at his shoulder? That arrogant popinjay who rules him now already thinks he owns the stars and the moon. He dares to counsel against an offensive because he thinks himself too high for even the Young King to rebuke. Yet if the Young King insists, he will abandon his reluctance and lead our forces to victory. And in gratitude, the Young King will place the very sun within his grasp. Can you bear that, Adam? What is he more than you, that he should receive such honor from royal hands? Were you not born of similar rank? Did you not both train for knighthood in the household of the great Chamberlain of Tancarville? Why should you not be the one who leads our ranks, the one who holds the Young King's ear? Why should you not be the one to claim the sun?"

Etienne had heard rumors that the Young King had entered into a secret alliance with the barons of Aquitaine and Poitou against the Young King's brother, Duke Richard. Was the Young King about to move beyond word into action? Etienne's blood flushed with excitement. Any "offensive" that would remove Duke Richard the Tyrant's ruthless grasp on Etienne's homeland could count on the steel of Etienne's sword. He leaned one hand on the wall and bent forward to listen to the rest.

"How?" D'Yquebeuf spoke the question, his voice thick with

frustrated ambition. "We have raised charges of *lèse majesté* to no avail. So long as the man's tournament victories continue to bring glory to the Young King, the Young King will continue to close his ears to the provocative battle cries that follow our popinjay onto the field."

"*Lèse majesté*," de Coulonces repeated coolly. "Treason is not committed in the open light of the tournament field. It is committed behind the Young King's back with the man he hates above all other men."

"He hates Duke Richard."

"Aye, but there is another he detests even more than his brother."

Etienne heard the sharp whistle of d'Yquebeuf's intake of breath. "King Henry?"

"Remember Adam of Churchdown?"

Etienne did. 'Twas the one memory that sometimes nettled his conscience about the wisdom of throwing in his lot with the Young King. His brother had tossed the Adam of Churchdown incident in his face less than an hour ago. Blazes! He needed another drink.

"Our popinjay would never so risk his neck," d'Yquebeuf protested.

"Not for himself," de Coulonces replied. "But he might do it for—"

Footsteps. Instinctively, Etienne flattened against the wall, then checked his alarm. 'Twas coming from the other way, from the direction of the exit.

"Ah," de Coulonces said. "Here you are. I was beginning to think you had changed your mind."

The newcomer answered with a jovial chuckle that echoed incongruously against the covert shadows of veiled conspiracy. "Nay, nay, Sir Thomas, I am a man of my word. And as I promised, I have found just the man to execute your scheme."

"How much does he demand for the task?" D'Yquebeuf asked with weary cynicism.

"'Tis not gold he wants, Sir Adam. That he already has in plenty."

"Then what?" D'Yquebeuf sounded baffled.

"You may speak," de Coulonces said when the newcomer answered with hesitant silence.

"A title," the newcomer replied. "To go with the lands granted him by King Henry II. He rules them now as a knight, but he wants a baron's title."

Another whistle of d'Yquebeuf's indrawn breath. "A baron's title? 'Tis more than I possess myself! Thomas, these men are mad!" D'Yquebeuf's voice rose dangerously in the dark.

"Nay, Adam," de Coulonces soothed, "it may be possible to do. When the dust has settled, King Henry will forgive his headstrong son as he always does. The Young King will insist that his father allow him to reward those who assisted in his victory against Duke Richard. If you wish, he will surely give *you* your pick of baronies from among the vanquished lords of Poitou or Aquitaine. Then no doubt a title can also be found for—"

"Nay, it must be a Norman title," the newcomer insisted.

"Norman!" d'Yquebeuf exploded.

The newcomer's laughter rang more nervously. "If you would only let me finish—"

"Nay, enough!" d'Yquebeuf said. "I would know the name of the man who makes this outrageous request."

A pause.

"Well?" de Coulonces prompted the newcomer gently.

Another pulse of silence.

"His name is Alun d'Amville."

A deep-throated growl from d'Yquebeuf greeted this announcement. "What trick is this? D'Amville is dead."

"Nay, sir, he is not."

"And how do you know he is not?"

"I have seen and spoken to him within this very sennight. Sir Alun d'Amville is my uncle."

"Thomas," d'Yquebeuf said, "raise the shade on your lamp. I would see this man's eyes to know if he speaks the truth."

Etienne pushed away from the wall as a shaft of light suddenly flooded the corridor. His blood had pounded at the thought of joining an assault that might "liberate" his homeland. Yet instead of stepping forward and pledging his sword to join d'Yquebeuf's cause, some irresistible instinct prodded him instead into a hasty retreat.

"Hold!" d'Yquebeuf's voice rang out after him.

But de Coulonces said, "Let him go. We will learn his identity later."

Learn his identity – Then they had not seen Etienne's face. But he had seen theirs in that brief instant before he had whirled and strode away with a betraying click of his boots against the floorboards. D'Yquebeuf and de Coulonces standing with a corpulent stranger with plump, ruddy cheeks and ginger hair . . .

"Chesnei," Etienne murmured.

Mathilde's fingers clutched around his. "I think he is the man who shot you on the tournament field."

Her words jarred him cleanly out of the past back into the present. *"Chesnei?"* he gasped. "Chesnei was the bowman who planted that curst bolt in my shoulder?"

"I-I think so. He wore a helmet so I could not see his face, but the bowman was fat, like Chesnei. I did not see another knight of that girth anywhere on the field or in Grantamur's hall the evening before. I could not be certain because of the helmet, but I told Girard what I suspected while he was making me put on these clothes. He said he would find Chesnei and question him. He told me not to say anything about it to you or Lord Therri until we knew for sure it had been Chesnei."

Etienne supposed it was possible. If the knight with the glittering, gold-flecked eyes who attacked him had in fact been d'Amville, it made sense that he should enlist the services of his nephew Chesnei in executing the assault. But why had they turned their violence on Etienne? Because he had overheard the conversation between d'Yquebeuf and de Coulonces? Had they only just now learned that his had been the ears that had eavesdropped on their conspiracy?

Once the last fumes of wine had cleared from his brain that night, Etienne had realized that the man with the stars and the moon in his grasp, the man threatened with charges of *lèse majesté*, must be William Marshal. As fiercely as Etienne wished to participate in a movement to free his homeland of Poitou from Duke Richard's grasp, he shrank from lending his name to any cause that carried as its accompanying objective the disgrace of Marshal.

Marshal held Etienne's highest admiration. Not only for his unparalleled battle skills which Etienne, like every other young knight in Christendom, sought to emulate. He admired Marshal's polished manners, his courtly bearing, his vigorous self-assurance in the presence of kings and princes. Marshal could be haughty at times, aye, but he was seldom truly arrogant. His counsel to the Young King had always been sound. His integrity was unimpeachable. And a keener eye for a winnable fight did not exist.

Was that why Marshal, according to de Coulonces, had taken a stand against attempting to depose Duke Richard, a goal that all the rumors suggested the Young King favored? Did Marshal believe that such an assault would fail? But even de Coulonces had said that if the Young King insisted, Marshal would lead their forces to victory.

Perhaps Marshal's reluctance merely stemmed from a disinterest in Poitou. Marshal, at heart, remained an Englishman. But Etienne was Poitevin. If an assault on Duke Richard succeeded, Richard's iron hand on Etienne's homeland would be replaced with the Young King's more negligent approach to government. The ancient freedoms that Poitou's Plantagenet overlords had so long trampled, the freedoms that Etienne's father had fought and died trying to reclaim, would finally be reestablished.

Etienne wanted to see his homeland rid of Duke Richard, with or without William Marshal's help. But whatever their differences on this issue, Marshal remained an honest man. Etienne's conscience would not allow him to stand idle while d'Yquebeuf and de Coulonces laid some snare to unjustly disgrace him.

Etienne had tried to warn Marshal about their plotting. But when Marshal learned that Etienne recalled nothing more than a vague threat to undo him in the Young King's eyes, Marshal waved the warning away. He was accustomed to jealousy from his rivals within the Young King's *mesnie privée*, Marshal had said with a weary smile. They had laid schemes to reduce his power before. Always, in the end, the Young King stood by Marshal. It would be no different this time. He appreciated Etienne's concern, but he knew how to guard himself.

As weeks had passed and d'Yquebeuf took no action against Marshal, Etienne had begun to think he must have misunderstood the veiled words. Perhaps they had not referred to Marshal after all. Perhaps his brain had been more wine-fogged than he had admitted that night.

He had nearly forgotten the incident altogether . . . until he had heard Chesnei speak d'Amville's name today. D'Amville was alive. The same instincts that told Etienne that, also told him that Marshal *was* the target. But without more proof than Etienne's "instincts", Marshal would not believe Etienne now any more than he had in Rouen.

"Mathilde, where is Girard?" he asked abruptly. Had her brother recognized d'Amville? Did he know about d'Yquebeuf's plot?

"I don't know. He told me to tell Lord Therri that he was leaving to raise his ransom for the tournament, but I do not believe he went to my father. He would have taken me with him if he had thought that journey was safe. Do you not think you should put your sling back on?"

He realized that he had released her hands and was rubbing his injured shoulder.

"I'm fine," he lied. In fact, the lengthy morning had begun to take its toll on him. A heaviness in his limbs warned him that he was pushing the bounds of his tenuously recovered strength. His shoulder ached, but he hated the restrictions of his sling. "Is there any more wine in that basket?"

"Yes. Shall I water it again?"

He nodded. She recovered the goblet, filled it, and handed it to him.

He drank and felt some energy seep back into his muscles. He set aside the goblet and used the fist of his right hand to push himself to his feet.

"Girard wanted to hide you from d'Amville " — he silenced her protest with a frown and finished his thought — "so he disguised you as a boy so that d'Amville would not recognize you. I can guess that much. What I don't understand is why he chose to send you to me and Therri — nor exactly how it is that d'Amville threatens you."

"D'Amville does not threaten me. He is — "

"No, Mathilde, he is not. The sooner you accept the fact that he is still alive, the sooner we can solve this puzzle of your danger."

She lifted her chin, clearly preparing to challenge him, but Etienne persisted.

"Your descriptions of d'Amville and the grey-haired knight are too alike to be coincidence. The man who attacked me had gold-flecked eyes as well. He was too lean to be Chesnei. It had to be d'Amville. I suppose he may have come after me because of what I overheard that night in Rouen. Perhaps he feared I might warn Marshal. But why would he threaten you and Girard?" He paused. Mathilde, at least, could have no possible link to William Marshal. He could conjure only one other motive. "Because of your father?"

He saw the flicker in her eyes. Her rebellious chin lowered.

"Mathilde — "

"Etienne, he can't be alive. He *mustn't* be alive."

He waited until she whispered out the kernel of her fear.

"If d'Amville is alive — I shall have to marry him."

Her chin trembled. He drew her down beside him on the log and put his hale arm around her shoulders, but he bit his tongue on vowing to save her from d'Amville. She had *wanted* to marry him once. He had to know why that had changed.

"You've not told me everything about him, have you?" he asked her gently.

She burrowed her face in the hollow of his uninjured shoulder. "I thought he was the kindest, most generous man alive."

"What made you change you mind?"

Her answer came muffled against the cloth of his tunic. He bent his head close to hers to follow her words more clearly.

"I heard him arguing with my father. Father wanted to annul our betrothal. D'Amville said that if he tried, he would see my father in prison." He felt the shiver that wove through her body and tightened his embrace. "They did not see me listening. Father said, 'I'm the one you hate, d'Amville. I'm the one who wronged you. Punish me, not my daughter.' I had always thought d'Amville's voice so beautiful, so melodic, but his soft answer held such menace that I remember the way goose-flesh rose on my skin, despite the summer's heat. 'The crime was not yours alone, Aymor,' d'Amville said. 'Caterine wronged me, too. I shall not be satisfied until I have stripped you of everything you both loved—including the daughter you made between you.'"

"Caterine was your mother?"

He felt her nod against his shoulder. "She died when I was born."

"And you do not know how your father 'wronged' d'Amville?"

This time her head shook in the negative. "No. But ever since he threatened my father, I have suspected that he fabricated the story that made King Henry accuse my father of theft."

He lifted her chin, then tilted back her hat to allow him to gaze into her face. Her love for her father shone clearly in her eyes. Etienne understood her desire to cast the blame somewhere else. Anywhere else but on a man who clearly meant the world to her. Etienne had preferred to remain blind to his father's crimes, too.

"Mathilde," he said gently, "though we none of us like to believe it, fathers, alas, are all too human. Sometimes, despite their best intentions, they—disappoint you."

She pulled away from his embrace, her eyes flashing a stubborn fire. "My father is not a thief! He told me that d'Amville lied about the ring."

"Told you when?"

"When—" she faltered, then raised her chin again. "When he told me that d'Amville was dead."

Etienne barely prevented himself from rolling his eyes.

"My father is innocent," she insisted, "and you promised you would help me prove it."

He opened his mouth to protest, then closed it again. He had promised no such thing. But he *had* pledged himself to protect her and however rashly, he had extended that pledge of protection to her father, as well.

He feared that if Mathilde persisted in her goal, the only "truth" she would learn about her father was that he had been a drunken, thieving young fool. Etienne remembered the pain of his own disillusionment when he had finally been forced to confront the tragic folly of his father's choices. Perhaps if he agreed to help her, he could find a way to soften that heartsick moment for Mathilde.

"Very well," he said. "I presume you have a plan for how we are to accomplish this?"

The fire died from her eyes, replaced by an expression of misty reflection. She had dreamed of this a long while, he knew. Dreamed that some knight-errant would come riding to the rescue of her and her father.

"There must be people who know the truth," she said, "but I do not know how to find them. I thought with your silver, with your influence, that you would be able to look where I cannot. To seek out servants, other men who served in the royal Wardrobe when my father was there. Someone must know who *really* took those things." The light in her eyes dimmed. "Only—only I did not remember that you had a brother. He must be your *older* brother, too, if he asked you to become his seneschal. You are not rich at all, are you? And your brother may not want to lend you the silver to help me."

Her mouth quivered. Saints! How he longed to still it with his. But the disappointment in her eyes cut him to the heart. He felt as though he had somehow betrayed her by his poverty.

"The only silver I possess is the ransoms I won in the mêlée," he admitted.

"What about the ruby on your surcote?"

"Ruby?" Ah. No doubt that explained her shattered misconceptions about his "wealth and influence." He felt a tide of embarrassment rising in his cheeks. "It is only glass, Mathilde. I thought its likeness to a ruby might attract more challengers in the mêlée, help me to gain more ransoms. If the silver I *did* win there were enough to buy proof of your father's innocence, it would all be yours. But—" he had to be truthful. She had been lied to enough. "Mathilde, it has been over twenty years since the Wardrobe theft."

"Thirty," she confessed.

"Thirty?" He had forgotten that Girard was ten years older than Mathilde. Her brother's memories would be ten years clearer, then. But it still might not be enough. "Even if d'Amville conspired with someone to steal from the Wardrobe and blame your father, their tracks would be thirty years cold. Memories will have faded or become garbled. It simply may not be possible to—"

He broke off as her pert little nose sniffed and her eyes misted again, this time with tears. Her chin trembled. Ah, saints, he could not bear to see her cry.

"Sweethear— Maude, don't. I—I will think of something. Just give me some time."

To his relief, her chin steadied.

"Do you think your brother might help?" she asked hopefully. "Perhaps he will know someone at court who could tell us—"

"He has no more influence in royal circles than I."

"But you said King Henry had pardoned your family."

"King Henry agreed to let us keep our lands and not cut off our heads. He did not agree to ever trust a de Brielle again."

She lowered her gaze, then drew off her hat. After several minutes, she began to twist it in her hands. "Then—if you have neither influence nor gold—what are we going to do?"

"*You* are not going to do anything," he said sharply, "except sit in our tent and play Therri's squire. Of course, the longer you do so, the more likely it is that Therri will see through your disguise. I sent Walter back to Rouen this morning, to prevent the possibility of him discovering your secret, but Therri . . . Not that I don't think we could trust him, but if he knew you were a woman, he'd probably insist that we find other—ah—arrangements for you."

She looked alarmed. "You mean—send me away?"

"Nay, I won't allow that," he promised. "At least not until I have figured out what the devil has brought d'Amville back from the dead."

"You are sure he is alive?" Her voice quavered.

"Aye." He stilled her nervous wringing of her hat with his hand over hers . "But I stand by my pledge to protect you. However your father wronged him, d'Amville will not use you for his vengeance."

She was silent for a moment, her head bowed.

"Etienne?"

"Hmm?" He had been admiring in the silence the way the autumn sun set a soft shimmer to her hair.

"Why did you lie about my ribbon?"

"Your ribbon?" He tucked a pale strand of hair behind her ear. The skin that veiled her high cheekbones gleamed with a delicate translucence. The memory of that silken cheek nestled in the palm of his hand brought a lump to his throat. One day her cheeks, her lips, her dreamy eyes would all belong to another man. But not, he swore, to a man who brought fear to her eyes. Not to d'Amville.

"You told Sir Nevell you lost my ribbon on the tournament field. But I know you still have it. Why did you lie to him?"

"Because he lied to me first. He lied about your betrothal, he lied about leaving you at your father's, and he no doubt lied about being sent by Girard. He had no right to your ribbon. Why the devil he thought I would give it to him—" He broke off, then reached into the breast of his tunic and slowly withdrew the object they discussed.

"You have been carrying it with you?" she asked in surprise.

He did not answer, but studied the strip with a frown. Dusty brown stains marred its whiteness and a portion of the gilt embroidery looked matted, as though some great pressure had ground it against the fabric. Hermaline's jealous foot, if Therri had told him aright. A swipe of his thumb revealed that several more stitches had come loose along the back. He turned it over and plucked broodingly at the threads.

"Why do you think Chesnei wanted it?" he wondered aloud. His thumbnail slid under a stitch and another string popped loose. Absently, he noted that the silk seemed to be lined with a coarser piece of cloth inside.

He chewed on his lip. Perhaps d'Amville had sent Chesnei after the ribbon. D'Amville had demanded the token from Etienne on the tournament field. He must have recognized the ribbon even then as Mathilde's. Perhaps d'Amville had been angered to see another man wearing his "betrothed's" favor. But had that been reason enough to attack Etienne with a sharpened lance?

He remembered the disturbing glitter in d'Amville's eyes. The same thought that had flitted through Etienne's mind then, flittered through it now. Was d'Amville, quite simply, mad?

All the more reason to keep a close eye on Mathilde. Perhaps Chesnei's demand had been a test to see if Etienne would betray some knowledge of her whereabouts so that d'Amville could seize her.

"You promised to give the ribbon back to me after the tournament," Mathilde reminded him.

So that she could return it to Girard and he to his harlot. The thought still angered Etienne. The musky scent of angelica had long since faded. The silk now lay stained and torn in his hand. Yet it would always sing to him of Mathilde, of her heart as pure as the once snowy cloth, of her smile as radiant as the gilded stitches when they caught the torchlight in Grantamur's Hall.

"May I have it now?" She held out her hand.

"I promised to give it back to Girard, not you. Let him ask me again if he wants it." Etienne would return it, aye, but not until he had first planted his fist in Girard's face for the slap he had dealt his sister.

He stuffed the ribbon back inside his tunic.

"But—"

"There they are!"

The shrill voice cut off Mathilde's protest. Etienne stiffened. Hermaline. He watched Mathilde jerk on her hat and pull it over her eyes.

A moment later, Hermaline appeared, trailed by Therri. Etienne started to rise, but Hermaline bounced over to the log and grabbed his arm. She pulled him back down beside her, almost landing atop Mathilde, except that Mathilde slid quickly aside to make room for her.

"Shame on you, sir," Hermaline chided. "You have had me in quite a tizzy of worry. You were gone so long, I feared you must have fainted away and your slow-witted squire had not the good sense to call for help."

A soft huffing sound came from Mathilde. Her arms folded across her chest in what appeared to Etienne a very feminine gesture of indignation.

Therri, thankfully, was too busy glaring at Hermaline to notice. He carried a basket twice the size of the one Mathilde had fed Etienne from earlier. "For someone in a 'tizzy of worry,'" he said to Hermaline, "you lingered a long time tittering with Chesnei."

"He was amusing," Hermaline said with a toss of her burnished head. "And he wore some very pretty jewels."

Etienne saw the covetous gleam in her eyes. But before his hope that she might turn her interest from him to Chesnei could climb too high, Hermaline sighed and ran her hand boldly along his arm, fondling his muscles through his sleeve.

"But I like you better, Etienne," she said with her sweetest smile. "You are much more handsome than Chesnei."

He pulled her hand away from his sleeve. Then his glance caught Mathilde. Her eyes were hidden by the brim of her hat, but the corners of her lips turned down in a frown. He had told her that he and Hermaline were as good as betrothed. If he did not play through the pretense, Mathilde would know he had lied about his reason for rejecting her. She would believe he had done it because she was homely.

He could not bear that. He raised Hermaline's fingers and kissed them. Just a kiss. Nothing more than he might have dropped on any well-born lady's hand. If Hermaline jumped to conclusions from the gesture, he could not be blamed for that.

Mathilde's mouth trembled, then stilled. Therri stared at him.

Hermaline fairly purred.

The basket Therri carried contained a lavish picnic lunch that Hermaline had brought from the castle. Etienne bore with Hermaline through the greater part of the afternoon, while Therri watched them with a puzzled frown and Mathilde took a fish cake from the basket and went to sit on the river bank with her back turned to the log. Hermaline sat uncomfortably close to Etienne's side as she coaxed him to eat, her plump hip brushing intimately against his. Each time Etienne shifted sideways along the log to try to place distance between them, Hermaline shifted with him, until he ran out of room to slide.

Bereft of escape, and resigned to maintaining his lie to Mathilde, he allowed Hermaline to nestle against him and fawn over him while she popped a seemingly endless string of picnic morsels into his mouth. Therri observed the scene with raised brows, but observing Etienne's apparent capitulation, made no comment until Etienne's endurance finally snapped.

As the autumn sun began its early descent towards the hills, Etienne could bear no more. His shoulder throbbed, his muscles felt like lead, and Hermaline's mindless chatter set his head in a spin.

At his first avowal of exhaustion, Therri was at his side, firmly insisting that Etienne return to the tent to rest. Hermaline pouted, but Therri's will won out, and soon Etienne found himself thankfully in his cot, while Therri escorted Hermaline to Grantamur castle.

Etienne lay on his back and listened to the dull clop of the horses' fading hooves. A numbing fatigue had almost lulled him to sleep when Mathilde's voice floated wistfully through the gathering dusk.

"Etienne?"

Fearful that Chesnei or d'Amville might be looking for her, he had forbidden her to leave the tent. She had lain in silence a long while, stretched out on Walter's former pallet beside Etienne's cot.

"What is it, Maude?" He heard the exhausted slur in his voice, but her sweet tones roused him to brush his thumb along her ribbon, which he had furtively rewound around his hand when she and Therri had not been looking.

"Have you thought any more about how we are to help my father?"

"Nay. My mind feels like mush just now. I'll think about it tomorrow, I promise."

Silence. He shifted, trying to ease the ache of his shoulder against the cot.

"Etienne?"

Clearly, she found the early evening hour too early to sleep.

"Yes, Maude?"

"Do you think I'm spindly?"

He had not believed anything could pry his eyes open again until morning, but her question brought them wide. A stretch of black canvas over his head greeted his gaze.

"Spindly?" he repeated.

"Chesnei said I was spindly."

Etienne recognized the mournful note in her voice and cursed that toad Chesnei.

With an effort, he rolled onto his side, then caught his breath when he found Mathilde's face mere inches from his. She had propped her arms along the side of his cot and rested her chin on the back of her hands. Her chin came up as his face swiveled close to hers, but she did not draw back.

Saints! Her mouth was near enough to kiss.

"You said I was ethereal," her enticing lips whispered. "I liked the sound of that. But I fear you were truly just being kind. Chesnei was right. My legs have as much shape as a stick."

Etienne remembered the way her squire's hose clung to the graceful curve of her calves.

"I was not being kind, Maude," he said huskily. "I know women who would give their eye-teeth for legs as shapely as yours."

As close as she was, he could not make out her features clearly in the dark. But he heard the smile in her voice.

"You really are the most splendid liar, Etienne de Brielle. I wish you had been rich—and free."

Before he could answer, her lips brushed his cheek, then her face vanished from the side of his cot.

"Goodnight," she breathed on a dreamy sigh.

"Goodnight." *My love.*

Twelve

Hermaline arrived at the tent shortly after dawn and determinedly attached herself to Etienne's side. She brought with her a chess board with ivory playing pieces, a wooden flute, and another basket stuffed full of food. Mathilde, forbidden by Etienne to wander out of his sight, sat on a stool and watched him and Hermaline play chess on the trestle table that Therri obligingly set up for them outside the tent before he rode up to the castle to pay court to Violette.

Mathilde cursed the fates that brought Hermaline to the tent so early, before Mathilde could consult further with Etienne about her father's plight. The question weighed upon Mathilde with a double urgency now. She wanted to find a way to restore her father's honor, as she always had. But now, the possibility of failure meant more than a simple continuation of his disgrace and poverty. If they could not prove that d'Amville had lied about her father, and if d'Amville should truly still be alive, then her betrothal remained in force and there would be no way to escape his demand of marriage. So long as d'Amville had power to threaten her father, Mathilde knew that Etienne could not protect her. She would marry d'Amville of her own free choice before she would allow further harm or shame to come to her sire.

Nay, she told herself, she must have faith in Etienne. He would not fail her. Like the brave heroes of the jongleur's ballads, he would learn the truth and punish d'Amville. He might have settled on a plan even now. If only she could talk to him alone.

But Hermaline continued to play chess and gossip, feed Etienne and gossip, squawk on her flute and gossip. Etienne endured it all with such patience that Mathilde knew he must be truly and deeply in love. He never once asked Hermaline to quiet the chattering tongue that threatened to drive Mathilde to distraction. True, a great deal of the time he looked abstracted—she hoped thinking of her father—and had to be nudged by Hermaline to make a move on the chess board or finish the cold venison he was eating. But he was not so engrossed in his thoughts that he failed to wince when Hermaline paused, as she did periodically in the game, and screeched a grating tune on her flute.

"Mathieu, you play the flute, don't you?" he asked at the conclusion of Hermaline's third mangled tune.

Hermaline's rose-bud lips pouted. "You do not like the way I play, sir?"

"Your music is charming," Etienne assured her quickly. "But I thought we might enjoy listening together to a soft, sweet melody while you and I concentrate on finishing this game."

Any reluctance Hermaline might have felt to surrender her flute to Mathilde was swept away by the beguiling smile that accompanied Etienne's words. Mathilde suffered a pang at the sight, worsened by the hungry way Hermaline gazed back at Etienne. Hermaline held out her flute to Mathilde without so much as glancing at the "squire".

Mathilde accepted the flute and returned to her stool, closing her eyes to shut out the couple by the chessboard as she cocked her head to consider what tune she should play. But the murmur of Etienne's voice, responding to Hermaline's revived gossip, confirmed in a heartbeat what Mathilde's melody should be. Softly, she began to pipe the strains of the jongleur's song of Prince Erec and his beloved wife, Enide.

Did Hermaline have any idea how blessed she was, Mathilde wondered as she played? Would Hermaline someday prove a worthy Enide to Etienne's valiant and faithful Prince Erec? How wrong Mathilde had been about Etienne from the first! If only she had not allowed herself to be so misguided by the maid's silly warnings about seducers, it might be *she* who . . .

Nay, he had loved Hermaline long before he had met Mathilde. The pain that quivered in her heart echoed in a wobbly note from the flute. She steadied her melody and finished it off with a delicate, shivery trill.

She opened her eyes as she lowered the flute, then stilled with it halfway to her lap. Etienne was watching her. She searched his gaze and saw something flicker in his eyes that set butterflies fluttering in her pulse.

"It is your move, Etienne." Hermaline reached across the table to pull on the sling Therri had made Etienne redon that morning.

Etienne glanced back at the chess board. Mathilde saw the lines of his face slightly harden as he pushed forward his bishop. She rebuked herself for the foolish notion that had flashed through her mind. For an instant, she thought the flicker in Etienne's gaze had reflected a subtle, tender yearning.

Clearly, she had been mistaken. Etienne leaned his chin on his hand and stared over Hermaline's shoulder, his former smile turned into a brooding frown. Hermaline picked up her rook and tapped it against her lips as she continued the chatter she had maintained throughout Mathilde's tune. She rattled on about the impromptu dance Violette's court had engaged in yesterday while Hermaline had picnicked by the river with Etienne and Therri.

"And while they were dancing, Cassandry said, Sir Bors of the Big Feet trod on Lady Basilia's gown and ripped it clear up to the knee. *To the knee.* Basilia must have been absolutely mortified, for she has the fattest calves, you know. And as if that weren't bad enough, Cassandry said Basilia had a snare in her woolen hose and when she tried to cover it up with her hands, her garter came loose and slipped down around her ankle. And one of the knights—you're not eating. Here, try some of this lamb."

She pushed a platter of sliced meat towards Etienne, then plopped her rook down somewhere in the middle of the board. Mathilde recognized it as a totally illegal move, but Etienne was still gazing off into the distance.

"One of the knights," Hermaline continued, "I think Cassandry said Sir Drogo, but it might have been Sir Bruno or Sir Hamo, shouted that Sir Bors should be a gentleman and tie the garter back in its proper place. Cassandry thinks he must have been in his cups, for when Sir Bors blushingly excused himself, Sir Drogo—unless it was Sir Bruno or Sir Hamo—gallantly offered to restore the garter himself." Hermaline tittered with shrill laughter. "He *must* have been drunk to have thought Basilia's legs worthy of such a risqué tribute."

Mathilde rose in disgust at this spiteful speech. Hermaline would *never* be a worthy Enide. How could Etienne—? Nay, it was not for her to question where he chose to bestow his affections.

Etienne's attention snapped round to her. "Mathieu, don't go wandering off."

"I wasn't going to—"

"Here, sit down and eat this fish cake."

He dug a cake out of the basket and waited for her to take it. She snatched it out of his hand, then determinedly reseated herself with her back to the table. Some woman would be doing him a favor to steal him away from Hermaline. If only his heart had not been involved, Mathilde might have tried.

Therri returned at dusk and sent Hermaline back to the castle, escorted by the servant who had accompanied him for that purpose. Therri was in a sour temper and vented it, pacing around the trestle table where Etienne still sat. Violette, Therri swore, had teased him mercilessly all day. First she had kept all her would-be suitors waiting in the hall till nearly noon. When she had finally appeared for dinner, she seated William Marshal on her right hand, "some other fop", Therri growled, on her left, and relegated Therri to a distant seat at one of the sideboards. During the games that followed the meal, she had laughed and flirted with every man but Therri, reserving for him only snaps of impatience.

Mathilde sighed. Therri seemed likely to grumble away the rest of the night. She would have to wait until morning to ask Etienne his plan to help her father. That is, providing she could snatch a moment alone with him before Hermaline descended again on the tent. Mathilde had as well go to bed.

But inside the tent she paused. Two more nights and she must rendezvous with Girard. Would her brother be pleased when she told him that Etienne was going to help their father? Or would he be angry and command her again to leave the matter alone? It did not matter. Etienne was her ally now. Once she had given the ribbon to Girard, she would return to Etienne and together they would expose d'Amville and prove her father's innocence.

But Etienne had stubbornly refused to return the ribbon to her on the river bank. From the belligerent look on his face when he'd said that Girard must ask for it himself, she feared that he harbored ill feelings towards her brother. Had Etienne quarreled with Girard over gambling debts, as Therri had? If so, she feared Etienne intended to use the ribbon as an excuse to confront her brother over the matter. It would make everything easier if she found the ribbon and returned it to Girard herself.

But where had Etienne hidden it? Surely he was not still carrying it about in the breast of his tunic? The thought of searching him for it while he slept brought a heated tide to Mathilde's cheeks.

She would search the rest of the tent first.

But there did not seem to be many places to look. Only the wooden chest in the corner that held Etienne and Therri's clothing, the two knights' saddlebags, and the cots. Therri and Etienne had piled their chain mail atop the chest, so she tried the saddlebags first. There was no sign of the ribbon in the first one she checked, although she did discover her mother's sapphire necklet, the one that Therri had broken in Grantamur Hall. This must be Therri's bag, then.

The necklet still in her hand, she started to reach for the second saddlebag when she heard footsteps. She whirled, stuffed the necklet back into Therri's bag, then dived onto her pallet and pulled the blanket over her head.

Therri was still talking to Etienne as they strode into the tent. "Vi told me to tell you, you are welcome to attend Sunday mass in her chapel tomorrow, if you are feeling up to the ride. She added, 'And I suppose, my lord, as Sir Etienne may still be weak and require your support, you may come too, if you like.'" Therri grunted. "As though she were extending me the same courtesy she would extend to a nursemaid."

Therri mimicked Violette's haughty tones so well that Mathilde had to stifle a giggle. Etienne murmured something soothing, but Therri continued to mutter complaints while he and Etienne stripped to their smocks. Fortunately, the autumn weather discouraged them from stripping further. Etienne had to step over Mathilde to reach his cot, but once he and Therri were abed, silence fell.

Mathilde lay listening to the two men's breathing, breathing that eventually evolved into soft snoring sounds from Therri. She had thought Etienne asleep, too, when he spoke softly to her in the dark.

"Maude, are you awake?"

She hesitated, then pushed back the blanket and stared up at Etienne's head hanging over the edge of his cot.

"Yes," she whispered.

"Then sit up so we can talk. I think Therri won't wake if we keep our voices low."

She sat up and wrapped her arms around her knees. The vivid memory of the night before, when he had turned suddenly on the cot and brought his face so near to hers, made her heart skip. She had thought, for an instant, that he was going to kiss her again. She had held her breath, wishing that he might.

When he had not, she had daringly stolen a kiss from him instead, albeit only a quick brush of her lips to his cheek. But that small salute of gratitude had sent a charge through her body that had driven the sleep from her eyes until nearly dawn.

Had she shocked him? No more than she had shocked herself. She had never believed she could be so brazen. And shameless. His kisses belonged to Hermaline. 'Twas wicked of Mathilde to covet them. Wicked to hope that she might tempt him to stray from his love.

"Maude, did you hear me?"

"What?"

"I said, I've been thinking all day about your father." He shifted himself onto his elbow. "I don't have the gold or connections to ask the kinds of questions that need to be asked. But Therri does. I think we ought to tell him."

"Lord Therri?" She glanced at Therri's cot, but he was only shadows of grey and black in the dark. Like the planes of Etienne's face. "Do you think he would help us?"

A week ago, it would not have occurred to her to wonder. Therri had been the Vision, the epitome of all her dreams of the courageous, valiant, resourceful knight whose only joy and calling lay in helping the troubled and oppressed. Now she knew that he was merely a man, susceptible to impatience and bad temper, as well as the nobler virtues of loyalty and friendship he demonstrated with Etienne.

"He'll help if I ask him," Etienne assured her. "He has a brother-in-law on King Henry's high council. And Therri has money. I wouldn't ask him to spend anything I cannot repay, of course. But he may know where we should begin to make some inquiries about your father. I'll talk to him tomorrow." He paused. "Or perhaps we should wait one more day. Tomorrow's Sunday and Violette is expecting us up at the castle for mass. 'Twould not be a good time to start another row between her and Therri. When she finds out that you— But we'll deal with that on Monday."

Mathilde did not know why speaking to Therri tomorrow should start a row between him and Violette, but Etienne lapsed into a silence that somehow discouraged her from asking.

"Don't worry about it any more tonight," he said at last. "Lie down again and go to sleep."

She leaned back onto the pallet and watched him lower himself to the cot. 'Twas shameful indeed, but she wished she had the courage to kiss his cheek again. 'Twould be worth it to savor the taste of him once more.

She stared for several minutes into the dark, then closed her eyes. Though the ground was hard and the blanket thin against the

autumn night, she did not feel cold. Or afraid. Even knowing that
d'Amville was alive, that he was waiting to use her to avenge
himself on her father . . . If she lay very still and listened very hard,
she could decipher Etienne's steady breathing from Therri's muffled
snores. And she knew that nothing, and no one, could harm her, so
long as he was near.

She had nearly drifted to sleep when something brushed
against her cheek. Without even opening her eyes, she knew
Etienne's touch. It sent little tendrils of fire through her.

"Maude?"

"Yes?" she whispered through a tightened throat.

"I forgot to tell you something."

"What?"

"I'll wager you have prettier legs than Lady Basilia."

She blushed in the dark at his teasing voice. He must be
remembering her disparaging remark about her legs the night
before. She opened her eyes. He lay on his stomach, his arm trailing
over the side of the cot, his fingers still dangling near her face. But
'twas not the proximity of his hand alone that made her catch her
breath. Her ribbon twined about his palm, its ends fluttering silently
on a ripple of air that stole into the tent. She raised a hand to pull
gently on one of the ends. The silken strand tightened rather than
loosened about his palm. He had wrapped it too securely to pull free.

But her thoughts were racing elsewhere than on her need to
retrieve the ribbon. "How do you know?" she asked. "Have you
seen Lady Basilia's legs?" The question popped out before she could
stop it.

"No, but I have seen yours."

In her squire's hose. His teasing carried even in his whisper.

"Hermaline said that Lady Basilia's legs were fat," Mathilde
whispered back.

"Just her calves. Not a fair contest, I admit, against slender
limbs like yours. But I'd lay odds of twenty to one that you have
prettier legs than any lady in Violette's court. Including Violette."

"Go to sleep," she said fiercely and pulled her blanket over her
head.

But she lay awake a long while wondering if "any lady in Violette's court" included Hermaline.

Sunday passed with excruciating boredom for Mathilde. She accompanied Etienne and Therri up to Grantamur Castle for mass and the dinner that followed. But as Etienne planted her in a corner of the hall and insisted that she keep her hat pulled over her eyes all day, she returned to the tent that evening frustrated at having been denied an opportunity to either examine Violette's exotic tapestries and table furnishings or survey the glittering throngs of suitors who came to woo their hostess even on the Sabbath.

But by Monday morning she forgot her disappointment, nervousness overcoming her instead as Etienne told her to wait outside the tent while he talked to Therri.

She sat on the stool by the entrance and strained her ears to hear what they might be saying. At first, all she could make out were murmurs. But ere long, the murmurs gave way to an ominous roar.

"He's *what?*"

Another murmur from Etienne.

The tent flap snapped back and Therri loomed in the open space, staring at Mathilde with a ghastly pallor in his face.

"Mathieu," Etienne called from behind his friend, "you'd better come inside."

She tried to obey, but Therri stood stock-frozen, blocking the entrance. Only when Etienne's hand clapped his shoulder, did he blink and step back so that Mathilde could dart around him.

"Tell me this is one of your jests," Therri pleaded, letting the flap fall back into place.

Etienne shook his head.

Therri raked Mathilde with a gaze so fierce she felt as though it might physically strip away her tunic.

"So," he said, clearly struggling to keep his voice level, "you're telling me that we've had a woman in our tent for a sennight—and I've been too thick-witted to know it?"

"You've been—preoccupied. With Violette," Etienne said carefully.

A strangling sound gurgled from Therri's throat. Mathilde marveled that he had any more color to lose, but he succeeded in going several shades whiter than he had been before.

"If Violette finds out about this—" he choked. "Great heavens, Etienne! She already suspects me of harboring a dozen lovers behind her back. She even accused me the other night of—" He broke off and sent a stunned, accusatory look at Mathilde. "Of smuggling one of them into my tent."

"I'm afraid Vi suspects the truth," Etienne confessed. "I mean she suspects that Mathieu is Mathilde. She told me the day after my fever broke. She remembered Maude's face from the tournament. I tried to convince her that she was mistaken, but—"

"The tournament?" Therri exploded. "*You* persuaded me to arrange for her to watch it from Violette's walls!" He dropped onto his cot and clutched his golden locks in both hands. "Fiend seize it, Etienne! Violette will never forgive me for this!"

"You haven't done anything that needs forgiving," Etienne insisted. "I'll explain it all to Vi. I'll tell her about Girard and that you've behaved with flawless rectitude towards Mathilde."

"How would you know?" Therri snapped. "You were unconscious for two days. I might have ravished her a dozen times while you lay fevered on your cot." He groaned, then growled in fury. "De Riavelle. When I see that shirking idiot again, I'll rip his throat apart with my bare hands."

Mathilde shivered. He sounded like he meant it. She had better warn Girard when she saw him tonight to deliver his ransom by messenger.

Therri lifted his head and glared at her. "Well, she can't stay here any longer. Send her back to her father. Send her anywhere! Just get her out of our tent."

Mathilde's heart shunted from her chest to her boots. He was not going to help them!

"Calm down," Etienne said. "We can't send her away. At least, we can't send her back to her father. She's in trouble. That's why Girard dressed her up this way and sent her to us."

"That doesn't make sense. How did he know we wouldn't take advantage of her?"

Etienne's gaze met Mathilde's. He raised his brows slightly, as though he shared Therri's question.

"He-He hoped to return for me before you realized I was a girl," she said. "And I'm sure he must have known from your reputations that I would be safe with you, even if you learned who I was before he came."

"My reputation?" Therri groaned again and dropped his head back in his hands.

"He's right," Etienne said. "Therri's been too reckless with his flirting. *I* know he would never harm you, but Girard would have thought the worst. Why *did* he hide you with us, Maude, and not with some other knight on this field?"

"I don't know," she lied, remembering Girard's command not to speak of the ribbon. "Perhaps—Perhaps it was because he owed money to Lord Therri. It gave him an excuse to send me here to pretend to be surety for his ransom."

"Pretend?" Therri ground out.

"I am sure he means to pay you," Mathilde said hastily. "When he comes back for me."

"And when will that be, exactly?"

Mathilde remained silent. If she confessed that she would see Girard tonight, Therri might insist that Girard take her away. Then how would Etienne be able to help her father?

"It doesn't matter," Etienne said. "I promised we would help her."

"We?" Therri's head bounced up. "*I* want her out of here." He pushed himself to his feet, reinforcing his demand with his formidable, glowering height.

His powerful build had once made Mathilde dizzy with delight. Now she took a dismayed step backwards.

Etienne must have seen her alarm, for he moved to stand beside her. "Stow your glares, Therri," he said. "We can't just throw her out. You're not as cold-hearted as that."

Therri shoved both hands through his hair again, then said with mingled exasperation and anger, "She can't stay here, Etienne. Not everyone is as slackwitted as I. How much longer do you think it will be before some other knight on this field sees through her disguise and starts spreading rumors? Think of *her* reputation, if not our own."

"I have thought of it. That's why I've kept her so close to me the last few days. But until Girard returns, I don't know where else to send her."

"Well, you'd better think of something," Therri snapped, "because I want her gone when I get back."

"Where are you going?"

"Up to the castle to tell Violette that Girard finally sent for his brother. At least if she knows that 'Mathieu' is gone, she might be willing to give me another chance."

"Therri, wait!" Etienne called as his friend strode out. He turned to Mathilde. "I'm going after him. Stay here, out of sight, until I get back.

"But Etienne, I—I don't think he is going to help us." *And I do not want to leave you.* Her heart pounded the panicked truth against her ribs. *I know you belong to Hermaline, I know you can never be mine, but I do not want to leave you yet.* "Please don't let him send me away," she whispered.

Etienne hesitated, then slid his arm around her shoulders. "Don't worry. Therri will listen once his temper cools."

Her knees wobbled, threatening to melt her body into his. She must focus on her father, she told herself, not on her own wicked longings.

But when Etienne's hand tightened on her shoulder, drawing her against him, she knew the yearning she had glimpsed in his eyes two days ago had been real. The same gleam darkened his gaze now as it slid over her cheeks and settled on her lips.

Her heart flipped over at least three times in the space of his smoldering contemplation. Anticipation licked over her flesh like a fever. She drew a slow, hopeful breath.

His tongue darted out to wet his lips.

Then abruptly, he let her go.

"I'll be back." The words croaked out of his throat, before he charged after Therri.

Mathilde made it over to his cot before her knees gave way. She had thought his flattery through these past few days and nights had been mere kindness. But in the dark green heat of his gaze just now, she had seen the truth. She tempted him. He wanted her, coveted her, lov—

Nay. A ball of ice formed in the pit of her stomach and spread to freeze away the residual warmth his gaze had left dancing in her veins. He did not love her. He had committed his love to Hermaline. But from the smoldering way he had just gazed at her, she knew she had the power to lure him, if not away from his love, then at least away from his loyalty. Saints! She had become the seducer she had accused him of being!

But she did not want to seduce him. She did not want his passions unless she could also have his heart.

'Twas the one thing he had made clear he could never give her. Had he not said as much that day beside the river? But if they continued dwelling side by side in this way, she sleeping next to his cot at night, he keeping her close beside him to guard her by day, he . . . they . . . might one day slip, despite their individual resolves to the contrary.

She picked up his bolster and breathed deeply of his masculine scent. She could not stay. After this night, she could not return. She hugged the bolster to her breast so hard it squeezed tears out of her eyes. Or perhaps they would have leaked forth anyway. She would take the ribbon to Girard and she would leave with him. Etienne, she knew, would still fulfill his pledge to help her father. Future communications could be done through a messenger, or in some public place with a chaperone at her side. His passion for her would die quickly once she was gone.

And he would thank her that his memories remained unstained by guilt when he lay in Hermaline's arms.

Thirteen

Etienne caught up with Therri half-way to Grantamur Castle. He had cast off his sling before he mounted his horse, but he winced more from stiffness than soreness in his shoulder as he reached out to grab the reins of Therri's mount. 'Twas the only way he could force Therri to slow his thundering ride.

Therri whirled in the saddle as Etienne forced both their mounts to a standstill. "Curse you, Etienne, why didn't you tell me?"

"Because Mathilde made me promise not to betray her," Etienne replied. "Besides, I knew if I told you, you'd react just like this."

Therri gave a caustic laugh. "Then you won't be surprised when I repeat that I want her out of our tent before nightfall."

He tried to spur his horse forward, but Etienne held onto the reins. "Blazes, Therri, I don't have anywhere to send her. Unless you want me to ask refuge for her with Violette?"

Therri's glare went glacial. "If you dare—"

"Then stow it. Another day or two isn't going to hurt now. Mathilde is in trouble. If you want to get rid of her, then help me to help her."

Therri's gaze thawed only fractionally, but it was enough to encourage Etienne to release the reins.

Therri did not try again to urge his mount away, but he exclaimed with renewed exasperation, "Fiend seize it, Etienne, the Lady Mathilde is no gutter-wench. If word gets out that she's been living and sleeping in our tent for a week—"

"It won't get out if you keep your mouth shut. No one knows the truth except you and me. Violette suspects, but she won't speak without more than mere suspicion to support her."

"We're not the only ones who know. Hasn't it occurred to you that this whole masquerade might be a trap?" Therri waved an impatient hand at Etienne's puzzled silence. "Girard. How do you know he didn't set us up? That he doesn't intend to come roaring into our tent any moment, shouting that we've defiled his sister and demanding that one of us marry her?"

Etienne had not thought of that. That Girard was badly in need of money, everyone in the Young King's court knew. Etienne, almost as poor as Girard, could not possibly be the target of such a desperate plan. But Therri might and his reputation made him vulnerable. The angry flush on Therri's cheeks betrayed the fact that he knew it.

But Etienne dismissed the possibility almost at once. If Girard schemed to marry his sister to wealth, he would surely have returned to make his accusations of "defilement" long before now. Besides, Girard knew that Therri shared a tent with Etienne. What if Etienne had decided to ravish Mathilde before Therri got the chance?

"No," Etienne said, "that's not why Girard sent her to us." He shared his reasoning with his friend.

Therri's cheeks cooled a bit, but he insisted, "But that doesn't mean that someone won't find out, and one of us will have to marry her just the same. I'm not going to do it, Etienne. And I know you've been attracted to her in the past, but are you sure you want to risk throwing your future away on a denier-less waif whose father, according to rumor, is under a cloud of shame?"

Etienne ignored the dull throb that always echoed in his breast whenever he thought about a future without Mathilde. He had almost kissed her again today. The pounding of his blood had warned him that if he indulged himself too many more times with embraces of "comfort", Girard might be justified to come roaring a demand of marriage.

Therri must have seen some of the struggle reflected in his face, for he asked abruptly, "It hasn't already gone that far, has it? I mean, while I've been up at Grantamur Castle, you and the Lady Mathilde haven't—"

Etienne hoped Therri could read his indignant outrage as easily as he had the desire that taunted him.

Therri cleared his throat repentantly. "No, of course you haven't. Not that I wouldn't have understood. We're none of us carved of stone, you know, and it's hard not to fantasize at least a little about what sort of figure might be hiding inside that shapeless tunic of hers. She does have curst fine legs, after all."

Etienne felt his hair bristle on the back of his neck. "You've been staring at her legs?"

"Not staring. But I couldn't help but notice, once you told me she was a girl."

Etienne choked down his irrational jealousy. Therri was besotted with Violette. He would forget about Mathilde's legs before the sun shifted another inch across the sky.

But Etienne wouldn't. Nor the misty violet of her eyes or her pert little tilt-tipped nose or her petal-soft lips that had let him taste of heaven . . .

"It's worse than I thought," Therri murmured. "You're in love with her."

Etienne realized he was gazing bemusedly at the horizon. Blazes! He was growing as dreamy as Mathilde.

"That's the real reason you don't want to send her away, isn't it?" Therri said.

Was it? Etienne had told himself that his only motive was to protect her. But he had not known she was in danger when he had first opened his eyes and recognized her angel's face hovering over him. Why had he not told Therri then? They had never kept secrets from one another before.

Because Therri was right. Etienne had known that Therri would insist that they send her away, and Etienne had not wanted to let her go.

He never wanted to let her go. But he knew that if he did not do so soon, the only man she would need protection from was himself.

"I know we can't keep hiding her this way," he said. "And however I feel about her, I also know that I can't marry her. I can't—I won't drag her or any woman from tent to tent and tournament to tournament while I try to scrape together enough coins to raise a family. I need to find a way to get her safely back to her father. But I made her a promise and before I send her away, I need to know that I'm going to be able to fulfill it. The trouble is—I require your help to do so."

Therri allowed his mount to take a few restless steps forward. Etienne nudged his horse to follow, but after a moment, Therri pulled up again.

"What is it you need?" he asked.

Etienne told him about Mathilde's father. Therri listened, frowning, but he did not interrupt until Etienne finished the story.

Then Therri shook his head. "I think we'll be chasing ghosts that don't exist, Etienne. If this fellow d'Amville had the ring, where else could he have gotten it but from her father?"

Etienne sighed. "I know. But I promised her I'd at least try to learn if d'Amville might somehow have planted the ring on her father. From what Mathilde says, there was some sort of grudge between the two men. The least I can do is ask some questions at court. Or rather, given my family's current state of disgrace, I have to find someone to ask them for me."

"I see," Therri said.

Their horses moved a few more feet in silence before Therri stopped again. Etienne watched his friend's face anxiously. Therri looked soberly reflective but not grim.

"Just where am I supposed to begin this wild goose chase?" he asked at last.

Etienne grinned, affection flooding through him along with relief. He had known he could count on Therri.

"I thought you could send a letter to Gunthar, ask him if he can compile a list for us of all the people who worked in or had access to the King's Wardrobe during the six months that Mathilde's father served there. That would at least give us a place to start."

"You're talking about the king's court thirty years ago. Gunthar would have been a child," Therri said of his brother-in-law.

"But he has connections. He will know men who may remember. And there must be ledgers of payments made to the king's staff. Perhaps he can compile some names from those." He saw the skepticism in Therri's face. "It can't hurt to ask him. But he won't do it for me. If you'll write the letter, I'll use my tournament winnings to pay for a messenger to cross the channel."

"Gunthar's not in England. He and Heléne are in Poitou. Something to do with your cousin Acelet."

Etienne's brows shot up. Acelet and the earl? To the best of Etienne's knowledge, his cousin had never met Gunthar, or Heléne, for that matter.

"Don't ask me what it is," Therri said. "I couldn't make heads or tails of it from Heléne's scribblings. She sounds a good deal more like herself, though. It went hard with her when she lost the child."

Therri paused, brooding over that memory. Etienne had grieved with him at the news, over a year ago now, for Heléne felt as much a sister to him as Therri did a brother.

"A messenger brought me a letter from her that day you went down to the river with Mathieu—I mean Mathilde," Therri continued after a moment. "I meant to let you read it, but it slipped my mind, what with Hermaline swooping down on our tent like a falcon after her prey. By the way, did you know she's hinting rather loudly up at the castle that she expects you to request her hand any day?"

Etienne winced. As he'd feared, a grain of attention was all Hermaline had required to believe that she had successfully sunk her talons into him. And the worst part was, that day he had sat with her at chess the thought had passed through his mind that trying to discourage her might not be worth it any more. If he could not spend his life with Mathilde, then why should he not at least fill its emptiness with Hermaline's land and gold? Perhaps her incessant chatter would eventually deafen him to the memory of Mathilde's wistful voice. Perhaps in the duties of the night, his arms would cease aching to hold Mathilde against his heart.

Therri spoke again, a little apologetically. "I didn't know if you'd want me to try to squelch the rumors she's spreading. The way you let her fawn over you that day by the river—I thought maybe you'd changed your mind about marrying her. If I'd known about Mathilde—"

"It wouldn't have mattered," Etienne said. "I can't have Mathilde. As for Hermaline—I don't know what I want any more. I suspect I won't be able to think clearly about it until Mathilde is safely back with her father." *And out of my life.*

"Then why don't you just send her home?" Therri asked. "It would remove her from our tent, appease Violette's suspicions, and restore some order to your brain." He softened his suggestion with a lopsided grin that hinted at more understanding of his friend's pain than his bracing words suggested.

Etienne sighed. It was time to stop making excuses just to keep her near him. "You're right. I should have done that at the first. She's afraid of d'Amville, that he will try to seize her and use her to avenge himself on her father. But I can hire her a guard with the ransoms I won in Vi's tournament. I think I'll go with her, though. Just to be sure her fears about d'Amville don't come true." He paused. "You'll write that letter to Gunthar?"

"I'll do it tonight. When will you leave with Mathilde?"

"I'll ride into town tomorrow and see if I can find some men for an escort. I don't imagine any of our comrades back there "—he jerked his head in the direction of the field of tents— "will be eager to leave until Violette has chosen a husband from among their ranks."

The familiar scowl settled back over Therri's brow. "I'd better get up to the castle, then, and see if I can't shoulder Marshal out of her sight before her choice alights on him. Although the way she's been smiling and sighing at him the last few days, I fear it may already be too late."

"Don't give up yet," Etienne said, trying to cheer him. "If she didn't care about you, she wouldn't be so incensed at the thought of Mathilde in your tent."

"Little good knowing that will do me if she marries Marshal in a fit of pique."

"It's been a sennight and she hasn't committed herself to Marshal yet. She's still hoping that somehow you'll prove all her doubts wrong."

"Aye," Therri said gloomily, "but how the devil I'm supposed to do that is what has me confounded."

Etienne rode slowly back to the tent. It was not yet midday. There was time to ride into town and begin his search for an escort for Mathilde. But he continued his unhurried progress towards the field of tents instead. One more day with her. One more night listening to the soft hum of her breathing, wondering what dreams caused her to sometimes murmur and sigh in the dark. Did she know how often he had waited for her to sleep her deepest, then reached down from his cot to sweep her cheek with a feather-soft touch?

This would be his last opportunity to caress her in the veils of the night, his desire to touch so much more safely checked by Therri's slumbering presence. The armed guard he would hire tomorrow would prevent even the small license of stroking her cheek as they journeyed to her father's.

He would accompany them, just in case d'Amville made an unexpected appearance. And it would give Etienne a chance to ask her father some questions. Perhaps the old man would remember some names that might be useful to Etienne's investigation.

Nay, Etienne did not care if her father recalled a single hour of his months on the Wardrobe staff. That was not why he wanted to accompany Mathilde, and neither, entirely, was a possible attack by d'Amville.

He wanted to squeeze every hour, every minute, every second of life that the heavens condescended to let them linger together, until he had wrung every last drop of joy from her companionship that he could.

The dark day of parting would come soon enough.

But he would not let it come today.

210

After indulging herself with a hearty bout of crying, Mathilde forced herself to dry her eyes. Her aching heart did not feel the least bit better in the aftermath of her tears, but she had made her decision. When Etienne lay deep in sleep tonight, she would unwind her ribbon ever so carefully from the hand where she had watched him furtively wrap it the last few nights, then she would steal away to meet Girard.

But if she were to leave and not look back, if she were to sever all ties beyond the most formal communication with Etienne, then she preferred to sever her ties to everyone who reminded her of him, as well. That included Therri. He had promised to mend the necklet he had broken in Grantamur Hall. But after his fearsome temper today, Mathilde preferred to take her necklet with her to her rendezvous with Girard. Her father would mend it for her when she returned home.

She slid the necklet from Therri's saddlebag and was on her knees, rolling it up in her pallet when Etienne's voice sounded behind her.

"Mathilde?"

She started guiltily and scrambled to her feet so fast that she stumbled over the pallet and fell across his cot.

He strode to her side and touched her arm as she pushed herself back up. "Are you hurt?"

"Nay, I'm fine. I—" Her breath snagged. He had as well have gripped her arm with hot tongs. Fire scorched down to her fingertips and up to her shoulder, then raged like a wildfire through her entire body. She struggled to drag air into lungs that felt as thick as if the conflagration had engulfed them with smoke. "I—j-just—tripped," she finally choked out.

He crouched in front of her, his fingers tightening on her arm. His eyes darkened, the way they had less than an hour ago when he had gazed so covetously at her lips. Only now he weighed her entire face. *'Tis not love,* she rebuked her leaping heart. *He desires me, but desire is not love.* She did not want to play the temptress. Yet she knew if he so much as leaned towards her now, she would sway to seek his mouth.

As if sensing the danger to them both, he shifted back on his heels. His grip on her gentled, then slid slowly down her arm until he found and lightly held her fingers. The fire still raged inside her, but ebbed enough with his subtle retreat to allow her to draw a easier breath.

"Lord Therri," she managed in a semi-normal voice. "Did you talk with him?"

"Aye." His voice sounded husky but controlled. "He has agreed to help you, Maude. And to let you stay another night. Perhaps two."

"And—and then?" Not that it mattered. She would be gone with Girard after tonight.

"Then . . . I will find some other way to protect you." He rose to his feet and drew her up with him. "Come."

He pulled her across the tent.

"Where are we going?"

"Outside."

Once in the open air, he released her hand and bade her sit on one of the stools beside the trestle table where he had played chess with Hermaline. He hesitated, then snagged the second stool with his ankle and pulled it across the ground next to hers.

"Talk to me, Maude," he said as he sat, clamping his hands on his knees.

"Talk? About what?"

"Anything. About your childhood. About your dreams. Just talk."

She wrinkled her brow. She did not think the autumn sun was hot enough to make his brain woozy, but it had only been a sennight since he had been ill with fever. Perhaps he had exerted himself too much by riding a horse so soon.

"Tell me about the jongleur," he said.

She cocked her head to one side. "The jongleur?"

"Aye, the one who sang to you in your father's hall. The one who told you the story of Prince Erec."

She hesitated. His hand left his knee to brush against her fingers, as though he meant to clasp them again, but at the last minute he checked himself. He darted a glance around the field. Most of the other knights were at the castle courting Violette, but a few of their squires lingered behind, drinking and exchanging jests outside their masters' tents or clustered in small groups tossing dice. Some of them glanced lazily at Etienne and Mathilde before returning to their game.

Suddenly Mathilde understood. He must have feared that inside the tent, desire might overwhelm him. But here, in the open, the squires' presence prevented him from acting rashly. She felt a stab of mingled bitterness and envy in her breast. Bitterness that desire should be all he felt for her. Envy that the faithful heart that restrained him from surrendering to that base passion beat for another woman.

He wanted her to distract him, to distract them both from the temptations raging inside them.

He was wise, as well as faithful.

She drew a steadying breath, then told him about the young jongleur, of his handsome face and dulcet voice, the lithe movement of his fingers across the harp strings, the faraway expression that hazed his eyes as he sang of the valiant knights of King Arthur's court.

"Prince Erec," Etienne said when she paused. "Tell me the story of Prince Erec."

She searched his gaze, fearful of finding laughter there, mocking, however gently, her attachment to the beloved tale. But no teasing light gleamed. Only that simmering desire mingled with a kind of hollow sadness.

"Erec was the son and heir of the king of Estre-Gales and a knight of King Arthur's court," she began. "No man was more handsome and valiant than he, nor more accomplished in deeds of chivalry. With his prowess and courage he won the hand of Enide, a lady renowned as greatly for her generosity and wisdom as for her beauty. Erec loved Enide with such an all-consuming passion that after their marriage he spent every moment, waking and sleeping, at her side. He completely forsook his former pursuits and cared no more for arms or tourneyings."

"His bride was fortunate," Etienne murmured, "to marry a man of such wealth that he could abandon practicality to follow the dictates of his heart."

"Nay," Mathilde said, "his bride soon became most miserable because the other knights mocked Erec and called him a recreant knight. She blamed herself for ruining his honor and reputation. One day Erec overheard her lamenting. He agreed that the rebukes laid against him were just. So he commanded Enide to don her most beautiful gown and immediately they set off to restore honor to his name by fresh deeds of chivalry."

"I suppose in this poet's fiction, the Lady Enide never suffered a moment's discomfort during their grand adventure," Etienne said with a frown. "A prince and his lady would surely have been accompanied by a multitude of servants to attend to their every command. No doubt they even traveled with their feather bed."

Mathilde shook her head. "Erec refused all attendants except his wife and at night, the two of them slept together on the forest floor."

She envisioned herself lying in a bed of leaves, safely clasped in the arms of the man she loved, their hearts beating as one in the silence of the trees. With a tiny stab in her breast, she pushed the image away. Those arms, that heart could never be hers.

"Alas," she said, her voice slightly stifled, "'twas not as romantic for Enide as it sounds."

"No," Etienne said roughly, capturing Mathilde's gaze firmly with his own, "it would not be."

Mathilde lifted her chin. "It would have been romantic, had Erec not taken it into his head that he must test poor Enide's loyalty and love. He harshly forbade her to speak along their journey, threatening her with the most dire punishments if she defied his command. Yet again and again, when she saw danger approaching, she cried out a warning to Erec. Each time he defeated the threat, three knights, and then five, and then a wicked count who wished to murder Erec and make Enide his mistress. Each time Erec afterwards rebuked poor Enide, yet all the while, in his heart he silently praised her. Repeatedly she proved that she cared more for Erec's safety than for his anger. Sooner would she have him alive and hating her, than risk his life through fear and blind obedience. And so in the end, Erec loved her more than he had before and swore ever after that he should be hers to command."

Mathilde sighed, remembering the shiveringly beautiful chord the jongleur had struck at the close of this poignant scene.

But Etienne looked surprised. "This is the hero you admire so? A man who rebukes and threatens the woman he loves and subjects her to tests that place her in danger at the hands of a covetous count?"

"He did not anticipate running into a covetous count," she said defensively. "As soon as Erec saw Enide's danger, he slew her would-be ravisher. Erec rode off with her cradled in his arms, and as soon as they were safe, he held her and comforted her and kissed her again and again. And each time Erec rebuked her, the jongleur sang of the love Erec concealed in his heart for his beloved Enide. In the end, their love was greater for the trials they had borne together."

She glanced down at where her hands lay clasped together in her lap. Etienne did not speak again for several minutes. When he did, he spoke her name softly.

"Maude."

His voice was not golden, the way she had imagined Erec's to be, or melodious like the jongleur's, or ringingly beautiful as Therri's had once seemed to fall on her ears. But it's tenderness made her heart quiver and wrapped her in blankets of painful longing.

"I pray one day you find your prince. And I hope when you do, that he has the consummate wisdom to trust from the first the loyalty that shines in your eyes and the wealth to devote his life to making your every dream come true."

Her lip trembled. *I have found my prince,* she wanted to cry. *I found you — too late.* Her hands blurred. Ah saints, she would not weep in front of him!

"Please," she whispered, "may I go back inside the tent?"

The way his own hands clenched, she knew he wanted to touch her. She knew it, because his knuckles were as white as her own.

"Go," he said softly.

She waited until she was out of his sight to cover her face and give way to her silent tears.

Fourteen

Mathilde had never conceived that love could hurt so much. The jongleur had sung of broken hearts, of unrequited affections, of torment and despair. His words had swirled her into endless, blissful hopes that someday, some man might suffer such exquisite agonies over her. She had dreamed of some handsome knight weeping at her feet, imploring her forgiveness, vowing to obtain for her the stars, if she would only so much as smile on him. It had all been so . . . romantic.

But there was nothing romantic about the tears streaming now from her eyes, or this piercing pain in her breast, so persistent, so racking that she longed to cry out.

But that would wake him. The hero who would forever stand at the center of a world she could never share with him. The man she had not even known she loved until she realized that she must leave him.

Etienne.

She sat up in the darkness, wiping away her tears with one hand while she gripped her mother's necklet with the other. The first gesture was useless. More tears splashed forth like a summer's rain. Her throat burned with smothered sobs.

Across the tent, Therri snored softly. From the cot beside her, Etienne's breathing sounded steady and deep. It was time. Time to leave her dreams behind her. Time to say good-bye.

She rolled onto her knees, crouching next to the cot in the dark. She had watched Etienne wrap the ribbon around his hand before he lay down to sleep, as he had each night before. He lay on his side, his hand reclining near his shadowed face. Gently, silently, she pulled at one end of the ribbon. He had wound it too securely around his palm. She set down the necklet and, breath suspended lest she wake him, used both hands to ease the ribbon free inch by cautious inch.

Etienne's breathing never altered. His body did not so much as twitch. The ribbon at last slid free. But Mathilde remained kneeling beside the cot. Could she leave him without touching his curls one more time? Could she leave without one last, tiny taste of him?

She caressed his hair ever so softly and instantly found her forefinger entwined in a silken loop. She had dreamed of the day when she could plunge both hands with abandon into his lush mass of coils. But they would never be hers to fondle now. She withdrew her hand and scrubbed at the tears on her face. Now for a final, stolen kiss. Surely he would not begrudge her that?

A deft peck on his cheek would be safest, she told herself. She leaned forward, hesitated, then shifted until she found the shadowed corner of his mouth. A quick, darting kiss that he would never feel . . .

Nay. Her lips lingered, lightly but stubbornly, savoring the salty tang of his mouth. Or perhaps the salt was from the tears that fell from her eyes in soft splashes on his face.

Only the fear of waking him finally wrenched her away.

"I love you."

The whisper slipped out before her hand could catch it at her lips. Thank heaven he slept! She must leave before she blurted out even more, before the temptation to shower his face with kisses overwhelmed her.

She gathered up the necklet with the ribbon, drew on her cloak, and slid quickly but silently from the tent.

Etienne pressed a hand to his cheek, as though he would trap her tears against his face. The corner of his mouth glowed warm from the touch of her lips. His heart pounded in the dark, echoing the words he had both yearned for and dreaded ever hearing her speak.

"I love you too, my little dreamer," he whispered. "But just what mischief are you up to now?"

He swallowed the guilty pleasure he had known as she caressed his hair and kissed him. It had taken every shred of will he possessed not to turn his mouth to hers. Hot desire still coursed through him, but curiosity over why she had taken the ribbon and fear that she was about to tumble into some sort danger surged more strongly still. He rose from the cot, dressed quickly in the dark, reached for his sword and followed stealthily in her footsteps.

The banner snapped smartly in the night breeze, alternately furling and unfurling the outlines of a charging boar. At least, Mathilde hoped it was a boar. It was difficult to be sure of the image with only a pale half-moon and a few stars defiantly dodging black cloud patches in the sky to light her view. Girard had said the banner stood beside a tent near the edge of the woods on the west side of the field. She had meant to reassure herself of the image before now, but Etienne had kept her so close that she had not had the chance. She waited for another gust of wind, then strained her gaze in the pale moonlight.

A boar, tusks curling, head down, foreleg pawing the ground . . . She was sure of it, even in the dim light. She turned and walked to the nearby trees. One of these must have a triangular stone at its base. She searched until she found the half-grown beech tree Girard had told her to look for, but before she could find the stone he'd described, the moon darted behind a cloud. She knelt, the dry autumn grass crackling softly, and probed the earth until she found the three-sided stone to the side of the tree. Three inches up in the bark . . . just as Girard promised, he had carved her a sign. A line, parallel to the ground. Two shorter lines at one end, each slanting backwards . . . An arrow? Pointing a southeasterly direction into the forest.

She shivered and pulled her cloak closer around her. How would she avoid becoming lost if she ventured into the forest depths? But Girard would not have left her to wander blindly about. He must surely be waiting just within, concealed amidst the trees. Still, she would have felt much braver had she been entering with her hand clasped against Etienne's strong palm.

She pushed the thought away, drew a deep breath, then turned herself the direction the arrow pointed and stepped into the trees.

She moved cautiously forward with one hand extended before her to help feel her way in the dark. Her other hand clutched the necklet and ribbon as if they could form a shield for her. Absurd, of course. What protection would such objects prove against some hungry animal . . . or bestial human?

Her shivers became a shudder. Nay, Girard would call to her any minute now. Unless, of course, she had inadvertently shifted in her path and was wandering in the wrong direction.

A rustling sound. She froze. "G-Girard?"

Silence. It must have been some forest creature. *A rabbit. Pray heaven, let it be a rabbit!* She forced her feet to move once more, but the tremors wove with increasing frequency through her body.

"Uuuhhh . . ."

The moan, muffled and weak, nearly made Mathilde jump out of her skin. She stifled a squeal, but a lump as large as a fist surged up and lodged, pulsing, in her throat. Who—or what—lay groaning in these woods? She leaned against a nearby tree, trying to steady her knees.

"G-Girard?" she called more loudly. "Costane? If you are there, please answer me!"

Another heartbeat of silence. Then another groan, fainter and more guttural than before. She *must* go forward. What if someone were hurt and needed help?

She pushed herself away from the tree and took a few trembling steps forward, then stopped as her foot struck against something that nearly made her trip. She hunched down and ran her hands over a fallen tree branch in her path. Thick and solid, but not too heavy. She picked it up and shifted it back against her shoulder. The makeshift club comforted her slightly.

"Where are you?" she called, moving forward again. "You must make another sound if you want me to find and help you—"

Something slithered directly in front of her feet. Mathilde gasped, then gave an earsplitting shriek when the creature rose up and clamped itself about her ankle.

She swung her club up over her head, preparing to bring it down upon the beast with all her might.

"Til—lot . . ."

"*G-Girard?*" The club dropped backwards out of her suddenly nerveless hands. She fell to her knees beside her brother's prone body as his hand fell away from her ankle. "Girard!"

He seemed to be lying face down on the forest floor. With an effort, she managed to roll him over and lift his head into her lap. His beard felt moist and sticky. The front of his tunic was wet.

"Girard, what happened?"

"Til . . . Tillot." The word scraped out of his throat. "Go . . . back. Take the . . . ribbon . . . and go . . . back . . ."

The ribbon. She had dropped it and the necklet with the club. But those trinkets meant nothing to her now. "Girard, what happened?" she repeated more frantically. "Who did this to you—"

A beefy arm wrapped around her waist and jerked her away from her brother. A hand clamped over her mouth, the palm, damp, plump, but strong, stifling her scream. The arm trapped her against a body padded with rolls of quivering fat. Her captor reeked of rank perspiration.

Mathilde writhed with terror and revulsion.

"Come now," a voice huffed into her ear, "be still and you won't get hurt. Just tell me what you've done with the ribbon."

Mathilde continued to strain wildly against his hold. His already moist hand slickened with sweat as he struggled to maintain his grasp over her mouth. The taste of his wet flesh sickened her as she gradually inched her lips apart beneath his slippery hold.

"I don't want to hurt you," he panted, "but if you don't quiet down I'm going to have to—"

Mathilde sank her teeth into the fleshy part of his palm.

Her captor howled. Mathilde wrenched her mouth away from his slackened hold and screamed.

Something whizzed past Etienne's face in the dark and landed with a *twang* in the tree just behind him. Adrenaline pumped with irritation through his veins. What sort of madman went hunting in the middle of a cloudy night? He turned and plucked the still quivering arrow-bolt from where it had embedded in the bark. He opened his mouth to shout an objection to being mistaken for some sort of wild game, but a second arrow came soaring, this one so close that he felt it brush his hair. Either the marksman was being incredibly lucky with the accuracy of his shots in the dark or he had uncanny eyesight. In which case, he must know that Etienne was not a deer or a boar, but a man.

The third time, he heard the click of the crossbow's release. He dove for the ground just as a third bolt whirred above him. He had an unpleasant feeling that had he not dodged, this bolt would have found its target straight through the center of his forehead.

His attacker had already demonstrated a grim determination. A fourth assault was certain. But it took time to reload a crossbow, and the direction of the arrows had betrayed his attacker's position. Etienne scrambled up. Such precision shooting in the dark could not have been accomplished from any great distance. He lunged forward, convinced that he would find his attacker reloading his weapon behind the first tree in his path.

Etienne moved quickly, but not quickly enough. A shadow surged up as he reached the tree. Etienne saw the dark lines of a crossbow leveled at his breast. But the bowman had apparently not expected to find his target confronting him so directly. A split-second's startled hesitation enabled Etienne to make a grab for the weapon. He forced the crossbow up, heard the click of release and felt a sear against his temple.

He swore at the pain, but tried to wrestle the crossbow away. The bowman clung tenaciously to his weapon. Etienne had half-expected to find himself struggling with the portly Chesnei—had not Mathilde guessed him to be the crossbowman who had shot Etienne in the mêlée?—but this man was small, with a lean, wiry strength. Etienne used the advantage of his greater height and own well-honed muscles to slam his assailant against the tree. After a brief, fierce tussle, Etienne tore the bow free.

His brow blazed where the arrow had struck it, but he flung the crossbow away, then closed a fist on the front of the bowman's tunic and dragged him nose to nose, trying to discern his face in the dark.

"Who the devil are you," Etienne demanded, "and why did you attack me—"

An air-splitting shriek sliced off his words. His head jerked towards the sound.

"Mathilde?" he shouted.

The bowman made a sharp move to break free, but Etienne restrained him with another shove against the tree.

"Ah, no. If you know where she is—if you have a hand in whatever threatens her—" He heard the furious shaking of his own voice.

The bowman did not speak. Each moment they stood here in confrontation, Mathilde's danger was surely increasing. Etienne drew his sword and released his hold on the bowman so that he could touch the point of his blade to the bowman's throat.

"You're going to take me to her. *Now*."

The bowman did not move. Etienne cursed him and pressed his blade a little closer to the man's flesh.

"Etienne? Mathilde?"

Etienne turned his head slightly, but kept his sword firmly in its warning position. "Therri?" he answered the calling voice. "Over here!"

A light appeared as his friend came crashing through the trees. Therri had brought a torch.

"I heard a scream," Therri panted.

"Mathilde is in trouble."

"I feared as much. I woke up and saw you leaving the tent with your sword. Mathilde was gone. I thought— What the devil happened to your head?"

Etienne's free hand swiped at the blood on his cheek. How badly was his wound gushing? His temple pulsed fiercely, but he could not let the pain muddle him now.

"It's nothing," he said curtly. "We've got to find Mathilde. And this fellow knows where she is."

He turned back to the bowman—and met the unblinking stare of Girard de Riavelle's squire.

Etienne ignored the inexplicable repugnance that always wove through him at the sight of this colorless, blank-expressioned little man. "Where is she?" he repeated. "Take me to her, or so help me, I swear I'll—"

Another scream, so piercing that it made Etienne flinch. But if she had freedom to scream, then perhaps she had power to call her direction. He grabbed the taciturn squire and flung him at Therri.

"Hold onto him," Etienne said, then shouted, "Mathilde! Where are you?"

"*Etienne?* Help me! He's killed Girard and—"

Silence.

Ah, Saints! Someone was with her. Someone who did not want to be found.

"This way."

Etienne turned at the squire's flat voice. The squire tried to pull away from Therri's grasp, but Therri jerked him back.

"If my master is dead, they'll kill her, too," the squire said, his voice as expressionless as if they discussed a bland summer's day.

Etienne hesitated only an instant, then gave a curt nod. Therri released the squire. The squire bent to retrieve his crossbow, but Etienne swooped the point of his sword between the man's hand and the weapon.

"We may need it, Etienne," Therri said.

He was right.

"Take it," Etienne snapped at the squire. "But my sword will be at your back."

The squire picked up his crossbow and led the way through the trees.

Mathilde clawed in vain at the lumpish hands cutting off her air. Her palms scraped on the faceted rings on the thickset fingers.

"I warned you to be quiet." The voice reverberated almost apologetically against the roar that was rapidly filling her ears. "My uncle wants you alive, but I can't have you screaming again. There, now, just faint away, then I'll search you for the ribbon." The voice paused, then added mournfully, "Pity you're not that plump morsel, Hermaline. I'd enjoy searching her for your brother's trinket."

Her hands gave one last, helpless tug at his choking hold. Her world, already black with the night, swirled towards oblivion.

A jolt. A grunt, and the choking hold freed. Consciousness flickered back, though her knees collapsed and she felt herself falling. She sprawled on the forest floor. But she could breathe . . . and she could see. Where was the light coming from?

"Curse you! You might have struck Mathilde!"

"Let me go. He's getting away."

"You clipped him," a third voice chimed. "He won't get far, I'll wager, not with that bolt in his arm."

She lifted her head from the dry grass and twigs beneath her cheek. Three men danced in an unsteady haze. Torchlight reflected brilliantly off the pale gold locks of the man who held the torch. Her gaze glided past him to the struggle taking place between a smaller man and one with a tumble of sooty curls.

"Etienne?" she croaked.

Etienne froze, then whirled towards her. The smaller man—she recognized Costane—broke from his grasp and ran into the trees.

Etienne let him go. Two strides brought him to Mathilde's side. He dropped to his knees beside her, scooped her into his arms, and rocked her against his breast.

"Saints, Maude! Are you hurt?"

She heard the fear in his voice and shook her head. Her throat ached where her captor had crushed it, but now that her breath came without a struggle . . . now that Etienne cradled her so close that she could hear the comforting thud of his heart . . . the hurt and fear ebbed away.

She shifted her head to gaze up into his beloved face—and saw his cheek smeared with blood, with more oozing from beneath the tangled curls at his brow.

"Etienne! Oh, *you* are the one who is hurt!"

"Nay, 'tis nothing."

She ignored his dismissal and pushed back his hair. The gash in his right temple foamed with thick, red blood.

"Etienne," Therri called.

Mathilde turned her head and saw Therri kneeling beside Girard.

The horror of memory rushed back, flooding out her concern for Etienne with fresh panic for her brother. She pulled away from Etienne and crawled frantically the short distance to Girard.

"Oh!" She gasped and covered her mouth with her hands. A long, brutal slice down his cheek had spilled blood into his beard, while the large, dark stain on the breast of his tunic stood evidence of a savage death blow.

Nay, not dead. Not quite yet.

"He's asking for you," Therri said. He drew her gently closer to Girard.

Mathilde tried not to shudder. But so much blood, her brother's slashed face . . .

She felt fingers pressing her shoulder. Etienne. She steadied herself without glancing at him and bent close to her brother.

"I'm here, Girard." She gently lifted his head into her lap once more. His gashed face blurred. "Don't die," she whispered through her tears. "Girard, please don't die."

His breath came in an eerie rattle. "Til-lot." Her name gurgled through his throat, as though it were filled with some sort of liquid.

Somehow, he pushed out the rest of the words. "The . . . ribbon. You must . . . must see . . . that it gets . . . to Ma . . ." He broke off, then dragged in a scraping breath. "To Mar . . ."

He started to choke.

"Girard!"

The fingers on her shoulder tightened. Etienne crouched beside her now.

Girard somehow dragged in another chestful of air, then exhaled in a hiss. ". . . shhh . . ." Suddenly, with a surge of unexpected strength, his upper body rose and one of his hands closed on the front of Mathilde's tunic. "Tillot! Swear it . . . to me!"

She shrank, alarmed and confused.

"Swear it to me!" he almost shouted. "Tillot, I can't see you. You must swear—"

His eyes stared straight into her face, but they had a frightening, glassy cast in the torchlight. "I swear. Girard, I swear I'll take the ribbon to—to—" Who's name had he been trying to speak?

He groaned and twisted as though some racking pain had gripped him.

"Girard!"

Another rattle, this one more hideous than before. He collapsed backwards and lay staring at the black forest sky. Staring and still.

"Girard!"

"Maude." Etienne pulled her into his arms. "Maude, he's gone."

"No!" She struck at Etienne in anger and grief. "He c-can't be—" A sob burst from her throat. Her fists thumped dully against his chest, then flattened, then suddenly curled into the cloth of his tunic. Anger fled, overwhelmed by grief. "Oh, Etienne, he c-can't be—"

"Dead," a voice finished her thought on a growl from behind them. "What a pity that your brother gave his life for a such failed cause."

Fifteen

Hazel eyes glittered in the torchlight with a hint of gold-flecked malevolence. Mathilde gaped through her tears at the looming, grey-haired intruder. Through his fingers trailed her brother's silken ribbon and her mother's sapphire necklet.

"He had to die, poppet," the man growled. He leaned on a cane carved of dark wood. "His death was sealed, even before I owed him for this." He tapped his thigh with the fist that gripped the cane.

Mathilde had a sudden, vivid memory of Girard loosing Costane's arrow bolt into this man's leg.

"Aye," he continued, "else how should you and I ever lay legitimate claim to your father's title? My final victory against Aymor. His barony — and you. For that, your brother had to die. My nephew attacked him here in these woods, but he was not man enough to strike the death blow. That pleasure he left to me."

She shrank in Etienne's embrace. This man had called her "poppet". No. Oh, pray heaven, *no!* It could *not* be him!

"D'Amville?" Etienne spoke the name grimly, his arms tightening around her.

The intruder looked surprised. "You know me?"

"I know *of* you. You're a . . . friend —" Mathilde heard the sarcastic slur in Etienne's voice " — of de Coulonces and d'Yquebeuf. The three of you are allied in a conspiracy with your nephew Chesnei to accuse William Marshal of *lèse majesté* — treason."

228

She followed Etienne's brief exchange of glances with Therri and saw the way Therri started at Etienne's words.

"Ah." The cool acknowledgment rumbled low from the man with the cane. "My nephew told me there had been an eavesdropper, but none of them quite caught your face. Pity I didn't kill you in the mêlée or that my nephew's aim was not more lethal. Never mind. I shall finish the deed before I leave these woods. Three men, slaughtered by outlaws, the lady carried off to who knows what fiendish fate?" His grin glinted evilly.

Etienne's arms tensed so hard about Mathilde that she felt his muscles tremble. Then abruptly, he released her and rose to his feet, drawing his sword.

Therri's sword immediately rang free, too. "You're outnumbered, d'Amville," Therri said.

The man laughed. "Two to one. And me with this wound in my thigh." With his free, beribboned hand, he pulled forth his own sword. "But I could still kill you both with one hand bound behind my back—or fisted on this cane. Shall I demonstrate? Which of you would like to die first?"

He tossed his glance from Therri to Etienne. Etienne stood the nearest to him. He raised his blade, necklet and ribbon dangling from his fingers.

"No!" Mathilde scrambled to her feet. She had thought it most romantic in the ballad when the faithful Enide had nursed her valiant Erec back to health after he had fainted from wounds incurred in her defense. But horrible reality had replaced her dreams. Girard was dead, his body slashed and bloody. And Etienne, however noble and brave he was, would be just as dead if d'Amville's blade landed in his chest.

D'Amville.

"It can't be you." Her voice cracked in pleaful dread. "You are nothing like him."

Etienne's arm stole around her shoulders.

The man with the cane turned his gold-glinting eyes on her. "And how is it I differ from your former beloved?"

"His—his hair was a reddish chestnut," she faltered.

The man shook his head so that his long, grey hair flopped about his shoulders. "The shock of death plays havoc with the body, poppet."

Mathilde shrank against Etienne's side. How would he know that endearment unless he . . . "And—and his voice was soft and melodious," she rushed on, determined to prove him an impostor. "Smooth, like honey."

"What, you do not care for my newly ragged tones?" he rasped. Something cold and deadly laced the gravely words. "Blame your father, poppet. I know *I* blame him—for this."

He reached up suddenly and jerked down the knot of the mantle at his throat. The torchlight gleamed red against a jagged scar that slashed an ugly, puckered line in his flesh from just below his left ear across his throat to the right side of his collar bone.

Therri had been slowly shifting forward, but he froze at the sight and muttered an oath.

Etienne's arm fell from Mathilde's shoulders. "Are you saying that Lord Aymor—"

"No!" Mathilde cried. "My father would never—"

"—cut a man's throat?" d'Amville finished harshly. "Or abandon him in the forest to die? But I didn't die, poppet. And I shall have my revenge. For Caterine . . . and for this." He pushed the knot of the mantle back up, veiling the brutal scar. "Now come. You and I have marriage vows to exchange . . . as soon as I have concluded my business here."

"You'll touch her over my dead body, d'Amville." Etienne raised his sword, but Mathilde saw the blade waver in the torchlight. Blood dripped from the wound beneath his curls. He could not be fully recovered of the injury to his shoulder, either.

Despite the cane, d'Amville moved with swiftness as he swung his own sword into the air and advanced. "Your death is the idea, stripling."

"No!" Mathilde sprang in front of Etienne. "Sir Alun, put your sword away and I will—"

Etienne swore. "Blazes, Maude, get out of the way!" His hand clamped on her shoulder.

Too late. D'Amville leveled the point of his blade at her throat. Her brother's ribbon, draped with the necklet through his sword hand, waved innocently on the breeze.

"Throw down your weapon, de Brielle. Your friend, too."

"You won't kill her," Etienne said, but Mathilde heard the breathlessness in his voice. "You need her for your revenge."

"Aye, and I would prefer her alive, but if you do not take your hand off her shoulder and do as I say, I will satisfy myself by carrying her dead body back to her father." D'Amville pressed the point closer to her flesh.

Mathilde shrank against Etienne's chest and felt the cold steel follow her.

"Drop it," d'Amville growled, "or I'll sever more than just her vocal cords."

Mathilde heard the soft thump of Etienne's sword as it hit the ground.

"And your friend."

"Therri—"

"It's already done," Therri answered, his voice taut with anger.

"Kick them away. Both of you," d'Amville said.

Etienne and Therri obeyed.

"Now then, poppet." D'Amville tilted up her chin with his blade and slowly nudged her away from her position in front of Etienne.

"Let them go," she pled. "I'll go with you. There's no need to kill them." To protect Etienne and Therri, she would leave these woods with d'Amville, the man who hated her father, who gazed at her with such sizzling, vengeful anticipation . . .

"They will try to stop us, poppet. I cannot have that."

"They won't follow us. Etienne, promise me!"

"Nay, look at the way his eyes flame at me," d'Amville said. "He will never speak the pledge you ask. Not that it would matter if he did. He has soiled you. As Aymor soiled Caterine. I thought better of you, poppet. I might have been gentle with you on our wedding night, had you come to me an innocent. But now you have sported with *him*." He jerked his head towards Etienne. "You are nothing but a harlot, like Caterine was. And I know how to deal with harlots."

His gaze raked her, stripped her, leaving her feeling as exposed and shamed as if his hands had followed his gaze. Instinctively, she crossed her arms over her chest and gave a muffled sob. Slowly, chillingly, d'Amville traced the point of his blade from her chin to the hollow of her throat. The steel paused. Then drifted further downward until it tugged at the neck of her tunic. This time, despite herself, her sob broke free.

"I've not touched her, d'Amville," Etienne said sharply. "And neither has my friend. Don't spoil her for your wedding night."

"Liar," d'Amville spat. "Aymor lied too, when I confronted him about Caterine. Why did you not simply give me this ribbon in the mêlée? Why did you cling so tenaciously to it, even with my nephew's arrow bolt in your shoulder? Because you thought it was hers, a symbol of her wanton passion for you, as Caterine's twin sapphires symbolized her treacherous passion for Aymor." The necklet trembled with the sword in his hand, its single blue jewel winking in the torchlight. "And you expect me to believe that you have not satisfied that passion while she's been tucked away in your tent in this absurd squire's garb?"

"That's just the point," Etienne said swiftly. "I didn't recognize her as a woman until this morning. She's been mostly in Therri's company while I recovered of my wound, and Therri did not know her face. She remains as virtuous as the day she was born."

"Well, now, we shall have to put that to the test." D'Amville used his blade to nudge her arms from their protective shield across her breast.

A footstep crunched.

"Hold, de Brielle!" The blade swooped back up to her throat. "Tell your friend to back off, too."

Mathilde cast a desperate glance at Etienne, who had taken a hasty step closer to her and d'Amville. She saw him freeze, then make a frustrated motion at Therri, who had also shifted further forward. Therri moved back, but Etienne stubbornly maintained the ground he'd gained.

D'Amville ignored him, confident in his security as long as his sword remained leveled at Mathilde. "Aye, poppet, you will be mine, soon. Mine, as your mother should have been. I swore that Aymor would suffer for taking her from me. I thought I could punish him and satisfy my hatred by stripping him of all he possessed, his lands, his castles, his honor . . . even Caterine's dagger, the one with the matching stone to this necklet, the gift she pledged with her own lips to grant me on our wedding day. She gave it instead to her lover, but I reclaimed it . . ." his mouth curved up in a triumphant grimace ". . . the day I claimed you."

"My father's dagger," she said, numb with fear, for herself, for Etienne . . . "The one he always wore, with the sapphire in its pommel. He stopped wearing it after you and I were betrothed. He said he'd lost it . . ."

"Nay, poppet. I took it from Aymor when I demanded your hand. Just slid it out of his sheath while he stood cursing me, but not daring to refuse me either dagger or daughter."

"If Lord Aymor has wronged you," Etienne said sharply, "then settle your quarrel with him. Mathilde has done nothing to you. Let her go."

"Ah, but my vengeance on Aymor will not be complete without her." The gold flecks in his eyes leapt eerily at her. "I saw the way Aymor watched you as you grew, poppet. You, more than these twin baubles of necklet and dagger, more even than your pathetic brother, were the true symbol of Aymor and Caterine's love. Caterine gave her life to bear you. Aymor's precious daughter. Born with Caterine's winsome smile and dreamy, violet eyes. It is Caterine he sees when he looks at you. But this time it is *I* who will possess you. This time, Caterine, it is *my* name . . . and my children . . . you will bear."

With a shock, Mathilde understood the significance of his glittering eyes. D'Amville, the man around whom she had woven her first girlhood dreams of love, the man who had betrayed her youthful trust — was mad.

"I am not my mother," she whispered. "I am not Caterine."

"You will be," he rasped. "And after I have finished punishing your harlot's heart, then I will make you love me. You *will* love me, as you did before."

Abruptly, his sword hissed away from her throat in a sideways arc. Mathilde did not realize d'Amville had dropped his cane until she saw both his hands on the sword hilt and the point of the blade poised at Etienne's breast.

"But *you* must die," d'Amville growled. "I don't believe you, you see. You knew who she was before this morn. She was with you when my nephew asked you for the ribbon. I stood a safe distance away while you conversed. While you toyed with Chesnei, I watched your squire. I knew her then. As you did. Aye, this fire in your eyes betrays you. You love her. Aymor loved her, and I made the mistake of letting him live to take her from me. But I will not repeat that mistake with you."

The sword swept up over d'Amville's head, preparing to descend on Etienne's breast.

"No!" Mathilde screamed

But Etienne's voice snapped across her cry. "Fine." He flung out his arms, baring his breast for the thrust. "Kill me then. Kill me, like the coward you are."

"Etienne!" she gasped. Had he lost his mind, too?

"No man calls me a coward!" d'Amville roared with sudden fury. The blade over his head trembled.

"*I* call you one!" Etienne shouted. "Striking down an unarmed man? That is the act of a craven. No wonder Caterine scorned you."

D'Amville bellowed a curse. He stepped back abruptly, then kicked Etienne's sword so that it spun to Etienne's feet.

"Pick it up," d'Amville barked. "I'll kill you anyway, and then I'll kill your friend." He jerked his head at Therri.

Etienne reached down and straightened with the sword in his hand. But not before Mathilde caught the way he shifted his feet to brace his balance. The trickle of blood down his face looked like it had slowed, but what if the graze had blurred his vision? What if his movements proved too sluggish to ward off d'Amville's blows?

D'Amville lunged. Steel clashed together as Etienne parried. Sparks exploded in the dark.

Therri regained his own sword, then thrust the torch into Mathilde's hands and turned to watch for an opening to aid Etienne.

D'Amville and Etienne circled, then fell together again. Their blades slashed the air, ringing and scraping against each other in blow after explosive blow. Although d'Amville limped slightly, his leg did not seem to slow him. But Mathilde saw Etienne sway. He blocked a thrust of d'Amville's sword, but the next strike stumbled him backwards. Mathilde watched with horror as his boots staggered just short of Girard's body.

"Someone's coming!" Therri shouted.

Hoofbeats. Mathilde turned towards the sound, then whirled back as a shout of victory rasped through d'Amville's scarred throat.

Etienne was on one knee beside Girard's body—and his sword was gone.

"Now, Aymor," d'Amville roared, "you shall die and Caterine shall be mine."

Mathilde screamed as d'Amville's sword sliced downward.

The same instant, Etienne's hand flashed in the torchlight and came up with a thick tree branch. Mathilde's club! Etienne whacked it full force into d'Amville's thigh.

D'Amville's injured thigh.

The blow to his wound set d'Amville howling. He lost his balance, his sword slicing the ground off center of his target before he crumpled to the ground. Etienne sprang unsteadily to his feet and kicked the sword out of d'Amville's hand.

Mathilde ran to Etienne as he stepped away from d'Amville. She threw herself against his chest, only just avoiding singeing his hair with the torch. Etienne took it out of her hand and held it out at a safer distance.

"Clumsy of me," he muttered into her hair. "I tripped over this stick. Thank the saints for that lame leg of his."

She wiped away the blood from his face, but before she could answer, four horsemen burst into view.

"Kill them!" d'Amville shouted. Still clutching his leg, he tried to roll to his knees. "Kill the men, but leave the girl to me!"

One of the horsemen tried to ride Therri down, but Therri dodged and swung round to block his attacker's sword.

"Get behind me," Etienne ordered Mathilde.

He thrust the torch back into her hands and shoved her into place. Therri's blows and parries whirred through the air. Etienne replaced her club with his recovered sword and launched into the battle. But his movements were slower than Therri's and during one brief lull, she caught the furtive way he rubbed at his eyes.

She picked up the club he had dropped. Perhaps she could deflect one of his opponents. That one. The corpulent one with the perspiration still streaming down his fat cheeks and a makeshift bandage wrapped around his arm. *Chesnei.*

She started towards him, but someone grabbed her from behind.

"Nay, poppet, you must not risk your fair neck amid the fray."

Mathilde twisted in d'Amville's grasp. He was back on his feet but she felt him stagger, still unsteady on his undoubtedly throbbing thigh. But despite her struggles, his clasp about her waist remained strong. She screamed. Not in fear this time, but in rage. Rage for her brother's death. Rage for how near he had come to killing Etienne. Rage for his threats against her father and his slurs on her mother.

She could not break free. Perhaps he needed some incentive to release her.

She threw down the torch at their feet. Flames crackled and leapt, fanned by the dry, autumn grass and the night's breeze. D'Amville flinched away from the surging blaze. Mathilde jerked free of his slackened hold, but she didn't run. She turned, furious, and thwacked the club into d'Amville's shoulder.

"Murderer!" she screamed.

"Maude!"

She heard Etienne's frantic shout. The flames licked after them as she hit d'Amville again and again, beating him back so far that he threatened to trod on Girard's corpse.

"No!" She thwacked the club into his leg, just as Etienne had. D'Amville dropped to the ground with another howl of pain.

"Maude, stop." Etienne grabbed her and pulled her away from both d'Amville and the flames. "Here, mount up and—"

She twisted out of his hands just short of the horse he sought to push her up on. "I can't go without the ribbon. I promised Girard."

"Maude!"

She ran back to d'Amville. He had dropped the necklet near Girard's body, but she struggled to wrestle the ribbon out of his hand. He tried to resist her, but he was still gasping from the renewed agony in his leg. Mathilde wrenched the ribbon free, then snagged the necklet's chain in her fingers just before Etienne scooped her up in his arms and swept her out of the path of the spreading blaze. D'Amville scrambled backwards, trying to escape the threatening conflagration.

"Curse you!" his voice rang out. "You'll not escape me, Caterine! I'll rise again, as I did before, and I'll find you. I'll find you!"

The flames swept between Mathilde and her last glimpse of d'Amville.

"Girard," Mathilde gasped, for the fire cut off her view of his body, too. "Etienne, the flames—"

"Mathilde, there's nothing we can do."

"But—"

He threw her up on the horse, then sprang up behind her. She leaned out, straining to see her brother's body, but the fire leapt too high. "Oh, Girard," she whispered on a sob.

Etienne's hand brushed her face, then he drew her back between his arms. "I'll come back for him," he murmured. "I promise. Maude, we have to go."

He spurred the horse forward, past a man lying face down in the grass—the former owner of their mount?—past Chesnei, who was attempting to weave his horse around the flames to find d'Amville. The other two horsemen had focused their attack on Therri.

"Ride on!" Therri shouted as Etienne reined in behind him and drew his sword.

"Therri—"

Therri dodged a blow from one attacker, then swung around to block a blow from the second. "Go!" he snapped. "I can take these two. Get Mathilde to safety."

Etienne hesitated, then slammed his sword back into its scabbard. With a flick of the reins, he and Mathilde thundered into the darkness of the trees.

***

The heat seemed stifling after the chill of the woods. Yet Mathilde could not stop trembling. She held out her hands towards the fire . . . the small, safely contained fire that burned cheerfully in the stone hearth at one end of Grantamur Castle's great hall. The warmth of the flames licked over her flesh, warming her outwardly, thickening her chest as if filling it with the steam of a sudden thaw. Yet the very center of her being remained untouched, a solid, frigid ball of ice.

She saw again the ghastly scar on d'Amville's throat, heard again the searing hatred in his rasping accusation. A hatred with her father at its core. She had unquestioningly believed her sire's protests that he was innocent of stealing from the King's Wardrobe. Evidence like rings and candlesticks, as she had insisted to Etienne, might easily have been planted. But one did not cut one's own throat just so that one might accuse an innocent man of attempted murder. Not even d'Amville could be *that* mad.

"Maude."

Etienne spoke softly from where he sat on the bench beside her. He took her hand in his and nursed it gently between his palms. But even the familiar heat of his touch failed to pierce the frost that gripped her soul.

Had he done it? Had her father tried to kill d'Amville? Why would he? Because d'Amville had framed him for the Wardrobe theft? Or because they had quarreled over her mother? But her mother had been dead for eighteen years.

Her shivers deepened. Whatever her father might have done, she was certain D'Amville would rise again, as he had promised. He would rise from the flames of this night, just as he had risen from the grave her father had vowed he lay in. And he would come for her.

Etienne's arm slid around her.

She pulled away sharply. "Should you not have someone look at your head?"

"I'm fine."

She did not need to glance at him again to know that his face was white. "You're not fine. You should be in bed."

"I can't leave until I know that Violette has agreed to help you."

She bounced up from the bench and drew closer to the fire. "What is taking her so long?"

"It's past midnight. She's bound to have been fast asleep."

Mathilde scarcely heard his answer. She stared into the flames, but all she could see was d'Amville's scarred throat and Girard's bloody face. She ran her hands up and down her arms, but the biting cold continued to gnaw away inside her. Her flesh was so hot. Why did this ice inside not melt?

A footstep sounded, then Etienne's arms encircled her from behind.

"You're the one who should be in bed," he murmured. "I will have a servant find you a room, and I'll talk to Vi alone."

So cold.

"Don't," she said.

His cheek rested atop her head. "Don't what?"

"Touch me."

His cheek came up and she felt his start of surprise.

"Please let me go." She heard her voice. Flat. Colorless. The way Costane might speak. Was it because the squire felt as cold and dead inside as she?

Slowly, Etienne's arms fell from around her. After a moment, she heard his step as he returned to the bench. He did not speak again, nor did she.

It came to her blindingly in the silence between them. This chill, this ice. 'Twas a blessing, a merciful gift from the heavens. She ceased trying to reach beyond it and drew it around her like a cloak of safety. Two images stood out starkly in the terrors of this night. Girard's dead body. And d'Amville standing over Etienne, his sword raised to plunge into Etienne's heart.

239

In his madness, d'Amville had claimed that Etienne loved her. Foolishness. Impossible! Pray heaven—

She trembled again and squeezed shut her eyes, trying to squeeze away the visions. Pray heaven, of all his mad accusations, let this one not be true! She could not bear it if Etienne loved her. Not now. Now that d'Amville had come for her. Now that she had witnessed the deadly power of his blade.

Etienne would try to rescue her, as all good heroes would. 'Twould be difficult enough to discourage him if he were driven only by motives of chivalry. But if he loved her—

Nay, he could not, must not. She must never covet it again. It had been an empty, dangerous dream to expect Etienne or any man to come riding to her aid and restore her father's honor. Such bold, effortless rescues were the stuff of jongleurs' ballads. But this night, as she had watched the life slip from Girard's eyes, she had learned that in real life, sometimes the villain won.

And sometimes the hero died.

She shivered again, but this time she welcomed the chill. 'Twas a comfort to know that Etienne's warmth could not touch her. She would no longer be tempted by his charms. No longer ache for the protection of his arms. This blankness of feeling was a blessing. She surrendered every joy, every exhilaration, every contentment she had ever known with him. She surrendered her dreams. And felt the fear flow away.

He would be safe. She vowed it from the depths of her winter-blown soul. D'Amville did not need to come for her. When the time came, she would go to him. Whatever could be done to salvage the shreds of her father's honor, whatever d'Amville demanded, she would give it. She would allow no hero to ever risk himself for her again. No more men would suffer for her foolish dreams.

Etienne. He had been her most beautiful dream of all.

A dream was a small price to pay to protect him from d'Amville.

Sixteen

Etienne slumped a little on the bench and raised a hand to rub his eyes. The wound at his temple felt like it had slowed to a sluggish trickle, but it had left him with a monstrous drubbing in his head. The pain blurred his vision. Mathilde's slender form swayed fuzzily against a blur of bright flames. He had sent some of Violette's men to battle the fire Mathilde had set in the woods and help Therri fight off d'Amville's henchmen. It sickened him to have left Therri surrounded with swords and flames, but with Etienne's pounding head and foggy eyesight, he knew he would be of little use to his friend. Mathilde was right, he should be in bed somewhere, sleeping this headache off.

But he could not leave her like this. He had felt the stiffness of her body when he embraced her, heard the cold remoteness in her voice. She had suffered shock upon shock this cruel night. He wanted only to hold her. He wanted to make her nightmare go away. But come morning, Girard would still be dead, d'Amville, if he had escaped the flames, would still be obsessed and insane.

No, Etienne could not ease the shocks she had endured this night. But she could not make him leave her. He would sit with her all night, if need be. Until she let the tears come. Until she cried the hurt and fear from her heart.

He picked up the ribbon from where she had left it with the necklet on the bench. Briefly, his blurred vision melded to let him

241

view the fabric strand clearly. Dust stained. The gilded embroidery matted. And half the stitches ripped out along the back. They must have tugged free in Mathilde's struggle to seize it from d'Amville. He tried not to shudder at the memory of orange, licking flames crackling and snapping around her. Would Girard's harlot appreciate the danger his sister had risked to retrieve a dying lover's token? Would Girard, had he lived, have given two snaps for Mathilde's fierce loyalty to a brother who slapped and abandoned her? The cur did not deserve her tears.

He flicked a thumb angrily against the torn stitches. The fabric parted to grant him for the first time a clear view of the lining within. Odd. Some sort of dark marks stood out starkly against—

"Pray, what is the meaning of this unseemly invasion of my hall at this hour?"

Etienne shot to his feet, then felt himself lurch as a white flash flooded his vision and a stab of pain erupted through his skull. He dropped back to the bench and lowered his head into his hands.

"Etienne!" Violette's haughty tones changed to alarm. "What is wrong with you?"

"Nothing," he muttered. "I'm fine. Just—stood up too fast." He bit his lip, fighting off a wave a nausea.

"He has a cut on his forehead."

Mathilde's voice echoed dully against the throb between his ears. He lifted his head and squinted at her, trying to see her face, but even had his vision not been so blurry she turned too quickly back to the fire.

A shadow fell across him, then a cool hand swept his hair back from his brow. Violette muttered an exclamation. She spoke sharply to a servant, sending her off to fetch a salve. Etienne winced as Violette's fingers probed the swollen flesh around his wound.

"How did you come by this?" she demanded.

"It doesn't signify," he said. "It's little more than a graze. I just need some sleep and I'll be fine."

Violette's hand fell away. He wished he could see her expression, but her face danced as hazily as Mathilde's.

"So, you've come to ask for a bed? For you and your squire?"

Her voice turned withering. "Forgive me, Lord Therri's squire. Does Therri know what you are about, Etienne? Or has he merely grown tired of his latest—servant."

Etienne hesitated. Therri would very likely murder him for this. But before he could ask for Violette's help, she had to know the truth.

"Vi, it's not what you think," he said. "If you will only give me a chance, I can explain all about Mathilde."

"Mathilde?" Violette's voice nipped like a shard of ice.

He rose, more carefully this time. Mathilde still faced the fire, seemingly disinterested in his exchange with Violette. All the same, he took Violette's arm and propelled her across the hall to stand next to one of the tapestried walls.

"This is no time to fly into a pique," he said. "Aye, that is Mathilde de Riavelle over there, but Therri didn't know her until I told him yesterday."

Violette's scornful laugh cracked with what might have been a sob, had he been able to clearly see her face. "You expect me to believe you now, after you lied to me? Yes, Etienne, lied to me! You swore to me that 'Mathieu' was the Lady Mathilde's twin!"

"Vi—"

She cut him off in a voice sliced with anger. "I did not believe you then and I do not believe you now. As soon as my servant has attended to your head, I want you both gone. Nay, I want you *all* gone. Off of my lands first thing in the morning."

"Violette—"

"Nay, I will not be mocked any longer by that—that—that libertine you call your friend. That p-profligate. That seducer of l-lewd and innocent w-women alike." Her words came out in a furious sputter.

"If you're talking about Therri, then you've got cobwebs in your brain. Blazes, Vi, when did you ever see him with a lewd woman?"

A crimson flush washed into her hazy face. "I don't need to *see* him. I have heard the rumors of his myriad lovers. And—nay, I take that back. I saw him kiss Lady Barbary."

"In front of a dozen other people. And Lady Barbary isn't lewd. A little bold, perhaps. But the kiss was part of the game. He'd have kissed *you* if Lady Barbary hadn't tricked him. He wanted to kiss you, Vi. He lov—"

She flung up a hand. "Do not say it. I will not listen to any more lies. Not while his very harlot is standing here right under my nose."

Etienne's hands fisted. If a man had spoken those words, he would have found himself on the ground.

"Mathilde is no harlot," he said softly. "And if you ever couple that word with her name again, you will regret it."

An empty threat, though he spoke it forcefully. He would never have laid a hand on Violette. But it seemed to quell her acid tongue. For the moment.

Her tongue, but not her intent. She turned to the servant who joined them. "Anoint Sir Etienne's head with that salve, then summon Hugon and have him show Sir Etienne and his—squire out."

"No!" He grabbed Violette's arm. "Vi, you can't send her away. Mathilde is in danger. Serious danger. That's why I brought her here."

"I will thank you to unhand me." Icicles fairly dripped from her voice.

"Not until you've heard me out."

Her arm was rigid beneath his fingers, but their pressure must have convinced her that his determination was as strong as her own. After a moment, she gestured to the servant, who moved a discreet distance away.

"Say your piece," Violette said stiffly, "then go."

He released her arm to motion towards Mathilde. Surely even Violette could see the forlorn droop of her shoulders? "Look at her. She needs your compassion, Vi, not your jealousy. She just found her brother murdered in the woods. That fat knave Chesnei attacked her and her father's mortal enemy is trying to carry her off and ravish her. On top of all that, she came within inches of being engulfed in a fire that's been set loose in your woods—"

"A fire?" Violette gasped and took an alarmed step away from him.

He caught her arm again. "Nay, I've already sent some of your men to see if they can contain it. And you had better pray they can, for I left Therri to battle the blaze and three men who were trying to cut him to shreds."

He wished he could see Violette's expression now. He heard her second gasp, this one gratifyingly louder than the first.

"Therri! You left him *where?*"

He hoped the panic in her voice betrayed her true emotions towards his friend.

"In the woods," he repeated. "With a fire. And three—possibly four if the one I clonked on the head has recovered—of d'Amville's armed and very deadly henchmen."

She wrenched her arm away. "How *could* you, Etienne! What if he— Oh, I must send more men to aid him!"

Her slippered feet scrunched against the rushes as she ran towards the exit of the hall.

"Your concern is flattering, my lady, but more men will not be required."

Violette skidded to a stop with a smothered exclamation. Etienne had not realized how tensely he had been holding his own body until he heard the sound of Therri's voice. In the back of a mind otherwise consumed with Mathilde, he had had visions of Therri caught in the flames or laid out dead, like Girard. Relief at his friend's safety swallowed up his guilt at abandoning him.

Etienne held his breath, hoping that her own relief would cause Violette to throw herself into Therri's arms. Instead, they both stood stock still. Etienne knew the message that Therri's heart must be pounding. But he could not see either of their faces clearly enough to know what might be passing wordlessly between them.

"My woods," Violette said at last, speaking with an awkwardness rare for her. "The fire—"

"Should be under control soon," Therri finished. "And aye, my lady, I escaped with my hair little more than singed, thank you for asking." With that waspish retort, he strode across the floor to Etienne's side.

Etienne rubbed his eyes, clearing his vision just long enough to see his friend's black streaked hair and the smudges of soot on his face before it blurred again.

"I'm glad to see you're still standing," Therri said, pointedly ignoring Violette. "That was some risk you took, baring your breast to d'Amville the way you did. How did you know he'd back off and let you retrieve your sword?"

"On the tournament field, when d'Amville attacked me, he growled, 'No man calls me a coward.' Chesnei told me that slur is a particular sore spot with his uncle. If d'Amville had struck me down unarmed, a coward is exactly what he would have appeared."

"Saints, the man is a raving lunatic! Calling you Aymor the way he did." Therri lowered his voice. "And what was it he kept calling Mathilde?"

"Caterine. Her mother's name."

Therri shook his head. "Lunatic." He broke off as Violette started in their direction. He said more loudly to Etienne, "Thanks for sending the help, but I routed our attackers before Lady Violette's men arrived. I think they'll be able to contain the fire, though. They shouldn't need our help to do so. Get Mathieu and let's go."

Etienne glanced at Mathilde. "It's not safe to take her back to our tent. That will be the first place d'Amville looks for her now."

"*Him,*" Therri said sharply. "You mean the first place d'Amville looks for *him.* We don't even know if d'Amville escaped the flames. The threat to Mathieu could be already be gone. Besides—you weren't thinking of leaving him here?"

The warning in Therri's voice was clear. Etienne hesitated, but there was no avoiding the step he had already taken.

"Vi knows," he said as Violette reached their side. Suddenly he was glad he could not see his friend's face clearly.

But he heard Therri's breath suck in. "You didn't—"

"Aye, my lord," Violette's voice broke in coldly on his strangled gasp, "he did."

Therri swore. Loudly. "Fiend seize it, Etienne, are you as insane as d'Amville?"

Etienne ignored him. "Violette, I told you that I could explain—"

"I don't want any more 'explanations'. You may all stay the night—only because Etienne looks ready to drop—but come morning, I want the three of you off my lands. *Gone.* My guards will be waiting to escort you to my borders in the morning." She started to sweep away from them, then turned back to ask with deceptive sweetness, "I suppose you will be wanting a room for three?"

Therri choked.

Etienne rubbed at his throbbing temples. "Blazes, Vi, if you could only swallow your injured pride long enough to listen—"

"My lord?"

The three of them turned at Mathilde's small, quavering voice. She had come up behind them.

"My lord," she repeated a little more steadily to Therri, "did you see him again? D'Amville?"

Therri hesitated. He cast a glance at Violette, then sighed and said defeatedly, "Nay. But it's likely he was caught in the flames and won't trouble you again, my lady."

"And—and Chesnei?"

The hesitation lasted longer this time. "I think he escaped. I'm sorry, my lady."

Etienne rubbed at his eyes. If he could only see her face. "No one can harm you behind Grantamur's walls, Maude. You're safe here. Isn't she, Vi?"

Etienne did not know whether it was the flat determination in his voice or some expression on Mathilde's blurred face that prodded Violette's unexpected change of heart.

"Indeed. Oh, yes, indeed! You are perfectly safe here, my lady. From *every* kind of threat."

She spoke a little too brightly for Etienne's comfort.

Violette suddenly flung her arm around Mathilde's waist and swept her towards the exit of the hall.

"Attend to Sir Etienne's head," she bade her servant, then said over her shoulder, "I bid you goodnight, gentlemen. I'm afraid you'll have to bed there in the rushes. I've just recalled that I don't have a room to spare. And don't give another thought's care for the Lady Mathilde. She shall sleep through the night at my side."

Soft, thick carpets of fur, like the coverlets that draped the huge, curtained bed at the center of the room, warmed the floor of Violette's chamber. To one side of the bed stood an elaborately carved chair with an embroidered, silk-cushioned seat and back. A trestle table was poised on the other side, with a painted pitcher molded in the shape of a rearing lion and a basin with a gilded rim.

Mathilde paused on a patch of cinnamon fur in front of the fire crackling in Violette's hearth. She stared at the tapestries that draped the walls, so vividly woven that their tiny figures threatened to leap to life in the flickering firelight. Surely Queen Guinevere herself could not have possessed a more luxurious chamber?

The thought flitted into her mind before she could stop it. She banished it at once. Queen Guinevere was the stuff of dreams. And she had sworn to abjure such foolishness from this night forth.

The bright hues in the tapestries flattened and dulled as the numbness spread through her again. She scarcely felt Violette easing her out of her squire's clothes to wrap her in a thick woolen robe, scarcely heard the murmur of her answers to Violette's soft-voiced questions.

"Pray, my lady," Violette asked, straightening the robe around Mathilde's shoulders, "what is this threat Sir Etienne has brought you to my castle to escape?"

"An enemy of my father's," Mathilde replied. Her voice sounded hollow in her ears. "He murdered my brother tonight in the woods. He tried to kill Etienne, too, but—but I will not ever let that happen again."

Violette's hands clenched on Mathilde's shoulders and turned her to stare straight into her eyes. "This is all truth? There has been such violence in my woods this night?"

Mathilde nodded. She did not want to speak of it any more. She did not want to think of it. But the images would not stop dancing in her mind.

Suddenly, Violette's hand brushed her cheek. To wipe away a

tear? Nay, Mathilde knew her eyes were dry. She was too cold to give birth to anything as warm as tears.

"Poor child," Violette cooed. She drew Mathilde closer to the hearth, then pulled her down to sit amid the furs. "Your hands are like ice! Here." Violette's hands, gentle on Mathilde's wrists, extended her fingers towards the fire.

She might have plunged Mathilde's fingers clean into the flames and Mathilde would not have felt the sting. There was nothing but this empty, merciless chill, gripping now not only her soul, but every fiber of her body.

"You have been most selfishly and cruelly used, my lady." Violette's soft voice sounded angry. "My guards will seek out the felons who have brought you such grief this night. Your brother's murderer will be punished. As for the other wrong that you have borne ... Nay, you must not think I blame you for the lustful weaknesses of men. You were not the first to fall victim to his dangerous charm. But I can, and do, assure you that he will never take such shameful advantage of you again."

Lustful? Dangerous charm? Etienne flitted into her mind. But he had taken no advantage of her. Except, of course, to have stolen her heart.

A heart that now lay thankfully dead in her breast. Aye, this numbness was truly a blessing.

Violette pressed something into her hands. A goblet, fashioned of gold and crusted with diamonds and rubies. Before tonight, Mathilde would have gasped at its beauty. But now, at Violette's prompting, she simply drained its contents without a word, without any emotion or sensation except for this wonderful, blessed chill.

She knew Violette meant the wine to warm her, but it surged down her throat without taste or the burning effect familiar from fermented brews.

Violette. So kind. Seeking so hard to be helpful. Mathilde tried to thank her. Her tongue felt thick, heavy. She tried to speak again, but the words came out in a slurring stammer. She felt her eyes drooping. Violette nudged her to her feet, supported her lagging footsteps over to the bed, slipped away the woolen robe ...

The furs Violette tucked snugly around Mathilde as her body sank into the feather mattress failed, like the wine, to stave off the chill. But a welcome cloud settled over her mind, stilling at last the violent memories of the night, as she slid into a dreamless sleep.

A heady scent of roses enveloped Mathilde, along with an absurdly smooth set of sheets. They lay soft as a whisper against her skin, a silken caress along her back, her hips, her legs. And this fur against her cheek, its pile so thick and soft . . .

Where was she? Certainly not wrapped in her own rough blanket on her pallet in Etienne's tent.

A thrill of panic shot through her. Not in his tent . . . Then where *was* she? And where was *he*?

She started to leap up from the foreign bed, then gasped and cowered back into the tumble of furs and sheets as she realized that her clothes were gone.

"Ah. I was about to wake you. Good morning, Lady Mathilde."

Mathilde blinked the haze of sleep from her eyes and stared across the room at Violette. She stood beside a tub of steaming water, dressed in an airy, long-sleeved chemise.

"I thought you might enjoy beginning the day with a bath," Violette said, her smile cheerful and bright. "And I hope you don't mind, but I have disposed of those ridiculous squire's clothes you were wearing. They were—stained, I fear."

Stained? The memories returned in a torrential shower of pain. Mathilde had seen the dark marks on the lap of her tunic as she'd stood beside the fire in Violette's hall last night. Girard's blood. She pressed a hand to her mouth. He was dead. Her brother was dead! Killed by d'Amville. A monster who would come for her next.

Violette took her hand and drew her from the bed. "Come," she said bracingly, "you will feel better after you have bathed and had something to eat. And I hope you will forgive me for the little trick I played on you last night?"

"Trick, my lady?"

"The sleeping draught I slipped into your wine. I thought you might need some help resting. I hope it did not trap you in any nightmares?"

Mathilde shook her head. She recognized now the sour taste in her mouth as the lingering effects of a draught. No, there had been no nightmares. But if there had, they could not possibly have been worse than the horrible realities of the night just past, or more hopeless than her Stygian future. Where was that merciful frigidity that had held her so blissfully emotionless last night? How could she bear to face the hellish days to come if she were to start feeling again?

Before she could utter a prayerful plea for a return to numbness, Violette nudged her over the edge of the tub and plunged her firmly into its steaming depths. Mathilde gasped at the scorching water, but even as she sputtered a protest, Violette scooped up some water with the lion-shaped pitcher and dumped it over Mathilde's head.

"What a shame that he cut off your hair," Violette mourned while Mathilde sputtered anew. "You had lovely hair, as I recall. But it does not surprise me. My husband sought to deceive me with a similar ruse, shortly after we married."

Violette rolled up her sleeves and set to work with a sponge to scrub away the grime and dust from Mathilde's body.

"It did not take long for me to see through his pretty-faced 'groom's' disguise," she continued as she worked. "It led to our first quarrel and to my first slap. After that, he put his little strumpet back in a dress and installed her in one of Grantamur's towers. Men! They are all abusive, lecherous beasts, all save for Sir Etienne and Sir William. The only two honest, decent men I have ever known. But you and I shall play victims to the rest of them no longer, my lady. If an angel can fall, then surely a compassionate hand can raise her back up. Come, we will make what is left of your hair shine like a halo."

She paused with the sponge to repeat her assault with the pitcher of water.

Mathilde gasped again and raised her hands to shove a thick, dripping web of hair out of her eyes. Flustered by the water in her ears, she was not sure she entirely understood Violette's speech. Except that for some incomprehensible reason, Mathilde feared she had just been compared with a strumpet.

She uttered an indignant defense. "My brother cut my hair to make me look like a squire so that Lord Therri and Sir Etienne would not recognize me and send me away. Girard was trying to protect me from d'Amville."

The sponge swiped across her back again, then stilled. "To protect you?" Violette stood up suddenly, then flung the sponge into the water so hard that it splashed around Mathilde. "Oh! That man is more vile than even I had thought! Seducing you into his tent would have been wicked enough, but to prey upon an innocent who was cast upon his mercy for protection—! And then to have the brazen gall to turn on me one of his golden smiles and expect me to melt in the false adoration of his sapphire gaze!"

Mathilde jumped as Violette dealt a hard kick to the side of the tub. The gleam in Violette's brilliant eyes betrayed a regret that her toes had not found their target on somebody's shin instead.

"I have not the power to punish the knave as he deserves," Violette said with fierce determination, "but I can see him driven off my lands forthwith. Be assured, my lady, you shall never suffer at his iniquitous hands again."

Mathilde clutched the rim of the tub and turned in puzzlement to watch as Violette marched to her chamber door. She wrenched it wide and shouted a servant's name. A freckle-faced girl came scurrying.

"Find Hugon and tell him to gather some men to escort Lord Therri off my lands," Violette said. "And if Lord Therri should protest and start a scuffle, Hugon has my permission to use full force to toss our unwelcome guest headlong across my borders."

Mathilde surged out of the water. She grabbed up the robe she had worn last night from the chair beside the bed and wrapped it around her still dripping body. "Stay, please!" she called to the servant. "Lady Violette, I don't understand what you think Lord Therri has done to incur your wrath like this."

Violette whirled on her and hissed, "He has ravished you, of course! Oh, you may think it was merely a seduction, or even that you succumbed to a mutual passion, but—"

"Succumbed to a mutual passion? With Lord Therri?" For a moment, Mathilde had a horrible fear that she had blurted out her early, naive dreams about Therri last night in her sleep. What else could possibly have caused Violette to think such an outlandish thing? "Oh, my lady, you are terribly wrong! Lord Therri has never so much as glanced at me. As a woman, I mean. He has thought I was a boy all this time, until Etienne told him the truth. No, truly! He was furious when Etienne told him. He threatened to turn me out of their tent."

Violette snapped the door shut in the servant's face, then turned her narrowed eyes on Mathilde. "I have extended to you my hospitality, my lady. I let you sleep in my bed and bathe in my own chamber. I have offered you a hand of friendship. If you think I shall tolerate being repaid with lies—"

"It is not a lie!"

"Lord Therri may be many deplorable things, but he is not stupid. You expect me to believe that you've been living in his tent for a sennight and he never even suspected you were a woman?"

"Etienne said he was too preoccupied with thinking about you. You are all Lord Therri talks about when he and Etienne are together. Even I can see now how desperately in love with you he is and how much it hurt him when you flirted with Sir William in front of him on Sunday." Mathilde drew a deep breath before continuing. "You wish me to be honest? Very well. When I first laid eyes on Lord Therri, I had a foolish hope that I could make him love me. He was the most beautiful man I had ever seen! I admit, I dreamed about him kissing me. But even in my dreams, they were not like real kisses."

Her fingers fluttered to her lips as she remembered the burning pleasure of Etienne's mouth on hers.

"Oh, no," she whispered, "not like real kisses at all."

Violette's voice broke stiffly across her memory. "And you now know the difference because—?"

Mathilde blushed and hurriedly dropped her hand. "Not because Lord Therri kissed me. He never did!"

"If not Lord Therri, then who? No one else knew about your disguise, except—" Violette's eyes widened. "Etienne?"

"They were only kisses!" Mathilde said quickly, her cheeks aflame with guilt. "And only a very few of those, and—and he repented very quickly. Oh, my lady, you will not tell Lady Hermaline? Truly, he has not betrayed her! Not in his heart. Only— only sometimes the flesh is weak. But he never, never let his wicked passion for me tempt him into more than kisses. And I am going to leave him now, I promise, so he will never be tempted again. He loves Lady Hermaline so very much. She does not need to know about me, does she?"

Violette stared at her, her lovely eyes glimmering with a mixture of shock and bemusement.

After a moment of silence, she seemed to collect herself. "You said you are going to leave him. Where is it you intend to go, my lady?"

"I-I shall find a way home to my father," Mathilde said. She lowered her gaze to her toes, saw the way they wriggled guiltily against the cinnamon fur, and hurriedly stilled them. She dared not speak the truth, that it was d'Amville, and not her father, that she must find. Violette might try to stop her, or worse, tell Etienne.

Oh, please, she prayed silently. *Don't let my heart start beating for him again.* But it was too late. No matter where she searched within her, she could not find that protective shell of frigidity that had held her so comfortingly through the night.

Perhaps she could find a way to slip from the castle without seeing him again? Without putting herself through the anguish of having to look into his beloved face, of standing near enough to touch him, to hear his teasing, tender voice . . .

She bit her quivering lip and swallowed the hot lump in her throat. Nay, she must not nourish those memories. The image she must cling to was of d'Amville standing over Etienne's kneeling form, sword raised to plunge into his breast. Next time, the sword might well find its deadly target.

She drew a deep, steadying breath. For Etienne's sake, she could find the strength to leave him. For her father's sake, she would find the courage to satisfy d'Amville's demands. Just as soon as she had fulfilled her pledge to Girard and delivered the ribbon to—

She stared suddenly at her empty hands. The ribbon. She had left it with her necklet in the hall last night. Pray heaven no one had wandered off with them!

"Is something amiss, my lady?" Violette queried.

"My mother's necklet," Mathilde said. There was no point in showing alarm over a tattered ribbon. "I must have left it downstairs in your hall."

"I will send a servant to look for it. Come, sit on the bed and have a bit of cheese to break your fast. We must talk more about you and—"

"Nay, I will run and look myself. If you will excuse me, my lady, just for a moment."

"But Lady Mathilde, you are not dressed—"

Mathilde had already opened the door and darted past the still hovering servant awaiting Violette's decision about Lord Therri. Mathilde sprinted down the winding stone staircase that brought her into the hall, then froze, the rushes prickling beneath her bare feet.

A handful of servants moved quietly about the high ceilinged chamber, trying not to disturb the two sleeping men stretched out in the rushes near the hearth. Therri sprawled on his stomach, covered by his cloak, his hair shimmering a pale gold in the glow of the nearby fire. Etienne lay on his back, his sooty curls tumbled over his brow, his hands moving softly with the rise and fall of his chest. Hands which clasped in one fist her mother's necklet, and in the other her brother's dust stained ribbon.

Last night, Mathilde had known the blessed chill of detachment and withdrawal. This morning, she had faced anew the painful stirrings of a love that could never be fulfilled. Through dispassion and turbulent emotion alike, her only resolve had been for Etienne's happiness and safety.

And how did he repay her? Would he let her leave him gracefully, quietly, without forcing a final, torturous confrontation between them? Nay! He must have known the twin objects of ribbon and necklet would compel her to come to him.

A blaze of fury flashed through her. Ungrateful wretch! If he wanted a confrontation, she would give it to him. With a muffled cry of frustration, she hurtled herself at him across the hall.

Seventeen

Etienne's eyes flew wide as an object with the force of a catapulted boulder landed on his stomach and drove the air out of his lungs. He had a foggy image of Mathilde's face crumpled with unaccustomed anger hovering above him, before the sight swirled into a desperate blankness as he struggled wildly to regain his breath.

Vaguely, he felt someone tugging at his hands and instinctively clenched his fists tighter.

"Let them go!"

The cry echoed against his urgent gasp for air.

"Ingrate! Knave! Let them go! Oh, why can't you just let *me* go!"

Her voice broke on a sob. His vision cleared as his breath returned. Mathilde. The cold remoteness that had so worried him last night had clearly vanished. Tears streamed down her flushed cheeks and behind the fury in her eyes swam so much pain, it nearly tore the air out of his lungs again.

Her nails clawed at his fingers, trying to pry them wide. He resisted again, then impulsively, shook her hands loose and flung his arms around her. He rolled her into the rushes, shifting himself to pin her beneath him.

"What are you doing?" she gasped. "Let me go! Oh, Etienne, please . . . let me go." She gave another scraping sob.

He brushed his hand with the ribbon against her face, wiping away her tears, trying to soothe her. "I can't," he whispered. "Heaven forgive me . . . but I can't."

The truth of those words scorched through him like the flames they had so narrowly escaped in Grantamur's woods. Let her go? Never feel the warm curve of her cheek beneath his palm again? Never still those sweetly quivering lips with his? Never see the soft mist of dreams gather again in her eyes?

That mist was gone now. Coldly, cruelly banished by d'Amville. But Etienne swore he would restore those dreams. If it took him a lifetime . . .

Her pain-filled eyes now flashed at him. She writhed beneath him, trying to free herself of his hold.

"Saints, Etienne, what's gotten into her?"

Her sobs and flailings had wakened Therri. A quick glance about the hall told Etienne that the servants were staring, too. He sat up and pulled her resisting body into his arms.

"Hush, Maude," he bade her gently. "All will be well, I promise."

She twisted in his grasp. "No! Nothing will ever be well again. Girard is dead, and d'Amville— I can't let him— Oh, just give me my necklet and the ribbon and go back to Hermaline!"

"Maude—"

"I can't let you— You mustn't— H-Hermaline will keep you safe. Oh, *please* go back to her!"

"But I don't want Hermaline. I want yo—"

She slapped her hands over his mouth. A faint shudder ran through her. "Don't say it! You don't love me. You *must* not love me. D'Amville will—"

She choked off the rest of her words and shook her head fiercely. He started to pull her fingers away, but his movement loosened his hold on her. This time she succeeded in jerking free. She jumped to her feet, grabbed hold of one end of the ribbon in his hand and pulled on it with all her might.

"I promised Girard! Give it to me, Etienne."

"Maude—"

"Give it to me!"

He heard the popping of the remaining stitches, ripping the seam wide before he finally let the strand go. Mathilde stumbled backward at the sudden release, tripped over the hem of her robe, and plopped down hard in the rushes.

Having gained the ribbon, Etienne expected her to scramble back up and come after the necklet next. But she did not move. She just sat where she was, staring at the ribbon. The skirt of her robe spread around her like a dark puddle, its bodice parted by her vigorous movements to give him a too tantalizing glimpse of her slender, white throat and the smooth ball of one shoulder.

A flush of desire washed through him. Nay, he told himself, she was not his yet. But the words he had spoken to her a moment ago were true. He could not let her go. He knew that irrevocably now. But if he were to claim her in good conscience, he would have to swallow his pride and lay aside his long-held ambitions. Aye, before he could revive her dreams, he would have to bury a few of his own.

A shadow fell over her. Violette, dressed in a flowing yellow tunic that brought out the rich highlights in her trailing mahogany hair, hunched down beside Mathilde. Therri scrambled to his feet, smoothed down his sleep-rumpled hair, then took a hesitant step across the floor to join the women. Violette and Mathilde appeared riveted in a study of the ribbon. Therri paused, then rounded behind them and bent down to join their study. After a moment, he raised his gaze to Etienne's.

"I think you had better see this."

Etienne eased himself up slowly, mindful of his disastrous, too quick rise the night before. But Violette's salve and a good night's sleep had restored his vision and eased the throbbing in his temple to a mildly irritating soreness.

"I don't understand," Mathilde said as he approached. She held the ribbon up to him. "What do you think it means?"

Therri straightened and moved to stand beside Etienne.

"What it means is trouble," he muttered into Etienne's ear.

Etienne took the ribbon and stared at its lining, fully exposed now by the ripped stitches. The dark marks he had glimpsed the previous night before Violette had distracted him were carefully printed letters. If he spread the torn ribbon out full width, they formed a message, with a signature —

Etienne felt the color drain from his face as he scanned back up to the name blocked out at the top left hand edge of the cloth.

"I told you. Trouble," Therri repeated.

"Violette," Etienne said hoarsely, "send your servants away."

Violette immediately chimed out the order, then bent down and helped Mathilde to her feet.

"I do not understand what such a message should be doing hiding in Lady Mathilde's ribbon," Violette said when the servants were gone. "But I presume it holds some significance to the two of you?"

Significance? Rage at this final act of monumental insensitivity on the part of Girard set Etienne shaking. If Mathilde had been caught with this message in her hands —

He grabbed Mathilde by the arm and dragged her back over to the bench by the hearth. "Sit down," he snapped, "and explain."

Mathilde obeyed his first command, but the blank look on her face bode ill for her ability to obey the second. Had she truly been ignorant, or had she known all along?

"Is this the reason you kept trying to fetch the ribbon from me?" he demanded.

She shook her head. "I did not know there was writing inside. Girard ordered me to get the ribbon back for him. 'Tis all I know."

He frowned and read the words on the ribbon again slowly, allowing the full impact of their meaning, both stated and implied, to sink into his brain. The message was brief, constrained by the limited space available in the length and width of the ribbon. The letters were small, compressed closely together to obtain the maximum wordage. Yet room enough had been found here, against the smooth white background of the ribbon's lining, to print in cold, condemning ink a warning to one king and a betrayal of another. In the brief space of its narrow length, the Young King's intent to invade his brother's domains in Poitou and Aquitaine passed beyond the realms of rumor into firmly established fact. But that was not what made Etienne's blood run cold. He detested the Young

King's brother, Duke Richard, and longed to see his homeland freed from the Duke's despotic control.

Nay, 'twas the name at the top of this ribbon that caused Etienne to shrink. *Henricus Rex*, printed carefully out in Latin. Not *Li Reys Josnes*, as they called the Young King in the Norman tongue. But *Henricus Rex*, the designation reserved for the Young King's sire, King Henry II of England, and despite their shared title, still de-facto overlord. That, and the signature scrawled into the last bit of cloth at the bottom edge of the lining. *Margarita Regina*. Queen Marguerite, the Young King's wife. Her use of the Latin title instead of the Norman proclaimed her attempted alliance with sire against son.

If this message found its way into King Henry's hands, the Young King's invasion plans would be summarily crushed by his father. A father the Young King already hated so fiercely that if he learned of this attempted betrayal by his wife or by the messenger who sought to deliver the words on this ribbon—

The messenger. Mathilde. Ah, saints . . .

"Are you thinking what I'm thinking?" Therri asked.

Etienne nodded and uttered hoarsely, "Adam of Churchdown."

Violette ranged herself behind Mathilde. "Who is Adam of Churchdown?"

Etienne and Therri both started to answer at once. Etienne bit off his words, but dropped protectively down on the bench beside Mathilde as Therri took up the explanation.

"He was the Young King's vice-chancellor after the Great War. He overheard a conversation between the Young King and certain members of his *mesnie* which, to Adam, sounded like a plot to renew the rebellion King Henry had just finished quashing. Adam attempted to inform King Henry by letter, but the messenger was intercepted by the Young King's men. The Young King, in a black Plantagenet temper, tried Adam for his life and was actually pondering a death sentence when the Bishop of Poitiers interceded. The bishop saved poor Adam's life, but the Young King's rage was not satisfied until Adam had been stripped and publicly whipped through the streets of Poitiers."

"Just for sending a message to his father?" Mathilde said.

"The Young King viewed it as treason," Therri answered. "Etienne, if we are found with that message—"

"You mean if Mathilde is found with it," Etienne said sharply. "It's written on her ribbon. At least, everyone will *think* it's her ribbon."

Mathilde's face went pasty. "You—you don't think the Young King would strip and whip *me?*"

Over my dead body, Etienne swore silently.

"I don't even understand what it means," Mathilde rushed on, her eyes wide with alarm. "What are these 'plans' Queen Marguerite is warning King Henry about? What is it the Young King intends to do in Aquitaine and Poitou?"

Etienne read through the message again. The limited space had forced the warning to be rather cryptically worded. But only to someone like Mathilde who was unfamiliar with the Young King's ambitions. King Henry would understand its gist. As would the Young King, if he discovered it before his father.

"Destroy it," Etienne said abruptly. "That's the only thing to do. Queen Marguerite will think it merely went astray somehow. Or that Girard was killed before he could deliver it and—"

"No!" Mathilde snatched the ribbon out of his hands before he could stop her. "I promised Girard I would give it safely to—to—to whoever it was he intended to give it to before he died."

"Blazes, Maude—"

She leapt up from the bench and danced away from his attempt to grab the ribbon back. "Etienne, I promised!"

"Have you lost your wits? If that message is found on you by one of the Young King's men—"

"*You* are one of the Young King's men," she said.

Etienne swore. He did not like being reminded of just how precarious his oath of loyalty to the Young King had become. The only reason he had ever considered marrying Hermaline had been to escape dependence on a man who showed increasing signs of irrationality coupled with erratic and dangerous bursts of temper. But with competent generals, the Young King might succeed in his bid to overthrow Duke Richard. And Etienne's hatred of the duke ran far deeper than his doubts about the Young King.

262

Etienne might be persuaded, reluctantly, to hold himself aloof from the coming conflict. Aye, to win Mathilde he might force himself, however unhappily, to abstain from supporting either side. But to actively participate in giving Duke Richard the advantage? That's what the duke would gain if this warning found its way to his father. And that was rather more than Etienne could stomach.

"Mathilde, give me that ribbon."

"No. I gave Girard my word."

He saw the white fear in her face. Therri's story of Adam of Churchdown had terrified her. But mingled with the fear was a fierce determination.

Saints, but she could be a stubborn wench.

And a loyal one. He tried to ignore a stir of pride at her courage. This was no time to praise her for a trait that just now threatened to thrust her headlong into disaster.

He tried reasoning with her, instead. "You don't even know who Girard intended to give it to. For all you know, he meant to carry it to England himself."

She shook her head. "He wasn't taking it to England. He said that I was to give it to someone named—named—" The corners of her eyes crinkled as she tried to drag back the memory. "He said 'Ma—' It sounded something like 'Mar—'"

"Marshal?" Violette's voice piped in so unexpectedly, it made both Mathilde and Etienne jump.

Therri muttered a curse at the name. But its voicing made the whole picture shift for Etienne. Shift and tilt until a simple plot to expose the Young King's invasion plans hung at a completely new and insidious angle.

"Marshal must have agreed to deliver this message to England for the queen," he said. "D'Amville's intention wasn't just to stop him. He wanted this ribbon found and its message revealed . . . in William Marshal's hands."

"How do you know—" Therri began.

A rhythmic clapping of hands cut him off. Etienne's head whipped around. A small man shrouded in a hooded cloak stood in the hall's entryway, applauding.

The man stopped clapping and slowly put back his hood. "Very clever, de Brielle. But Laurant's question is well asked. How do you know about D'Amville's plot against Marshal?"

"Costane!" Mathilde exclaimed. She took a hesitant step towards the squire, but Etienne rose and caught her arm.

"How did you get in here?" he demanded. He had heard Violette's guards returning from the woods last night, ordering that the gates be sealed until further orders from Violette.

Costane spread his hands and executed a small bow in Mathilde's direction. "I have come to escort my late master's sister safely home to her father, along with my poor master's body."

"Girard—" Mathilde whispered.

"His body is in a cart in the bailey, my lady," Costane said, his voice flat with empty emotion. "But I trust your brother did not die in vain." His gaze, eerily unblinking, returned to Etienne's face. "I ask you again, de Brielle. How do you know about d'Amville's plot?"

Costane slid one hand inside his cloak as he spoke. The gesture parted the garment long enough for Etienne to catch a glimpse of a wooden crossbow beneath the voluminous folds. Something cold and deadly flickered in the flat depths of the squire's eyes. Did he think Etienne was allied with d'Amville? Or was *Costane* the ally who feared that Etienne meant to thwart d'Amville's scheme? True, Costane had wounded d'Amville's nephew, Chesnei, last night with one of his wretched crossbolts. But had Chesnei been his target? Or had he really been aiming at the bearer of the ribbon—Mathilde? Someone had betrayed Girard's rendezvous with his sister in the woods, else how had d'Amville known when and where to find them? And who better to know Girard's movements, than Girard's squire?

Etienne challenged him forthrightly. "What happened last night with Chesnei? You went after him, but he returned and brought d'Amville's henchmen with him."

Costane's unblinking eyes gave nothing away. "They were waiting in the trees. There were five of them. I picked off two with my crossbow, but a third one rounded behind me and struck me on the back of the head. As soon as I recovered, I made my way back to the clearing. By then a fire had been set and you and Lord Therri were gone. I helped Lady Violette's men contain the blaze. That is why they let me through the gates this morning."

"Struck you on the head," Etienne repeated. Costane's empty face was not a face that invited trust. But there was one way to be sure. He crossed the floor and lifted a hand towards the squire's head. "May I?"

Costane hesitated, then bent his neck forward. Etienne plunged his fingers into the squire's pallid hair. Aye, there on the back of his head he probed a lump the size of a goose egg. It gave Etienne some satisfaction to feel the unsettlingly impassive fellow wince beneath his hand.

"Then if it wasn't you," Etienne said, taking a step back from Costane, "how did d'Amville know that Girard would be waiting for Mathilde last night in the woods?"

"First," Costane replied, "you will tell me how you know about d'Amville's intention to trap Marshal with that message."

Etienne saw a tightness about Costane's body, an implacable hardness in his usually expressionless eyes that warned Etienne that too much provocation might result in an unwelcome appearance of Costane's crossbow. Safer to humor him, Etienne decided . . . at least for the moment.

He told Costane about the conversation he had overheard in Rouen between Chesnei and the Young King's men, d'Yquebeuf and de Coulonces.

"No names were spoken beyond d'Amville's," he said as he finished. "And Adam of Churchdown's. I knew they were conspiring to trap some man as poor Adam had been trapped. But it was not until the next morning that I began to suspect they meant Marshal."

"Why did you not warn him?" Costane asked.

"I tried, but Marshal dismissed d'Yquebeuf's plotting as an empty threat."

Etienne shot a glance at Therri to gage his friend's response to his revelations. But despite Therri's current jealousy of Marshal,

Etienne knew he was not capable of such poisonous malice as ate away at men like d'Yquebeuf and de Coulonces. Therri scowled, but gave an approving nod at Etienne's actions.

"Marshal has too much overweening pride," Costane said, a shade of disgust in his voice. "He believes no suspicion or slander can topple him from the Young King's affections. From what I have observed of the Young King's fickle nature, I fear that Marshal is wrong. A day of reckoning is coming for him. But it shall not come today." He extended his hand towards Mathilde. "If you will give me the ribbon, my lady, I will see that it arrives safely at its destination."

She stepped towards the squire, but Etienne caught her arm again.

"Not so fast," he said. "Before we trust you with a message that could cost our heads, I want to know who betrayed Girard. Who told d'Amville that Mathilde would be meeting her brother in the woods last night?"

Costane's unblinking gaze weighed him.

"We're not your enemies, Costane," Etienne said. "If we'd wanted to stop this message from reaching King Henry, we'd have thrown it in the fire before you arrived."

No need to tell him that's exactly what Etienne had wanted to do.

Costane's only answer was to slide his hand inside his cloak.

Etienne tensed and shifted himself in front of Mathilde. "One shout, and Lady Violette's guards will come running. You can't kill us all, Costane, before they cut you down. What will become of your message, then?"

He saw both Therri and Violette start. They must not have glimpsed the crossbow, but Therri took the alert from Etienne's words and moved to take up his sword from where it had lain beside him all night in the rushes. Costane's gaze shifted from Therri's blade back to Etienne's face. Slowly, he drew his hand out empty from his cloak.

Etienne flashed a glance at Therri. His friend understood the unspoken message and went to stand near enough to the hall's exit to sound an alarm if necessary. Costane's empty eyes followed the movement too, then slid to Violette. Had she seen the silent exchange between Etienne and Therri? She must have, Etienne thought, or perhaps she merely trusted two men she knew more than this stranger, for she lifted her proud chin at Costane and directed a curt, approving nod at Therri's action.

Etienne, reassured that the squire recognized the advantage had been turned against him, took Mathilde's hand and drew her down beside him on the bench. Her fingers flexed briefly, convulsively about his. Then she jerked her hand away and laced it stiffly with its twin in her lap, the ribbon trapped between her fingers.

Costane's shoulders lifted in an almost indiscernable shrug. "Very well. I suppose I owe the Lady Mathilde that much. You were betrayed by your brother's lover, my lady."

"His lover?" Mathilde repeated blankly.

Etienne stared. "Girard told one of his strumpets? Why would the queen entrust such a compromising message to a man of Girard's reputation? Didn't she know what an incompetent, loose-tongued braggart he was?" He bit off this insulting description of Girard too late. He saw Mathilde's pale cheeks turn rosy at his words.

"The queen allowed her judgment to be swayed by that 'strumpet'," Costane said, "because she happened to be concealed beneath the facade of one of the queen's trusted ladies-in-waiting."

Mathilde stopped frowning at Etienne as her eyes grew round with awe. "Girard was in love with one of the queen's ladies?"

Costane's revelation amazed Etienne, too. He ran his memory through the glittering blondes, brunettes and redheads of Queen Marguerite's circle of noble waiting women, wondering which of them could possibly have been so desperate as to take Girard for a lover.

Before he could ask for a name, Therri inserted an impatient question. "If Queen Marguerite wished to spite her husband by betraying his invasion plans to his father, why didn't she just hand this devilish message to Marshal herself and avoid all this rigmarole with Girard and that blasted ribbon?"

"Because," Costane replied, "while Marshal was willing to help the queen, he was not willing to risk any exchanges that might be . . . misinterpreted."

Etienne understood. "He's been trying to distance himself from her, hasn't he?" He looked at Therri. "You've seen the way the Young King ignores his wife. And the way she responds by trying to fan his passion by flirting with other men. She's done it with you a time or two. She's even done it with me. And she's frequently done it with Marshal." He cocked a brow at Costane. "Only in his case, perhaps it was more than mere flirting?"

He thought of the smiles the queen bestowed on William Marshal. They were different than those she shared with other men. Warmer. More . . . intimate.

"She is fond of him," Costane admitted. "Overly fond, I fear. I have warned her not to risk her husband's temper. The Young King would not hesitate to pack her back off to her brother, the King of France, if she gave him sufficient provocation. Fortunately, Marshal seems to recognize that more risks than advantages attend an illicit affair with the queen. He wants land and a title, neither of which the Young King would ever allow an unfaithful wife to bestow upon him. So Marshal cultivates the queen's friendship. He serves her. He may even love her. But he will not risk being caught in a compromising exchange with her. And he will vent his ambitions and passions on a safer target than she."

Etienne shot a look at Violette. Her face went even redder than Therri's at this last statement.

"You seem to know a great deal about the queen's affairs," Etienne remarked, "for being a mere squire of Girard's. Who are you really, Costane? A servant of the queen's? Or of Marshal's?" How else would Costane know so much about their plans?

Costane stood silent for a long, unblinking moment. His utter stillness unnerved Etienne. Saints, was the man even human? Since his aborted attempt to reach for his crossbow, he had done nothing but shrug so faintly Etienne might have imagined it and slide his eyes back and forth in a face as blank as a stone. Well, perhaps this would bestir him. Etienne clamped his hand over Mathilde's, further trapping the strip of cloth she held.

"If you hope to convince us to surrender this ribbon to you," Etienne said, staring a hard warning into Costane's empty gaze, "you had better tell us everything."

Another frozen moment, and then the statue cracked. Costane rolled his shoulders and linked his hands behind his back. "To be precise," he said in a voice so dull he might have been speaking of the weather, "I am a servant of King Philip of France."

"France?" Etienne scarcely felt the way Mathilde shook off his clasp as the hair prickled along the back of his neck. Conspiring with France had led to Etienne's father's downfall. If the French were involved in the queen's and Marshal's plans and it became known that Etienne had, even for the briefest of time, been a carrier for their message, he would suffer a punishment far worse than a painful and humiliating whipping.

Again Costane's eyes moved, flicking from the ribbon between Mathilde's fingers to Therri and his sword beside the exit. A breath that might have been a sigh exhaled from between his bloodless lips.

"When Queen Marguerite learned that her husband was planning an attack on Poitou," he said, "she determined to inform King Henry. Perhaps, as you say, it was in spite for her husband's neglect. However, I believed her when she told me that she, with Marshal, simply hoped to preempt an assault they honestly believed was doomed to failure. The queen wrote to her brother, King Philip, asking him to send her a servant whom she could trust, for she knew the servants her husband had given her owed their loyalty to him above her. King Philip did me the high honor of selecting me to serve his sister."

"Did King Philip know why she wanted you?" Etienne asked. "Did she tell him about the Young King's plans?"

"Nay. Though French by birth, she was raised in King Henry's court and her loyalties to the Plantagenets are strong. She might be willing, for her own purposes, to play father against son, but betray them, even to her brother, she would not."

Etienne drew a breath of relief and relaxed as Costane went on.

"I came to her secretly and helped her lay her plans. Originally, she hoped to send me with the message. But France has too great an interest in disrupting the peace of King Henry's family, and I knew that King Henry would suspect any report, even one signed by the queen, that was delivered to his hand by a Frenchman. 'Twas then the queen whispered William Marshal's name. It was Marshal to whom King Henry entrusted the youthful tutoring of his heir, and Marshal whom he has continued to trust to keep his heir safe. If Marshal added the weight of his judgment to the queen's, King Henry would listen. And act.

"Marshal agreed, on a few words murmured during the course of a dance with the queen, to bear the queen's message to King Henry. But how was the message to be delivered? Both the queen and Marshal feared being caught and punished by the Young King, as Adam of Churchdown had been."

Therri gave a short, skeptical snort. He stabbed the point of his sword into the rushes and leaned against the hilt. "The Young King would never have dared to whip the queen, as he did Adam of Churchdown."

"No," Costane said, "but he might well have sent her back to France in disgrace. I believe she even feared he might, if angered sufficiently, attempt to divorce her, as her father had divorced the Young King's mother. The Young King could too easily claim that she has, to this point, proven incapable of bearing him an heir."

As the proud and flirtatious Eleanor of Aquitaine had failed to do for her French husband, King Louis VII. The irony was, Etienne thought, after her divorce from Louis, Eleanor had married King Henry II of England and borne him four stout sons and three daughters. Poor King Louis had had to marry twice more before he had gained a male heir to *his* throne. Queen Marguerite was the daughter of his second wife, who had had no more success in bearing male children to the French king than Eleanor had.

Etienne saw Costane weighing Therri and motioned to his friend. Therri's lip curled in disdain of the smaller man, but he straightened his posture and wrapped his hand more firmly around his sword's hilt.

Costane's mouth quirked faintly, but he remained as unreadable as ever as he continued. "That was when the queen struck upon the notion of concealing the message inside the lining of an innocuous hair ribbon. I insisted that she borrow one from one of her ladies, to avoid the trinket being traced back to her. She agreed, and much to our misfortune, she selected the Lady Beata."

"Beata?" Etienne remembered the tall, exotic woman in the queen's circle, her lovely, oval face framed by a cascade of ebony curls. Her voluptuous figure had half the men of the court panting for her favors. "Lady Beata was Girard's lover?" Even for Mathilde, Etienne could not smother the fresh incredulity in his voice.

"Aye. Beata had won the queen's trust through the years as wife, and later widow, of one of the Young King's household knights." Costane paused, then added, his flat tones taking on a rare hint of bitterness, "The queen, alas, did not deem it sufficiently significant at the time to mention to me that Beata's uncle was Sir Alun d'Amville."

Etienne started. Mathilde gasped from beside him.

"Not that the name would have held any meaning for me then—"

"D'Amville is Beata's uncle?" Etienne interrupted, stunned at this twist. "Then Chesnei—?"

"Is her brother." The squire's bloodless lips twitched, acknowledging Etienne's shock.

Etienne asked, "Why did I never see Chesnei at court before that evening I glimpsed him in the shadows with d'Yquebeuf and de Coulonces?"

"The Young King scorned him because he lacked skill in the mêlée. When his ineptitude cost the royal team winning points in a tournament seven years ago, the Young King banished Chesnei in a fit of peevish temper. Chesnei begged Marshal to intercede for him, but Marshal refused. 'Twas a grudge against Marshal that Chesnei has never forgiven."

Etienne studied Costane through narrowed eyes. The man had gone very stonelike again. "I've been in the Young King's court for four years, yet you know more about past court affairs than I do."

"Ah. That is because I have spent the past sennight . . . persuading the truth out of Beata."

Etienne could not stop his gaze from flicking to where he knew the crossbow hid behind Costane's cloak. He could not possibly mean . . . Of course he didn't. All the same, Etienne shifted his body just a little closer to Mathilde, leaning forward as he did so to thrust his shoulder protectively between her and Costane.

"Then you returned to Rouen after the tournament?" Etienne asked him. "Is that where Girard went, too?"

Blazes, he felt Mathilde leaning to peer around him to watch Costane.

"Aye," Costane said. "Girard flew back to Beata in a panic after he realized d'Amville was alive and knew about the ribbon. He did not know she was Chesnei's sister and was too besotted with her to suspect her loyalty to him. But I knew we had been betrayed by someone. Beata was the only person besides the queen and Marshal who had known about the message. I concealed myself and watched as Girard told her that the ribbon was in his sister's hands, then he told her when and where they were set to rendezvous. Beata soothed him, praised his cleverness, took him away to 'reward' him—and while he lay sleeping, I followed her as she slipped away to send a message to Chesnei."

That explained how d'Amville knew where to find Mathilde.

"But why did the queen choose Girard to give her message to Marshal, instead of you?" Etienne asked.

"Beata suggested Girard at d'Amville's command. She told the queen there would be less risk should the messenger be intercepted if that messenger could not be traced directly back to the queen. Beata seduced Girard and won his consent to deliver the ribbon. He was to join the tournament at Grantamur Castle, where Marshal would also be fighting. There, amidst the many distractions that accompany a grand mêlée, she assured him he would have no difficulty passing the message to Marshal.

"I was not prepared, however, to trust the queen's message, and possibly her future, to a man who was, to me, an unknown. I convinced Girard to accept me as his squire, so that I could keep him under my eye. He thought I was sent to him by Beata. I gave his former squire a bag of gold and persuaded him to take his new-found wealth and enjoy his fortune far away from Rouen." The bland gaze flicked to Therri. "He was far more cooperative than *your* squire, when I made a similar suggestion that he ride away from Grantamur Castle. I'm afraid I had to enforce my . . . suggestion . . . to him by less than gentle means."

Therri thundered an oath. He took a step towards Costane, fist clenching on his sword hilt. "If you have harmed the boy —"

Costane flung up a hand as though he might have been brushing back an annoying moth for all the alarm he showed at Therri's scowl.

"Nay, he has merely been bound and gagged and held in a hut in the depths of Lady Violette's forest. I thought his removal would facilitate your acceptance of the Lady Mathilde in his place."

"Oh!"

The soft exclamation came from Violette. Etienne saw how her eyes widened and darted to Therri. His friend gave a triumphant "hmph!" as he met her gaze. Costane's words proved at least that Therri had not seduced Mathilde into their tent. Violete took a step in Therri's direction, then stopped. Something flickered in her eyes, still holding her back.

"Why Therri's squire and not mine?" Etienne asked. After all, *he* had been the one who had unknowingly held the queen's message.

"I encountered Laurant's squire first," Costane said with what was clearly a shrug this time. "Girard was desperate to hide his sister from d'Amville, who had recognized her on the tournament field, while I needed to retrieve the ribbon. It seemed a way to satisfy both ends. We thought she would be gone from your tent before either of you discerned her masquerade." When Therri swore at him again, he added with an edge to his colorless voice, "Be grateful I treated your squire as gently as I did. The Lady Beata could bear witness to how ruthlessly I deal with impediments . . . or traitors . . . to the queen's cause. If the Lady Beata could speak."

Etienne bit his lip, not wanting to ask the question, yet feeling compelled to do so. "What happened to her?"

Costane gave another careless shrug, though this one hitched his cloak in such a way that Etienne caught the slight bulge of the weapon that lay concealed beneath it.

"After proving so wonderfully informative, I convinced her to join Girard and me on one of the queen's hunts. Unfortunately, someone's arrow went astray when the party loosed a volley at a stag. A sad end for so much beauty."

Etienne shuddered. He remembered again the coldly loosed arrow that had so narrowly missed Mathilde in the woods. Impulsively, he covered her linked hands with one of his. She stiffened, but his fingers closed firmly over hers. Blazes, he had the right, whether she knew it yet or not. He *would* make her his. And a man had a right to protect his own.

Her gaze, darkened with an emotion he could not interpret, darted to his, then away again so quickly it appeared but a violet blur. Her posture remained stiff, but she did not attempt again to draw away from his grasp.

Encouraged, he resumed his questioning of Costane. "I presume that Lady Beata told Chesnei about the message concealed inside her ribbon and that Chesnei told d'Yquebeuf and de Coulonces. So they hoped to trap Marshal with the queen's message? But why did they bring d'Amville into their scheme?"

"D'Yquebeuf's and de Coulonces' jealousy of Marshal was well known. Marshal was constantly on his guard against them and any of their men. But no one would suspect d'Amville. Everyone thought he was dead. D'Amville's orders were merely to watch and wait for Girard to place the ribbon in Marshal's hands. Only then was he to summon d'Yquebeuf's knights, who would arrest Marshal for the attempted delivery of the queen's treasonous message.

"But when he saw you, de Brielle, wearing the ribbon instead of Girard in the tournament, he must have thought Girard had gotten wind of d'Yquebeuf's scheme. I suspect he feared that Girard had enlisted accomplices and meant to pass the ribbon from confederate to confederate in hopes that d'Amville would lose track of who held it and it could ultimately be passed to Marshal without d'Amville's knowledge. D'Amville must have decided the only sure way to trap Marshal would be to hand him the message himself."

"Which is why he was so determined to wrest the ribbon away from me on the tournament field." Etienne paused, thinking over all that Costane had said. "I understand the jealousy that drove d'Yquebeuf and de Coulonces and the grudge that fired Chesnei, but what was in this plot for d'Amville? In the conversation I overheard in Rouen, Chesnei said something about a title."

"Beata told me that d'Yquebeuf promised to obtain the de Riavelle barony for d'Amville," Costane replied, glancing at Mathilde, "but d'Amville did not trust d'Yquebeuf to keep his word. 'Tis why he wanted Girard chosen as the messenger. Once Marshal's 'treason' was exposed, no one would blame d'Amville if he fell upon the treacherous knight who had served as go-between and punished him for betraying his oath of loyalty to the Young King. And if, inadvertently, d'Amville's punishment went too far and Girard died, the deed would scarcely be noticed for the uproar surrounding William Marshal."

Etienne's hand tightened over Mathilde's. The thought had not occurred to him before. But with Girard's death, Mathilde became heir to what land remained to her father. And his title would go to her husband.

Little good that would do Etienne. A penniless title would still leave him without means to support a wife. But d'Amville already held all of Mathilde's father's castles. He undoubtedly intended to claim the barony as well by marrying Mathilde.

She surely must have realized d'Amville's plan as well as Etienne did? Yet she gave no sign of dismay at Costane's words, other than to ask rather breathlessly, "Last night, when you helped Lady Violette's men put out the fire, did you find d'Amville's body in the woods?"

"I regret not, my lady. 'Tis why I am wearing this." Costane gestured at the hidden crossbow, though to everyone but Etienne it would appear he indicated his voluminous cloak. "If d'Amville is alive, then he knows you still have the ribbon and undoubtedly expects you to pass it on to me, now that Girard is dead. I hope he did not recognize me approaching the castle this morn, but just in case . . ." He turned to Violette. "There is a postern exit, I presume, to Grantamur Castle?"

Violette hesitated, then nodded.

"Then if I might have the ribbon?" He held out his hand again, palm up, towards Mathilde.

Mathilde turned towards Etienne, her violet eyes pleading. "I know you do not wish me to give it to him. But Girard gave his life for this." Her voice trembled and tears pooled in her eyes.

No, Etienne did not want this message delivered to King Henry, but he saw her determination. It was her choice to make, not his. Besides, he suspected it was the only way to rid themselves once and for all of Costane and his menacing crossbow. Etienne had wrung an explanation from the fellow, but even with Therri standing at his back with a sword, Etienne sensed Costane had no intention of leaving without a deadly attempt to obtain his prize if they tried to resist him. More than he wanted his homeland freed of Duke Richard, he wanted Mathilde safe from all threats the ribbon had brought upon her . . . including Costane.

He allowed her to draw her hands away and hold out the ribbon to Costane. Costane slid his hand inside his cloak. Etienne coiled his muscles and nearly shouted to Therri, but Costane merely pulled out a pouch to slip the ribbon in.

Etienne blew out a breath of relief. "So what now?" he asked.

"D'Amville has left me with no choice," Costane said. "I dare not give the ribbon to Marshal now. I shall have to carry it to England myself. Though King Henry may well doubt my story, I hope to at least convince him to visit Rouen to investigate the matter. That will force the Young King to delay his invasion plans, and perhaps even frighten him into abandoning them altogether. My lady," he said to Violette, "if you will be so kind as to show me that postern exit?"

"But what about Girard's body?" Mathilde protested. "You said it was in the bailey."

"My duty is to the queen," Costane said in his flat, cold voice. "I can do nothing more for your brother, my lady."

"But—" Her lower lip quivered, but she stilled it quickly with her teeth. "Then . . . then I must take him home to my father myself."

Etienne regained her hands and squeezed them. "I will hire a guard to escort us, just in case d'Amville should be watching for us on the road."

276

"No!" She snatched her fingers free and jumped to her feet. "I thank you, but—I do not want you to come. Etienne, this—this is something I must do for myself."

"Maude—"

"I will not go alone. I am sure Lady Violette will be kind enough to lend me an escort."

"Escort or no, if you think that I am going to sit here doing nothing while you risk yourself with d'Amville—"

Her eyes flashed violet fire at him. "Etienne, it is not your affair! I don't need you to protect me anymore."

"Mathilde—"

"No! I don't need you. I don't w-want you. Just go back to Hermaline and leave me be!"

He sprang up from the bench, but she pushed past him and ran up the stairs that led out of the hall.

Eighteen

"Etienne, stay," Violette said as he started after Mathilde. "Let me speak to her."

"So you can encourage this ridiculous fancy she has that I'm in love with Hermaline?" he challenged. "I think not."

Violette swept across the floor to block his path to the stairs. "She is still too distraught about her brother's death to listen to your declarations of devotion to her. Give her time."

Etienne tried to step around Violette.

She grabbed him by the sleeve and said more insistently, "Let her go home to her father. Let her grieve. I will provide a safe escort for her. If your passions for one another cannot survive a few sennights separation, then they were misplaced to begin with."

Grudgingly, he let her words check him. Perhaps she was right. Mathilde had not had time to recover from the shock of either Girard's death or d'Amville's violent reappearance and horrific accusations. She would need time alone with her father. Time to sort out the truth.

And *he* needed time to arrange a future they could share.

He drew off his jacinth ring and handed it to Violette. "My pledge to her," he said, "that I will come to her in a fortnight. And tell her that when I do, she shall become Enide to my Prince Erec. The only way I will ever ride forth to the world again is with her at my side as my wife."

Violette's eyes widened. Her exquisite lips silently mouthed the word "wife". Her gaze slid from him to Therri. When it finally shifted back to Etienne, the glow of her brilliant eyes had misted. Her fingers moved from his arm to find and press his hand.

"I will tell Hermaline as well," she said with a small smile. She released Etienne and turned to Costane. "If you will come with me, sir."

Costane followed her out of the hall.

"You're going to marry her then?" Therri asked when he and Etienne were alone.

Etienne's chin rose defensively at his friend's surprise. "Aye."

He refused to even contemplate the possibility that Mathilde might continue to rebuff him. Once her shock had worn off, she would respond to him as she had before. With fervent kisses, her gentle fingers caressing through his hair. With dreamy sighs from petal-pink lips and mists of longing in her violet eyes . . . longing that he ached to banish forever with the fulfillment of his love.

"I thought you could not afford a penniless wife."

Therri's reminder of Etienne's repetitive refrain interrupted his swiftly smoldering imagination. He gave a regretful sigh and pushed aside a vision of Mathilde steamily tangled in his arms.

"I can't," he agreed, "as long as I remain penniless myself."

"So . . . ?"

"I'm going home, Therri. I'm going to accept Triston's offer. We won't be rich, but Mathilde will never have to wonder where her next meal is going to come from."

The astonishment on Therri's face was so strong that it briefly banished his perpetual frown. "But what about Duke Richard? Your brother has sworn fealty to him. If the Young King invades Poitou, Triston will have no choice but to require every man of his house to raise his sword in Duke Richard's defense. Including you."

Etienne's mouth tightened. Defending Duke Richard was the one compromise he did not think he could make. "I'll find a way to avoid it," he said. "Triston detests Duke Richard as much as I do. He only swore the oath for his wife's sake. I think he will not press me too hard, so long as I bite my tongue and refrain from any conduct

that might call his own loyalty into question. That much I *can* do."
He hoped.

He waited for Therri to chide him, to rebuke him for all he
would be giving up ... his dreams of an independent future, his
hopes to someday possess a castle and land of his own, the freedom
to choose for himself where to bestow his allegiance among the
devil's brood known as Plantagenets.

Therri shook his head, but the wry smile that twisted up his
mouth was empty of disappointment or mockery. "I doubt Mathilde
understands the sacrifice you are making for her. But I'd give up as
many dreams of my own if it would only thaw Violette's proud
heart."

The last of Etienne's self-doubts melted away at Therri's words.
Buoyed by his friend's response, he grinned and clapped Therri on
the shoulder. "Vi will come around yet. I saw her face when Costane
suggested that Marshal was looking for a titled, landed wife to 'vent
his passions on' and distract him from his love for the queen. Do you
suppose Vi is any less outraged to know that he has been spouting
false devotion to her while coldly calculating her benefits as a
marriage partner, than she has been at you merely because you
accidentally kissed Lady Barbary in front of her?"

"It's more than just Lady Barbary and you know it," Therri
muttered gloomily. "She thinks that Mathilde and I—"

"No she doesn't. Not anymore. Costane explained why
Mathilde was in our tent and Vi knows I would never marry a
woman who had been another man's mistress. Especially *your*
mistress. She knows her suspicions about Mathilde were false. It will
not be long before she begins to wonder if *all* her doubts about you
have been misplaced."

Therri's face brightened. "Do you think so?"

"I am sure of it. As for Vi's pique over Lady Barbary ... I've an
idea for how to amend that misstep, as well."

Therri listened to Etienne's plan, his mouth quirking eagerly at
his suggestion.

"But what if Violette won't agree?" he asked when Etienne
finished.

"You have a fortnight to persuade her." Etienne dug a teasing elbow into Therri's ribs. "Remember, practice is the key. If you can convince Vi of that, the rest of my plan may be unnecessary. But we'll play the game nonetheless when I return with Mathilde."

When I returned with my wife. His blood pounded at the thought, but his heart floated curiously light. A sacrifice, Therri had called his decision to go home to Poitou. But it did not feel like a sacrifice now. The decision rested sweetly, peacefully in Etienne's breast. But excitement thrilled through him, too, a joyful anticipation for his future with Mathilde.

A fortnight. Fourteen days and she would be his. What could possibly go wrong in that time?

Mathilde stared at the jacinth ring winking in her hand. Her heart quivered with dismay.

"You must be mistaken, my lady," she protested. "Surely he meant you to give this to Hermaline?"

Violette smiled and gently pressed Mathilde's fingers until they enclosed Etienne's token. "There is no mistake, my lady Mathilde. Hermaline never fired the light in his eyes that I saw this day. Etienne is quite completely, utterly head-over-ears in love with you."

Mathilde's quivering heart vaulted into a tumble. The ring burned against her palm, branding into her flesh the pledge that Violette had repeated as she'd placed the jeweled object into Mathilde's hand.

Etienne loved her. Enough to plight his life to her. Enough to make her his wife. 'Twas her most precious, shimmering dream come true.

He was her Erec. She blinked away a tear. Nay, he was her Etienne. Her gentle, brave, faithful Etienne. And she would protect him as doggedly as Enide had sought to protect her own valiant, headstrong knight. Such men were too quick to dismiss their own mortality. But Mathilde would never make that mistake again.

She extended her fist with the ring towards Violette, thankful to see that her hand did not shake. "Tell Sir Etienne that I thank him, but I c-cannot—" Her voice threatened to betray what her steady hand did not. She must not falter now. She drew a deep breath and finished with resolute composure, "I do not return his love."

She spread her fingers and waited for Violette to take the ring from her palm.

Violette made no move to do so. Her dark eyes searched Mathilde's face. Mathilde knew how easily her blushes betrayed her. But she had only to remember d'Amville's sword raised above Etienne's breast to keep her cheeks cold and her eyes dry with determination.

Violette continued to study her in silence.

Impatience to have the deed done, the link to Etienne severed, lent an brittle edge to Mathilde's voice. "Pray, return this ring to him for me and tell him—"

One of Violette's dainty hands flew up. "I beg your pardon, my lady, but I am not a messenger. You shall have to tell him yourself the next time you see him."

She turned away on the words and swept across the fur carpets to the wardrobe door that stood in one wall.

Mathilde's dignified composure deserted her. "But my lady, I will not see him again. You must—"

"Of course you will see him," Violette cut her off, "when he comes to your father's manor to collect his ring and replace it with a wedding band. If you do not love him, you must tell him so to his face. I am not going to do it for you."

She pulled open the door and vanished inside.

Mathilde stared after her. She could not tell Etienne herself! He would insist that she look into his eyes when she said she did not love him, and if she did that he would know it was a lie. It had taken every shred of will she possessed not to melt into the shelter of his arms today when he'd sat so close to her while they had listened to Costane. If he touched her again, if he held her . . . if he kissed her . . . she might forget d'Amville and surrender herself, body and soul, to the blissful fulfillment of her dreams. But such a moment of weakness might prove fatal for Etienne. She could not allow that to happen.

But how to stop it? If Violette would not help her —

Violette emerged from the wardrobe with a small carved chest. She set it on the table beside the lion-shaped pitcher, searched through the chest's contents, then shook loose a gold-linked chain from a tumble of jewelry. Mathilde went weak with relief when Violette returned to her side and plucked the ring from her hand. She had changed her mind —

Violette slid the ring onto the chain and slipped the chain over Mathilde's head. "It would not do for you to lose this ere you return it to Etienne."

The metal links prickled cold along Mathilde's neck, but the ring, warmed by her hand, sank into the folds of her robe and nestled its promise against her skin.

Mathilde wondered that the leaping of her heart did not send the ring flying.

Violette stepped back and surveyed her with a little smile. "You have played squire long enough, I think. We must turn you into a lady again before we send you home to your father. I fear you are too tall to wear any of my gowns. Wait for me here while I borrow you something from one of my ladies."

Mathilde waited until she was alone in the room, then sat down on Violette's fur-tumbled bed. Her thoughts had been so tightly entwined about Etienne that they had almost choked out her concern for her father. Soon . . . too soon . . . she would have to confront him. The King's Wardrobe. The scar on d'Amville's throat. Did she truly want to know the truth about either anymore?

But there would be no way to avoid asking the questions, not now that Girard was dead. Her brother's loss would break her father's heart. And when he learned that d'Amville still lived, that d'Amville had struck the death-blow . . .

D'Amville, d'Amville! If she had not been a guest in Violette's house, she would have seized that lion-shaped pitcher on the table and hurled it against the wall.

She covered her face with her hands to prevent them from succumbing to the temptation. Without Violette to strike a pose for, there was no reason to fight the trembling in her fingers, the soft shiver of her palms against her cheeks. It did not matter what her father might have done. She could not leave him to d'Amville's mercy.

She must find d'Amville. Or allow him to find her.

She did not realize that one hand had slid away from her cheek and stolen inside her robe to close about Etienne's ring until the door opened and Hermaline stepped across the threshold, a rust-colored surcote and dull-gold tunic draped across her arms.

"Violette said I was to bring you this."

The words were simple, but the unspoken accusation in Hermaline's summer blue eyes flushed Mathilde's face with guilty heat. She released Etienne's ring as though it had become a firebrand. The abrupt movement bounced the ring out of the folds of the robe to land against the outside of the fabric.

Hermaline drew in a sharp breath. The accusation flared into rage. "He gave you *that?* The ring the Young King gave him?"

Violette entered the room a half-dozen steps behind her stepdaughter, in time to hear Hermaline's wail. "My dear, I told you that Etienne and Mathilde were—"

"Etienne is *mine!*" Hermaline flung the clothes in her arms onto the floor. Her soft, round face screwed up in distorting fury. "I'm not going to surrender him to this—this drab little—*scarecrow.*"

"Hermaline!"

She ignored Violette's rebuke and rushed on, "Do you think your false blushes fooled me, *Lady Maude.* Lady, indeed! That oh-so-coy game you played with him before the tournament, demanding your token back, pretending you were too virtuous to kiss him—" She swung round to Violette. "It was sickening, Violette, the hungry way he gazed at her, and the eager way she gazed back. Etienne said she was his childhood friend, but from what I witnessed between them, his trollop is more like it."

Violette gasped.

Mathilde shot up from the bed, too indignant to be relieved that Hermaline did not appear to recognize her as Therri's squire. "I am not a trollop! Etienne never did anything more than kiss me."

"He must have done a great deal more, if he now feels obligated to marry you," Hermaline said with an angry smirk.

All of Mathilde's self-sacrificing intentions suddenly dissolved in a heartbeat. *Hermaline will keep you safe*, she had told Etienne. Nay, marriage to Hermaline might protect him from d'Amville's mad jealousy, but this gilded-haired harpy would make Etienne's life miserable.

There had to be some lady, somewhere on the face on the earth, who would guard him for Mathilde more gently than Hermaline would?

"Etienne and I are not lovers," Mathilde insisted. "We are not even childhood friends. We met for the first time here at Grantamur Castle, the night before the tournament when he asked to wear my favor. He has behaved as nothing but a gentleman towards me — except for those lies he told you about us. And I can think of no reason why he spoke such an outlandish tale, unless he simply wanted to avoid wearing that atrocious veil you were trying to thrust upon him."

"Oh!" Hermaline gasped, fury etched across her face.

"There was a time," Mathilde went on, "when I feared that I had stolen his affections from you. I thought it was only lust he felt for me. But now I know . . ." Her fist closed again, boldly, defiantly around Etienne's ring. "Now I know that he loved me all along."

Let Hermaline think that Mathilde intended to wed him. Hermaline would be forced to look for some other man to snare. Before Mathilde left Grantamur Castle, she would make Violette swear to find Etienne a gentle, worthy wife to protect and cherish him . . . anyone but Hermaline.

But Hermaline jeered, "Loved *you?* With your scarecrow body and your funny straw hair? What on earth have you done to your hair?"

Mathilde reached up defensively to the cropped ends of the locks that brushed her shoulders. They did not feel like straw. Their texture was fine and soft, almost as silky as Etienne's wayward curls. Etienne had not seemed to be put off by the blunt cut Girard had dealt them. Or by her "scarecrow" body.

"A man would have to be desperate to find his passions fanned by a woman as scrawny as you," Hermaline sneered.

"I am not scrawny," Mathilde uttered, goaded into an impulsive response. "Etienne says I am 'ethereal' and that my legs are even prettier than Violette's." She stopped, her hand flying to her lips.

But Violette did not look offended. Laughter danced in her dark eyes. "I have been very careful not to flaunt my legs in front of men, including Etienne. He must be well and thoroughly smitten with you, my lady, to hazard such an opinion without knowing the competition. Or else your legs must indeed be exceptional."

Mathilde giggled and blushed.

"How would he know," Hermaline challenged, "unless she has been flaunting her legs for his view. Or unless they were lovers."

"We are *not* —"

"He undoubtedly glimpsed them," Violette broke blithely across Mathilde's protest, "when the wind caught her skirts and lifted them teasingly above her ankles. I own, such an embarrassing occurrence has happened to me a time or two. So perhaps Etienne had more evidence than I thought for his bold statement."

Mathilde threw her a grateful look for protecting her squire's disguise. What spiteful tales Hermaline would spread if once she made that connection made Mathilde shudder.

"Give it up, my dear," Violette said to Hermaline. "Etienne does not love you. He never did, and your land and gold are no longer enough to lure him. We will find you another husband. What about that ginger-haired gentleman I saw you laughing with on Sunday? What was his name? He seemed quite taken with you. If the jewels he wore are any indication of his wealth, you will like him even better than Etienne."

"I don't!" Hermaline pouted. "He is fat. I thought it wouldn't matter, that this ring would be worth —" She waved her hand in the air as she spoke. Mathilde caught a glimpse of an emerald enclosed in a circle of twinkling diamonds before Hermaline saw Violette's frown and thrust her hand behind her back.

Mathilde's heart skipped. She had seen that ring before. It was one of many that had flashed from Chesnei's plump hand the day that Therri had introduce him to Hermaline outside Therri's and Etienne's tent.

Violette's gaze narrowed on her step-daughter's face. All humor fled from her brilliant dark eyes. "Worth what? Where did you get that ring?"

"Where I got it is none of your affair," Hermaline muttered. "I don't want to marry Sir Nevell. I don't care how rich he is. His hands sweat too much and his mouth is too wet and he puffs like the blacksmith's bellows when he—" She caught herself up, then whined, "I don't want him. I want someone handsome and tall and slim like Etienne. I know it would be different with him."

"What would be different?" Violette demanded.

Hermaline answered with a sullen stare at the floor.

Violette's mouth tightened. "Lady Mathilde, would you excuse my step-daughter and me for a moment?"

Mathilde hesitated, then slipped obediently out of the room. But she paused on the other side of the door.

Clearly Violette had not connected Hermaline's ginger-haired suitor, Sir Nevell, with Chesnei. Mathilde racked her brains, but could not recall that during the discussion with Costane, Chesnei had ever been referred to by his Christian name. No doubt Violette had so many suitors of her own that she could not put names and faces to them all.

When had Hermaline obtained Chesnei's ring? And why had he given it to her? Men did not bestow such expensive gifts on ladies without expecting something in return. Even Etienne hoped for a concession from Mathilde in exchange for the token that now hung around her neck. What had Hermaline promised Chesnei?

Or had the payment already been made?

She remembered Chesnei's hungry gaze at Hermaline outside the tent. *His mouth is too wet and he puffs like the blacksmith's bellows when he –* Mathilde shuddered, thankful that Hermaline had not finished the sentence. The thought of Chesnei caressing a woman with even a fraction of the passion that Etienne had showered on Mathilde twisted her stomach with revulsion. No, no. Hermaline could not have surrendered more than a few kisses to him.

Could she?

Mathilde suppressed another shudder. Even Hermaline's rude behavior could not justify Mathilde's allowing her to become entangled in d'Amville's nasty family tree. She must warn Hermaline and Violette.

She reached out a hand to the door latch, but had no more than cracked the door open when Hermaline's sulky voice checked her.

"I didn't even like it. His fat, clammy hands and his sloppy mouth— I thought I could close my eyes and pretend it was someone else, but he just grew too disgusting. It would be different with someone like Etienne."

Violette stood with her back to the door, but Mathilde saw her rigid outrage. "As if Etienne would touch you with a ten-foot staff after this! " Violette exclaimed. "And you had the *gall* to impugn Mathilde's morals. A kiss is one thing, Hermaline, but this—! If your father were alive, he would beat you black and blue for such lewdness."

"Then he would have been a brutish hypocrite," Hermaline replied, her round face crumpling into a belligerent scrunch from where Mathilde viewed it over Violette's diminutive shoulder. "He sported with a different woman every night. Why should I not use men to satisfy my desires, the way he used my mother to satisfy his?" Hermaline held up her hand shamelessly this time, twisting and turning it until the stones of Chesnei's ring sparkled in the light. Whatever expression she caught on Violette's face turned Hermaline's eyes mocking. "Oh, don't look so shocked. I did not give him what he wanted most. Just enough to leave him panting and hopeful. I told him I could not surrender more before our wedding night."

Violette gave a ringing gasp. "Are you saying that you promised to marry him?"

Hermaline tossed her head. "I have no intention of doing any such thing. I already have what I want. If he says I made him any promises, I will simply deny it." She smiled smugly down at the ring.

"What good will that do you if Sir Nevell decides to boast of your tryst? People—especially men—are too eager to believe the worst where women are concerned. Especially when the woman flaunts a man's jewels on her hand."

"Mathilde is flaunting Etienne's ring, but you defend *her* honor."

"She is going to marry him, Hermaline. Nay, don't you dare fly into a fit about that again. Etienne would not take you now anyway. No man wants a wanton for a wife, particularly one who has been wanton with another man. There is no help for it now. You shall have to wed Sir Nevell."

"Marry that toad? I would rather die!"

"You should have thought of that before you allowed greed for his ring to allow him such liberties with you."

Hermaline stamped a foot against the floor. "I won't marry him! You cannot make me! And I shall win Etienne yet. Just as soon as that little scarecrow is gone from Grantamur Castle—"

"Nothing you can do will win you Etienne now." Violette flung up a hand to silence Hermaline's angry protest. Mathilde could not see Violette's face, but something in her expression must have given Hermaline pause. "I shall confront Sir Nevell myself and insist that he do the honorable thing by you. And if you think I do not have the power to enforce this marriage, you are very much mistaken. I gave the Young King three bags of silver for the privilege to choose my own husband and a fourth bag for the privilege of choosing yours. I was willing to allow you a voice in the matter, but now—! I fear your actions have spoken for you. Sir Nevell it must be, and none other."

Mathilde pushed the door open. As fiercely as she disliked Hermaline, she could not allow her to marry Chesnei.

"My lady, forgive me," she stammered when Violette swung round at her sudden entrance. "I did not mean to overhear, but— You must not do this. Sir Nevell—you do not realize who he is."

Violette stared down her haughty little nose at Mathilde, manifesting her displeasure at the interruption. "I know that he has besmirched my step-daughter's reputation," she said coldly. "Whoever he is, whoever is to blame—" she shot a crushing look at Hermaline "—he must now make the matter right."

"But my lady, I recognized Hermaline's description, and his name—Sir Nevell—it is Chesnei. D'Amville's nephew. I am sure of it."

Her words succeeded in taking Violette aback. "Nay, how would Hermaline come to be involved with d'Amville's nephew?"

"She met Chesnei outside Etienne's tent one day. I saw how Chesnei admired her, but I did not realize he meant to pursue her, much less that she would permit him to—"

"You vile little eavesdropper!" Hermaline cried. "I ought to tear off your ears! Now I expect you will spread the tale, so that Etienne will spurn me the more!"

She started across the floor towards Mathilde, her fingers curling into claws. But Violette swept in front of Hermaline and caught her by the shoulders.

"Is it true?" she demanded of her step-daughter. "Does Sir Nevell go by the surname Chesnei?"

"What if he does?" Hermaline said, glaring at Mathilde. "What does it matter what his surname is? I don't want him and I won't marry him. And I won't give back his ring!"

Violette groaned. "If you don't marry him, you will be branded a wanton. If you do, you will be marrying a murderer's kin. Would your father were alive to see this day! He might have flogged some sense into you ere you brought us to this impossible pass."

Hermaline shook herself free of her step-mother's grasp. "Sir Nevell, kin to a murderer? He offered no threat to me. Oh, he grew zealously bold, but he made no attempt to prevent me from withdrawing from his caresses."

"Then you were fortunate, my lady," Mathilde said, "for I assure you, he can be most dangerous." She touched her throat, remembering the crushing force of Chesnei's hands cutting off her air.

Hermaline observed Mathilde's gesture. She cocked her head. "Was he dangerous to you, my lady?"

"He . . . tried to injure me, yes."

"Why?"

Mathilde's first instinct was to refuse to answer Hermaline's question. Her family's affairs were none of this spiteful girl's business. Hermaline, she suspected, would take too great delight in publishing the embarrassing details of her father's past if she learned of them. And if she knew that Chesnei still posed a threat to Mathilde, she might even be malicious enough to tell Chesnei where to . . .

. . . find her.

And Chesnei would tell d'Amville.

Mathilde swallowed hard, then answered the way she knew she must. "He did it for his uncle, Sir Alun d'Amville. I was betrothed to him once, but my father revoked it and Sir Alun grew angry. He . . . he still wishes to marry me. So he sent his nephew Chesnei to find me and . . . bring me to him. Only Etienne rescued me. Now I am going home to my father, where I will finally be safe from Sir Alun and—" she found Etienne's ring and deliberately closed her hand around it "—where I shall I have peace to consider my decision to marry Etienne."

A lie. That decision had been made for her by d'Amville. But she must appear to remain in competition for Etienne if she were to push Hermaline into the action she wanted.

Hermaline frowned at Mathilde's fist about the ring. Then the corners of her mouth lifted in a slow, speculative smile.

"When do you leave to return to your father, my lady?"

Hermaline's inquiry dripped with sudden sweetness, a ludicrous contrast to her shrieking anger only moments before. Mathilde had read Hermaline's vindictiveness aright. At her first opportunity, she would meet with Chesnei or send word to him of Mathilde's whereabouts. Hermaline's eyes glittered with such eager anticipation that Mathilde almost hated to dash her hopes.

"As soon as your step-mother's guards are ready to accompany me."

"Guards?"

Mathilde was hard put not to laugh at the way Hermaline's face fell. "Indeed, yes. She has most kindly agreed to lend me an escort so that Sir Alun might not seize me along the way." She turned to Violette. "But you are quite right, my lady, that I cannot travel this way." She gestured at the robe she still wore.

Violette moved to pick up the tunic and surcote from where Hermaline had flung them onto the floor. She said to Hermaline in a lowered voice, "We will settle this matter of you and Chesnei after Lady Mathilde is gone. And I will not hear one more rude word to her, do you understand?"

Hermaline gave a sullen nod.

Violette laid the clothes on the bed and began to smooth them, then sent an impatient glance at Hermaline. "You forgot to include a chemise. Fetch one from my wardrobe. Bring some stockings, too, and a pair of my shoes. I hope they will not be too small for your feet, my lady," she said to Mathilde. "The chemise will undoubtedly be a bit short, but no one will notice beneath the tunic."

Hermaline obeyed her step-mother's orders with a sulky pout.

Mathilde waited until Hermaline brought the chemise and Mathilde had exchanged it for the robe, before remarking to Violette, "I shall be glad to be home again. There is a place on my father's manor where I sometimes go when I am confused and need to sort out a question in my head."

Violette handed her a pair of silk stockings and murmured with a sympathetic smile, "Like what to do about Etienne?"

Mathilde nodded. She rubbed the sleek fabric between her fingers, then sat down on the bed to draw the stockings on.

"Where is it you go on your manor to . . . think, my lady?" Hermaline asked.

Mathilde saw Violette's sharp glance at her step-daughter and hastily fastened on the garters. Perhaps 'twould be safer if Violette were not in the room to hear her answer.

She slid one foot into Violette's slipper. White silk, like the stockings, only the shoes were encrusted with gold embroidery done in elaborate scrolls. It did not surprise Mathilde that the delicate object did not fit her foot. She did not think her feet were overly large, but Violette's were tiny, in keeping with her diminutive frame. It gave Mathilde the excuse she needed to divert Violette.

"They are too small, my lady. And I very much fear that Lady Hermaline's would be too big." Hermaline colored, as though suspecting her of a deliberate insult, but Mathilde's only intent was to deprive Violette of an excuse to send Hermaline on the errand Mathilde wished Violette to undertake. "Perhaps one of your other ladies will have a pair that will fit me more comfortably. Do you mind asking them? Perhaps something in a sturdy leather for traveling. I will take the greatest care of them, I promise."

Violette hesitated, then nodded and started towards the door, but she paused to warn Hermaline softly, "I will be gone but a moment. Help Mathilde lace up her surcote . . . and see that you mind your tongue while I'm gone."

Mathilde slid the dull-gold tunic over her head, then followed it with the rust colored surcote. She turned her back to Hermaline and said over her shoulder, "If you would be so good, my lady?"

Hermaline began lacing up the back. "This place on your manor where you like to go. Where is it, my lady?"

She was pathetically obvious, Mathilde thought. Hermaline might as well have said, "Pray tell me where d'Amville can find you and I will be sure he gets the message."

Mathilde suppressed a bitter smile and feigned an attitude of casual conversation. "The old threshing house at the south end of our fields. 'Tis more of a shed, really, that a few of the serfs erected to thresh and winnow their wheat in my grandfather's day. My father built a newer, larger barn after our last good harvest several years ago that he lets the serfs use for their wheat as well as ours. No one goes to the old threshing house any longer. Which is why I like it there. It is quiet and private. I do not think even my father knows how often I go there to untangle my thoughts."

She knew from the agitated jerking of the surcote's strings that Hermaline could scarcely contain her excitement. How quickly would she impart this information to Chesnei? Would she entrust it to a written message or deem it safer to reveal it in person? If Hermaline went herself, what if another of Chesnei's jewels caught her eye and she decided to endure his embraces again to obtain it. This time, Hermaline might not escape Chesnei's lust so easily.

Mathilde's conscience stirred uncomfortably. She was not responsible for Hermaline's greed, she told herself. Or her jealousy. Hermaline did not have to betray her to Chesnei.

But Mathilde knew she would. And she knew she would not try to stop her.

Nineteen

Etienne drew off his gloves and bent to warm his hands at the hearth in his brother's hall. It had been an exhausting sennight and five. It had required a punishing pace to inspect his brother's three grand manors in so short a span of time. Triston had not questioned his brother's urgency. He had conducted the tour with rare patience and a keen agricultural eye that Etienne had never known his brother possessed.

But what had amazed Etienne the more was his own swift comprehension of the nuances of manor management. He, like Triston, must have absorbed more rustic knowledge in his youth on Vere Manor than he had realized.

Triston mounted the hall's dais and sprawled his large frame in one of the two carved chairs set there. "Well?" he demanded, eyeing his young brother with a weighing gaze.

Etienne stole a covert look around the hall before answering. Gone was the stark coldness his father had embraced after his mother's death. The cheerful tapestries his father had torn down had been restored to the grey stone walls. Mingling their fragrance with the rushes beneath Etienne's boots were trellises twined with flowers, propped strategically along the walls in the spaces between the weavings. Although the flowers were a foreign touch, they lent the chamber a familiar warmth. The hall was alive and vibrant, the way it had been in his youth. Before his mother died.

"You are back!"

Etienne turned at the singing, feminine voice and saw his sister-in-law sail into the room. Triston immediately straightened in his chair and held out a hand to her, but while her glowing blue eyes betrayed her longing for his clasp, she turned instead towards Etienne.

"The matter is settled, I trust? You will be staying with us, will you not?"

Etienne cursed himself for his rudeness, but he could not resist staring at her, as he had at their first meeting a sennight and five ago. Her resemblance to his brother's first wife was as startling now as it had been then. She appeared to have taken pains to lessen the likeness by piling her golden hair into a mass of curls on top of her head and draping her shapely figure in an elegant, exotically patterned surcote. Etienne had seen similarly rich attire in the Young King's court, but never in Vere Castle's quiet environs. Certainly never worn by his brother's shy, reserved first wife! Yet this face was so like—

The merry mouth twitched into a frown. Nay, Triston's former wife had never borne such a twinkle in her eyes, or ever displayed such firm but controlled displeasure.

"Do not tell me that you are still debating the matter?" she said. She swung about towards the dais. "You've quarreled with him, haven't you?" she accused her startled husband. "I warned you to say nothing of—"

"I didn't," he interrupted her swiftly. "We did not talk politics once." His dark eyes shot a glance at Etienne. "Although you know it is something that we must discuss eventually?"

Etienne nodded. He rubbed his flame-warmed fingers at the knots of tension throbbing along the back of his neck. The time had come for decision. He cast another glance about the hall. The chamber was not large. It might have fit comfortably into any one of the grander halls of his brother's new inheritance. But in a pang of sharp realization, Etienne knew that this was all he had ever really wanted. A modest hall, like this one of his youth, someplace he could call his own.

Given time, he might someday win such a castle and manor for himself. But he was no longer willing to wait. He had learned from his father how empty such a hall could be. Without the woman one loved to warm the walls, as his brother's wife had warmed these for Triston, Etienne knew the victory of castle and lands would be empty indeed.

"Better a servant in my brother's house," he murmured, "than lord without Mathilde."

"I beg your pardon?" Siri, his brother's wife, turned towards Etienne at his murmur, her fair eyebrows raised in question.

Etienne shook his head. "'Twas naught." He smiled and took her hand, then led her onto the dais and placed her fingers in his brother's large, brown palm. "I think I have never seen you so happy, brother," he said, seeing the way Triston's eyes warmed at the transfer of Siri's clasp to his.

Triston laughed and pulled his protesting wife onto his lap. "In truth, this sprite brings light to all she touches . . . including my dark, benighted soul." He grinned at her embarrassed struggles.

Etienne had difficulty reconciling Triston's teasing manner with the quiet, solemn brother he had grown up with. But the tight lines about Triston's mouth, etched in a youth burdened by Triston's own overblown sense of responsibility, were gone, as were the haunted shadows that had sobered him yet further through the tragedies of his first marriage.

"One kiss, sweetheart," Triston insisted, his dark eyes clear and bright with laughter. "It has been well-nigh a fortnight."

Siri pushed against her husband's chest, but so tiny a woman had small hope of escape from Triston's powerful arms. "Triston, 'tis not the place for—"

"Come, 'tis only before my brother. He will forgive my impatience, I think, for I suspect he is suffering a similar restlessness of his own."

By the time Triston had soundly kissed his wife and allowed her to slip into the chair next to his, Etienne knew his face was as red as Siri's.

"How do you know that I—"

"Nothing causes a man to swallow his pride faster than a headlong fall for a woman," Triston broke across his brother's confusion. "What else would bring you 'crawling back' to me, after telling me six months ago that I could go to blazes?"

Etienne grew hotter. "I have not come crawling—"

Siri slapped her husband's arm. "No, of course he hasn't. Shame on you, Triston. 'Tis you who needs his help far more than he needs yours."

Etienne swallowed his resentment and cleared his throat uncomfortably. "Well, as to that . . . Triston, I won't deny that your offer has become more . . . attractive—" he bit off the word *imperative* "—since we last talked. And though I clearly have much yet to learn, I believe I could learn it quickly. And I hope you do not doubt that I would serve you loyally and honestly—"

"Of course I do not doubt it," Triston said, his dark face settling into its more familiar planes of soberness. "'Tis the reason I came to you in the first place. We have had our differences through the years, but I've always suspected a cool head lay beneath the impetuousness of your youth. Rash though it was then, your fidelity to Father was unswerving. You showed courage in your defense of him, as well as faithfulness. I have need of both qualities in the man I entrust to govern the inheritance that Siri brought me."

Triston rose from his chair and moved to place a hand on Etienne's shoulder. "You are no longer a boy, Etienne. Perhaps I did not make it clear that I recognized that when I came to Rouen. You have grown into a man of thoughtfulness and conviction. One whom I am proud to call 'brother.'" His fingers tightened against Etienne's tense muscles. "And, as my sweet wife says, one whose talents and loyalty I find myself much in need of at present."

Etienne felt a lump swelling in his throat. He had never known how much he craved his brother's approval until this moment.

"But Triston, why?" he forced himself to ask. "From all I have witnessed during the tour of your manors, you are more than capable of governing Siri's lands yourself. Why do you need me or anyone to serve as seneschal?"

Etienne wanted this position—needed it, if he were to claim

Mathilde—but still his spirit shrank at the fear that his brother had offered it out of pity.

Triston dropped his hand. Etienne caught the wariness that stole into his brother's eyes, although Triston answered with a studied nonchalance.

"Duke Richard is demanding my presence more frequently in his court. The rumors are becoming louder of an imminent assault on Poitou by the Young King's forces. And with our family's record of tarnished loyalty—" Triston's laugh was harsh now, empty of the amusement he had displayed earlier. "Well, let us just say that Duke Richard prefers to keep me under his eye."

Etienne drew a deep, resolute breath. "Triston—"

Triston held up a forestalling hand. "I know, I know. You refuse to swear fealty to Richard." He tossed a glance at his wife before adding, "Nay, Etienne, I do not intend to quarrel with you about it again. I shan't require it of you. But my oath must stand for my house, and if in truth an assault is launched by the Young King—" He paused with an inquiring lift of his brows at Etienne. Etienne bit his lip but said nothing, and after a moment Triston calmly repeated, "If an assault is launched by the Young King, I cannot allow you or anyone to put my lands and the lives of my house at risk by taking up arms for Duke Richard's rival."

"I know that," Etienne said. "And I give you my oath that I will raise my sword for neither side. 'Tis the best I can offer you. I need this position, as you have discerned—but I cannot—I will not fight to keep Richard the Tyrant on his throne."

Triston weighed him for a moment, then gave a curt nod of his head and held out his hand. Etienne gripped his brother's arm in a hard, firm clasp.

"'Tis done then," Triston said with a smile. "You shall play seneschal while I dance attendance upon the Tyrant."

From the curl of Triston's lip, Etienne knew his brother nourished as bitter a dislike of Duke Richard as Etienne did himself. But for the protection of his wife and lands, and because of Triston's integrity in keeping the oath he had sworn to the duke, Etienne knew that his brother would spill his own blood to defend the Tyrant's throne.

Siri flew up from her chair and caught Etienne's hand away from Triston. "Well spoken, my love," she said to her husband, then to Etienne, "I have gained not only a brother, but if Triston is right, I shall soon have a sister as well. Oh, but you must tell us all about her, Etienne!"

"Aye," Triston said, a mischievous gleam in his eyes, "tell us about the 'willow-maiden' who has entranced you."

Etienne stared at him. He had dreamed of Mathilde every night, but surely he had not blurted out that description of her in his sleep? "What makes you think she is a 'willow-maiden?'"

Triston flashed a lopsided grin and Siri gave a warm chuckle. It took a moment for Etienne to realize that they were gazing over his shoulder.

He turned. A woman stood in the arched entryway of the hall, a tendril of pale gold hair escaped from her snowy white veil. She was not beautiful, but an elusive charm sparkled from her striking, silvery eyes. Gone from her tall, slender figure was the awkward uncertainty Etienne remembered from their youth. She stood before him a confident, dignified matron. Saints! Five years wed! It made him feel an old man.

"Heléne!" He sprang from the dais and caught her in his arms, swinging her once around in joyful greeting before setting her back on her feet with a brotherly kiss.

She returned his embrace with a quick, fierce hug. "Oh, Etienne, how glad I am to see you again!"

"And you, my dear. I feared never to lay eyes on you again after Gunthar snatched you off to England."

"He brought me back over a fortnight ago, because Acelet— Oh, but I will tell you all about that later."

Etienne shot a look at Triston. He had said nothing about their ramshackle cousin, but Triston only shrugged and smiled as Heléne continued, "Hugh is so good to me, Etienne. I hope your willow-maiden will be as good to you."

Etienne dropped his arm from about her. "You know as well?"

She ducked her head in a gesture of guilt. "'Twas in the letter Therri wrote me, along with his request to Hugh to compile for him some names from King Henry's Wardrobe staff. You do not mind that I told your brother, do you?"

So that's how Triston had known. The sly dog, making Etienne think he had been a sleep-talking fool.

"Nay." Etienne grinned at her and slid his arm back around her waist. "She is a little like you, Heléne. Not quite so tall, and without that touch of gold in her hair, and her eyes are violet instead of silver, but—"

Heléne laughed. "She does not sound like me at all. False-flatterer."

"Nay, 'tis not her looks, but her manner, the way you were before you married Gunthar. She does not believe me when I tell her that she is pretty. But she is, Heléne. She is lovely! An angel's face with a sweet dusting of dreams in her eyes, and lips as soft and fragrant as the petals in your mother's rose garden."

"Oho," Triston laughed from the dais. "You have sampled her lips, have you? You move along apace."

"I trust you are all speaking of his willow-maiden," a new voice drawled, "else I must bear sore suspicions about the way he is embracing my wife."

Etienne flushed and hurriedly dropped his arm from Heléne. The Earl of Gunthar leaned with his broad shoulders propped against the entryway, eyeing Etienne with a mixture of amusement and some less pleasant emotion in his steady grey eyes. Etienne remembered that Gunthar had once been irrationally jealous of his friendship with Heléne.

Gunthar straightened and joined his wife, passing a possessive arm around her shoulders.

Heléne sent another guilty glance at Etienne. "You do not mind that I told my husband about your lady, too? I was so happy for you, Etienne, that I could not resist sharing the news." She smiled up at Gunthar, then looked back at Etienne. "I saw you and Triston riding past my father's manor this morning, on your return to Vere Castle. I suggested to Hugh that we ride over and bring you the information that Therri asked my husband to search for."

"The Wardrobe list?" Etienne looked sharply at Gunthar. "You have it?"

"Aye," Gunthar drawled. "What bee has Therri taken between his ears now, to hold such urgent and uncommon interest in the workings of the King's Wardrobe staff thirty years ago?"

"Actually, I am the one with the 'uncommon interest,'" Etienne admitted. "'Tis for Mathilde . . . my willow-maiden." He sent a crooked grin at Heléne before turning his attention cautiously back to Gunthar. "I was not sure you would agree to help me after . . . well, considering what lay between us. So Therri sent you my request in his name."

"If you are thinking of the dagger you once tried to plant in my breast, I have long pardoned you for that," Gunthar said, "as I hope you have forgiven me for snapping your wrist and threatening to have you drawn and quartered."

Despite the generosity in Gunthar's wry response, Etienne still found the memories uncomfortable. "Thank you, my lord," he uttered gruffly, then said, to turn the subject, "Do you have the list with you?"

Gunthar pulled some folded parchments sheets from a pouch attached to his belt. "This was sent to me by William Hallet, a former servant of King Henry. Hallet is now three score and ten and can scarce recall what he had for dinner last noon, but his memory of names and events from the past is remarkable. Nevertheless, I thought it judicious to back up his recollections with ledger accounts, as much as was possible. But some of the ledgers have been lost or misplaced and could not be recovered in the short amount of time Therri stated in his request."

Gunthar waved a hand at the dais and Etienne adjourned with him and Heléne to the table set there. Triston and Siri joined them as Gunthar smoothed out the sheets out on the tabletop.

"These are the men on the staff that Hallet recalls from his days of service in King Henry's Wardrobe." Gunthar gestured at the sheet that lay on top. "Because Therri seemed unsure of the exact dates, I thought it wise to allow a ten year span for your search, stretching from twenty-five to thirty-five years back."

Etienne followed the sweep of Gunthar's finger as it traced down the column while Gunthar spoke the names aloud.

"Cloué, d'Anvau, Bonnard, Faulkner, d'Avenant . . .

"Do any of them ring familiar?"

Etienne shook his head.

Gunthar continued, "De Valmé, de la Roque, Margéury, Clifford, Fairfield—"

"Fairfield?" Etienne repeated. "An English name. I asked specifically about the staff of King Henry's *Norman* Wardrobe."

"Hallet assures me this is what this is. No doubt Fairfield was an English transplant to the staff. Perhaps his mother was Norman. Is it significant?"

Etienne hesitated. "I don't know. I am not sure what I am looking for. Go on."

Gunthar shrugged. "D'Aiguillon, Conalle , Dubois, Chesnei, Tourdeville—"

"Chesnei?" Etienne gasped out the name. "*Chesnei*. Are you sure?" He swept Gunthar's hand away from the parchment and stared at the name scrawled there. He felt a lurch of excitement, but caution quickly reined it in. "But he is even younger than you," he said, frowning at Gunthar. "He could not possibly have been on King Henry's staff thirty years ago."

"Who?" Triston asked.

"Sir Nevell de Chesnei. Unless . . . Might it have been his father? What do the ledger copies say?"

Gunthar shifted through the pile of parchment until another leaf lay on top. Again he ran down the list, muttering the names, until he came to the one Etienne sought.

"Bevis de Chesnei. According to this, a man by that name served in the King's Wardrobe between 1150 and 1167."

"A Chesnei on the king's Norman Wardrobe staff thirty years ago," Etienne murmured. "And D'Amville's sister married a Chesnei." His hand formed a triumphant fist. He banged it lightly twice against Sir Bevis' name. "Ah, Maude, I think we have just found the missing piece to your puzzle."

Mathilde shivered in the afternoon mist and drew her thin cloak more tightly around her. She had spent so many hours pacing in front of the old threshing house that she could see the matted, indented path her footsteps had left in the stale hay. She swept a wild hand through hair disheveled by the low howling wind. She had come here every afternoon for the last thirteen days. This waiting would drive her mad!

Mad. She smiled bitterly. That malady would make her a suitable bride for d'Amville. If her father had known that his enemy still lived, he would have barricaded her inside their manor house . . . or sought to banish her to some far flung corner of another realm where her betrothed might never find her.

But he would find her. Today, tomorrow . . . nay, dear heaven, let him not come tomorrow! Tomorrow would be the fortnight's end, and Etienne . . . D'Amville *must* come before Etienne arrived. If the two men met again . . .

Her heel swiveled, carving another notch in the softened earth at the end of her path as she whirled to pace back the other way. Her father thought her long hours away from the house were spurred by her grief for Girard. She had told him that his son had been cut down by thieves in the woods. Guilt niggled her that she and her father ought to be spending these days grieving together, comforting one another.

But Mathilde had no time for grief, and only the sure knowledge that her father and Etienne were safe from d'Amville would ever have the power to comfort her.

Hoofbeats. Mathilde froze, then slowly turned, her fingers clenching on the folds of her cloak. D'Amville emerged like a figure in the mists of a nightmare. Black-cloak swirling in the wind, hazel eyes glinting in the muted afternoon light. He drew rein and sat, hulking, silent, menacing in the saddle of his midnight-coated horse. Then he leaned down and spoke in that rough, graveled voice that made her flinch at the memory of the scar that had robbed him of his former, honeyed tones.

"Well, poppet?"

She tried to speak but her throat was too tight.

303

"I would have thought your father would guard you better than this."

"He—I-I have been waiting for you," she choked.

"Have you?" He swung off the midnight horse. He did not limp now as a quick step brought him to her side. "But where is my victory, if you come to me so easily?" One gloved finger slid under her chin and lifted her face to his gold-flecked gaze. His long grey hair snapped in the wind. "You sent me on a right merry chase, my dear, after your brother's squire. We have been playing cat and mouse for days on his way to the coast. I was forced in the end to let him elude me. D'Yquebeuf will not be pleased to learn that I failed to stop the queen's message. But I understand that your swain comes for you tomorrow, and I was not prepared to lose you or my revenge against your father."

"You will not harm him?" she pled. "If I go with you—if I m-marry you—you will not harm my father?"

"It has never been my intention to harm him, poppet. At least, not his body." He circled behind her, then bent to murmur on a hot breath against her ear, "His mind, his spirit . . . his heart . . . ah, now, that's another matter."

She refused to give him the satisfaction of a shudder. She felt him straighten, then lean forward again until his mouth almost brushed her ear on the opposite side.

"But what about your swain?" he growled. "What about de Brielle? What will he do when he comes for you tomorrow and you are not here?"

"He will do nothing. I do not love him, Sir Alun. I have left him a letter, telling him so." It was in her bedchamber, beneath her pillow. When she did not return to the manor house, her father would search for her and find it.

"Ah, sly wench. Like your mother. De Brielle will not believe you, any more than I do. No matter. I shall know how to deal with him when he follows us."

"He will not—"

"He will, poppet. I saw the flame in his eyes for you. As Aymor flamed for your mother." D'Amville's arms suddenly slid around

304

her waist and jerked her back against his chest. "He will steal you from me if he can, as Aymor stole Caterine. But this time I shall not lose you. Aymor shall live to see you give me all that Caterine gave to him. Her beauty . . ." His mouth nuzzled the skin at the base of her ear.

Her stomach flopped in disgust. She pried at his forearms, but his strength held her fast.

"Her passion . . ."

His rough lips moved downward along the side of her throat, coloring her revulsion with panic.

"Eventually, I trust, an heir." His arms tightened as her struggles to free herself grew more frantic. His voice thickened. "This squirming excites me, poppet. You tempt me to step inside that threshing house and demonstrate that, despite my grey locks, I am not yet too old to play a husband's part."

She froze at the threat. A sob worked in her throat, but she choked it down. Perhaps if she stood very, very still the wind would cool him.

"Aye," he murmured, shifting his head so that his rough, leathern cheek scraped against hers. "We shall get a son between us, poppet. Your father should thank me for that, don't you think? A nice, stout grandson to replace your clod of a brother and to bear your father's title when he's gone. A d'Amville for an heir, bred with Caterine's beloved daughter. Aye, that will be sweet revenge, indeed."

He eased her around in his arms, until they stood breast to breast. She felt his hands in the small of her back, molding her with quiet, determined force against him. The sob almost bubbled free this time, but she clenched her teeth tight to subdue it.

But he saw her fear. She knew it when his leathern cheeks creased in a grimacing, malevolent smile. 'Twas not madness that glittered in his eyes now. Nay, as their hazel depths fixed on her mouth, they darkened with something more frightening than madness . . . something more obscene.

Still holding her against him, he took a step towards the threshing house.

Fear shot up hot from the pit of her stomach. She dug her heels into the ground, trying to stop him. "Sir Alun, we—should we not be going? My father may come looking for me."

"But this is your own private place, is it not?" Hunger roughened his already harsh voice. "Even your father does not know that this is where you come when you wish to be alone. Is that not what you told Lady Hermaline?"

She gulped. "But—but he will be alarmed when I do not return to the house. He will scour the manor for me and—"

"Are you afraid he will find you sporting in the hay with his worst enemy? Sweet justice that would be. I only regret that Caterine should not be at his side to witness the return of her sins upon her daughter."

His mocking laugh lapped away on the wind. Two more strong, purposeful strides, and he had dragged her to the door of the threshing house. He held her arm tight with one hand while the other groped to wrench open the latch.

Mathilde twisted desperately, clawing at his fingers. "If my father comes upon us he will kill you!"

"I do not think so, poppet. He tried once before and failed. He shall pay dearly for this scar on my throat, as he will pay for the rest of his betrayal."

Mathilde knew from previous trial that the warped wood of the door would cause it to stick. D'Amville shouted a curse into the wind, raised a booted foot and kicked the door in.

One quick jerk and he had pulled Mathilde onto the threshold.

"No!" She no longer cared that the word broke from her on a scream, that the sob tore wildly out of her throat. She sank to her knees, pleading despair the only defense she had left. "Sir Alun, please, do not do this! I will go with you—I will marry you—I will be your wife in very deed. But please, please do not do this—not here, not like this. Do not shame me before our wedding—"

"Shame?" His hands clamped on her shoulders. He dragged her back to her feet and slammed her into the doorjamb. "You speak to me of shame? *You*, Caterine?"

Caterine. The gold flecks in his eyes seemed to leap at her. In an instant, lust vanished . . . and madness returned.

"Where was your shame when you forsook your vows to me? When you gave yourself a harlot to Aymor?"

"Sir Alun, please," she whispered. "I am not Caterine, nor am I a harlot."

"No?" he cut her off harshly. "Then what is this?"

His gloved hand slapped against her throat before the fingers curled as though grasping at something there. The chain. He must have seen it when he had kissed her neck earlier. He gave a jerk, and Etienne's ring popped free of its home against her heart.

"*He* gave you this, didn't he?" D'Amville yanked the chain so that it scraped against her throat. "Aymor. Before he made love to you. Before you became his strumpet."

Ah, Saints! How had she been so foolish as to think that she could hide the ring, that she could cling to this one, secret reminder of her lost dream and that d'Amville would never know?

She tried desperately to soothe him, to restore his rationality. "No, Sir Alun. I am Mathilde, not Caterine. Aymor is my father. And Etienne de Brielle gave me that ring. Only — only I intend to return it to him. I meant to leave it with the letter, but — but I forgot."

"Liar!" He shouted the word in her face, then dropped the chain and struck her with a blow that stung no less for his hand being gloved. "Liar, Caterine! You lied to me then, as you are lying now. I should have killed you. I should have killed you both. I should have shown you Aymor's blood, red on my sword, before I plunged my blade into your traitorous heart."

His hand closed on her throat, shoving her head against the splintered wood of the doorjamb. For a moment Mathilde feared he meant to strangle her. But though his grasp made swallowing difficult, it did not completely cut off her air. He had already demonstrated sufficient strength to restrain any attempt to escape. She could do naught but stare into his glittering eyes and pray.

"It is not too late," he growled. "Perhaps that has been my mistake. I thought that Aymor's ruin would quiet this pounding rage in my head. I have torn his lands from him, stripped him of his heir and his honor. I have held his last child in my hands —" his gloved palm briefly cupped her bruised cheek — "but still my brain burns."

The hand at her cheek fell away, but the other remained clamped at her throat.

"Might I have been wrong? You, Caterine. Perhaps it is your grief that will quiet me at last, not his. Aymor I have punished . . . but where was *your* suffering? Where was your grief to match my own?" His choking hold slackened. "Aye, 'tis your tears I will see. You, weeping over Aymor's slaughtered body, you, counting my blows in his flesh. And you will know 'twas your own treachery that brought my blade upon him. Had you been faithful to me, Caterine . . . I would have let him live."

He released her so abruptly that she had to catch the doorjamb behind her to steady her balance. The wind whipped back his cloak as he stepped away from her and closed his hand on his sword hilt.

"Where are you going?" she shouted after him into the wind.

"There." He gave a curt nod towards the distant silhouette of the manor house. "Does Aymor not wait for you there?"

Her father. He was going to kill her father!

Mathilde ran after him and seized his arm. "Sir Alun, no! I pray you—"

His strides only quickened, so that she stumbled in her attempt to maintain her hold on him. She could think of only one way to stop him. If she could not fight his madness, then perhaps she could manipulate it.

She tugged on his arm. "Sir Alun, there is no need for this. Aymor is nothing to me. It was all a mistake . . . a blind, foolish error on my part. I never loved him. I only love you."

He swung on her, rage in his eyes. "More lies, Caterine?"

"No!" She tried not to flinch in fear of another strike to her cheek, but his hand remained clenched on the sword at his side. When she realized that a blow would not fall, she repeated more steadily, "No. I was wrong. I own that freely. Aymor—Aymor dazzled me for a time. But—but however else I betrayed you—my love for you was always true."

She saw the disbelief that cracked his mouth and impulsively put up her hands to his face. "I love you," she whispered, because she could not speak the words aloud with conviction. "Always you.

Only you." She moved her palms over his rough, leathern cheeks in what she hoped were calming, quieting strokes.

The skeptical smile slowly dissolved. When he drew in a slow, husky breath, she feared he had found her touch more seductive than soothing.

"Will you prove it, Caterine?"

She followed his glance to the threshing house behind them.

"I will prove that I am not a harlot," she said, gruffening her voice to hide her fear. "And you will prove to me that you are not the coward men call you by dishonoring me before we speak our vows." As she'd hoped, she saw the responsive glitter in his eyes when she reversed Etienne's trick of attacking his courage in the woods. She had nourished the idea in her mind just in case d'Amville proved impatient. Pray heaven it would turn his mind from the threshing house and give her time—however little!—to steel herself for the inevitable. "Take me away from here," she said. "Away from Aymor. Make me your wife first and I will prove to you that my love . . . my desire . . . burns only for you." There. She had spoken it without a stammer.

The ruse worked. He gave a curt nod, but said hoarsely, "A kiss then. You never let me kiss you before, Caterine. If you speak truth . . . if you love me . . ."

Mathilde hesitated, then stretched onto her toes and brushed her lips against his.

She would have retreated then, but his hands clamped about her head and dragged her mouth back. His gloved fingers twisted into her hair, while his lips—

Bitter. Like foul, corrosive acid. Scorching her mouth, not like the sweet flame of Etienne's kiss, but consuming her in raw, caustic hunger. She found his shoulders and tried to thrust him away, but his assault only deepened until nausea gurgled up in her throat.

I must either be sick or faint, she thought. She struggled valiantly to suppress both weaknesses, until at last he released her with a groan that she hoped signaled his temporary satisfaction.

"I have waited . . . so long." His lips moved in a harsh whisper against her brow.

She squeezed shut her eyes, wishing she could squeeze away the taste of him as well as the sight. "We will share more, Sir Alun," she forced out the assurance. "After we are married. After you take me away from here."

Away from her father. To ensure his safety, she would find a way to endure a wedding . . . and its inevitable aftermath.

"Aye," d'Amville growled, "but first—"

His hand closed once more on the chain that suspended Etienne's ring. D'Amville gave it a quick, violent jerk. Mathilde cried out in pain as the thin strand of metal scraped and blistered her skin. Another fierce yank, and the chain broke away.

He flung chain and ring down at her feet. Gold flecks leapt again in beds of hazel malevolence. "If he follows us, Caterine, I will kill him. Aymor . . . de Brielle . . . whatever your lover's name. If you betray me again, you will wish that you and he had never been born."

"They will not come," she insisted. They *must* not come. When Etienne read her letter, he would understand why he and her father must stay away.

But Etienne's ring winked a contradictory promise at her as d'Amville swept her up in his arms and carried her to his midnight horse.

Twenty

"Sir Etienne de Brielle, my lord."

Etienne strode into the manor hall behind the threadbare servant who announced him. The rushes scrunched beneath his boots, dry and brittle, their fragrance stale as though they had not been changed for days, perhaps weeks. Smoke from a poorly vented hearth tickled his throat. Soot had stained the chamber's walls a dreary grey and dulled the colors of the tapestries that hung there.

The gentleman who sat beside the hearth looked up with a start when Etienne's name was announced. Etienne experienced a brief, confused sensation of staring into Girard's resurrected face. The gentleman lurched up from the chair and stepped sharply towards him. Etienne's confusion faded as he saw streaks of grey in the dark brown hair and beard.

"*You* are Sir Etienne?"

Etienne nodded and favored the gentleman with a respectful bow. "And you are Lord Aymor, I presume? Lady Mathilde's father?"

"Aye, aye," the gentleman answered impatiently. "But what do you know of her, sir? Who are you? And where has she gone?"

Something clenched in Etienne's gut. "Gone?"

"She has been missing since yesterday afternoon," Lord Aymor said, a frantic note in his voice. "I thought perhaps she had gone for a ride and taken a spill, but all the horses remain in the stable. I've drafted every serf on this manor to search for her. This morning one of them brought me this." In one hand, Lord Aymor clutched a folded sheet of parchment, but 'twas the other hand that he extended now. In the palm lay Etienne's ring on a broken gold chain. "It belonged to her," Lord Aymor said. "I saw her toying with it one day about her neck, but when I started to ask her about it, she made an excuse and left the hall."

Etienne's mouth went as dry as the day he had awoken from his fever. "The ring is mine. A pledge to her that I would—" He raised his gaze to Lord Aymor's tortured eyes and told him straightly, "I came here to ask for your daughter's hand, my lord. I had hoped to convince you of my worthiness to bear her away as my wife." He took the ring from Lord Aymor's hand, leaving him the broken chain. "Where did you find this?"

Lord Aymor swept Etienne with a quick, assessing gaze before he answered. "The serf said it lay on the ground beside the old threshing house. There were footprints in the softened earth, he said, one set large like a man's, the other small like a woman's, and a horse's prints a little further away. The threshing house door was broken open, but he could not tell whether anyone had been inside."

Two sets of footprints and a horse. Etienne's mouth tightened grimly. "Then she did not go of her own accord."

"So I thought . . . until I found this." Lord Aymor gestured at the parchment. Etienne glimpsed both an unstamped seal of red wax and the scrawl of his own name along the top. "She knew you were coming?"

Etienne gave a curt nod.

Lord Aymor frowned. "A servant brought this to me after she searched Mathilde's room this morning." The parchment fluttered. "It was under Mathilde's pillow. I was about to break open the seal and read its contents . . . but she clearly intended this letter for you."

Etienne slipped on his ring and shifted impatiently from one foot to the other, waiting for Lord Aymor to hand him the parchment.

Lord Aymor made no move to do so. "I gather you met and courted Mathilde at Grantamur Castle?" he said in hesitant tones.

Etienne nodded again.

"Did you have a rival, my boy?"

Etienne stared at him. "A rival?"

Lord Aymor shrugged. "She cast off your ring and left you this letter . . . perhaps because she did not want to see you."

The implication of Lord Aymor's words sank in slowly. "Are you suggesting that Mathilde has eloped with someone else?" Etienne's impatience popped and sizzled. "Blazes! Didn't she tell you about d'Amville?"

The white shock on Lord Aymor's face answered Etienne's question.

Etienne could bear it no longer. He snatched the parchment out of Lord Aymor's hand and broke the seal.

Etienne, Mathilde had written, *if you are reading this, you will know that I have gone with d'Amville. I was wrong to encourage you at Grantamur Castle — wrong to kiss you — wrong to let you think I loved you. I do not. I asked Violette to tell you so and return your ring, but she refused. So I tell you myself. I do not love you. I never loved you.*

"Never," she had underlined thrice. Despite his alarm at seeing his apprehensions confirmed, Etienne felt the corner of his mouth quirk up. The "r" in the word was blotted, as with a tear.

I know you will find a worthier object for your affections, she continued. *Only pray, do not marry Hermaline. She would bring you much unhappiness, I think. You are a brave, valiant knight, and deserve a kind, faithful lady like the beautiful Enide. I know you will find her — oh, soon!*

Again, the ink in the word "soon" was smudged and the parchment slightly warped in that spot, as though touched by another drop of moisture.

Because you are such a valiant knight, I fear you will feel duty-bound to rescue me from d'Amville. You must not do so, because I do not need to be rescued. I go with him willingly. He is not coward enough to harm me before we are wed. Etienne's fear eased slightly at the line. *But he will harm you if you follow me, so you must not do so. And you must not let my father follow me either. Please, please, Etienne* — the two "pleases" were again thrice underlined — *if you wish to bear me one last service, you will*

313

*guard my father and see that he does nothing foolish. D'Amville will not
harm him if he will only stay away. Do this for me, I pray you, and you will
earn my eternal gratitude.*

In what appeared a hastily added postscript, she dashed off at
the end, *I wish I could have loved you – but I do not. Forgive me. Maude.*

More tear splashes blotted and warped the bottom of the page.

"Oh, my heart," Etienne murmured, "you protest your lack of
affection rather too loudly, I think."

"What does she say?" Lord Aymor demanded.

Etienne passed him the letter and let him read it. The
parchment shook in the older man's hand. His face went ashen.

"What does she mean, 'I have gone with d'Amville?' D'Amville
is dead!"

"And you know that because you thought you had cut his
throat?" Etienne spoke more roughly than he'd intended, his voice
harshened by his fear for Mathilde.

Lord Aymor stumbled backwards, then collapsed into the chair
beside the hearth and dropped his head into his hands. "My child,
my child! What have I done?"

Etienne pitied the older man's distress, but he had not time to
indulge it. *He is not coward enough to harm me before we are wed.* So she
had used his own ploy to try to protect herself. But Etienne had seen
the lust in d'Amville's mad, gold-flecked eyes. According to Lord
Aymor, she had been missing since last night. What if d'Amville had
already found a priest? Nay, Etienne forced himself to shove the cold
fear out of his mind. Mathilde's safe return was all that mattered.

Her safe return. How was he to manage that, when he did not
know where d'Amville had taken her? He began to pace the hall,
frustration causing him to lash out at her father.

"You ask an apt question, my lord. What *have* you done?
Mathilde and I have both seen the scar on d'Amville's throat. He
says you put it there."

Lord Aymor dropped his hands and Etienne saw his handsome
features twist with anguish. "I was defending my child! Defending
Mathilde! He said that he would—that he—" A long, violent
shudder ran through the older man's frame.

Etienne struggled to master his temper and fear. He stopped and turned to face Lord Aymor. "Forgive me, sir, but if I am to know how to fight d'Amville, I must know what lies between you."

Lord Aymor appeared to wrestle his agitation under a fragile veneer of control before he answered. "D'Amville and I quarreled about his betrothal to Mathilde. I wanted to annul it, but he threw his old threat in my face to see me imprisoned for the Wardrobe theft if I tried. Either way, he said, he would make Mathilde his. I knew he still had proof of the theft. If I went to prison, there would be no one to protect Mathilde."

"What about Girard?" Etienne asked.

"Oh, Girard was fond of Mathilde in an offhand, careless way, but he was weak and easily manipulated. I dared not leave him to fight d'Amville alone."

Etienne recognized a firmness about Lord Aymor's chin, a quiet strength in the depths of his anguished eyes that Girard had never possessed.

"I would willingly have paid the price of imprisonment, if only that would have contented d'Amville," Lord Aymor said. "But once he fixed his mad eyes upon Mathilde, he left me no other choice. I have never been a violent man. But that night, I took my sword and rode forth to meet d'Amville in the woods. I begged him to do what he would to me, but to release Mathilde from their betrothal. He refused. And then—" Lord Aymor's hands fisted. "Then, in that smooth-as-honey voice of his, he began to tell me, detail by vicious, lustful detail, how he intended to use my daughter on their wedding night."

As though spurred by the explosive memory, Lord Aymor shot to his feet. Etienne saw him shaking, but knew that this time he trembled with anger rather than shock.

"D'Amville's foul mockery finally drove me over the edge of fury. I seized my sword and fell on him. But he had come armed as well, and he deflected my blows. His skill was greater than mine. He might have easily killed me, but he wanted me to live, to see him 'complete his revenge on Caterine,' he said. I thought I must have misunderstood him, but he repeated it twice more as we fought. He thought Mathilde was Caterine!

"I saw his madness then, as I had only suspected it before. 'Twas the madness made him careless, I think. He had me down on my knees and thought me defeated. He lowered his sword for an instant—an instant!—and I sprang back up and swung. My eyes were so thick with sweat, I feared my strike would go wild. But this time, I felt my blade meet flesh. And when I wiped the sweat from my eyes, d'Amville lay at my feet, a bloody gash across his throat."

Lord Aymor ran a shaking hand through his dark, grey-streaked hair, then turned his haunted gaze on Etienne. "I thought him dead. I swear, I thought him dead! I left him there in the woods and rode home. When Mathilde came in, I told her that d'Amville had been killed by outlaws in the forest. I never heard word about the body being found. I presumed it had been ravaged by wild beasts. At least, that is what I prayed for every night. That by the time they found what remained of his body, it would be too late to trace his death to me."

"Only someone else must have found him before the beasts," Etienne said, "realized he was still alive, and nursed him back to health."

Lord Aymor closed his eyes on a groan. "Are you sure 'tis d'Amville? Might you not be mistaken?"

"No, sir. I gather that he has altered greatly since you knew him, but even Mathilde recognized him at last. And now she has gone with him—"

"To protect me," Lord Aymor choked. He covered his face again with his trembling hands. "My child, in that monster's power!"

Etienne battled his own taunting images of Mathilde with d'Amville. "'Twas not lust alone that seemed to drive him," he said, grasping at memory and again at the line in her letter. "D'Amville wanted to marry Mathilde, not just rape her. Where would he have taken her, do you know?"

For a moment, he feared Lord Aymor was too wrought up in his anguish and guilt to hear his question. But at last, the older man replied in a stifled voice, "I suppose—if he means to mock me with her, he has taken her someplace close by. Perhaps to his castle on the other side of the river."

316

So near? Then the likelihood that d'Amville had already found a priest— The icy dread Etienne had been struggling so fiercely to hold at bay, rippled down his spine. "I saw a church as I rode through your village," he said hoarsely. "Would the priest have recognized d'Amville? Would he have agreed to wed Mathilde against your wishes?"

Lord Aymor lowered his hands and shook his head. "I do not think so. But Father Bernard has been absent from the village for the past sennight. I gave him leave to visit his ailing mother. He is due back today. I expect him near noon."

The chill dread ebbed ever so slightly. Noon was still an hour or more away. "Then there is time," Etienne breathed. Pray heaven, let him be right.

"Time?" Lord Aymor shouted. "She has been gone an entire night! What if d'Amville has—"

"He hasn't," Etienne broke in sharply. "You said yourself that he wished to mock you with her. If he had harmed Mathilde last night, he'd have been on your doorstep at the crack of dawn to boast of it."

To his relief, Lord Aymor seemed to check his panic, then gave a slow, concurring nod.

"I'll bring her back to you, my lord," Etienne swore. "I give you my oath on that. But until your priest returns, I believe she is safe."

He resumed his pacing while he racked his brains for some method to fulfill his vow. How was he to storm d'Amville's castle alone? He should have asked Therri to meet him here, to bring some of Violette's guards. But he had thought Mathilde would be secure in her father's house. It had never occurred to him that she would deliberately give herself into d'Amville's hands. Curse his blindness! He had known there was nothing she would not do to protect her father.

"D'Amville's castle is small but well-fortified," Lord Aymor said, "and I have only a few dozen serfs at my command." He swept Etienne with another glance, taking in his unpretentious but well-tailored clothes. Clearly he hoped they bespoke either wealth or position. "You have men you can summon to our aid?"

Etienne shook his head.

"Then how are we to rescue Mathilde?"

Etienne's ears pricked at the pronoun. "*We* are not going to do any such thing."

"She is my daughter—"

"And she is trusting me to protect you. I said I would bring her back, my lord."

Lord Aymor's pallor fled, washed out by a crimson tide in his cheeks. "I am not going to stand idle while d'Amville abuses Mathilde with his insane lust." He shouted a name and the threadbare servant who had announced Etienne reappeared in the entryway. "Fetch me my sword and saddle my horse." He swung back to Etienne, determination writ across his face. "I will confront d'Amville as I did before, and 'tis more than his vicious throat I will slice open this time."

Etienne moved quickly to block Lord Aymor from following the servant out of the hall. "More likely he will have his men hold you down while he slices open yours," Etienne retorted. "D'Amville would like nothing better than to ravish 'Caterine' before your eyes, then make her watch while he kills you."

"For all we know he has already ravished Mathilde!" Lord Aymor roared, a note of hysteria in his voice.

Etienne drew a deep breath to maintain his own calm. "Sir—my lord, I pray you will not provoke d'Amville with your passion like this. As I said before, I do not believe he will harm Mathilde before he marries her . . . unless some careless action on our part goads him into acting precipitously." He allowed his voice to sharpen, hoping to jolt Lord Aymor into the cool headed self-control they both needed if they were to deliver Mathilde safely from d'Amville's mad intentions.

Lord Aymor glared at him, but made no further effort to leave the hall.

"Sit down again, I pray you," Etienne said. "Tell me how this malice between you and d'Amville began." He hoped the tale would distract Lord Aymor and give himself time to think of a plan to rescue Mathilde.

After a moment, the color faded from Lord Aymor's face. He sank back into his chair on a sigh. He looked as though he had aged twenty years since Etienne had strode into his hall.

"D'Amville frequently visited the palace in Rouen when I served on the Wardrobe staff," Lord Aymor mumbled, as though he found it difficult to focus on the memory. "Ostensibly he came to call on his sister and brother-in-law —"

"Bevis de Chesnei. He served with you in the Wardrobe, did he not?" Etienne said.

Lord Aymor looked surprised. "Aye. How did you know?"

Etienne shook his head and merely bade the older man continue.

"Chesnei had introduced d'Amville to Caterine de Guerre, the daughter of a minor knight serving in the Royal Treasury. D'Amville had little wealth in those days, but he had a fine, silver tongue. He won permission of Caterine's father to court her, and for a time, she believed herself in love with him. But his occasionally erratic behavior eventually began to frighten her. When d'Amville and her father pressed for a wedding, she looked about for an escape."

Etienne saw the anxious lines in Lord Aymor's face soften.

"I had long watched Caterine with hopeless, adoring eyes. We talked — oh, often, and she had begun to confide in me. Learning of her distress, I offered her my services. She asked me to escort her to her grandfather, whom she said would sustain her in her refusal to marry d'Amville. I intended to do no more than see her safely to her destination . . . but along the way, the impossible happened. Caterine confessed that through our weeks of friendship, she had fallen in love with me. She showed me the sapphire necklet her father had given her, and the dagger he had fashioned with a similar stone in its pommel. Her father had forced her to pledge the dagger to d'Amville, but she had brought it with her. Twin jewels to represent twin souls, she said, as she pressed it into my hands. Then she kissed me, and pled with me to seek out a priest in the small Norman town where we had stopped to rest. I had not the heart to resist her. We married, and consummated our union in a roadside inn."

The lines in the old man's face deepened again. "But d'Amville had followed us in a rage and burst upon us while we slept. He refused to believe my proofs of marriage. He called Caterine a harlot, shouted that she had betrayed him, and drew his sword. He undoubtedly would have killed us both had Caterine's father, who accompanied him, not intervened. He dragged d'Amville away, and I carried Caterine to the safety of my father's estates."

"But you returned to the Wardrobe staff," Etienne said.

"I was still a younger son, dependent on royal service to maintain my new wife. I did not see d'Amville again until ten months later, just after Girard's birth. D'Amville came to the palace to visit to his uncle. Ah, but he was a smooth-tongued devil. He persuaded me that he had forgiven all, invited me for drinks at a tavern in Rouen, and lured me into a game of dice. I was still celebrating the birth of my son. I let d'Amville and his friends buy me drink after drink, until the dice swam before my eyes. I don't remember passing out. But when I woke the next morning, I was in my own bed at the palace with a pair of royal guards standing over me. They accused me of theft of ring, candlesticks and plate from the Wardrobe treasury. D'Amville himself had signed a letter of witness against me, with the ring I had 'stolen' and gambled away to him as proof of my guilt."

"A ring that might as easily have been stolen by his brother-in-law as by you," Etienne suggested.

"Indeed," Lord Aymor said bitterly, "but I had no evidence to prove that. My father interceded at great cost to save my head, but he could not restore my honor. He banished me to this manor with Caterine. A year passed. 'Twas easy enough for d'Amville to make our next meeting appear casual. His lands marched close to this manor. My brother was then on his deathbed, my accession to position as my father's heir imminent. Again d'Amville and I met in a tavern over a game of dice. I allowed d'Amville to bait me and, convinced as I was that he was responsible for my shame, I accepted his challenge to stake one castle of my future inheritance against his fortress on the other side of the river. I threw the dice . . . and lost."

"Sir Nevell de Chesnei, Bevis's son, said that you initiated the challenge that lost your father's castle," Etienne told him. "He said you called d'Amville a coward."

"Aye, that much is true. D'Amville had fixed the dice to fall in his favor. But when I grabbed the dice up to prove he had cheated, one of his companions knocked them from my hand and kicked them through a crack in the floor. I was livid. Oh, I am quite sure I called d'Amville a coward that night, and a good many other things. D'Amville was at my throat in a flash, but the glitter in his eyes bespoke something more unsettling than simple rage. As his companions wrestled him off me, he screamed that his revenge had just begun. 'You will pay for stealing her from me, Aymor,' he shouted. 'And Caterine shall pay for betraying me, as well.'"

Etienne moved over to one of the narrow windows and studied the position of the sun, a faintly glowing disk shining through a thin layer of grey autumn clouds, before asking, "Having lost one castle and knowing that d'Amville was a cheat, why did you agree to further games of risk with him?"

"I didn't," Lord Aymor said curtly. "A month later, d'Amville approached me again, all quiet and smooth as butter once more. I thought it was over, didn't I, he purred. I thought myself safe because my father had bought my pardon from King Henry. But suppose other items from the Wardrobe theft began to appear, he said. A candlestick here, a jeweled plate there. And suppose . . . just suppose . . . some of these items surfaced in the possession of some French baron. King Henry was but newly seated upon his throne in England, and France, as ever, was eager to nip away at his heels, particularly here in Normandy."

"I understand," Etienne said with a taut smile. "Theft King Henry might pardon, but selling his treasury to his enemies in France he would undoubtedly view as treason."

"Precisely." Lord Aymor gave a weary sigh. "'Twas a threat d'Amville repeated over and over through the years. I must give him this castle and that castle and tell everyone that I had gambled them away. He took my lands, my gold, my jewels, my reputation— At last, he left me with naught but this manor, and even then he forced me to surrender half my fields to him. D'Amville continued to torment me until the night that Caterine died giving birth to Mathilde. He disappeared then, going off to lord it over my inheritance, so I heard through the few friends that remained to me. Then suddenly, one day he returned and set eyes on Mathilde. She had just turned twelve. She did not have her mother's beauty, but she had Caterine's eyes, long-lashed and violet and sweetly misted with dreams even then."

Etienne glanced away from the sky as Lord Aymor paused.

Lord Aymor's face darkened. "Ah, but d'Amville knew how to play upon those dreams. He courted Mathilde slyly with his curst honeyed tongue and showered her with romantic trinkets. Mathilde thought he walked amidst the clouds. It amused him to mock me by winning her childish trust. When he demanded a betrothal, I refused, but Mathilde begged me to change my mind and d'Amville drew me aside and threw his old threat in my face. So at last I agreed, hoping that when the time arrived for marriage, I would find some way to avoid it. And then . . . But I have already told you the rest."

Etienne nodded. The sun had slid higher during Lord Aymor's long narration. The priest would be returning soon.

An idea stirred in Etienne's mind. He repeated more strongly than before, "I will restore Mathilde to you, my lord, you may rest assured of that."

Lord Aymor gazed at him with hopeful eyes. But he said, "I have nothing to give you in return for risking yourself against a madman. And if you hope for Mathilde's hand, I must tell you that I will not force her to marry you or any man against her will."

Etienne smiled. "I do not intend to take her against her will."

Lord Aymor gestured at the parchment he had dropped on the floor near the hearth. "But her letter—"

"If Mathilde does not love me, she must tell me so to my face. I think even you will agree that is a fair request to make."

Lord Aymor considered these words, then nodded. "But if she does so?"

Etienne remembered Mathilde's slender fingers caressing his hair in the dark when she thought he was asleep, her lingering kiss on his lips, her tears splashing softly against his face . . .

"She won't," he said with quiet conviction. He bent to pick up her letter, folded it and slid it inside the breast of his tunic. "Leave Mathilde and d'Amville in my hands."

"Where are you going?" Lord Aymor demanded as Etienne strode towards the hall's exit.

"To fetch your daughter," Etienne tossed over his shoulder. *And my wife.*

Twenty-One

Mathilde chafed her hands along her sleeves beneath her thread-bare mantle in a vain effort to warm herself. The grate in the hearth had been left cold through the night, but she had not dared complain. That might have brought d'Amville back into the room. It had been dreadful enough to be locked all night in his bedchamber. She had spent the long, chill hours in terrified expectation of hearing the key scraping in the lock. A click, a footstep, d'Amville at her side with a priest before them, vows exchanged, the priest dismissed, and then—

Then. 'Twas that word that had driven the sleep from her eyes all night and held her fixed stiffly in the chair directly across from the door. Since he had kissed her outside the threshing house, d'Amville no longer seemed to see her as Mathilde. The mad glitter in his eyes terrified her. But his rasping words had been soft, almost caressing before he had left her alone in his chamber.

"Soon," he had whispered, his gaze flicking at the large, curtained bed. "'Twill be our chamber soon, Caterine."

She shuddered and wiped away a cowardly tear. She must find the courage to see this through. If she could persuade d'Amville that he had indeed won Caterine's heart, he would have no more reason to hate or threaten her father.

Grey light seeped around the edges of the shutters, but she knew it was long past dawn. A drear autumn day to reflect her bleak future. She stood and tried to warm herself by pacing, then stopped beside a large, carved chest at the foot of d'Amville's bed. This must be where he stored his clothes. Perhaps she would find a warmer cloak inside.

A thick layer of dust coated the lid, the same as had blanketed the chair before Mathilde had wiped it clean with a corner of her thin mantle. The lock on the chest had rusted. Wherever d'Amville had been hiding through the years of his "death," it had not been in his old castle near her father's manor.

She tried lifting the lid of the chest, but the rusty seal held. There must be a way to break it open? She looked about the room. Next to the empty hearth leaned an iron poker. It too showed signs of rust, but she picked it up and slid its tapered end into the lock. She turned the poker, jiggled it, jabbed it, until she finally heard a *pop*. Then she knelt beside the chest and lifted the heavy lid.

Something glistened at her in the dark recesses. She reached in a tentative hand and lifted out a sleek, long-bladed dagger. Gold threads wound around the leather-covered hilt. A large sapphire studded the circular pommel.

Her father's dagger. The one that bore the twin stone with the sapphire in her mother's necklet.

The dagger d'Amville confessed he had stolen when he confronted Mathilde in Grantamur Forest.

"What else do you have in here that does not belong to you, Sir Alun?" she queried softly.

She had to tumble out several layers of clothing, including a thick, fur-lined cloak that she tossed around her shoulders, before she found the answer. Two caskets of jewelry. She did not recognize their contents, but several of the settings suspiciously had etched on the back initials that accorded with her father's and grandfather's. She searched the chest again. More clothing. And beneath them, at the bottom, a candlestick . . .

"Caterine?"

Mathilde started to her feet, the candlestick in her hand. D'Amville's gaze shifted from her to the silver object. The mad glitter in his eyes slowly ebbed.

"So . . . poppet . . . you have found me out."

Found him out? Slowly, she tilted the candlestick to view its base.

"You recognize the royal seal?" d'Amville mocked. "I presume you've discerned the origin of these, as well." He swept to her side, bent over the chest, and thrust another object into her arms.

Mathilde had already glimpsed the jewel-rimmed plates stacked alongside the candlestick in the bottom of the chest. She did not need to turn over the plate she now held to know that it, too, bore the seal of King Henry Plantagenet.

Anger briefly washed away her fear at d'Amville's reappearance. "You stole these from the King's Wardrobe and blamed my father."

An ugly laugh rasped out of d'Amville's throat. "'Tis not all I have stolen from him, poppet. But I'd wager your father would count all this as dross in exchange for your safe return to him." He dealt a savage kick to one of the caskets, scattering her father's jewels over the floor. The dagger she had left atop the clothing caught his eye. He picked it up. "Ah, the symbol of Caterine's betrayal. Your mother pledged this to me, poppet, then gave it to her lover. But I reclaimed it . . . as I have reclaimed you."

He tilted her chin with the tip of the blade. The metal, chilled by the long years in d'Amville's abandoned chest, bit like ice against her skin, but the hungry gleam in d'Amville's eyes flushed Mathilde with panic. She drew a shaking breath, determined to choke down the ball of terror rising in her throat.

"I sent that fool, Chesnei, to fetch us a priest, poppet," d'Amville muttered. "You do not know how hard it has been for me to wait for his return." He circled behind her slowly, sliding the edge of the dagger to the side of her neck. "It is difficult to restrain myself, poppet, when both revenge and pleasure lie so near to hand. I have not held a woman in my arms since the night your father murdered me."

She had borne the steel against her skin without flinching, but her heart lurched when he tossed the blade aside and replaced it with caressing fingers along her neck.

She stepped away from him before he could feel her shudder, then turned to meet his gaze. Relief that he had not tried to restrain her leant a rough composure to her voice. "You appear very much alive to me."

"No thanks to your father," he snarled, "who left me to bleed away my life on the forest floor. Fortunately for me, there were outlaws in the wood who found me and recognized the value of the clothes I wore. When they realized I was yet alive, they bound up my wounds, thinking they could demand a fine ransom for me. They sent their terms for my freedom to my nephew. Their reward for that folly was Chesnei's crossbolts through their hearts and my dagger in their leader's back."

"It has been three years since you . . . disappeared," she said. "Why did you wait so long to come back?"

"I wanted to keep your father off his guard. So I let him think I was dead and permitted Chesnei, as my heir, to parade about in my jewels. Ah, forgive me, your father's jewels. I extorted them from him before your birth, so you would not have recognized the chains and collars, the girdles or rings my nephew wore."

Rings. Like the one that Chesnei had given Hermaline? Had that belonged to her father, too?

The indignation that flared in her breast suddenly flashed an escape through her mind. She held out the candlestick and jewel-rimmed plate. "When King Henry learns that I found these concealed here, in your own castle, he will know that you were the thief, not my father. 'Tis you who will be cast into prison now."

D'Amville's twisted smile mocked her. "What, betrayed by my own wife? I think not, my dear."

"I am not your wife." Perhaps now she need never be. If she could only reach the door . . .

But in a movement so swift she did not have time to dodge, d'Amville swept candlestick and plate out of her hand. They clanged against the cold, stone floor as his fingers crushed into her shoulders.

"Make no mistake, poppet," he growled, "as soon as Chesnei returns with the priest, you will speak the vows that will seal you mine. Mine, as Caterine should have been."

327

His angry gaze dropped from her face to the soft curve of her throat. As the hazel orbs darkened, Mathilde saw their golden flecks begin to flicker once more in a glittering dance. When he spoke again, she knew his mind had shifted back into madness.

"But you did not wait for a priest to play harlot with Aymor, did you, Caterine? All the while you were speaking soft words of love to me, you were sporting with him behind my back."

Mathilde did not know whether she feared his madness or sanity more. But hope was a difficult flame to squelch. He had left the door ajar behind him. If she could only break free of this room, the evidence of royal plate and candlestick would end d'Amville's threat to her father forever.

She tried to twist away, but his grasp clenched on her shoulders until it forced a moan from her.

His rasping voice trembled. "Have you any idea of the agony that seared my soul when I finally caught you in his arms? Have you, Caterine?" He shook her so hard that her teeth snapped together. "Then why should I wait, Caterine? If you love me as you say, what do wedding vows matter between us? We can speak them afterwards, can we not? As you did with Aymor?"

He bent his head, seeking a kiss from her lips but she twisted her head to avoid him. His mouth found her cheek and nuzzled it with brutal pressure. She thrust a hand against his jaw and pushed with all her might, trying to force him away from her. When he resisted her strength, she curled her fingers against his cheek and raked.

D'Amville jerked back with a howl. Mathilde broke free in his moment of surprise and sprang for the door, but she hesitated on the threshold. She could not leave without evidence of d'Amville's crime. She turned to grab up the candlestick.

A fatal delay. D'Amville caught her from behind. As he spun her around, she swung the candlestick at his head. His hand flashed up to catch her wrist, stopping her intended blow short. His fingers pressed, squeezed, crushed until with a cry, she dropped her makeshift weapon.

Fury raged across his bloodstained face. "They were lies, weren't they, Caterine? You never loved me. You were trying to protect *him* when you said you did. So long as Aymor de Riavelle lives, you will never give your heart to me."

He hurled her so hard across the room that she fell through the bedcurtains and landed in a sprawl across the bed. Darkness enveloped her. Her heart pounded in terrified expectation of d'Amville snapping back the curtains, of him flinging himself upon her—

She heard a footstep. Two. *Receding.* She scrambled up and tore the curtains aside.

D'Amville was striding towards the door.

Confusion at his retreat transfixed Mathilde for only an instant. Then she saw the sword in his hand.

"Where are you going?" she cried, though she already knew the answer.

"To put an end to my rival once and for all."

Her father! What use to expose d'Amville's theft to the King if d'Amville murdered her father? "Sir Alun, no! Wait, please!"

D'Amville stopped, but not because of Mathilde's plea.

Sir Nevell de Chesnei had appeared on the threshold, jeweled chains twinkling across his plump chest. *Those jewels belong to my father.* The thought flashed through her mind before the significance of Chesnei's arrival drained the blood from her face.

D'Amville lowered his sword. "So, nephew, you return at last." He tossed over his shoulder at Mathilde, "A respite for your lover, Caterine. It seems I will make you my bride after all before I plunge my sword through Aymor's heart."

Mathilde's hand clenched on the bedcurtain as the last of her hopes shriveled and died. *Fool. Why did you scratch him, why did you fight him?* D'Amville would never again believe her if she said she loved him. How was she to protect her father now?

"Well?" d'Amville demanded impatiently of his nephew. "You have brought the priest, I presume?"

Chesnei's mouth opened and closed, but no sound came out. Mathilde saw beads of perspiration dotting his broad brow. One large drop rolled slowly down his plump cheek, but he made no attempt to wipe it away.

"The priest!" d'Amville shouted as though faced with an imbecile.

Chesnei's mouth worked again, but the voice that rapped out the answer did not issue from his damp, mobile lips.

"He's not coming, d'Amville."

Mathilde's spine stiffened at the strong, familiar accents. *Etienne.* Her gaze flew in panic to d'Amville's sword. *No, no, no! Etienne, you must not be here!* Her head told her to scream out a warning, a plea for him to flee, but when his dark face appeared over Chesnei's shoulder, her heart pounded a different response.

His green eyes locked briefly with hers before sweeping back to her captor. "The priest had better things to do today, d'Amville, than give you license to ravish an innocent woman."

"You," D'Amville spat. Mathilde saw the white-knuckled grip of his hand on his sword hilt. "Your lover comes for you, Caterine. Said I not that he burned for you? Said I not that he would follow?"

"Let her go, d'Amville," Etienne demanded. "Or I'll slice up your nephew like a Christmas ham."

Chesnei's eyes bulged as Etienne's sword moved from his back to press ominously against his side. "Uncle!"

"Silence!" d'Amville roared at him. "You were a fool to bring him here."

"He found me at the church, waiting for the priest. He said if I did not give him access to your castle he would cut me down where I stood."

D'Amville's gaze flicked coldly from Chesnei to Etienne. "Go ahead," he growled. "You will save me the trouble of spitting him myself."

Etienne hesitated, then slowly lifted his sword. Chesnei cringed and gave a terrified whimper. D'Amville smiled grimly and waited.

Oh, saints! Mathilde pressed her hands to her lips. Surely Etienne was not going to—?

With a quick, powerful *thump*, he banged the hilt of his sword into the back of Chesnei's head. Chesnei's bulging eyes rolled up and he sank to the floor in a quivering, unconscious heap.

"He has served his purpose," Etienne said. "He got me past that motley crew of men who guard your castle, but I did not think the rest would come so easily." He stepped away from Chesnei and dropped into a battle stance, sword leveled at d'Amville. "Come then. I've no crossbolt graze on my brow this time, and my shoulder is much improved since last we met in Grantamur Forest."

"I will slaughter you before her eyes," d'Amville swore, raising his sword. "Aye, Caterine, you will see what your folly has wrought when you see him writhing in agony on the point of my blade."

"You bluster like a bag of sour wind, d'Amville," Etienne jeered.

His baiting of d'Amville appalled Mathilde. "Etienne, don't! Go away. Take my father with you. D'Amville will kill you both."

"I'm not leaving without you, Mathilde."

A hot tear splashed down her cheek. If Etienne could defeat d'Amville, if they could escape together from this room with evidence of d'Amville's theft— But d'Amville's blade had only to slip beneath Etienne's guard for an instant—an instant!—and Etienne would never leave this room at all. She could not let him risk his life for her. She *would* not let him do so.

"Sir Alun, you gave me your word that you would not hurt my father or Etienne if I married you!"

D'Amville cast a skeptical glance at her. "Your mind changes like an unsteady flame, Caterine. A moment ago you were clawing my face."

"You may punish me for that as you please. Let Etienne go, and I will ride with you wherever you wish to find a priest. We may leave this very moment—"

"Stop it, Maude," Etienne snapped. "I don't want your sacrifice and neither does your father. If this lunatic thinks he is going to ride anywhere with you, he is going to have to go through me first."

Etienne spoke truth. He stood firmly planted blocking the doorway. It would be impossible for her and d'Amville to leave the room without Etienne's acquiescence. And from the kindling fire in his eyes, she knew that no power she possessed would convince him to step aside.

Etienne shifted and clanged his sword lightly against the tip of d'Amville's blade. "Why do you hesitate, d'Amville? Don't tell me you're afraid?"

D'Amville's leathern face twisted. He exploded with a curse, just as he had in Grantamur Forest when Etienne had challenged his courage there. D'Amville brought his blade down with a crash on Etienne's. Mathilde smothered a scream, but Etienne shoved d'Amville back and disengaged. D'Amville recovered swiftly. A flurry of blows erupted between the two men.

They circled the room, striking, parrying, striking again.

"I will kill you, Aymor! I will grind you into dust, and Caterine shall be mine!"

D'Amville's demented shouts jarred Mathilde's already shredded nerves, but Etienne made no reply to the taunts. Grim determination tightened the lines about his mouth. He fought silently, eyes alert, hand steady.

D'Amville continued shouting at him, detailing the agony he intended to inflict upon his "rival". But though his offensive was clearly driven by insane rage, his assault fell in measured, potent blows. Each time his steel flashed at Etienne, Mathilde flinched. Her hand ached from fisting it so hard on the bedcurtains, but fear held it locked on the cloth, as dread kept her gaze riveted to the combat.

The jewels d'Amville had earlier kicked over the floor crunched beneath the two men's boots. Once Etienne nearly slipped on a brooch, but he regained his balance in time to parry the jab d'Amville aimed at his breast.

It was the only time Etienne faltered. D'Amville had decades of experience over his opponent, but Etienne had the stamina and agility of youth. D'Amville's breath began to come in quick, shortened spurts. Perspiration sheened his face. In Grantamur Forest, the graze to Etienne's brow had made his vision and aim unsteady. Now he slowly but inexorably drove d'Amville back with blows that were well-measured and powerful.

Gradually, by degrees so small she did not recognize the flickers until they had sprung into a full-fledged flame, hope began to glow anew in Mathilde.

Etienne was winning! Her hero might rescue her yet.

D'Amville's panting breaths betrayed frustration as well as weariness. "You have improved since we last fought, Aymor. Your blows were reckless and haphazard then."

Etienne made no attempt to convince d'Amville of his true identity. "Yield," he demanded. "There are no confederates to come to your aid this time, as there were in Grantamur Forest. This time, d'Amville, it is just you and me . . . and I am not the one who grows tired."

"Ah." Calculation glittered alongside the madness in d'Amville's eyes as he blocked one of Etienne's forceful blows. "But it is has never been just you and me, Aymor. It has always been you and me . . . and Caterine."

D'Amville dodged Etienne's swing, swooped down, and came up with the King's jewel-edged plate in his hand. He hurled it at Etienne's head. Etienne ducked, but his defensive reaction gave d'Amville time to whirl towards the bed.

In the split second that she stared into his eyes, Mathilde realized that he meant to seize her, to use her as a shield as he had in the woods at Grantamur. On the floor glinted her father's dagger. She dove for it as d'Amville sprang for her. Her knees scraped as she skidded across the stone floor, but she grabbed up the dagger and scrambled about with the blade extended to hold d'Amville off.

D'Amville checked his pursuit of her a single pace away, turning to thrust his sword warningly at Etienne who had taken a quickened step after him and Mathilde. The reach of d'Amville's blade was greater than that of the dagger. If he'd wanted to, he stood close enough to swing about and pierce her before Etienne could stop him. Etienne halted, alarm flashing across his face.

But Mathilde knew that d'Amville wanted her alive.

She hoped he was less certain that she wanted him the same.

"Stay back," she warned as he edged towards her, his sword still trained on Etienne.

One of his twisted grimaces cracked d'Amville's face. "The blade shakes in your hands, Caterine. You do not want to kill me."

"If you harm Etienne or my father—"

"Their fate rests on your head, Caterine. Had you not lied to me, had you not betrayed me, this man would not have to die." His sword hissed as he swung it away from Etienne to level it at her breast. "I stand with my back to you, Aymor. Shall you reach me before I reach her, do you think?"

Etienne lowered his sword.

"Etienne, don't!" she cried. "He won't kill me. Don't give up your sword!"

"Too late," d'Amville rasped a hoarse whisper at her. "Your lover hesitates . . . while my confederate awakes."

Mathilde's gaze flew to the door, expecting to see one of the evil-visaged men who guarded d'Amville's castle standing on the threshold. Instead, her gaze locked in horror on a recovering Chesnei. Although still blurry-eyed from Etienne's blow, he had managed to heave himself to his feet and at his uncle's shout, lurched forward to grasp Etienne's arms and twist them behind his back.

Taken by surprise, Etienne nonetheless managed to hold onto his sword. He recovered his wits quickly and pitched forward at the waist before Chesnei could solidify a firm grip on him. Chesnei's balance tottered. Etienne's foot slipped around Chesnei's ankle and jerked. At the same time, he rolled his upper-body to flip Chesnei sideways. Chesnei's grasp on Etienne's arms slipped free as he struggled to avoid hitting the floor headlong. Etienne whirled. His fist landed on Chesnei's chin in a resounding *crack*.

Chesnei slammed into a wall.

And d'Amville seized his moment.

With a bloodcurdling scream of victory, he whipped away from Mathilde and lunged at Etienne. Mathilde shrieked a warning. Etienne turned, but his half-raised sword met with a vicious kick of d'Amville's foot to his wrist. Etienne's defense sailed out of his hand.

D'Amville might have ended the conflict with one swift plunge to Etienne's chest.

Instead his sword's tip swooped to Etienne's throat and forced him back against the wall where Chesnei slumped.

"A thrust to your heart would be too easy, Aymor. I want Caterine to watch you die bit by agonizing bit."

Etienne cursed him, but his empty hands could only fist in impotent frustration.

The sword's tip traced a line teasingly across his throat. "I owe you a slash here first, do I not?" d'Amville growled. "Never fear, I shan't slice deeply enough to kill you—yet. Only enough to let Caterine see your blood flow, to hear you groan in agony, to steal from you the voice that Caterine loves . . ."

D'Amville smiled, a malicious, self-satisfied grimace, and slowly shifted the sword, methodically angling it for the promised incision.

Mathilde scrambled to her feet and stumbled forward. D'Amville's movement bared his side. He did not see her, did not realize his own vulnerability . . . Her hands clenched on the hilt of her father's dagger.

"Sir Alun, let him go, please!" *Please do not make me kill you.*

"You should have loved me, Caterine," he rasped at her without turning his head. "Aymor's groans, his screams, his blood— his death—you have brought it all upon him, all. If you had only loved me . . ."

The sword flashed up, preparing for the measured strike.

She saw the blur of Etienne's dodge in the same instant that she flew at d'Amville and thrust. The dagger's blade punched through d'Amville's side. He gave a startled groan. The sword wobbled in his hands. She released the dagger's hilt with a shudder and backed away, a sob raking out of her throat.

Through blurred eyes, she saw that Etienne had thrown himself sideways and landed in a sprawl, his hand stretched inches short of regaining his sword. He stopped reaching at d'Amville's groan and turned to stare as d'Amville swayed.

Swayed but did not fall. Mathilde backed away. Why didn't he fall?

D'Amville glanced at the hilt protruding from his side, then slowly turned to gaze at her with his glittering eyes. "The ultimate betrayal—eh, Caterine?"

He lurched a step towards her, then sank to his knees. Panic sheered through her as his hand closed on the skirt of her dress. Etienne sprang to his feet and started towards them.

"Curse you, Caterine," d'Amville rasped. "I would have loved you. All I ever wanted . . . was to love you . . ." His voice broke. "Why . . . could you not love me?"

Behind the dancing madness in his eyes, she glimpsed a flicker of bewildered grief. Then the lids slid closed and he slumped silently to the floor.

She shook her skirt free of his slackened grasp and hurled herself into Etienne's arms.

Twenty-Two

Mathilde burrowed her face against Etienne's breast as she flung her arms around his neck. She could not cling to him tightly enough. She had come so near to losing him. She would never, never let him go again.

Etienne held her hard for long, silent minutes, his face pressed into her hair. "Maude."

The violent tremors in her body had not ceased when he finally uttered her name.

"Come, sweetheart, there's nothing more to fear. It's over."

Over. An odd gruffness colored his tender comfort. But his hand stroked her cheek with exquisite gentleness. Warm fingers brushing her skin. Blessedly live fingers. She turned her head and darted a quick kiss against them.

His palm cupped her cheek. Shouts sounded somewhere in the distance, but she gave them no heed. How could she, when Etienne pressed his mouth to her brow, coupling her trembling relief with shivers of fiery pleasure?

But she could not ignore the horrified gasp that scraped the air immediately behind them. She and Etienne turned their heads together to see Chesnei clambering to his feet, his gaze riveted in panic on d'Amville's slumped form.

One glance from d'Amville to Etienne, and Chesnei lurched from the room.

Etienne released Mathilde on an oath and started after him.

She grabbed his arm. "Let him go!"

"We need him to help prove your father's innocence."

"There are more candlesticks and plates in that chest. 'Tis all the proof of d'Amville's guilt we require." She could not bear to risk Etienne again in another confrontation.

But an angry glint lit Etienne's eyes. "Chesnei tried to strangle you, Maude, and planted a crossbolt in my back. If you think I am going to let him go with no more rebuke than my fist against his chin—"

He tried to pull free of her fierce grasp on his sleeve, then suddenly stopped struggling and tensed. Mathilde froze too.

More shouts. Closer now. And footsteps, scuffling, pounding up the stairs . . .

Had Chesnei summoned d'Amville's men? This time she allowed Etienne to shake her free so that he could retrieve his sword.

But before he could slam the door shut, a familiar voice shouted, "Etienne! Mathilde!"

Etienne shot a startled glance at her, then stepped into the doorway. "We're here, Therri!"

A moment later, Therri's hand clapped on Etienne's shoulder and pushed him back into the room.

"I knew you were coming to fetch Mathilde today," Therri said, grinning at Etienne's surprise as he strode into the chamber with Violette's servant, Hugon, at his heels. "Violette lent me an escort to meet you, just in case d'Amville was lurking about watching for a chance to cause more mischief. Mathilde's father sent us here. I hoped we'd arrive in time to help you defeat d'Amville—" He broke off and hitched one of his fair, heroic eyebrows in the direction d'Amville's crumpled form. "We intercepted Chesnei in the hall below, but I see that you have taken care of d'Amville yourself."

A faint, ruddy flush rose in Etienne's cheeks as he followed the direction of Therri's glance. "Maude has taken care of d'Amville for us," he said.

Mathilde heard the renewed brusqueness in his voice, but the memory of her dagger plunging through d'Amville's flesh submerged her puzzlement in a fresh shudder.

Therri knelt beside d'Amville and laid his fingers to the base of the fallen man's ear. He threw a sharp glance at Etienne, then slanted it towards Mathilde. "He's not dead, Etienne. Did you think he was?"

Mathilde gave a little gasp. Tears of relief stung her eyes. She did not regret striking d'Amville. He had left her no choice. But that she had taken a man's life, even d'Amville's, was more nightmare than she wished to live with.

Etienne must have sensed the delayed shock that threatened to buckle her knees, for he swept her up into his arms. He gave a curt nod at d'Amville. "Bind up his wound," he said to Therri. "Do what you can to keep him alive, at least until he can sign a confession."

"Confession?" Therri repeated.

Hugon picked up the jewel-rimmed plate that had come so near to cracking Etienne's head, looked at the base, then handed it to Therri.

Therri gave a low whistle at the royal seal stamped there "So she was right. D'Amville *was* the thief."

"There is more in that chest," Etienne said. "Gather it up. Mathilde and I will wait downstairs."

Etienne carried her out of the room and half-way down the steps that led in a downward spiral towards the hall. Mathilde tightened her arms around his neck while she struggled to choke back the sobs that threatened to convulse her. Dimly, she could hear the murmur of voices, one of them Therri's, from the bedchamber behind them. More voices mingled below in the hall. She guessed that was where Therri's men had forced d'Amville's defeated guards to gather.

Etienne paused as a gulping sob escaped her. Abruptly, he lowered himself onto one of the steps, cradling Mathilde in his lap.

"It's all right to cry, sweetheart."

At Etienne's gruff reassurance, Mathilde stopped gulping, buried her face in the warm crook of his neck and burst into tears. He embraced her gently, cooing soft words of comfort in her ear, until she finished weeping out her tangled emotions of shock and relief.

"I th-thought d'Amville was g-going to k-kill you," she whispered between the little hiccups that lingered from her tapering sobs. Her hands found and caressed his throat, so narrowly escaped from d'Amville's fury.

"He might have, if he had just cut instead of drawing back for a deeper slash," Etienne said. "The blade's retraction gave me a chance to lunge out of the way . . . but my hand still fell short of my weapon. I was bracing myself for his sword in my back when I heard him grunt from your blow." He paused. "You saved my life, Maude."

The muscles of his neck tightened beneath her hands. She leaned away from him to look into his face and saw him frowning. "Etienne?"

He wiped the tears from her cheeks, but avoided her gaze. "Never mind. It is over now. The threat to you and your father is gone."

She shivered, unable to push it all so easily from her mind. "D'Amville has recovered before. After my father—" She broke off, the vision of d'Amville's scarred throat sending a brief, violent tremor through her. She pressed a quick kiss to the warm, hale flesh of Etienne's neck. "And—and he escaped the flames in Grantamur Forest."

"But he'll not escape a Plantagenet's wrath. As soon as he's recovered sufficiently to travel, he and Chesnei will be sent to give an account of their actions in King Henry's court. D'Amville may be too insane to give reliable evidence, but I'll wager Chesnei will crow out the truth fast enough if it means the difference between imprisonment and a rope around his neck."

"Do you think they will hang d'Amville?"

"I don't know. Your father will have to testify, too. But when all the facts come out, he should have no difficulty reclaiming his lands and wealth from d'Amville." Etienne's mouth curved ruefully. "Your father will think I only want to marry you for your money now."

He spoke lightly, but there was something in his voice, in his face . . . She studied him anxiously. Questions about d'Amville slid away as she sought to decipher the brooding cloud on Etienne's brow. "Do you, Etienne? Do you truly want to marry me? What about Hermaline?"

He snapped his fingers with reassuring promptness. "That is how much I ever cared for Hermaline."

"But you said —"

"I never said I loved her, Maude. I only let you think so because — because I had nothing to offer you. I could not marry you then. But you were so determined to think I had rejected you because you were plain. I much preferred to hint that it was because I loved another woman to that."

She searched his eyes. "Is that what is troubling you? That I will think you came after me only for my father's wealth? But you did not know my father would regain his lands when you gave me that." She touched the ring on his hand, the one she had worn for so long close to her heart.

He drew it off and slipped it onto her finger. The ring was too large. He smiled when she crooked her finger to keep it from falling off. "I will replace that with one that fits when we exchange our wedding vows. No, sweetheart, I'm not afraid you think I want you only for your father's lands. 'Tis a plump windfall for me, of course . . . but I was prepared to carry you off to my brother's manor and serve as his lowly seneschal. We'd not have been rich, but you would have been safe and comfortable." He tucked a strand of hair tenderly behind her ear. "Until I had at least that much to promise you, I could not tell you that I loved you."

"We shall have that much and more after the King restores my father's lands," she said shyly, "so may I hear you tell me now?"

He laughed and moved his hands to cradle her face. Behind the shadow in his eyes glowed a steady flame of adoration and desire. "I love you, Mathilde de Riavelle. I am becharmed by your little tip-tilted nose . . ." He dropped a kiss on this member. "And your rose-mantled cheeks . . ." A dozen more kisses rained over her blushing face. "And ah! your angel lips!" His mouth settled over hers in a deep, tenderly possessive caress that ignited a sprinting fire of bliss down her spine.

Mathilde surrendered to his melting assault for a handful of heartbeats. But when the flame had swirled clear down to her toes, she twined her arms about his neck. The last threads of d'Amville's

341

horrors fled as she answered Etienne with kiss after hot, fervent kiss of her own.

After several sublimely scorching minutes, Etienne's hands slid into her hair and gently but firmly pulled her away. "Blazes, Maude, you scatter my wits when you kiss me like that. I was not finished cataloging the attributes that hold me in thrall."

"You cited my nose, cheeks and lips," she said impatiently, "What more can there be?"

"These." He closed her eyes with a soft brush of his thumb across her lids. "For here are where your dreams reside." His mouth pressed warmly, lingeringly against one eyelid and then the other.

Mathilde sat very still. She could sense the change in him, the fresh tension in his body.

"Ah, Maude."

His voice cracked a little, but she kept her eyes closed. He would tell her more easily without her trying to look into his soul.

"I wanted to be the one to fulfill those dreams. I wanted to be your hero, your Prince Erec . . . but I muddled it. In the end, you had to do the rescuing for us both."

She felt for his cheek to stroke it, but instead felt his mouth press a kiss into her palm. She murmured, "Even Prince Erec needed his Enide by his side on occasion to help him escape from danger."

Silence. She cracked open her eyes to peep at him through her lashes. He looked as though he were trying to remember something. The jongleur's story she had told him once?

"I needed you, Etienne," she insisted when the frown continued to hover at the corners of his mouth. "If you had not come when you did, d'Amville would have murdered my father. He was on his way to do so when you arrived. I do not think I would have been able to stop him again if you had not ignored my letter and appeared in the doorway just when you did." This time her hand safely found his cheek. "In my moment of darkest despair, you appeared. In the very instant that I needed you, I looked . . . and you were simply there." Her eyes prickled with tears at the miracle of it all.

"As you were there for me," he murmured, "in a moment when I needed you." He kissed her in a slow, candid mingling of their

342

hearts and souls. When he finally drew back, the cloud on his face had lifted. "How did you say your jongleur closed his story? 'In the end, their love was greater for the trials they had borne together.'"

His smile warmed her almost as deeply as had his kiss. With her arms still looped around his neck, she rested her head on his shoulder. "I came to Grantamur Castle searching for a hero to save my father. I did not find Prince Erec. But I found you, Etienne. The brave, valiant, chivalrous knight of my dreams."

"And I found a selfless, loyal, courageous . . ." He paused. A familiar teasing light stole into his eyes. ". . . delightfully kissable lady. The latter is indispensable, you know, in a heroine."

She giggled. "Or in a hero."

They were confirming this vital characteristic in one another when Therri's tread on the step interrupted them.

"Practicing for that game of hoodman blind you promised me, are you?" he said with a laugh.

Mathilde blushed, but there was no mockery in Therri's tones. He was really breathtakingly beautiful, she thought, with that scowl gone from his face. At least, he would have been to any woman whose breath had not already been snatched away by another.

Etienne grinned at his friend but made no effort to loosen his possessive hold on Mathilde. "I trust you've followed my advice and have been practicing the same with Violette?"

"She's been reluctant about that," Therri answered. "It took a deal of persuasion just to convince her to give me one more chance at the game. But I persisted as you said I should and demanded of her how I am to guess her kiss correctly this time when it has been so long since I have tasted her lips?" His jewel-hued eyes twinkled with a charm too long buried beneath a wounded temper. "After a good deal of coyness, she finally agreed to surrender one kiss before we play the game again. I claimed it before I left Grantamur Castle and drew it out long enough to make her cling to me a bit. I told her I needed to be thorough to make sure there would be no chance of my mistaking her lips again."

Mathilde looked back and forth between the two men, puzzled by their exchange. But Etienne only laughed.

"There won't be, I trust?" Therri said, his voice taking on an uneasy edge. "Any chance of me making a mistake, I mean?"

To Mathilde's surprise, he sent a sharp glance at her.

"None," Etienne assured him, then scooped Mathilde up and pushed himself to his feet. "We'll see you at Grantamur in a fortnight."

"A fortnight?" Therri thundered as Etienne carried Mathilde down the stairs. "I can't wait another fortnight!"

The soft-glowing embers in Etienne's eyes sent a thrill of promise through her. But he sighed and called over his shoulder, "A sennight then. In the meantime, take care of d'Amville and Chesnei for us. Whatever you do, don't let d'Amville die before he reaches King Henry's court!"

"But, fiend seize it, Etienne, where are you going?"

"To find Lord Aymor's priest and wed my Enide."

She saw the bewildered look on Therri's face. "Enide? Don't you mean Mathilde?"

Her laughter mingled with Etienne's rich chuckles. He paused on the stair. "I'll explain it to you later," he promised Therri. His eyes twinkled meaningfully into Mathilde's. "But . . . we may be a day or two late."

The glower descended once more onto Therri's fair brow. "A sennight. You said a sennight, Etienne. Not one day more!"

Etienne closed Mathilde's eyes again, this time with two soft kisses against her lids. "A sennight," he called, adding in a voice lowered with wistful hope, "if we don't get lost in Maude's dreams."

He swept her around the curve in the stair, away from Therri's sight before his friend could protest again. Mathilde rubbed her cheek against Etienne's broad, solid shoulder while her hand played with one of the silken curls that lay along the back of his neck. Her curls, now, to caress and fondle as boldly as she pleased. Soon the rest of him would belong to her, as well.

She smiled. Sometimes reality could be more splendid than a dream.

Epilogue

A Sennight Later

M athilde lowered the flute with a sigh. "How much longer must I play?" she queried her husband. "My mouth is getting tired."

Etienne bent down from where he stood beside his wife's high stool to investigate her complaint. He found no sign of weariness in the zealous way her lips responded to his kiss. Seven days of heaven. Seven nights of paradise. And if the heat of their present exchange were any indication, he could look forward to a lifetime of the same to come.

Mathilde jerked away, her cheeks washing with color as she darted a glance at the laughing circle gathered before the hearth in Grantamur Castle's great hall.

"Shame on you, sir," she chided. "You are unchivalrous to embarrass me before Lady Violette's court."

"And you were less than truthful, my lady. Your mouth appears to retain a great deal of energy to me."

She tried to frown at him, but ended by coupling her blushes with giggles. Fortunately, the circle before the hearth was too engrossed by the game in progress there to have witnessed the moment's telling passion between the game's musical accompanist and her husband.

A victorious shout drew Etienne's gaze away from the glow on his wife's smooth cheeks. A tall, thin man with crimped brown curls stood at the center of the circle of brightly gowned ladies, his eyes covered beneath a crimson hood turned to the rear, pinned up to leave bare the lower portion of his face. His hands planted boldly on one lady's hips, he announced with a triumphant smirk, "This whiff of rose-petals betrays you, my lady. By the rules of the game, you must surrender your plump charms to me. The prize is mine, gentlemen! I claim the Lady Violette de Maloisel, mistress of Grantamur Castle!"

Laughter roared through the circle. Someone lifted the hood from the gentleman's face. The triumphant smirk vanished, replaced by a look of almost comical dismay as he stared down, not into Violette's imperious countenance, but into the round, pouting face of Hermaline.

The gentleman jerked his hands from her hips as if he'd been stung by a wasp. "Forgive me, my lady," he stammered. "I thought 'twas—"

Hermaline's face crumpled with sulky wrath. "'Twas *not*," she hissed. Her toe snapped into the gentleman's ankle. "And I am not *plump*." When Violette rebuked her, she whined, "'Tis a game. I'll not play any more," and flounced away from the circle.

Three paces from the edge she stopped, her eyes locking with Etienne's. Violette had made Hermaline return Chesnei's ring to Mathilde. But Etienne knew 'twas not the loss of that trinket alone that had set Hermaline in such a foul temper. He racked his mind in search of some words he might speak to calm the angry flush on her cheeks. Then he felt a slender hand on the back of his neck drawing his gaze away, his head down . . . and his mouth firmly back to Mathilde's.

This time their kiss did not pass unnoticed. Chortles erupted from the circle. A sly shout or two, encouraging Etienne to still bolder action, rumbled from a few of the men. Such comments died quickly, no doubt shriveled by the frigid glare of Grantamur's mistress. Or so Etienne imagined in the one corner of his mind still able to function. The rest of his brain Mathilde's kiss had set on fire, along with the surging blood in his veins. How many more hours until he could whisk his wife away from this tedious game?

Her hand found his cheek, caressing it briefly before she pushed him away.

"There, she is gone," Mathilde murmured.

It took Etienne a moment to master his breath. Regrettably, he sensed that the satisfied smile on his wife's rosy lips was not due to the skill of his kiss alone. He slid a glance to the empty space where Hermaline had formerly stood, then grinned and tweaked a tendril of Mathilde's shoulder-length hair. "Wicked minx."

"Well, it quite served her right," Mathilde said, although her cheeks warmed with embarrassment again at the amused attention focused on them. "She said such horrible things to me, Etienne. No, I shan't tell you. I just wanted her to know you are mine."

"You have demonstrated your command of me to the whole of Vi's court." He flung out a hand at the chuckling men and ladies turned their way.

Violette preempted Mathilde's blushing reply with two smart claps of her hands. "Let us resume the game, gentlemen. Else Sir Etienne will be the only one enjoying the pleasures of wedded bliss this night."

The men who had been formerly milling about at the outer ring of the ladies' circle, instantly turned their attention away from Etienne and Mathilde to clamor with unseemly eagerness to become the next wearer of the crimson hood.

All except for those gentlemen who had already played the game and lost. One of these strolled across the floor to Etienne and said, with a rueful nod in Violette's direction, "I see the trick she plays, now. While her ladies confuse us with teasing lures and laughter, she strikes a position and stands silent as a sentry, so there's no finding her by ear. She's dressed every one of her ladies in a silken gown with identical girdles, and pinned up all their hair the same way, so that it's impossible to identify her by touch. Like Sir Ivo, I thought to locate her by that rose-scent she always wears. But hang me if she hasn't doused all her ladies in rose water, too!"

Ah, Etienne thought, that explained the panicked look Therri kept throwing his way. Now that Violette had sent Marshal off with a flea in his ear, and with her suspicions of Mathilde shattered,

Etienne had been certain Violette would allow her proud heart to thaw towards Therri. Indeed, the glow in her eyes when she thought no one was watching her gaze at him betrayed the true depth of her feelings. But she had stubbornly clung to her pique over Therri's misguess of her kiss in the game of hoodman blind at Rouen. The solution to Etienne had seemed simple. Arrange a second game and this time make sure Therri guessed aright.

But not only had Violette refused to surrender any further preliminary kisses to Therri to help him in his judging, at the last minute she had been persuaded to raise the stakes of the game. The other knights still assembled at her castle recalled that prior to the tournament, she had promised them all an equal chance for her hand. She had rejected another contest of arms, stating that she would not risk further bloodshed. But when she announced the game of hoodman blind, one of the knights had been struck by a brilliant idea. If Violette would not agree to another tournament, he said, then let her new husband be chosen by a different contest of skill. The man who could correctly identify her from among her ladies while his eyes were hooded should this very evening, he insisted, have the privilege of claiming her for his wife.

Before she could protest, he and his fellow knights had set the terms. They had even sent a servant off to summon a priest. After a few unnaturally flustered moments, Violette had regained her composure and smiled stiffly upon her court. She had given her word before the tournament, she admitted, painfully avoiding Therri's gaze. She would not go back on her promise now.

From the thundercloud on Therri's brow, Etienne knew that Violette's sudden attack of integrity had infuriated his friend. Therri's glares at Violette had grown steadily fiercer throughout the game. Etienne suspected that Therri viewed her attempts to make it nigh impossible for the men to identify her as a spiteful trick aimed directly at himself.

But Etienne had glimpsed the relief on her face each time the gentleman wearing the hood misidentified the lady he caught. Violette was not trying to evade Therri. She was trying to buy him time to be the one to find her.

Fortunately for Therri, Etienne had come up with a foolproof way to guide his friend to the woman he loved.

"Look," he said to Mathilde. "Therri's got the hood. At least—no, don't let Sir Drogo twitch it away, you fool." He tried to catch Therri's eye to signal him that it was time to put their plan into action, but Violette settled the matter herself.

"Sir Drogo, you will tear the hood if you continue to yank on it like that and if the hood is torn, I shall pronounce this game at an end. Lord Therri had it in his possession first. I vow you may wear it next . . . if my lord fails to find me, as have the rest."

The playful smile on her lips looked strained to Etienne. The roses that normally graced her cheeks had been conspicuously missing all morning. But she turned with composed dignity and gestured to Mathilde.

"My lady, if you will resume your music, we will proceed with the game."

Mathilde exchanged a quick glance with Etienne, then raised her flute to her lips and began to pipe an airy tune. She had volunteered to accompany the game with her music at her husband's request. Although Violette and the others would think the melodies little more than a pleasant background to the game, Etienne had coached his wife carefully. He caught Therri's anxious gaze and returned a confident smile. This time nothing could go wrong.

Therri pulled the hood over his head with a jerk. Etienne thought he caught sight of a tremor in Violette's hands, but she laced them firmly beneath her bosom—almost, Etienne thought, in an attitude of prayer—and wove herself silently through her ring of ladies before she selected a position in which to stand and wait for the game to play itself out. Two of Therri's rivals were allowed to turn him, rather roughly, about three times before retreating out of the circle.

Therri steadied his balance, then moved cautiously forward, hands extended before him to help feel his way.

"Pipe sprightly now, sweetheart," Etienne bade his wife. "Lady Cassandry seeks to lead Therri astray."

The bold redhead whisked herself directly into Therri's path. His hands landed on her shoulders, but warned by a string of sweet staccato notes from Mathilde's flute, he announced, "Nay, too square by half. My lady's shoulders slope with elegant grace."

Etienne darted a glance at Violette, but her face betrayed neither pleasure nor disdain at Therri's compliment. Therri released Lady Cassandry and stepped to the right. The wrong direction. Mathilde's tune picked up speed, skipping through a series of zestful notes. Therri hesitated, then took two measured steps to the left. Mathilde's tune gradually slowed as he shifted closer to Violette.

The other women tried to confuse him. They laughed and teased and mimicked Violette's imperious tones. Between his hooded eyes and the brazen way some of the women thrust themselves in his way, Therri could not avoid colliding with a few of them. Each time he did so, Mathilde's tune quickened. Therri submitted the would-be decoys to a diffident investigation, announced: "Too tall." "Too thin." "Too—ah—buxom." And determinedly moved on.

Guided by Mathilde's alternating tempos, he slowly but inexorably advanced towards his prize. The increasingly languorous strains of the flute at last brought him directly in front of Violette.

Etienne touched Mathilde's arm. Three beats of silence. That was to be the signal that Violette stood before his friend.

Only the three beats of silence didn't fall. Therri hesitated as the notes deepened, their low, sensual tones lingering seductively in the air. But when they failed to fade for those few significant moments, he slid another step to the left . . . away from Violette.

Though it quivered over her face for only an instant, Etienne saw Violette's pang of disappointment. He tightened his grip on his wife's arm, but the presence of the gentleman at his side prevented him from doing more than mutter out the side of his mouth, "Maude, sweetheart, what are you doing?"

Her melody, caressive and dulcet, continued in a deep, languid drawl. Therri appeared confused. The notes clearly signaled to him that he was near his target. But without the telling pause to stay him, he shifted still further away.

"Maude." Etienne glanced down at her and saw not only that her eyes were closed, but her face bore a soft, abstracted expression, one that he had become intimately familiar with over the past seven days.

She was lost in some rapturous vision, visions that she had assured him for a long while now had woven around him. Or rather, she would correct herself shyly since their marriage, now wove around *them*. In the mornings she awoke at his side with a blissful shimmer of mist in her eyes. In the afternoons, while he sat in her father's hall and conversed with Lord Aymor about the testimony they would all soon give in King Henry's court, he stole covert glances at his wife, usually sitting near the hearth with her recently lowered flute on her knees, her eyes closed on a dream that promised her husband fresh bliss of his own when the sun sank behind the trees.

Etienne had sworn he would restore her dreams, and he had done so. The knowledge usually swelled his chest with contentment.

But just now, it filled him with so much alarm for Therri that he abandoned caution before the gentleman standing beside him and shook his wife's arm.

"Mathilde!"

Her eyes snapped open, misted and confused. She lowered her flute. "Etienne?"

Pulse one.

"You're not paying attention," he whispered fiercely. "You just let Therri—"

"Am I Lady Violette or am I not?" a haughty voice rang across his rebuke.

Pulse two.

Etienne glanced sharply at the circle and saw a lady very near Violette's height and build step slyly into Therri's path. She wore a scarlet silk gown, and she simulated Violette's accents well-nigh perfectly as she laid a hand against Therri's chest.

"Taste my lips, Lord Therri," she purred, "and see."

Pulse three.

"Your flute," Etienne whispered hoarsely. "Maude, your—"

Too late. Therri lifted the lady's chin and lowered a kiss to her mouth.

Mathilde, her eyes stricken, instantly piped a frantically paced melody in an desperate attempt to impart to Therri his mistake. But Etienne feared her bright tune might signal a triumph to Therri instead of a warning.

Etienne shot a glance at Violette. Her face was rigid, but something in the half-lowered lids of her eyes raised an unpleasant suspicion in his mind. Her ladies had used myriad techniques to confuse the other gentlemen, but only with Therri had one sought to do so with the offer of a kiss. Had Violette deliberately sent the scarlet-gowned lady forth to test him?

If so, thanks to Mathilde's momentary distraction and Etienne's reckless interruption of her melody, 'twas a test Therri was sure to fail. Etienne had to do something, find some way to disrupt the situation before Therri made his inevitable, disastrous announcement that the scarlet-gowned lady's kiss belonged to Violette.

When the gentleman beside Etienne moved closer to the circle to better view Therri's imminent response, Etienne reached over and pulled the flute from Mathilde's mouth. "Maude, do you think you could fake a swoon?"

She stared at him.

"Just a small swoon," he said. "I vow I will catch you."

Understanding came into her eyes, but she nodded towards the circle. "I think it's too late."

Etienne looked back with dread. Therri still held the scarlet-gowned woman by the chin, but his handsome mouth wore a puzzled frown.

"Nay." Therri spoke the word slowly. "Nay. I know it should be right . . . but 'tis not."

Etienne scarcely dared trust his ears. A murmur passed through the circle. Violette stilled it with a lift of her hand. An expression of guarded hope flickered across her face, but her brilliant eyes narrowed. She moved to stand directly beside the scarlet-gowned lady, then gestured her rival away. An elegant curve of her finger brought forward a lady in a pale yellow gown.

"Perhaps you will like these lips better, Lord Therri," Violette said in her most honeyed accents and guided his fingers to the yellow-gowned lady's chin.

Therri held the new woman uncertainly for a moment. Etienne's brief flicker of relief died. Had Therri recognized his love's true tones? The touch of her hand on his? Would he allow these familiarities to lead him into a trap of defeat?

From the steely determination in Violette's face, Etienne doubted that even a swoon by Mathilde would deflect Violette from her purpose. She meant to try Therri thoroughly this time. And if Therri failed her test, Etienne had an unpleasant feeling Violette would ensure the next knight to play the game would receive sufficient hints to successfully win her for his bride.

Mathilde drew Etienne's hand into hers and squeezed it as Therri lowered his head and kissed the yellow-gowned lady. "Etienne, would you know my kisses if your eyes were hooded?"

He looked down at her. Apology mingled with a sweet wistfulness in her violet gaze. He brushed his thumb across her rose-petaled lips.

"I would know your kisses if I were struck eternally blind," he replied. "Though I would rather you not put me to such a test as Vi is subjecting poor Therri to."

She blushed faintly. "No, I will not. Only I think that if Lord Therri truly loves Violette, he would not need my music to guide him to her."

"He misguessed her once before."

"Yes, I know. You told me. But this time it is different. This time . . ." She trailed off with a curiously wise little smile and motioned with her flute towards the circle.

Etienne held his breath as Therri released the yellow-gowned lady.

"Someone seeks to trick me," Therri said, his voice edged with impatience. "These are not Lady Violette's lips."

Frowns from the men, awed whispers from the ladies. Etienne let out his breath, but almost immediately sucked it in again. Violette silently dismissed the yellow-gowned lady and slipped into her place in front of Therri. This time when she took Therri's hand, the chin she guided his fingers to was her own.

"And these, my lord?" she queried softly. "How do you judge *these* lips."

Therri hesitated, clearly suspecting another trap. But given no other choice, he cautiously lowered his head and kissed Violette.

"Now watch," Mathilde whispered, "and you will see."

Five seconds. Ten. Therri's kiss deepened. Fifteen. His hand slid from Violette's chin to cup her cheek. Twenty seconds. Twenty-five. His other palm came up to possessively cradle her face.

The tension eased from Etienne's body in the same excruciatingly slow degrees that the stiffness appeared to drain from Violette's. Therri prolonged the kiss until she had fully melted against him.

He raised his head then and said quietly into the straining silence that had fallen over the circle, "Lady Violette. Only a slackwitted fool could ever have mistaken another's kiss for the sweetest lips in Christendom."

In one neat breath, he mocked his own past blindness and wreathed his lady in forgiving smiles.

Violette pushed the hood back from his eyes. In her chiming laughter, Etienne recognized the small catch of tears.

"Gentlemen," she announced, "the fates have made their choice . . . and now I make mine. As soon as Father Denis arrives, you are one and all invited to attend my wedding to Lord Therri de Laurant."

A few initial groans of disappointment gave way to reluctant laughter from the men and hearty blows of congratulations thumped against Therri's back. Therri hooked a possessive arm around Violette's waist. His grin of relief and joy made him glow like a young sun god.

"I told you he would know her," Mathilde said to her husband. "He did not need our help at all."

"You had more faith in him than I," Etienne admitted. "Why could he not remember her kiss in Rouen?"

"Because before it was only a game," Mathilde said. "But this time, he was playing to fulfill the dream of his heart."

He gazed down into the soft glow of her eyes. *As you, Mathilde de Brielle, have fulfilled the dreams of mine.*

Now that Therri's crisis had ended, Etienne allowed pride to swell his chest again. *Mathilde de Brielle.* She bore his name now, just as she bore his heart in her delicate-fingered hands. What visions had she been lost in when she had so nearly guided Therri astray? Etienne felt sure the answer would be best sought out in someplace more private than Grantamur Castle's great hall.

He dropped a quick kiss to the promise of his wife's lips, then pulled her off the stool. "If Therri did not need our help to find his love, then he certainly has no need of us now."

"Where are we going?" Mathilde asked as he drew her towards the exit of the hall.

"I don't believe you have ever seen Grantamur's gardens."

"You are going show them to me now? Why?"

"Because, my sweet life, the wonderful thing about dreams is that there seems to be an endless supply of them. And I think Violette's roses are the perfect place to weave a few more."

No two persons ever read the

same book

The great writer Edmund Wilson once said, "No two persons ever read the same book."

I suppose in the same way, no two persons ever see quite the same flower or the identical cloud in the sky or even taste a cookie exactly the same way. That is what makes each of us unique.

What book did *you* just read? Would you be so kind as to take just a minute or two to write a review of *Loyalty's Web* and share with others what made this story unique for *you*?

Mathilde, Etienne, and their author will thank you!

Glossary of Medieval Terms

Aquitaine: A region of southwest France that was ruled by Henry II of England during the Middle Ages; assigned inheritance of Henry II's second son, Richard

Bailey: The courtyard of a castle

Chemise: A woman's loose undergarment

Coif: A hood made from metal rings (i.e., **mail**), worn beneath a knight's helmet

Crenellation: The gaps or notches along the top of a castle wall for firing arrows or launching other types of ammunition

Curtain wall: The outer wall that lies between the towers of a castle

Dais: A raised platform in a castle's **hall**

Denier: a French coin of little value

Destrier: A knight's war horse

Embrasure: The space between two **merlons** on a castle wall

Favor/Token: Trinkets that ladies awarded to knights to denote him as her "champion" in a tournament; favors/tokens might include handkerchiefs, **girdles**, tassels, sleeves, gloves, scarves, ribbons, etc; these favors/tokens were worn in the knight's helmet or about his arm and might be kept after the tournament or returned to the lady

Fealty: The loyalty sworn by oath by a knight to his lord

Fortnight: Two weeks (from fourteen nights)

Girdle: A belt worn around the waist

Hauberk: A long tunic made of chain mail that covers the upper body

Jongleur: An itinerate minstrel, poet, or entertainer in medieval France

lèse majesté: Literally "injured majesty"; a crime such as treason committed against the king

Mail: A flexible armor made of small, overlapping metal rings

Mêlée: A mock battle between two opposing teams of knights that formed the tournament of the 12th Century

Merlon: A part of the fortified castle wall that juts up between two crenels (gaps or open areas)

mesnie privée: A lord's inner circle of most trusted knights, specifically those who travel together with their lord to fight in tournaments and wars

Normandy: A region of northern France bordering the English Channel, ruled by Henry II of England during the Middle Ages; assigned inheritance of Henry's eldest son, Henry, the Young King (along with England and Anjou)

Parchment: Material made from animal skin; used for the pages of books or other writing

Poitevin: A resident of Poitou

Poitou: A region of west-central France ruled by Henry II of England during the Middle Ages; assigned inheritance of Henry II's second son, Richard

Pommel: A counterweight, usually in the shape of a circle or ball, at the top of the handle (hilt) of a sword or dagger, often intricately decorated; derived from Latin word for "little apple"

Postern: A hidden door in a castle's **curtain wall**

Refuge: Roped off areas set apart on a tournament field for knights to rest or rearm during the combat; also called *recets*

Romance: A long narrative tale recounting marvelous adventures and deeds of chivalry

Rouen: Capital of **Normandy**

Sennight: One week (from seven nights)

Seneschal: Official in a medieval household responsible for the supervision and management of a nobleman's estates

Smock: A loose, blouse-like garment

Surcote: Also known as the surcoat or super-tunic; a secondary **tunic** worn over an under **tunic**, usually more elaborately decorated; also worn over a knight's armor, decorated with the heraldic device of his house

The Great War: A civil war that erupted between Henry II and his sons in 1173-1174; also called the Great Rebellion and the Great Revolt

The hall or great hall: The central living space of the castle; the ceremonial and legal center

Tunic: A sleeved, loose fitting outer garment worn by both men and women; could be worn alone or under a **sucrote**; for a man, could be knee or ankle length

Ventail: A piece of **mail** that protected a knight's throat and chin

Wardrobe: A room or (for a king or great noble) a series of rooms in a castle that housed his robes, jewelry, and other personal valuables (including spices!), as well as cash and important documents; the King's Wardrobe included his personal treasury

Join my Medieval World!

Sign up for Joyce's newsletter to receive announcements on new releases, special promotions and offers, participate in monthly giveaways, get subscriber-only glimpses into writing updates, book recommendations, historical trivia, and more! You are free to unsubscribe at any time.

Sign up at joycedipastena.com

Suggested Reading List

(For readers interested in a further study of subjects addressed in *Dangerous Favor*)

Chrétien de Troyes and His Poetry

Chrétien de Troyes: Arthurian Romances (Penguin Classics): translation and introduction by William K. Kibler. (*Erec and Enide* translated by Carleton W. Carroll.) London and New York: Penguin Books, 2004.

William Marshal; William Marshal and Queen Margaret (Marguerite)

Crouch, David. *William Marshal: Court, Career and Chivalry in the Angevin Empire 1147-1219.* New York: Longman, 2003.

Duby, Georges. *William Marshal: The Flower of Chivalry.* New York: Pantheon, 1985.

Rivalry between Henry the Young King and Duke Richard of Aquitaine

Barber, Richard. *Henry Plantagenet: 1133-1189.* New York: Barnes & Noble Books, 1964.

Warren, W.L. *Henry II (English Monarchs)*. Berkeley and Los Angeles: University of California Press, 1973.

Adam d'Yquebeuf and Thomas de Coulonces/Conspiracy Against William Marshal

Crouch, David. *William Marshal: Court, Career and Chivalry in the Angevin Empire 1147-1219*. New York: Longman, 2003.

Duby, Georges. *William Marshal: The Flower of Chivalry*. New York: Pantheon, 1985.

Adam of Churchdown

Crouch, David. *William Marshal: Court, Career and Chivalry in the Angevin Empire 1147-1219*. New York: Longman, 2003. (Cites city of Argentan instead of Rouen)

Meade, Marion: *Eleanor of Aquitaine: A Biography*. London and New York: Penguin Books, 1977. (Cites city of Rouen)

Warren, W.L. *Henry II (English Monarchs)*. Berkeley and Los Angeles: University of California Press, 1973. (Cites city of Rouen)

12th Century Tournaments

Crouch, David. *William Marshal: Court, Career and Chivalry in the Angevin Empire 1147-1219*. New York: Longman, 2003.

Gravett, Christopher. *Knights at Tournament*. London: Osprey Publishing, 1992.

Keen, Mauarice. *Chivalry*. New Haven and London: Yale University Press, 2005.

Acknowledgments

Few books achieve the joy of publication in a vacuum, and *Dangerous Favor* is no exception. I owe the deepest gratitude to the following for their help in this story's journey:

Lisa Messegee, Sara Fitzgerald, and Rebecca Wade for their insightful feedback on and unwavering encouragement of the earliest versions of this manuscript.

Monique Luetkemeyer, Heidi Murphy, Rachel Rager, Tina Scott, and Peggy Urry for sharing their time, talent, wisdom, and enthusiasm in later critiques of this work. And Shanda Cottam, who gave me the final boost of courage I needed.

Finally, I wish to express my gratitude to those men and women who likely will never know this book or its author exists, but whose love for history and the people who lived it prompted them to write the resource books that make researching my historical novels a joy.

About the Author

Joyce DiPastena dreamed of green medieval forests while growing up in the dusty copper mining town of Kearny, Arizona. She filled her medieval hunger by reading the books of Thomas B. Costain (where she fell in love with King Henry II of England), and later by attending the University of Arizona where she graduated with a degree in history, specializing in the Middle Ages.

When she's not writing, Joyce loves to read, play the piano, eat chocolate, and spend time with her sister and friends. A highlight of her year is attending the annual Arizona Renaissance Festival.

Joyce is a multi-published, multi-award winning author who specializes in sweet medieval romances heavily spiced with mystery and adventure. She lives with her two cats, Nyxie and Calypso, in Mesa, Arizona.

Email her at joyce@joycedipastena.com.

Visit her website at joycedipastena.com.

Made in the USA
Las Vegas, NV
12 May 2024